Rose Tremain is the author of six novels: SADLER'S BIRTHDAY, LETTER TO SISTER BENEDICTA, THE CUPBOARD, THE SWIMMING POOL SEASON, RESTORATION, which won the *Sunday Express* Book of the Year Award in 1989 and was shortlisted for the Booker Prize, and SACRED COUNTRY, which won the 1993 James Tait Black Memorial Prize and the 1994 *Prix Femina Etranger*. She has also written three volumes of short stories: THE COLONEL'S DAUGHTER, which won the Dylan Thomas Short Story Award in 1984, THE GARDEN OF THE VILLA MOLLINI, and EVANGELISTA'S FAN. She has written numerous plays for radio and television, including TEMPORARY SHELTER, winner of a Giles Cooper Award. Rose Tremain lives in Norfolk and London with the biographer, Richard Holmes.

SCEPTRE

Also by Rose Tremain and published by Sceptre

The Colonel's Daughter and Other Stories
The Cupboard
The Garden of the Villa Mollini
Letter to Sister Benedicta
Restoration
Sacred Country
Sadler's Birthday

The Swimming Pool Season

ROSE TREMAIN

SCEPTRE

Copyright © 1985 by Rose Tremain

First published in Great Britain in 1985 by Hamish Hamilton
First published in paperback in 1986 by Hodder and Stoughton Ltd
A Sceptre Paperback

10

British Library C.I.P.
Tremain, Rose
The swimming pool season
I. Title
823'.914[F]

ISBN 0-340-39269-x

Printed and bound in Great Britain by
Cox and Wyman Ltd, Reading

Hodder and Stoughton
A Division of Hodder Headline PLC
338 Euston Road
London NW1 3BH

For Richard Simon

My grateful thanks to Maureen Duffy for her
help with the poem on page 125

CONTENTS

ONE

POMERAC

Here, at dawn, the first sound is the calling of Gervaise to her cows. Standing with her wrists on the metal gate, put in this summer to replace a wooden five-bar so rotten and moss-covered it was returning itself, limb by limb, to the crumbly earth, Gervaise floods her peasant head with a superstitious prayer: Thank you, Our Lady of Jesus, for this gift of a metal gate. Bless our English neighbour who understands the need for it. Amen.

Then the cows lollop slowly to her, white, muddy rumps swaying through the white September mist. They're heavy with nourished flesh, huge with milk, and this woman calling to them, Gervaise, is a little stick of a person beside them, so meagrely fleshed, her breasts lie flat on her ribs like soft purses. Yet she it is, her knowledge of soil and weather and sickness and crop, who gives this warm steaming health to these cows. She it is – not her husband, M. Mallélou still rolled up in his flannel sheets and snoring at the whitewashed wall – who opens the gate now and drives the cows under the window of Larry Kendal, her English neighbour, and on up the rutted lane where Larry's tomato-coloured Granada is parked, opaque with dew, its rear bumper squatting in briars and brambles, on past the car and over a small incline where the cows' hooves slip on loose stones.

As the village clock chimes six, Gervaise follows the animals into the barn where one day, she has promised herself, she will install a modern milking parlour, kind to the teats, self-cleaning. As she begins to milk the cows, she croons a lullaby so honoured by time it has passed into her veins. Gervaise wants to still the quivering udders to the rhythm of her voice, but the cows begin to tremble and stamp. Very often they do this: they refuse to be calmed as her sons were calmed at her breast by Gervaise's singing, yet every morning she sings.

Gervaise's English neighbour, Larry Kendal, wakes as the cows come toiling past his Granada. Buried under the lane where they pass is the cheap septic tank he installed four years ago, when the house was a holiday home, occupied for a few weeks only each summer. This year, the stench from that septic tank has been sickening. Little froths of sewage have bubbled up onto the stones and weed. The cow flops smell sweet compared to that rancid human waste. It's the meat we gobble and the alcohol we sip . . . Something will have to be done about the tank. No use pretending the problem will go. Larry hears six o'clock from the bell-tower and sighs. The chime is both familiar and utterly alien. It's the sound of the village, Pomerac, on its silent hill, in a country he's trying to make his own, but which refuses to enter his blood or his language or his longings or his will. It's like a hopeless mistress, beautiful, frigid, cold, dry. And the effort of possession is tiring. He's trying still, but he's tired out. And it's at dawn that his strivings kill him most, with that long day ahead. The light falling in his room is white and dense, yet utterly flat, casting no shadow anywhere, so the room seems featureless like the day.

But Larry Kendal thinks of his car and feels comforted. The interiors of cars have always soothed him: the smell, the comfy seats, the exquisite functioning of small switches. Once, when he had planned to leave Miriam, to drive a hundred miles to another city, to another life, it had been enough just to go round and round Oxfordshire all night and take his Renault 16 to breakfast at a Post House. Odd this, how the car had been both the vehicle of and the argument against a dramatic change in his entire way of life. Like a devil's advocate or a clever friend. But he hates what sun and air and rain are doing to the Granada. He wants to apologise to it for his failure to shelter it. He has a plan: he'll buy the bit of land at the top of the lane where Gervaise's old milking barn is slowly shedding its tiles. He'll refurbish the barn as a garage, with a proper up-and-over door, a window and a strip light. Here, too, will he install the swimming pool plant: the heat exchanger, the pump, the backwash, the sand filter, the pipework to sump and skimmers, the vac, the winter cover, and the anti-algae compounds. Yet fears for his plan are growing: he doubts he has the power – or the money – to make Gervaise sell him the barn. She 'owes' him for the gate he put in to stop her cows from eating Miriam's flowers, but her need of the barn is so old and obvious, she's too sharp, too sensible to let anyone take it from her. Even to Miriam, the plan seems vain. 'Don't be stupid, Larry. What about the winter? The cows would simply die.' But the Granada, he wants to wail. Rust is coming. The damp and the dew. It's clapping out . . . But these words tail off. They're futile.

Miriam sleeps. Larry can feel, a few inches from the sighs that keep heaving and falling, heaving and falling inside his ribcage, the lovely warmth that is his sleeping wife. Her hair on the pillow is a burnished colour, the colour of those broad-shouldered radiators his parents used to have; and the heat her body gives, he compares it to central heating, warming the core, the centre of himself. He doesn't know whether he should call this feeling of being warmed 'love'. Love has always seemed such a sumptuous word to Larry Kendal that he has held it apart from his private vocabulary, like a medal kept hidden in a leather box and never pinned on. Earned of course, but just not worn, not displayed. But no, he decides, it isn't precisely love that he's feeling, in this dull white dawn, not precisely, yet he's not ashamed of what he does feel: the warmth of Miriam in his bed is right, perfectly right, and he is grateful for these calm moments of certainty. Miriam and his car: to these he belongs. He is theirs, they his. This is *right*.

Larry turns his back on Miriam, pulls the sheet up to his eyes to shroud the light and tries to drift back to a sleep which, all night, seemed hardly to hold him so that he kept falling in and out, in and out of it like out of a boat or a tipping hammock. He tries his most effective sleep trick: think up three inventions, or if you're not asleep after three, think up five. Inventions are like sleeping pills: they satisfy that bit of the brain that won't shut up, they knock it on the head and you get drowsy. So he lies still and warm with Miriam's breathing at his back and concentrates first on a ready-pasted disposable toothbrush to be sold in vending machines in public toilets everywhere, called the Rush-Brush, no, the One-up Brush, no, the Brush-up Brush, yes that's it, the Brush-up Brush, and men in floppy suits with airline breath and perfumed women smelling of escargots de Bourgogne (to name but two categories of people) reach for these gratefully and the quick cleaning of their mouths alters the next few hours of their lives. But through these lives, as they hurry to kiss lovers or mistresses waiting at arrivals gates or in hotel lobbies, creeps a queer, primitive noise which sends them and the toothbrushes, though they try to cling on and have substance, back into the nothingness they stepped out of and Larry is there in the white room, empty of inventions, listening but not wanting to listen to Gervaise singing to her cows. Disturbed by these songs, Larry's brain sets up a ferocious conversation: if Gervaise won't sell me the barn, how much might it cost to lay a driveway to the right of the house down the length of the boundary and build a new garage there? Too much. Money he hasn't got. Money he has he must spend on the pool. Unless Miriam does well out of this exhibition she's planning. What are the chances? Not bad, perhaps. Watercolours are back in fashion. People want small, pretty, familiar things again. They're tired of being baffled. Art is creeping back inside frames. And Miriam's work, since she's found all these wild flowers in France (far more here than in Oxfordshire because it is Gervaise who rules this corner and not a business consortium), has got brighter and a little freer. But would Miriam agree to a garage? She feels nothing for the Granada. Hates cars, she says. Which is odd. She's fifty next month and there are slits of grey in her radiator-coloured hair, yet she hates cars. You're meant to love comfy, luxy things more as you age. Larry does. Take the swimming pools. He loved, *loved* those swimming pools. But Miriam didn't. She admired them, but she didn't love them. Though why is he using the word 'love'? Even for the pools, it wasn't exactly love. Just, he was so proud of those pools, they were so sparkly and new. This new azure jewel replacing nettles or a field, this superb manifestation of design and plumbing and know-how where before there was only wasteland . . .

On it goes, this talk that won't stop to let sleep edge through. The bell chimes the half hour. The light behind the thin curtains expands in brightness. Larry, in this foreign hamlet he must now think of as home, feels a prisoner of all the waking and beginning going on outside the window, and opens his eyes to listen.

M. Mallélou's sepulchral voice is calling up dark wooden stairs: 'Klaus! Klaus!' Mallélou has set out bread and coarse ham and three bowls for the strong coffee he makes every morning. His hands fuss over this making of coffee, measuring, pouring. He's a small sinewy man with cavernous speech. Larry Kendal refers to this man, always, as 'old Mallélou' and he seems, to those who don't know, more like the father of Gervaise than the husband. Klaus must be the husband, they decide, despite the German name: Klaus is the husband and Mallélou the father or the uncle. And Gervaise aids this misconception: in the evening, sitting by the stove, one elbow on the oilcloth table, she places a naked yellow foot tenderly in Klaus's lap. He takes it in his red German hands and massages and warms it.

Mallélou worked on the outskirts of the city once, a poor job on the railways, tapping the line. Then he was promoted to signals. In the perched-up signal box he felt content. 'The life of a signalman,' he told Gervaise, 'it's all right. I would have been comfortable with that.' And now, years later, he often thinks about the fugged smell of the signal hut, the tin mugs of coffee, the ashtray the shape of a woman, and mourns the passing of something agreeable. The thing he'd liked every morning was you stubbed out your first cigarette in that woman's pussy. And you felt okay. You looked out at those sloggers on the line and thought, *imbeciles*. But when the father of Gervaise died, Mallélou went back with her to the old man's bit of land. The brothers wouldn't go. They had jobs in the print in Angoulême, jobs too good to leave for a few hectares. And Gervaise had never, in her simple head, left those fields. The soot of the railways had made her wring her hands. 'I don't feel sane,' she'd say, 'in this smog.' So they returned. It was dawn-to-dusk work, the farm. No walking home with the lights glimmering in the city rain and thinking, that's it for now, a day off, get out tomorrow and see a Hollywood film. You never got out from Gervaise's farm. It cried and bleated and sang to you in every season.

Klaus descends. There's a roguish majesty in all his movements. Standing at the table where Mallélou has set out the ham, Klaus dwarfs the older man like a giant Goth. His skin is pink, pig-pink fleeced with curly gold that lightens in summer; his mouth is a sweeter colour, the purple-pink of the smoked ham. Mallélou has a secret plan for Klaus: to get him to Paris to meet Claude Chabrol. He trusts absolutely Chabrol's willingness to turn the weighty Klaus into a star. But Klaus shows no sign of wanting to go to Paris. He seems happy with his slow, labouring life. He seems, in fact, one of the most contented men Mallélou has ever met. Yet why? His trade was bread. There was money in the city bread shops. He was doing well and he chucked it. Just chucked it and stayed on with Mallélou and Gervaise, listening out the winter evenings by their fire.

'Go and call her, Klaus. Tell her the coffee's hot.'

'No. She'll come in when she's finished.'

'Well she's late today.'

'So? She's late.'

'I'm not waiting for her then.'

'Don't wait.'

But they hear her now, that flip-flap of her rubber boots. After her meal she will measure the milk into churns while Mallélou drives the cows back to their pasture. She comes in, her breathing audible but shallow, her skimpy hair flat on her forehead under the soft scarf, her little flinty eyes bright like an animal's. Klaus draws back a chair for her and smiles, as if a king or queen had dropped in for tea. Mallélou turns back to his coffee on the hob.

The post van bouncing on the rutted lane wakes Miriam. Miriam Kendal, née Ackerman, makes the transition from sleep to alert wakefulness elegantly, without fuss or sighing. At almost fifty she's well fleshed but not soft, large but not fat. Dependable, she seems, stoic, healthy. Larry envies his own son his robust mother, yet often feels that for a wife he might have chosen someone more fragile, with a greater need of him.

Miriam puts on a garment she privately addresses as la robe. Sometimes she paints wearing la robe. Sometimes she goes out to the flowers in la robe and thinks of Sissinghurst and Vita Sackville-West and her friends wearing those strange clothes they wore. Mainly la robe is a comforter. Larry calls it 'that thing'. 'Why're you in the garden in that thing, Miriam?' 'It's not "that thing",' she wants to say, 'it's la robe.' She loves it. It's loose and full of pockets. She designed it and made it herself with a remnant from Dickins and Jones. She made it for the French holidays, for summer and a terrace. Now she's in it all year till winter.

She can hear Larry talking to the postman. The way Larry speaks French makes him sound both eager and helpless. This isn't merely true of Larry, Miriam has noted, it's true of almost all the English men. Somehow, the women manage this language better. Or perhaps the eagerness, the helplessness is simply less embarrassing in a sex the whole terrified patriarchal world is hoping will retain its last shred of docility and willingness to obey. It's odd though, she flinches when Larry talks French. She has this thought of displacing him to Germany where, in hard monosyllables like *gutt* and *Gott* and *nicht* and *nacht* he might regain some missing strength, some sort of dignity.

The door of the post van slams. Miriam at the window watches it reverse almost to Gervaise's yard and bounce up the lane. Letters don't often come. The Kendals' absence in England is no longer new. It's assumed they've 'made a life for themselves'. Only Leni writes every month. You can measure date and season by Leni's letters.

'Is it from Leni, Larry?'

Miriam comes down the uncomfortable staircase. Larry stands in the wide kitchen-living room. For some reason he's slung a tea towel over his shoulder and he holds this in just the same way as, twenty-seven years ago, he held their baby, Thomas. Men slung with tiny babies make them seem so light. Larry's a well-built man, his legs just a little too short for his torso. His face is wide and his blue eyes generous and kind. His hair is wild, curly and grey.

'No. Not Leni. It's not her writing. But it's postmarked Oxford.'

'Oh? Who, I wonder?'

'Addressed to you.'

The mist has cleared. On the flagstone terrace, expertly laid by Larry, the sun is falling on straggly geraniums in plastic urns painted to look like stone. Old Mallélou has admired the lightness of these pots. His own existence is hedged with weightier things.

'I'm off then, Miriam,' says Larry. He wears shorts and a sweat shirt. His sturdy, short legs beneath these move him rather jerkily to the hook where he hangs his car keys.

'Off where, Larry?'

'Périgueux. It's time I looked up those pool suppliers.'

'I thought we were going to wait till the spring now.'

'I don't want to wait. I want to get on with it.'

Miriam goes to the fridge and takes out a carton of orange juice. The orange juice in France tastes of sugar and chemicals. Miriam mourns her Unigate delivery.

'Well. What time will you be back?'

'Oh, not sure. Car needs a spin. I'll go via Harve's and see if he wants anything. You'll be working, won't you?'

'Yes.'

'Remind me, when I get back, there's something I want to talk to you about.'

'Talk to me now.'

'No, no. It's not that important. Just a thought I've had about the car.'

'The car? You're not thinking of changing it in are you?'

'We should trade it in this year. But I don't think there's any question. Next year perhaps, after the pool's in.'

'So what *about* the car?'

'Nothing, Miriam.' Larry is agitated now, wanting to leave. The Périgueux road goes past a waterfall. Perfect spot, this, he always thinks, for a car commercial, and imagines himself in a spanking new Datsun Cherry or a VW Scirocco. 'It's just a little scheme which, like all my schemes, will come to nothing.'

'What are you upset about, Larry?'

'Upset?'

'Yes. You seem upset.'

'I'm not upset, Miriam. I'm just keen to press on.'

'You'll get a beer and a sandwich or something for lunch?'

'Yes. Don't worry about me.'

Miriam smiles. 'Larry, you've still got that tea towel over your shoulder.' Larry doesn't smile. He seems fussed with rage. He snatches the towel off and leaves without another word.

In the lane, his passage to his Granada is temporarily blocked by Gervaise's cows slipping and swaying past his house on their way back to the fields. Mallélou with his stick and Larry with his car keys exchange a silent greeting.

Miriam sits down at the heavy wooden table – bought in Eye, Suffolk, for six pounds – and opens the letter. It is, after all from Leni Ackerman, but written in black biro by someone else.

> 25 Rothersmere Road
> Oxford

Dearest Miriam,

> *Kind Gary – you remember my lodger, Gary? – is going to help me with this letter because at the moment my silly hands refuse to do anything practical, like holding a pen.*

> *I'm not writing to worry you, but I have been ill. Dr Wordsworth talks about a 'respiratory infection' but the old rascal means pneumonia and I was in hospital for a while. Now I'm home and a nurse comes. She gets paid with that BUPA thing I've kept on since your father's death. I think they rake it in, those private insurance schemes, but now I'm grateful for it and my nurse is called Bryony which I like as a name, don't you?*

> *I hope I shall be up soon and back at my desk. And perhaps at Christmas you might afford the trip over. I do miss you, Miriam darling, and have thought of you so much in this recent time. I hope those plans you had for a new exhibition are going on well. With love and blessings from your loving mother, Leni. PS. Where is Thomas? I've forgotten where he is or what he's doing? If he's in England, please ask him to come and see me.*

Miriam reads this letter twice and tears gather quickly in her
grey eyes and begin to fall. When Miriam cries, she cries
copiously: 'Look at Miriam's tears!' Leni used to say delightedly.
'They're so round and perfect!' And Miriam can still feel the
scented dabbing of Leni's lawn handkerchiefs and hear her
screechy laugh. Leni. Impossible to imagine you dying. Impossible. Miriam wipes her eyes with the sleeve of la robe. Get well,
Leni. Get strong again. Don't leave me. Don't.

But Miriam's mind has already heard, in some hard and buried
part of itself, this certainty: Leni is dying. She pushes away the
orange juice, lays her arms on the table and weeps. Outside,
she dimly hears the Granada start up and thinks for a moment
of calling Larry back to comfort her, and tell her it isn't so. Yet
it is so. Miriam knows. She prefers to be alone with this
knowledge and let it bow her.

Gently, on her bed in the spacious old Oxford house, Miriam
lays out her mother's dead body. At her back, out of sight behind
the door, students fuss and whisper, boys mostly, bringing
flowers. Miriam selects a dark dress, thin with time, with
clusters of sleek, soft feathers at each shoulder. The Crow
Dress. A hat used to go with it: more feathers and a velvet-
flecked veil. She finds this and lays it down while she touches
the fine, fine contours of the face, eyes vast in their sockets, a
nose like Napoleon's in the Delacroix painting, angular and fierce.
Leni Ackerman. So beautiful.

At the waterfall, Larry turns left up the steep drive that leads
to Harve's house. There's a mush of chestnut leaves on this
track and the green husks of conkers. Autumn begins, then the
winds come and it starts to feel like winter. Harve's house is
two centuries old, with a stone turret and brown, echoing cellars.
He's been alone in it but for a maid, Chantal, for years now.
He's fifty-one and a bachelor: Docteur Hervé Prière, known to
Larry affectionately as 'Harve'. He's a slim and careful man with
a proud forehead and slow exquisite speech. Larry loves him
for this, his care with language. He was the first Frenchman
Larry could understand.

He's in a room he calls the bureau with his straight, dry legs resting on a hard sofa. These legs are in plaster from heel to knee, the vulnerable imprisoned feet covered with woolly socks like egg cosies. His long hands flurry with a medical journal but he's not reading it; the broken legs disturb and reproach him. Where will the next years lead him? To what precipice? He's become so somnambulist. The night he broke his legs, he flew down the stairs.

Chantal is away. Some dying parent or cousin in Paris. Poor old Harve slithers round the wood floors of his mansion on flat, sinewy buttocks, wearing a dark shine into his grey trousers. He prefers this slithering to walking with crutches, believes it's quicker, doesn't mind if he looks like a seal. And he says people in the village are kind: Nadia Poniatowski cooks him chicken with chestnuts; the de la Brosse widow lends him her maid to make his bed and do his washing. The practice is suffering, though. The young locum sitting in Hervé's consulting chair is too shy of bodies; has let slip he'd rather be a vet.

Larry parks the Granada on the gravel sweep. Harve's home, in its high isolation, always impresses upon Larry the lowliness of his own house, its hopeless nearness to Gervaise's south wall, the pretensions of its terrace. He feels diminished by Hervé's turret, by his sundial, by the wistaria dressing the stone with mauve cascades. This is elegance. This is nobility and money and roots. Larry has begun to fear that life led without the comfort of these is oddly futile.

'How are you, Harve?'

Larry has walked past dusty leaning suits of armour in the impressive hall and found his friend in the bureau, staring at his legs.

'Oh, Larry. Good. Good of you. So bloody boring all this. Imagine the war-wounded. What do they do? Restricted motion kills. It's killing me.'

'Yes. Or the man chained to his desk.'

'The man chained to his desk! That's good. Yes. What does he do? Dies. Have a drink, Larry. Sherry or something? A little morning cassis?'

Hervé waves feebly at a mighty oak cupboard where these drinks are kept. Larry has had no breakfast. He feels hollow and slightly unsteady. He imagines Miriam poaching her solitary egg, making a small pot of coffee, taking these into the sunshine.

'Well, a cassis . . .'

'Yes. Me too. I like cassis in the morning. Gets the stomach nice and warm. You pour them.'

Sunshine comes in the flat squares the colour of amontillado on the polished floor. Larry sits a few inches from Hervé's woolly toes and they sip gently at the strong blackcurrant. Hervé says, 'Did I tell you, I've sent for Agnès?'

'Agnès?'

'My niece. The elder one. Didn't get her place at the music school. All upset and mopey. So I told her mother, send her to me. She can play that old Bechstein and help me about. She's a sensible girl, not one of those young frights. She'll like these woods and this autumn air.'

'I'm glad, Harve. You need someone . . .'

'Yes. Another three weeks in this armour. My heart's not used to an invalid life. My blood pressure's up, I can tell without taking it. That's Agnès in that photograph. The one on the right.'

Hervé points to a picture on the mantelpiece of two windswept girls with their arms round each other's shoulders, smiling in what seems to be a Welsh or Scottish landscape, craggy and cold. They wear warm patterned jerseys; their hair is the colour of weak tea; they are clearly sisters. Larry is surprised by how English these fresh faces look. They could be English princesses on holiday at Balmoral.

'They look like princesses,' Larry remarks. Hervé smiles and sips his drink.

'Agnès was about seventeen then and little Dani fifteen or sixteen. Their mother is English. They speak the two languages very well.'

Larry looks at the photograph. Pale light on the smooth skin. No blemish anywhere. Better these radiant daughters than poor old Thomas going grey at twenty-seven with a pocked and crazy face the colour of a blanket. 'Oh, I would have liked a daughter,' Larry says.

'You have just the boy, Larry, haven't you?'

'Yes. Thomas. We don't see much of him.'

'If I remember, he has some antiques business.'

'Antiques? No. Wish it was. Modern. Marxist furniture, he calls it.'

'Cheap stuff?'

'No. There's the irony. Not cheap. Sick jokes for millionaires.'

'Oh yes?'

'One's a lamp. It's a giant naked bulb on a flex with a great piece of plaster attached to it. So it looks as if your ceiling's falling down. Don't ask me to explain the logic. Don't ask me why anyone would want that, but they do, it seems.'

'Well. Very odd. Comfort of course has always been regarded as bourgeois. As corrupting even. Perhaps your son believes the rich might buy broken ceilings as a kind of absolution.'

'Beats me, Harve. Miriam pretends to understand what he's doing, but she doesn't really. She's as baffled as I am.'

'Sad for her. Most sad. How is Miriam?'

'Working hard. Got this exhibition coming up, did I tell you? A gallery in Oxford.'

'I admire those watercolours. Would she bring a few paintings to show me before they go to England? I could buy some little flowers or a scene to put in Agnès's room.'

'When's Agnès arriving?'

'The end of the week.'

'Who will meet her, Harve?'

'Oh, she'll get the train to Thiviers. Then I shall pay a taxi.'

'No, no. Don't pay the taxi. I'll go and fetch her.'

'No, Larry. The taxi can come . . .'

'I'd enjoy it. Be a pleasure. I like to feel useful.'

'Have some more cassis, Larry. This is kind of you. But the Paris train's a late one. Nine-ten, something like that.'

'I'd like to do it, Harve. Any excuse to get out in the car.'

So, as the Granada takes Larry on to Périgueux, he finds himself dreaming of this princess of a girl, this Agnès. What would he have called his own daughter? Harriet? Emily? He likes names that sound like the names for stern-faced china dolls. Agnès he likes very much: old-fashioned, simple and fierce. He feels his heart lift. If a young person is going to arrive, all the more reason to press ahead with the pool. Then, next spring, he will invite her to sit among the urns, on the first hot days. He imagines the imprint of her wet feet on his terrace.

Nadia Poniatowski has dreamt of her French husband Claude Lemoine, incarcerated still in his 'Adjustment Home' in the Pas de Calais flatlands. He begged her, with sticky stewed eyes, to release him and take him back, him and his name and the thousand insanities busy inside his skull. No, she said, no, Claude. I changed my name back to Poniatowski, and the children's names, they're Poniatowski now and I'm teaching them about their Polish ancestors. You must stay where you are.

Nadia was grey at thirty-five with the madnesses of Claude Lemoine. Now, at forty-eight, she dyes her fine hair champagne blonde. She uses an English preparation called Nice 'n' Easy. She detests hairdressers. They complain about the thinness of her hair. And she's a proud woman. She won't listen to complaint about herself. She's reached the plateau beyond the murky valleys of her marriage and must not be dislodged from it.

Once, she and Claude owned two properties in Pomerac. When Claude finally went, she sold one of these to Larry and Miriam and lives in a small flat above the garage of the other house, empty now after another English family tried and failed to plant their hearts in it. She's got used to the flat. Her bed folds away into the wall. She cooks behind a Japanese screen on a second-hand Calor gas cooker. Polish recipe books are on a stained shelf above this. When she gives dinners, the silverware is still grand.

Talking is what Nadia Poniatowski loves. The details of lives, their longings and tragedies. She envies marriage counsellors their daily glut of private knowledge. 'Tell me, tell me,' she implores. She, alone in the village, knows that Hervé Prière has started sleepwalking. Secrets spill out to her in sighs and shivers and she breathes them in through a fine sensuous nose. Yet in her sympathising, in her giving of advice, as she lifts her white neck and pats her hair, she makes errors of grammar and syntax, gets the carefully learned colloquial phrase exquisitely wrong. People have momentarily forgiven and forgotten the most wounding betrayals trying not to grimace at Nadia's language. Claude in his infirmary still carries tender basketfuls of his wife's peculiar sentences in his drugged and dopey brain.

Towards noon, as old Mallélou sits on his step, staring at the yard where chickens and guineafowl disdainfully scratch, Nadia in white slacks and a tight turquoise blouse comes down the lane to Miriam's door. Miriam, still wearing la robe, has anaesthetised her grief with strong black coffee, but sits at the table still with an unwritten letter to Leni inside her head and a feeling of weariness in her hunched shoulders.

'Miriam!' calls Nadia, and taps with little stubby fingers on the heavy front door. From the south window of her flat she has seen Larry drive off in the Granada and knows that Miriam is alone. In the past – but never when Larry's there – Miriam has talked about the failures that brought them to their peculiar exile, about the birth and death of *Aquazure*, the swimming pool company, brainchild of the hot summer of '76, the one-time jewel in the plumbing of Larry's heart. But Nadia knows she hasn't been told all. Behind Miriam's dignified quiet, there's more. A breakdown, goes the delicious rumour. Larry has had a nervous breakdown.

'Miriam!' Nadia taps and taps.

'Who is it?' Miriam's voice is barely raised.

'Nadia, darling. Can I pop in? Aren't you working?'

Old Mallélou lifts his head. What a woman, that Poniatowski. Puts her husband in a nuthouse and never so much as visits him.

The door opens slowly on Miriam. Even to a less practised eye than Nadia's, the recent crying would be visible. Miriam turns away. Nadia follows her. Sometimes, Nadia reminds people of a shrill little dog.

'Sorry, Nadia, I'm not dressed . . .' Miriam's voice tails off. The presence of another person chokes her.

'Well, my God, Miriam, what's happened?'

'Nothing. Just a letter from Leni.'

'Leni, your mother?'

'Yes.'

'To tell you what for?'

'She's ill.'

'Oh my God, so serious?'

Miriam goes back to her chair. She folds her arms round herself, as if for protection from this intrusion.

'I don't really know, Nadia. I think it may be. She's seventy-eight.'

'Oh and you the single child, Miriam. You must go to England of course.'

Miriam sighs. 'Well, that's what I've been trying to decide. I don't want her to see me and be frightened, but on the other hand . . .'

'Who is looking at her?'

'Nursing her, you mean?'

'Yes. Looking at her.'

'A nurse. And Gary's there. He wrote the letter for her.'

'Who is this Gary?'

'Her lodger. He's been there for years. She mothers him.'

'Well at least she has some companion. But if I were you, Miriam, I would go there. Let me come with you.'

'Oh no. I'd be perfectly all right.'

'But this is too upsetting, I know. Like the terrible one time I visit Claude and see all those people round their rockers . . .'

'Leni isn't "round her rocker", Nadia. She's just getting old.'

'And what does the doctor saying?'

'She's had pneumonia. Badly, I think, because she's too ill to write. Perhaps her heart is weak. I don't know. I think maybe I should go to England.'

'Yes. And let me come, Miriam. I can do all these arrangements.'

'No, Nadia. Larry can fix the travel. He loves this kind of little chore, and he's very good at it.'

'Oh but I must come.'

'No, no. You stay and keep Larry company.'

'Poor Larry also.'

'Why "poor Larry"?'

'With the swimming pool question.'

'That's in the past, Nadia.'

'But these such things are never past, Miriam, I don't think.

Even now Larry would be dreaming of all that swimming pool disaster.'

'Dreaming of it? Well, perhaps he does. But he's thinking of trying to start the business again, out here. The climate's a lot better here.'

'But not the people, I don't see. Larry will not sell any swimming pool to those Mallélous!'

Miriam laughs. For a moment she imagines Gervaise, Mallélou and the mighty Klaus standing and staring with awe at this wonder Larry has sunk in their chicken yard.

'No. Not to the Mallélous. But there are a lot of holiday houses . . .'

'But mostly British, no? You hear them all at Riberac: "Sorry old bean, chippy-choppy old buffy bean." Old bean all the time but not money for pools I'm thinking. Anyway, Miriam, we must talk of your mother.'

'Sit down, Nadia.'

'Thank you. You are loving your mother a good much, Miriam?'

'Yes I do.'

'I think the single child is always loving the parent.'

'Maybe? Love or hate. But Leni is . . . like a rare species. Something beautiful going forever. I used to think when I was little, she had a kind of magic, because everyone seemed to love her and want her to like them.'

'And your father is Don?'

'He was a history professor, yes.'

'And dead?'

'Yes, he's dead. He died in '75 very suddenly.'

'So your Leni is so on her own now.'

'Well she's not entirely. She's never moved from Oxford, so she has a lot of friends. There's even this man who wants to marry her.'

'And seventy-eight, my God! Why is there no kind rich man wanting to marry Nadia?'

'You're not divorced from Claude, are you?'

'No. But I get this divorce any time. Just I say look where he is in this loony bowl and the judge divorces me straight away.'

'Would you want to marry again?'

'My God yes! Where I am I have no money. Down on my
bum end, you might say. Perhaps in Oxford there is some old
choppy bean for Nadia.'

And so an hour passes. The sun is hot on the terrace, the
geraniums in need of water. But Miriam and Nadia sit on at
the table and talk of Oxford and madness and marriage and
death.

Larry reaches Périgueux and parks the Granada in a square
behind the St Front cathedral. The ornate shoulders of this
building appeal profoundly to Larry's sense of design. He has
already decided to offer a 'St Front Pool' as part of the new
range he has nervously planned for his reconstituted company.
The thing is to build his own first – the show pool. Use the St
Front colours in the mosaic trim on the side and steps. Maybe
use the ground plan of the basilica as a kind of template for the
shape. Put in two or three sets of steps at different angles. Give
the customers the idea of something utterly new. Let them see
that pool-building is art. He feels light-headed with hope. The
sky above St Front is azure and the domes gleam. Larry wonders
fleetingly whether this surge of optimism comes direct from
God.

It takes him almost half an hour to locate the pool suppliers'
ramshackle premises, designated *Piscines Ducellier Frères*, by
which time it it is mid-day and a blue-coated employee is tugging
a sliding grille across the shop front. Larry curses the way, in
France, twelve o'clock hangs like a guillotine over the galloping
hours of the morning. No matter how early you wake, the slam
of mid-day always sounds too soon. And then time slows and
drags. You sit in a café waiting for life to start again. You drink
beer and fill up with wind. You feel randy and sad.

It has been market day, but the market, too, is over: the
meat and cheese wagons have gone, the ground by the fish stalls
is slushy with ice; a tired woman, making pancakes since dawn,
snatches down her sign: *crêpes sucrées; chocolat confiture grand
marnier*, men with wide, tattooed arms pack boxes of women's
underwear and overalls and blouses; an elaborate display of

bridal sweets, smelling of burnt sugar, is taken down and loaded into a car; crates of live chickens ride away in a caravan.

Larry finds a pizza stall and carries his wedge of pizza, wrapped in a paper napkin, to a sunny café with orange plastic chairs. He orders a *demi*. The pavement at his feet mills with people. One man carries a larch tree in a heavy tub. He seems to walk jauntily nonetheless and in time to a sweet, long-ago song that surfaces in Larry's head as he sips the cold beer: *Hello Mary-Lou, goodbye heart*. The larch-carrier passes out of sight, but Larry can still see the tip of the tree bobbing above the heads of the people. He likes this busyness. He likes the hard commercial buy-sell brightness in the women's eyes. Perhaps this is where he and Miriam should be, in the city. Consumers. *Consommateurs*. With so much to have, to wear, to swallow. *Consommations*.

But then he remembers the eagle. He's seen it twice now. A week ago on the roof of Gervaise's milking barn, then this morning there on the boundary wall, his wall. On the barn roof, high up, it didn't look so vast. A hawk, he told himself, a kestrel, a buzzard . . . But close to him, no higher than his head, you couldn't doubt it. The first eagle he's seen in his life and it sits on his wall like some tame sparrow! Miraculous things occur so disappointingly seldom, Larry has come to believe you have to *make* them happen. That feeling of shivering, of the self becoming small. Superb. The eagle dwarfed him. He was afraid to watch it take off and reveal the great width of its wings. No wonder these birds are a protected species. If we let all the wonders go we'll become crazy with our sense of loss. When *Aquazure* collapsed, Larry was wounded so much less by the sad reproaches of his employees, by the grim sighings of the bankers and solicitors, than by the loss of the thing itself, the pools. The pools became so magnificent, after he'd lost them. He remembers his first pool: oil-heated in the days before electric heat exchangers had become the thing; a Roman-end pool, concrete, no vinyl anywhere, real mosaic tiles, dive board and slide, non-slip surround, underwater light, and a pool house converted from eighteenth-century stables, fitted with kitchen-ette, changing rooms with basins and mirrors, a toilet with a rainbow blind. He'd looked at this finished miracle like God upon creation and was well-pleased. But, unlike God, he couldn't alter the weather. The summer after that pool went in, it was used for less than three weeks. The same year, building other pools by then, the work hampered and made difficult by rain, Larry met an American meteorologist on a London tube train. This meteorologist said English scientists should be exploring the possible use of the Rosenblum Crystal in weather control. 'Ah, the Rosenblum Crystal,' said Larry, as if he knew, 'yes. Why aren't they exploring it?' The meteorologist shrugged. 'Dunno. Perhaps they like this climate.' Larry never discovered what the Rosenblum Crystal was but there were many days, hundreds even, when he thought about it: a magical particle, roseate, he imagined, dispersing cloud like tear gas, making pathways for the sun.

The café fills up. Near Larry, a dominoes game begins. The men shout. Larry marvels at how quickly they get into the game. The comfort of routine, repetition. He has no routine now. No one waits for him, watching a clock. He waits for no one. Next only to the pools, he mourns his office. It was a functional place, never beautiful, never plush, yet it constantly reaffirmed an order of things with which he felt content. Larry envies the men not only the domino game but the day-to-day patterning of time that brings them to this café at this hour. He senses that they never miss a game. Just as he, well or ill, never missed one day at *Aquazure*. Not one. So no wonder, when it all went, he felt helpless, like a rape victim, fouled up and helpless. And it was Miriam who decided one day, it's enough. We must try a new start. The new start was France. The house at Pomerac. Now, a year after that start, Agnès Prière is arriving. And an eagle perches on the wall. Larry orders a second beer and waits patiently for two o'clock.

There are fifteen houses in Pomerac. The grandest is the Maison de la Brosse, a square, gated house, nicely settled behind pollarded limes. The other houses seem to have grouped themselves round this one without attempting to form a street. Lanes pass round them, through them. Dogs sleep in these lanes, sidle crossly away when cars hoot. It's a village without a centre, a

hamlet which expects no visitors, no traffic, and no map-makers.
There is no shop, no church and no café. The forty or so
residents possess between them seven motor cars, twelve
mopeds and twenty-two bicycles. There are few children. Animals outnumber children by far. Mainly, it's a village of people
growing old, people born there like Gervaise and just carrying
on. When they die, an ugly hearse takes them down a main road
to the great squat church of Ste Catherine les Adieux to be
buried in unfamiliar soil. They buy their plots at Ste Catherine
in advance and the frequent visiting of relatives makes them
feel, perhaps, that they 'belong' there. Yet this church is badly
sited, near a sewage plant. Huge tankers scream past. You can
imagine the bones jiggering in their shaken graves.

The oldest living inhabitant of Pomerac is M. Foch, known to
all the villagers as 'The Maréchal'. He's a stooped and serious
person with springy white hair and eyes like owls' eyes, circled
by time. He's been widowed for years now, lives out each day
in fumbling solitude, sucking down the broth that keeps him
alive, sucking on a blackened pipe. He makes baskets. Mme
de la Brosse arranges the sale of these for him in Périgueux and
Angoulême. His baskets are neat and strong. You can't recognise
the ninety-year-old Maréchal in them. He knew Gervaise's
father and grandfather. Gervaise cooks a hen for him at
Christmas and Easter and on All Saints Day. Mallélou is afraid
of him because he mistrusts strangers and, to Foch, Mallélou is
still a stranger. When the English started to come to the village,
he raised his hooded eyes to glance at their shiny, big cars and
their marble faces and merely shrugged with despair
and disbelief: 'C'est la comédie humaine, non?' Larry, deviat-
ing from village custom, always refers to the Maréchal as
'La Comédie Humaine'. He has the notion that the sight of a
swimming pool in Pomerac would cause the old man's heart
to cease.

Gervaise dreads this death. The Maréchal is in her first
memories: looking for *cèpes* in the forests behind Ste Catherine
the Maréchal wearing a sacking apron with a big pouch, putting
her child's hand inside this pouch and feeling the warm *cèpes* like
minute limbs of flesh, smelling of leaves and earth, and feeling

afraid, as if she'd touched something private and forbidden. Then
her grandfather's funeral: crying for Grandpapa, not knowing
where he'd gone, not believing they'd boxed up his body. The
Maréchal took her out of the church and she sat with him in the
cold November graveyard with a light snow beginning to fall.
'He went to America,' he told her. 'All spirits go there because
there's room for them there on the prairies. When the prairie
grass whooshes and sings, that's the spirits calling.' But the
word 'prairie' sounded lonely, far too lonely for Grandpapa,
with his wine-breath and his chatter about governments, so she
wept and the Maréchal gave her his handkerchief, which was
red and white and smelt of lavender. The Maréchal was perhaps
fifty then. His wife, Eulalie, was a seamstress from Thiviers.
To Gervaise, this couple always seemed old and, when Eulalie
died, she wasn't really surprised. But she got used to the
permanence of the Maréchal. His going would tug deep at her
heart.

The Maréchal owns no land now. Bit by bit as he aged he
sold it off to his neighbours. The de la Brosse family bought
most of it and Mme de la Brosse is now the largest landowner
in Pomerac. She also owns a milk pasteurising plant. Gervaise
has always thought of the de la Brosse family as being rich. A
maid is employed at the house. Mme de la Brosse buys her
clothes in Paris. Yet the house has a neglected feel. Most of its
rooms are shuttered. For long periods of the year, Mme de la
Brosse is away. Only at Christmas does she offer hospitality:
after Mass on Christmas Eve, the villagers are given hot wine
and cinnamon cakes. For the children, there are lollipops and
sugar angels. Some don't bother to turn up. 'To another year,
Mme de la Brosse!' someone says and the slim little widow
raises her glass and answers: 'To another year!' But you sense
she's tired. She's not more than sixty – young enough to be the
Maréchal's daughter – but exhaustion seems to hang in the limp
folds of her eyelids, in the vexed lines at the corners of her
mouth. 'Life,' says this creased and bedraggled skin, 'has never
been much.' The only person in the village who seems to interest
her is Klaus. Perhaps their mere size difference astonishes her.
Last Christmas, Klaus made a sumptuous Bûche de Noël,

decorated with holly, and brought this to the Christmas Eve party, carrying it aloft in his wide, red hands. Mme de la Brosse clapped and blushed: 'How kind, how kind . . .' She stood and admired it like a statue. Klaus put a knife into her neat white hand and held his own over it, like a bridegroom. Mme de la Brosse laughed a trembling laugh. As the knife cut into the rich chocolate cream, she felt ecstatic. And many of the Pomerac women, it seems, yearn for Klaus. None can understand why he's there among them or in what way he belongs to Gervaise. Is it true that he's her cousin? None remember him in her childhood. Or is he part of the years when she was away, living in the railway house outside Bordeaux? Was he her lover then? Has old Mallélou turned a blind eye? Could Klaus be the father of her sons? Is this why he stays with her, handsome Klaus, with old Gervaise, nudging fifty? Mallélou isn't saying, nor Klaus, nor Gervaise. When you call on them on a winter evening, there they sit, very close to each other, the three of them by the fire. So the question of Klaus remains the most potent mystery in Pomerac, a community so obedient to the seasons it has little heart or time for concealment. Birth, death, aspiration, longing, failure, love: the knowledge of these things passes from mouth to mouth like the giving of kisses. Only the English newcomers are not embraced in this way.

When Larry returns from Périgueux, oddly depressed by his afternoon struggles with *Piscines Ducellier Frères*, he finds Miriam in her studio, not painting, but staring critically at pictures already finished. It's careful work. The brush strokes are quick, clean. You sense Miriam's love of sky, of churches, of wild flowers. Larry enjoys the quiet artist in his wife, feels proud. Miriam looks up from a watercolour of Pomerac seen from the main road, a little huddle of stone on the shoulders of a green hill. She stares at Larry without quite focusing her eyes and says blankly: 'Leni's dying.'

Larry sits down on a corner of paint-spattered work table. Leni Ackerman was never much to him. She disapproved of him, in fact. Seemed to enjoy making him feel stupid. But none of this counts now. He knows the quality of Miriam's love for

her. More obstinate love for a parent he has never encountered.
'Shit,' he says, and sighs.

Miriam looks down at the picture of Pomerac. She's changed
out of la robe and wears a faded blue skirt and a blue and yellow
blouse. Her eyes are dry but the skin around them seems
stretched and grey, as if with fatigue.

'You won't mind if I go to England?'

Larry feels panicky. Yes, he minds. Winter's coming. The
bed, without her, will be a tomb.

'When?'

'As soon as possible. I'd get a flight from Bordeaux, if we can
afford it. Or, if not, the Thiviers train to Paris, then on to
Boulogne and the ferry. I thought you might fix it tomorrow,
Larry.'

'Yes. I'll fix it.'

'Nadia offered to come with me, but I don't want anyone.'

Larry recognises this statement for what it is, a warning. He
understands. If Leni must die, then Miriam wants to be the sole
custodian of that death.

'What's she dying of, Miriam?'

'Heart. Her heart.'

'Is she being cared for?'

'Yes. There's a nurse. And Gary will be there.'

'Oh, Gary. Still calls Leni "Mother", does he?'

'I don't know, Larry.'

'I suppose it flatters her. What a trial he must be to live with,
though. Worse than a house plant.'

'She's fond of Gary.'

'Is she? I'm amazed. Still, better old Gary at her bedside than
me, I suppose.'

He didn't mean to say it. Christ. Why couldn't she have died
one spring? It's the winter that makes it bad.

'Sorry, Miriam. Sorry.'

'I know you don't like me going. For anything else, anyone
else I wouldn't.'

'I know. Yes, I know . . .'

'I couldn't live with myself if she died and I wasn't with her.'

'I *know*, Miriam.'

'It may only be for . . . quite a short time.'

'Yes.'

Useless. He feels useless. When they talk about Leni, it's as if there's some faceless higher authority, some Politburo kind of thing slamming them each in separate cubicles. Leni waits in the corridor, listening, knowing. It's so lonely in his cubbyhole, he could die.

'How did Nadia get to know?'

'She called in. She saw I'd been crying.'

'Have you cried?'

'Of course I've cried.'

There's silence in the small room. Outside, Larry can hear one of Gervaise's guineafowl screech.

'Best if you fly, Miriam. I'll telephone Air France from Nadia's.'

'Thank you, Larry. How were the pool people? Helpful?'

He'd forgotten *Ducellier Frères*. He feels too anxious to reveal the subtle ways in which this firm showed its mistrust of him.

'So-so. I'll work something out with them.'

'Oh, I meant to ask you, have you got a name for the new company?'

'Oh, *Aquazure* again. I'll stick with that. No danger of anyone here pronouncing it "Aquaisha".'

'I think you should change the name altogether.'

'What's wrong with *Aquazure*?'

'It's tainted.'

'With what?'

'With the bad luck.'

Larry gets up. He must go and pour himself a gin. He's seasick with this day. Up, down, up, down. God Almighty. He could kill Leni Ackerman. Stick a knife in her bony chest. He hopes, as he goes down the stairs, that she'll die quickly, before Miriam can reach her bedside.

That evening, towards six o'clock, the wind settles and dies and the air seems suddenly warm, like a summer night. Gervaise watches the pale, bulky shapes moving slowly in the dark field and feels grateful that time has brought her to this meadow, to this September.

Larry sits alone on his terrace. Thoughts slide and slip. This is his third gin. He feels flushed and breathless, his face a pink lamp in the quiet descending dusk. He's trying out the solitude to come. Wearing it. He admires the slow declining of light. His silly, shiny face like a beacon embarrasses him. He'd like to decline with the dusk. Become weightless, invisible. *Slipslidin' away* . . . Damn Miriam for loving her mother. Why had there never been a daughter, his daughter, who would love him in this same, fierce way? He'd asked for a daughter. So often. Oh, one of these days, Larry. One of these days . . . But all the days passed. Now, all there will ever be is Thomas. That raspy voice he's inherited from the Ackermans. And grey already. Thomas is *grey*. He'll be bald next. Old years and years before his time, making excruciating furniture. But there should have been someone else to replace him, a daughter. Except it's too late. For Miriam. Not for him. For him and Miriam, but not for him. Why not a baby somewhere else? Start again. Yet the baby could be a son. Grow up like Thomas, looking ancient before he's hardly alive. No point in that. Unless . . . Unless it was to stop the coming loneliness, this confrontation between his round face and the dark. He closes his eyes. His thoughts revolve. *The nearer your destination, the more you're slip-slidin' away* . . .

Inside Gervaise's house, Mallélou and Klaus are reverently watching their favourite weekly serial on a black and white television, so many times superceded by the year-in year-out production of newer models, it's as if the celluloid ghosts of the old programmes still palely turn beneath the programmes showing now. Thus, during this latest episode of *Devil or Man?* (*Homme ou Diable?*), Mallélou for a split second sees American canyons and tumbleweed, hears a dry wind. He nudges Klaus. 'What's that?'

'What?'

'Something peculiar there.'

The picture's streaking, dividing. Bodies are pinched sideways. Klaus gets up and thumps the set. The sound grows in volume, but the people are still pulled.

'Oh leave it. Leave it, Klaus.'

Klaus returns to his chair. Robert X, hero of the programme, this week masquerading as a surgeon, is about to insert an amplifier the size of a pinhead into the voice box of a beautiful singer, thus assuring her a rich and starry career and a scene in which he will go to bed with her. What appeals most to Mallélou about this programme is the way the hero is able to become, at will, numberless things. One week he was a tennis star. Mallélou didn't know how they'd filmed the climax to this scene, at the French Open Championships. Mallélou would like to write to the TV channel suggesting an episode in which Robert X was chief signalman at an important metropolitan junction. He has the germ of a story. A beautiful provincial girl is on one of the trains. On another is a beautiful Parisian girl. At the terminus, a stranger waits. Which train will arrive first? Aloft in his box, Robert X, the signalman, controls the destinies of these people. Stories. It makes Mallélou tremble to think he could escape his life inventing stories.

Gervaise comes in. She hates the harsh, sad light the television gives. And the quivering, growling pictures, they seem remote to her, meant for city people in apartment houses with their hearts boxed up in street names. They remind her of the years when she was a signalman's wife in that no-man's-land where the city hurls its debris of worn tyres, broken glass, rusting crates, and the countryside flings its poorest seeds, willowherb and ragwort and dock. In her head, she knew where, not far down the line, the city began and where, not far up the line, it ended absolutely and silence started and the earth was deep and rich. It seemed wrong that anyone should live in that in-between place. Leave it to the trains, she thought, and the dumped cars and the sodium lights. When her children were born, she was shamed by the world she showed them, just as these days it embarrasses and shames her to watch television. The stories they tell her, Mallélou and Klaus, after the Friday evening hour of *Homme ou Diable?*, stories of a person so 'advanced' he can alter in seconds the lives of ordinary people, they seem stupid to her, pathetic, sad. She wishes that Klaus at least didn't like them so much. She has no idea that Mallélou is seeing canyon ghosts and composing letters to the television company. She begins to set the table for supper. Robert X is now in a satin bed with the beautiful singer. Mallélou is smiling a satisfied smile. In the jumpy, vexing light, Gervaise puts out a tender hand and touches Klaus's head.

The morning is grey. Nadia Poniatowski has turned on her electric fire. Beyond her damp windows, a blanketing drizzle shrouds the village, so that the limes of the de la Brosse garden are no more than flat shapes and the house behind them invisible. Nadia hates this kind of smothering weather. She feels lost in it. She's glad when the telephone rings. Such a relief to hear a voice, to remember she's far from friendless . . .

'Good morning, Nadia, my dear. Hervé here. What a most unpleasant morning, uhm?'

'Oh Hervé. My dear dear. Yes. Too very miserable.'

'Now. May I ask a small favour?'

'Oh yes, dear Hervé. Always from Nadia.'

'My niece is arriving on Monday. Agnès, whom I believe you once met . . .'

'No. Not your niece I meet, but your sister . . .'

'Oh yes? Well.'

'Or sister-in-law.'

'Ah yes.'

'I think I am meeting your sister-in-law, Hervé.'

'Ah. Well, no matter. Now, the question is, would you mind bestirring yourself in this very unpleasant mist to give Larry a message from me.'

'Larry and Miriam?'

'Yes. Or, in this case just Larry, who has kindly offered to meet the Paris–Thiviers train for me, and bring my niece up to the house.'

'Oh but of course, Hervé my dear. I will do this collecting.'

'Thank you, Nadia. Will you tell Larry, then, that the Paris train gets in at 9.18 on Monday evening and Agnès will be on this?'

'But why I am telling Larry?'

'What?'

'No. Well I'm not bothering to tell Larry.'

'You can't?'

'Oh no. Nadia will do this.'

'I'm so sorry, Nadia. You seem to have lost me . . .'

'Why am I bother telling Larry, when I am meeting your girl?'

'Well, just the day and time, Nadia. Agnès called me a few minutes ago to say which day she would be coming.'

'Nadia will go.'

There is silence at Hervé's end of the telephone. Near him, on a mahogany balustrade table is a silver box engraved with the signed names of members of his father's regiment. Hervé does not understand why he has always found the feel of these names beneath his thumb soothing and sweet, but he does. He touches them now, trying not to feel angry with la Poniatowski.

'Let's start again, Nadia. All I am requesting is that you should go down to Larry's house and tell him the time of Agnès's train.'

'Well all right, so, Hervé. You don't trust Nadia to drive?'

'What?'

'You think, oh a woman and a Pole into the boot with some Slavic perversion doesn't stop at the red light or something? You think this woman doesn't use her feet?'

Patience. Hervé strokes the dead names: Patrice Armoutier . . . Guy de Rocheville . . .

'What are you talking about, Nadia?'

'You think so a precious girl won't safe with Nadia? You think I'm not driving in all directions since I was eighteen years old?'

'Nadia, Nadia . . .'

'Is this what? Aren't you knowing I'm always conducting Claude the moment he is composing his headaches and always stopping at red lights?'

'What are you *talking* about, Nadia?'

'Talking about? I am talking about trust!'

Nadia thumps down the receiver. Despite the buzzing which tells him she has rung off, Hervé disbelievingly repeats her name a few times more while his fingers caress the box lid: Alain Dunoyer . . . Yves Bonnetard . . . Slowly, he replaces his receiver. He remembers angrily that the night he broke his legs, Nadia's high and sorrowing voice had somehow entered his dreams.

Nadia puts on her old beige raincoat. Claude used to puddle

about in this garment and it still smells faintly of the tobacco he
kept in its pockets. She blows her nose on a piece of kitchen
paper, picks up her key and goes quickly down her stairs out
into the silent, shapeless day.

At Gervaise's barn, she pauses. Klaus, a heavy black mackintosh over his head, is shouting at the cows bumping and slipping
down the lane. Nadia calls good morning but the little greeting
is lost in the mist. Klaus doesn't see her and strides on, slamming
the animal's rumps with a long hazel-switch.

Nadia picks her way between new cow-flops to Larry's door.
She knocks with a little fist still clutching the piece of kitchen
paper. Before she's withdrawn her hand, the door opens and
Larry, also wearing a beige raincoat, collides with her.

'Nadia! I was just coming up to see you.'

'Oh Larry. I'm talking now just to Hervé.'

'What?'

'He's not trusting me with his niece in the car.'

'What, Nadia?'

'This Agnès or what her name is.'

Larry glances back into his house which is dark on this morning
of drizzle. Upstairs, Miriam is still sleeping after a wakeful night
spent mourning Leni. Too drunk to comfort his wife with more
than sighings and belchings, Larry had stumbled off to bed and
slept soundly, dreaming of his own face, round and luminous like
the moon, up there in the firmament.

'Miriam's asleep, Nadia. Can we go on up to your flat? I need
to make a telephone call to Air France.'

'Oh you were coming?'

'Yes.' Larry moves Nadia out into the lane and closes the
door behind them.

'I think it's best if Miriam flies to London. I don't know how
ill Leni is, but neither of them would ever forgive me if I didn't
get her there in time.'

'Well, forgive you! If Leni is knocking up the daisies, she can't
forgive you or not!'

'No. That's quite true.'

'You are so nervous of women, Larry.'

'Nervous? Am I? I don't like Leni Ackerman, that's all it is.'

'Such a dreadful beauty, isn't she?'

'Yes. That about sums her up.'

'I know this kinds of woman. My Polish mother is being like this: very beautiful and all the men's heads are coming off in the street and they're spreading the red carpet over the puddles like Sir Raleigh, but then at home we have no carpet and my mother is always complain, look at this bloody puddles, and I'm not putting my foot in it.'

Larry giggles. He thinks of Claude in his prison. He hopes the poor man is granted some silence there on those buried battlefields.

'Why do you laugh, Larry? She isn't like my mother, this Leni?'

'Well, I don't know your mother, Nadia. Leni is probably quite all right with people she likes. She never liked me, however, and she's chosen, over the years, to make this very plain.'

'Oh what did you doing, Larry! Some practical fun? You put a whoopee pillow on her seat?'

'Metaphorically, yes. She thought the noise of my conversation was beneath her.'

They are almost at the doorway to Nadia's stairs now. The other houses in the village are still shrouded and no one moves in the lanes. Even the dogs are chained up, under cover. Nadia takes a key from her pocket.

'Well, you know Larry, I am so most upset about Hervé.'

'What's he done, Nadia? I didn't understand what?'

'Well this bloody niece or what she is. I say I will go for the Thiviers train in my car and lift this girl to Hervé's house. But no, he is saying, I am not putting my faith in you, Nadia. You will risking life and limb in your Polish driving.'

'Oh I see. Well I don't know why he couldn't trust you. But he did ask me to go for Agnès.'

'So you go, you go. Okay, I say Larry is a man, but who is going on the left, you or me? Maybe Larry is daydreaming he's rolling to Stonehinge and just forgetting right is right. No?'

Nadia unlocks her door. Immediately beyond it is a tiny lobby where she hangs Claude's mackintosh. Her blonde hair, now soaked, clings to her head like a cap. Larry, his mac over his

arm, follows her up. Nadia at once disappears behind the
Japanese screen and Larry hears her filling a kettle. At least, at
Nadia's, the tea is always good. They sit and drink this tea for
half an hour. Nadia alternately pats and prinks up her damp hair.
Larry's Burberry slowly dries in the heat of the fierce little fire.
Nadia steers the conversation from Hervé's seeming lack of
trust in her to the question of trust and betrayal in general. We
are all deceived, runs her threnody: the people or things we put
our faith in alter and disappear before our very eyes, like
mirages. Take Claude. Take the swimming pools. Claude was
a healthy man, vigorous, sexually potent, with a sense of humour
and springy chest hair. And then what happens? The health of
his mind begins to go, his limbs become weak and his fine pelt
turns wispy and grey. He is no longer Nadia's Claude. His poor
little sex dangles there like the lolling dead neck of a chicken.
His laughter fades. 'And the pools, Larry? The same with the
pools, no?'

Larry thinks of pink bird necks and dead laughter and shivers.

'So sparkling, no?'

'Yes.'

'Like my Claude. So beautiful sparkling eyes. I'm sorry you're
not seeing them.'

'I'm sorry, Nadia.'

'And I am never seeing those swimming pools. But I imagine.'

'Can you?'

'Oh yes, yes. Like those David Cockney painting, this loops
of brightness and all the lying people in their skin reflected. I
can imagine very good. No?'

Larry is silent. Nadia pours more tea, waiting for him to yield
up the dark confusion that came with the collapse of his dream.
But, oddly for Nadia, she has said it all for him: the phrase 'loops
of brightness' ransacks his mind like a lost song.

Miriam sorts paintings and folds clothes. Now that her flight is
booked, she does no more crying for Leni, but meticulously
prepares herself for her re-entry into what is left of her mother's
life. She remembers the house, the street, the neighbours, the
smell of autumn in North Oxford. Her desire to be there now is

like a sudden home-sickness. She wants to talk about it all, reminding herself that she can still belong there. It's just a question of arriving. She packs her tin of watercolours and her box of pastels. The act of closing the lids on these and putting them in the suitcase gives permanence to her stay in England. She looks up guiltily at Larry's anxious, grizzled head. 'It's no use,' she says, 'wondering if you'll be all right. I know you'll have the moments of loneliness. You'll just have to telephone me from Nadia's. And I'll write. Of course I'll write. But I have to go. You understand this.'

'Yes.'

He's never felt so distant from her. Miriam. His chestnut woman. His careful wife. The daily monitoring of what makes her happy, this is a habit he's never asked himself to break. Even when he was ill and depressed, he tried to 'get on' with each bitter day as she instructed him. He dreaded losing her then, when he had so little to give her. He had nightmares of Leni, then, waiting with her disdainful eyes, waiting to snatch Miriam from him. That he survived that time, that Miriam helped him so lovingly is a kind of miracle to him. He's never thanked her. The way he yearns to show his gratitude is by getting *Aquazure, France* started. He could do it, surely? The summers are long. Thousands come from England – and from Paris – to holiday homes. The public pools and lakes are overcrowded in July and August. He can beat *Piscines Ducellier Frères* at their own game, because he's not merely a pool builder, he's a pool *artist*. Consider the St Front idea; no mere pool installer would have found inspiration in a Roman-Byzantine basilica. He pictures the St Front pool installed beyond the terrace for Miriam's return, his gift for those months of patience.

'Have you packed up all the paintings yet, Miriam?'

'No. Not yet.'

'Harve asked me, could he see some before you go. He'd like to buy one for his niece's room.'

'His niece?'

'Yes. She's arriving on Monday, to help out.'

'Well I can't sell a painting. I need everything for the exhibition.'

'Just a small one, he said. A little still life or something.'

'No, Larry.'

He's begun to hear Leni's voice in hers. He thinks, she's hardening her heart. He can't bear to stand and watch her packing, yet he wants the comfort of her. He feels desolate, humble.

'You may be away for your birthday, Miriam.'

'Yes. Never mind.'

'I mind.'

'Why?' Leni again. Hardness. Curt questions.

'I wanted us to have a proper celebration this year. A party, even.'

'Who would we invite?'

'Nadia . . . Harve and his niece . . . Mme de la Brosse . . .'

'And the Mallélous, I suppose. Watch Gervaise eating with her mouth open.'

Larry ignores this, though it worries him. Miriam brought them here to live. Now, she's found an excuse to leave Pomerac and run back to Oxford.

'I thought we'd get Thomas out here for once . . .'

'Well, I'll be seeing Thomas.'

'I won't.'

'No. That can be my birthday gift then: seeing Thomas.'

She's packed two suitcases: almost all the clothes she owns are laid gently in. Left in the wardrobe are just the soft summer things. She's also bought Leni's favourite peach jam, sachets of *tisane somniflor* and a tin of Périgord *foie gras*. Larry imagines Leni's fragile lips opening and closing on this delicacy, her heart stopping as its poisoning richness enters her blood.

The mist and rain of Saturday linger on Sunday. The dampness quells the stench of the septic tank. Larry examines the Granada for signs of rust. Pomerac inhales moisture into its old stones and the interiors of rooms are dark and cold. Larry, wearing the Burberry, surveys the site of the new pool. A casualty of the pool will be the walnut tree Miriam is fond of and which now reproaches Larry with an exemplary crop of bright green fruit. Miriam wanders out and stands near him by the tree. She looks shabby, he thinks, in her bulky mac, and he touches her shoulder tenderly. At least she doesn't have Leni's sharp bones. Miriam reaches up for Larry's hand and presses it tightly. She, who is running, running to the bedside of her mother, feels in this moment like a mother to Larry. His blue eyes have a helpless look.

'Start the pool if you can. If the weather's good.'

'Yes. We'll need some building, though, to house the filter plant.'

'A shed?'

'Yes. Or I thought we could run a driveway by the wall, curve it round to a garage, there.'

'Too expensive, I would have thought. And we don't really need a garage.'

'Well, handy though. And I'd fit the plant at one end of it. Nice short run from there to the skimmers.'

'Our trouble was we always did things too grandly. Why build a garage?'

'You must conceive grandly! Or not bother.'

'A hut would do.'

'No. Not for me.'

Miriam lightly tugs away her imprisoned hand. 'You've got to stop dreaming, Larry.'

And she walks away from him slowly towards the house; the mother withdraws her love, slaps the child awake. Larry sighs. His heart is throbbing.

By the time her plane leaves on Monday, he's ready to feel relief at her going. On Monday morning, he sees the eagle again. It stares at him with an eye so flint-hard, he senses a challenge and he feels his spirit lift. When the eagle takes off, he knows it will return. What he dreads is to see its mate come, the pair. Only in its isolation does the bird inspire him.

At Bordeaux airport, it is still raining. In Miriam's mind, Oxford is cloudless, the stones yellow in afternoon light. All light has gone from the tarmac as she follows the crowd to the plane. Unseen by her, Larry waves, but she doesn't turn. As he climbs wearily back into the Granada he thinks of Agnès hurtling south on the Paris train, to be met, at last, by Nadia's waiting gabble. Travel. Change. Arrival. Loss. *Hello Mary-Lou. Goodbye heart.*

*   *   *

News of Gervaise's youngest son, Xavier, comes to Pomerac.

At twenty, Xavier Mallélou kissed a bitter goodbye to his job
on the railways, told his boss, in fact, that he could stick this
particular job (the laying of sleepers on a new stretch of the
Bordeaux-to-Biarritz line) up his grandmother's cunt, and went
to work for a certain Mme Motte who ran a cheap restaurant
for long-distance truckers in Bordeaux. Neither Gervaise nor
Mallélou had ever met Mme Motte, nor seen the small premises
where she offered a five-course set meal (soup, cold hors
d'oeuvres, hot dish, cheese, sweet) for thirty-five francs, but
Xavier had written one letter to say he had some responsibility
in this new work. He wasn't just waiting tables: he was negotiat-
ing with a new wine supplier and was 'getting to know properly'
the regular customers. He'd also convinced Mme Motte to get
little cards printed with the name and address and the price of
the menu on them. Business was brisk. On winter days, he was
warm by the chip-fryer instead of freezing to death on that bitch
of a line. Mallélou shrugged, remembering the signal box and
the coffee and the thighs of the ashtray. He didn't blame his son
for wanting to be warm, but he considered the railways to be 'a
fair master', whereas a widow running a café, what kind of boss
was this for a young man? Klaus reassured him. He'd worked
for a woman once, learning the bread business. They could treat
you fair. Yet Mallélou felt disappointed in Xavier. He wrote to
his son and advised him never to trust Mme Motte and never
to do her favours, sexual or otherwise.

Now a letter comes from the police. Xavier is accused of
stealing seventeen cases of wine, and three hundredweight of
potatoes from Mme Motte over a period of six and a half
months. Bail has been set at eight thousand francs. The accused
is being held in custody until this sum has been raised. The
accused has no visible means of support.

Gervaise weeps. That wasteland, that no-man's-land,
poisoned the heads of her sons. Everything they touched was
foul. They played football with old cans, they made swings with
worn tyres, they fished in a dead river. And the language. That
language of the hard, mucky wasteland boys. *Fuck and suck.*
Cunt. Arseholes. Nigger-lovers. Kill the Socialists. She weeps

for all of that which was, or should have been, their childhood and which, in its own bitter words, fucked them.

She goes up to the Maréchal's house. The mist and damp are still heavy on the village. The Maréchal sits by his range with a half-made basket on his knee. The pipe, barely alight in his mouth, is shiny with spittle. When he sees Gervaise, his owl's eyes take fire and he holds out his arms to her. She stoops and plants a little gobble of a kiss on each of his papery cheeks, then unwraps her gift to him, a roasted guineafowl. He looks at it in surprise, grabs the pipe out of his mouth.

'It's not a Feast Day, Gervaise.'

'No. She needed killing, that one. She was a screecher.'

'Very kind of you. Very kind . . .'

Gervaise sits opposite the Maréchal. She reaches out and touches his knee.

'I've not just come with the bird. I've come with a favour to ask.'

'Good. You ask, Gervaise.'

'My Xavier's in trouble. I'm ashamed. And sad. I'm so sad for him.'

'Well, a child is heartbreak. I told you, Gervaise . . .'

'Yes, you told me.'

'My children are dead. I've outlived them, eh?'

'I know.'

'Outlive your children! You don't imagine that.'

'No.'

'Perhaps you'll outlive your sons. With your strength, Gervaise . . .'

'Who can say. I think people die younger in the cities.'

'They like the city?'

'Yes, they say they do. They got used to it when they were small.'

'I'll eat that bird, some of it, this evening.'

'Yes. You enjoy it.'

The Maréchal eats, sleeps, lives in one room now. Upstairs, the old bedrooms are shuttered. Down here, he shuffles between the range and the small table and a tumbled, smelly cot. Outside, on the other side of the wall is a wash-house and a damp privy. On winter nights he pisses in a china pot rather than endure the cold. He has a saying: 'Winter's got me licked, where many women failed.' This one room hugs him and keeps him alive.

'Xavier's in prison, Maréchal.'

'Xavier?'

'Yes.'

The Maréchal puts his pipe back in his mouth, sucks on the embers. To him prison is wartime. Eating your own misery and loss, living on these until it was over. Like being kept alive on vomit. He's not sure how he survived it. He thinks part of his brain died, to save the rest.

'Where?'

'Bordeaux.'

'You need the bail money.'

'We have two thousand put away and Klaus has offered us three thousand. We need another three thousand. As a loan of course, Maréchal.'

The Maréchal gently lifts the basket off his knee. He remembers the day Gervaise was born. He got drunk with her father and they walked back from Ste Catherine wearing their trousers round their necks like scarves. After the two sons, the birth of a girl was a quiet miracle. And thank God for that stupefying, joyful night. Thank God for that baby, Gervaise.

He kneels down and from under his bed tugs a canvas bag, like an army kit bag. He leans on it for a moment, then pushes it towards Gervaise.

'You know the old tin where I used to keep maggots, in that time of the pike fishing?'

She knows the tin. Once, when she was a girl, it had a yellow and red label on it saying *Biscuits Chérisy Fils Paris*. She didn't know where or how the Maréchal had come by these delicacies, but gradually the label faded and peeled off, the tin grew dull and rusty and smelled of river slime. Now she holds it in her lap and it feels light. It's rusty, but clean. No trace of the maggot smell.

'You take out what you need.'

It's not the first time. She's borrowed from the Maréchal

before. She pays him back slowly, over months and months. The hens and vegetables she brings are the interest still owing.

She takes out three thousand francs and folds the money in the crease of her small breasts. She closes the tin and pushes it back into the bag, where it's padded out with ancient bits of clothing, some the Maréchal's, some his dead wife's and some, though he's forgotten what's what, belonging to his dead sons.

Gervaise's heart lifts. Tomorrow Mallélou will go to Bordeaux. By Wednesday Xavier must be released. And in this case the Judge must be lenient – a young man too big for his boots, a first offence . . .

'He didn't kill, did he?'

'No, Maréchal.'

'Your boys wouldn't kill, would they?'

She shakes her head, her lips tight. *Mother-fuckers. Fagsuckers. Jewish shit. Kill the Commies.* She feels tears start.

'No. I don't think they would.'

'Then it's all right. You take the money. And don't you worry about it.'

'He robbed a woman.'

'Well. Jewels, was it?'

'No. Wine and potatoes.'

The Maréchal's face creases into a thousand laughter lines. 'Potatoes! Potatoes! You tell him, just you tell him that's a waste of time. We've got plenty of potatoes here, eh Gervaise?'

Yes. Gervaise touches her eye, where the tears twitch. Yes. It's pathetic. Her sons are pathetic. Not like she wanted them to be. It's Mallélou's fault. It must be. In that sooty, overheated signal hut his blood and his semen grew too stale and hot.

Mallélou doesn't like it when Gervaise borrows from the Maréchal. In the days when he worked on the railways, he never borrowed and he has tried to teach his sons: never *owe* anyone. It humiliates him, in particular, to take money from a man who doesn't like him, who gives it to Gervaise because he's seen and known more of her life than anyone else. He's convinced himself that the Maréchal actually saw Gervaise born, was actually there, gawping at the mother's spread fanny when

her little peasant head came pushing out. It's become the thing
he resents most about the old man, this and the way he treats
Klaus with contempt. Who does the old bugger think he is?
Some tribal chief? Mallélou likes modern hierarchies, hates
primitive ones.

So when Gervaise comes back with the three thousand francs,
he quashes a momentary fear that the Maréchal wouldn't give
it to her this time, and snatches it from her breasts without a
word. Watching this, Klaus feels angry but says nothing.

Hervé Prière compares the touch and scent of his niece, Agnès,
to the touch and scent of falling blossom. Everything he notices
about her is light, gentle. Her voice, her straight shiny hair, her
feet. She plays the Bechstein with a touch so light, she turns
concertos to water music. 'Play *Clair de Lune*', Hervé asks.

And this piece of music enters his willowy soul and moves it.
He sees rivers and minnows and stars. His shoulders relax. His
restless fingers are still. If he could only hear this music in his
dreams, instead of the things he does hear . . .

She's been there three days. She drives his car and he laughs:
'You look like a kid behind the wheel of that car.' She's twenty.
Small like her mother and sister, with the mother's English
peachy skin. Her eyes are green, flecked with brown. She wears
pale, soft clothes – little rabbity jerseys, grey skirts – and flat
bright buds of shoes. She's neat in all her ways. When she
cooks, she dabs and wipes as she goes. And she likes food to
look pretty and neat. Under the baked egg dishes she fans gold
maple leaves, she tosses mint flowers onto the potatoes, she
arranges cheese on a criss-cross of washed twigs. Hervé is
enchanted, captive to these careful ways. Then he starts to
wonder about her. He wonders why, at twenty, she gives these
things such attention. Like the blossom she reminded him of,
falling from the old walled trees of his youth, she seems both
old fashioned and somehow lacking in substance.

After dinner, when she's washed the plates and dishes, and
put everything away, she arrives in the sitting room with a sad
smile. This sadness, there now and then in her playing, is what
moves him in her. *Mourning becomes her*. She doesn't see it.

He understands why the music school rejected her. She doesn't. If you'd found that – that grave bit of you – and shown it, they would have accepted you. She may grow old not knowing, not really knowing this.

She mentions a boy called Luc. Her own age. Doing his two years in the army. She thinks they'll marry when he comes out. She shows a photograph: a smiling, thin-faced young man. Shiny buttons. Hervé nods, approves. 'Do you love him, Agnès?'

'Yes.'

'Really love him?'

'We write every week. He's stationed at Lyon.'

'Could you die for him?'

'No, Uncle Hervé. I don't want to die. I think, it's silly to die for other people. I think it's a silly question.'

'Do you? Yes, you're probably right.'

But he has his answer: she doesn't feel love. What she may never discover, however, is that she doesn't feel it, letting the substitute for ever – mercifully? – obscure the thing. He hands her back the photograph. He feels both jealous of and sorry for this boy, Luc. He remembers what it is to be twenty and in the army and writing letters to a girl. The girl he wrote to was called Denise. She had spotty twin brothers and an obese mother and he dreaded she would become ugly like them. In his letters, he warned her not to eat chocolate cakes or drink alcohol. All his life, he has feared the blemishes women acquire. He couldn't have married Denise and watched her grow old. He preferred to remember her as she was, with unlined satin skin and long straight eyelashes like brushes. He knows this fastidiousness has prevented him from feeling the kind of passion which, these days, is expressed in close-ups of pushing sweating limbs in the cinema. He knows his old age will probably be lonely, but better this than sleep with the bad breath of some loyal decaying woman, better this than go mad with the gross imperfections of the domestic world, like poor old Claude.

On the morning of Friday, Agnès's fifth day at Hervé's house, Larry's fifth day without Miriam, the Granada bounds up Hervé's drive, splattering gravel, and stops at Agnès's feet. The mist has gone and the sky is cloudless. Agnès has been picking flowers for the drawing room, late roses and Michaelmas daisies. Walking sedately to the front door with her bouquet, she looks like a bridesmaid in rehearsal for a smart wedding. When the car surprises her, she stops absolutely still, as if at some appointed station of the marriage procession, and stares sweetly at Larry. He tugs on the handbrake, his mouth dry. Though he has imagined the wet footprint of Agnès by his pool, he has never clearly enough imagined the girl. She's wearing a mauve angora jersey the colour of the daisies, her neck and face above this are pale in the bright September light; her feet, in brown pumps, stand neatly together. Larry's mind frames this picture of her, then he looks away, as if from a snapshot of loved people long dead. He fusses with the car interior, closing the ashtray, winding up the window, extracting the keys from the ignition. Agnès walks on into the house, carrying her flowers. Larry gets out of the Granada and stares at the place where she stood a moment ago. He remembers he's come with some apology to Hervé, but can't think now what it might be. Unless it's to apologise for being there at all, which feels right. He thinks of Miriam in Leni's Oxford house. Oddly, the picture he makes of these two older women is comforting. He doesn't know why. He reminds himself to telephone Miriam from Nadia's flat.

Hervé is in the bureau as usual. His legs are still in plaster, but crutches are now propped against the mantelpiece.

'She's making me walk, Larry.'

'Well, it's time you did. You're wearing your trousers out on the floor.'

'Miriam gone? You never brought me a watercolour.'

This was it. This was the apology. Larry smiles with relief.

'No. I asked her, Harve. In the upset about Leni, she forgot. There are one or two hanging in the house. You could have one of these.'

'But they're not recent?'

'No.'

'Agnès loves flowers. Bright colours.'

'Yes, I saw her.'

'Oh you saw her. Well I shall call her and introduce you to her.'

'No. Don't disturb her. I expect she's busy arranging those flowers.'

'But you must meet her. Stay to lunch. She's making a courgette soufflé.'

'My word, Harve . . .'

'Yes.' Then a whisper: 'She's an extraordinary girl, Larry. She knows haute cuisine like a middle-aged châtelaine and she never seems to tire of the little domestic things: arranging this, shining that. I thought young people weren't meant to be like that any more. I don't know what's got into her.'

Arranging this. Shining that. *Exquisite*. A daughter of mine would have been that kind of person, Larry decides. The extreme opposite of Thomas with his obscene fabrications. Everything quiet and tidy and clean.

Then she comes in. She carries the flowers that were meant for the drawing room and sets them down on the balustrade table. In shadow now, the regimental names lie bedded in the box lid, just within reach of Hervé's fingers. He holds one hand a few inches above the box (a constant precaution) and with the other gestures Agnès round to the fireplace where she stands, demure and formal, in front of Larry.

'My niece, Agnès Prière. Agnès, this is my good friend, Larry Kendal, who is English. Larry's wife is the very fine artist I was telling you about.'

'Oh yes. Good morning.'

She holds out a hand that is still the firm, plump hand of a child. Larry takes it and presses it to his lips in the most un-English gesture he has ever made. It smells of the Michaelmas daisies, an almost bitter smell.

'Enchanté, Mademoiselle.'

Ridiculous. He sees the little tableau and himself in it as profoundly ridiculous, so he straightens up immediately from the kiss and lets go of the hand.

'Do you come on holiday to France, Mr Kendal?'

'On holiday? No, no. I live here. In Pomerac. My wife is on a kind of holiday – in England.'

'Oh yes?'

'Yes. Her mother's ill.'

'Oh I'm desolated. I hope she will recover.'

Hervé moves his brittle legs. 'Have a cassis, Larry. Agnès, get us both a cassis and you have whatever you want.'

Larry shakes his head. 'I musn't. I'm trying not to drink.'

'Why?'

'Dunno really. Just feel I musn't while Miriam's away. Afraid I'll start feeling sorry for myself.'

'Well. Have one cassis.'

'No. No cassis. A glass of white wine . . .'

'Yes?' Agnès smiles. The smile is so clear and brimming, it chills Larry's heart. 'Uncle Hervé has a nice Mâcon in the frigidaire. I'll get this.'

'Thank you.'

She goes out. Larry glances up to the mantelpiece. The photograph of Agnès and her sister has been replaced by one of Agnès alone wearing a long evening dress and holding a cello. There is something disconcerting in this picture. Larry can't yet see what it is but believes he will discover. A small silence hangs between him and Hervé. Hervé strokes the box.

'Well, what do you think of her?'

'I think you're very lucky, Harve.'

'Yes, I am. So fortunate the music academy didn't want her!'

'Is she upset about this?'

'I don't know. I would have been, at her age. This would have been her one chance of a career perhaps. Yet she doesn't seem to mind. I think she's very good-natured, like her mother. I like good-natured women. They age more slowly.'

Larry ponders this. If the reverse is also true and bad-natured women age rapidly, then Leni should look ninety by now. Yet she doesn't. She hardly looks her age. 'How long will she stay?'

'Agnès? Well. Till I can walk at least. Then I might give her some little work to do for me at the surgery, if she's not homesick for Paris by then.'

'You're looking better already, Harve.'

'Am I? My blood pressure's still up. And I'm putting on weight with all this cooking Agnès does. Please stay for lunch and help me out with courgette soufflé, Larry. I'm not hungry.'

Grated, the courgettes look like plankton, Larry decides. This dish isn't as aesthetically pleasing as it might be, though the soufflé itself is light. They eat it in Hervé's dining room off fine plates on lace mats. The room smells of polish and musty fabric. Months have passed since Hervé Prière entertained in here. But Agnès says she likes the dining room. She likes the right rooms to be used for the right things. While her sister eats television suppers, she spreads her little meal on a table. Arrange this. Shine that. It's the precision of Bach that makes him her favourite composer, not his so-much-vaunted soul.

She isn't shy. She has quiet poise. She tells Larry how much she enjoys going to England. Her mother has relations who live in Chester Square. She loves cashmere. Once she was taken to Newmarket Races and saw the Queen come out of her box onto a flat roof. She was surprised that there was no railing round the roof to protect the Queen. In France, this wouldn't happen. The President wouldn't step out onto something unprotected.

She asks Larry about Oxford. She's never been there. Her sister, Dani, is studying hard, hoping to go there to study medicine. Medicine is in the family. Music isn't. She doesn't know where her talent for music comes from.

'I don't think talents do "come from anyone",' says Larry; 'parents like to think their children get this or that directly from them – as long as what they get is good. But heredity is never the answer to genius.'

'Oh, genius?' says Agnès. 'I don't think I'm talking about genius, in my case. I just have a small talent.'

'A "small talent" is wonderful,' says Larry. 'I wish my son had a "small talent".'

'Larry's son is a furniture-maker,' Hervé says.

'Oh yes? How interesting,' says Agnès.

'Could be,' says Larry, wiping his mouth on a lace napkin. 'But it isn't. He makes rubbish.'

'I thought about what you said, Larry,' says Hervé. 'About the high prices he charges. I think this is perfectly in line with his revolutionary ideals.'

'Yes?'

'Yes. He's fooling the rich clients, don't you see? To sell a rich man a broken light bulb is clever.'

'The light bulb isn't broken, just the piece of ceiling.'

'Even more clever.'

'Oh, is this what he makes?' asks Agnès with a little furrowed glance at the neat place settings she has laid. 'Broken things? I hear about some things like this in Paris. Very new-wave.'

'New-wave?' says Larry, sipping his wine. 'Micro-wave to me – chuck it all in the oven and burn the lot of it! It's nothing but travesties.'

'Travesties?' Agnès says the word with hushed revulsion. 'Yes. I can't bear this.'

Hervé glances at Larry. The look says, you see, she is an odd girl, out of her time, so goody-goody. Like girls used to be told to be. But Larry sees this message coming and looks away.

That same evening, Larry walks up to Nadia's flat to telephone Miriam. Nadia and Mme de la Brosse possess the only two telephones in Pomerac. Normally, it irritates Larry, this telephoning from Nadia's. He remembers the time of the *Aquazure* office and his desk with two telephones on it, one blue, one white. Tonight, however, he's glad to have an excuse to visit Nadia. His own house feels cold. It's almost October. For the first time, he feels a bond with Nadia, in their separate solitude.

She answers the door, wearing a pink candlewick dressing gown. Moths have fed at the elbow of this garment. Occasionally, Nadia dreams of Lingerie Departments and satin quilted robes. When she sees Larry, she folds her short arms under her breasts and apologises.

'Oh, Larry. I don't expect you. I am just taking a bathe.'

'Is it too late to come up, Nadia? I feel I ought to telephone Miriam, if that's alright with you?'

'Yes. Come. Come. You're not minding I have my bed out of the wall?'

'No, Nadia.'

'I will make you some hot drink.'

It's not yet nine o'clock. There is something sad, Larry thinks as he climbs Nadia's stairs, in the way lonely people put themselves to bed so early. As if they've become children again, excluded from all the downstairs conversation. He's becoming one of them, too. Far away in Oxford, the adult world whispers round Leni's bed. As he asks for the Oxford number and is told to wait, he senses how little this telephone call matters to anyone there. It is simply an intrusion. The sob-sob of a child.

To his surprise, Leni answers. The voice sounds unchanged.
'Leni?'
'Yes. Who is this?'
'It's Larry. How are you, Leni?'
There's a long silence. Larry waits. He fancies he hears the sucking of the sea above the telephone cables. He imagines the million drowned voices chattering chattering back and forth between England and France. Or do conversations bounce now? Do they zip up into space and bounce off a dish and down again? He doesn't know. He sighs. In the 1980s, one should know these kinds of things. He looks round Nadia's room, cluttered, garish. Behind her Japanese screen, Nadia is boiling milk.
'Leni? Are you there? Leni?'
Still no sound. The tide comes in at Dieppe, at Calais, at Le Havre. The tide at Dover, at Ramsgate recedes . . .
'*Leni?*'
'Miriam here, love. How are you?'
'Oh Miriam. Was that Leni I just spoke to?'
'Yes. She has the phone by her bed.'
'Why didn't she talk to me?'
'She's not well, Larry.'
'She sounded all right. She sounded like she normally sounds.'
'She's been terribly ill.'
'Well. She could have acknowledged me, said hello or something.'
'How are you, Larry?'
So it's still there, the normal conspiracy. Leni is defended – even her worst rudenesses. 'How's the house?' says Miriam.
'The house is fine. Why wouldn't Leni speak to me, Miriam?'
'I've told you. She's not at all strong. Where are you? Are you at Nadia's?'
'Of course I'm at Nadia's. Where else? Or did you imagine the engineers had finally got round to laying the requisite number

of metres of telephone cable so that our house can actually be connected to the outside world?'

Silence again. Night falls on Cherbourg. Night falls on Southampton.

'Why did you phone, Larry?'

'Why did I *phone*? To talk to you, Miriam. You are in Oxford aren't you, or did I imagine your departure? I do sleep alone in our bed at night, or did I imagine this too?'

'Why waste money being angry?'

'Waste *money*?'

'Yes, you're wasting Nadia's money.'

'It is not Nadia's money, Miriam. It is my money. I do not make calls from here without reimbursing Nadia, as you perfectly well know, so what on earth is wrong with you?'

'Nothing's wrong with me. You're angry and I don't know why.'

'I was simply reflecting, Miriam, that if Leni is well enough to say "Who is this?" she is well enough to acknowledge me and ask me how I am . . .'

'Larry . . .'

'But no. Once again she can't resist it: put Larry down, pretend he doesn't exist!'

'Larry. Why don't you call me tomorrow? Then we can have a proper talk. There's a lot to tell you.'

'What? What is there to tell me?'

'Oh, about things here.'

'How long's she got?'

'What?'

'Leni. How long's the old vulture got?'

'I simply cannot talk to you like this, Larry. I will not. Please give Nadia my love.'

Miriam hangs up. Larry slams the receiver back into its cradle and bangs his fist on Nadia's floral wall. Nadia's face, still pink from her bath, peers at him with frightened eyes over the screen.

'Fucking bitch!'

Nadia comes round the screen and puts a little stubby hand on Larry's arm.

'Oh, Larry . . .'

'I don't know what that woman does to Miriam. Jesus Christ. I've spent my whole life trying to please those two, trying to succeed . . .'

'And there you are. What we struggle is never appreciated. So ironical thing. All our hard working and someone is spitting in our nose.'

'Up my nose. Up my bloody nose she gets, that cow.'

'So shame she isn't dying, Larry.'

'Too right, it's a shame.'

'Then you are spitting on her tomb.'

'I wouldn't go near her tomb. Let her rot, unvisited.'

'You want Ovomaltine, Larry?'

'Yes. Okay. Unless you've got any whisky.'

'No. I have this eau-de-vie your Gervaise is giving me on Tuesday. That Mallélou was here telephoning to some avocat.'

'Lawyer? Telephoning a lawyer?'

'Yes. Some prison trouble with the Xavier boy. You want eau-de-vie, my darling?'

'Yes. It'll do.'

'I don't like it. But I can't refuse. I think they're spending fifty francs on this talk to the avocat.'

'What's the boy done?'

'I don't ask. Did you ever see that Xavier Mallélou?'

'No. They'd gone, both the sons, by the time we moved here.'

'Well he's so handsome, my God. You can't imagine Gervaise and Mallélou making some boy like this. But cruel. Like all the handsome boys in Nadia's life! Such cruel face. Sit down, Larry and take some deep breath. Forget this bloody Leni woman. Nadia will get the eau-de-vie.'

Larry sits on Nadia's bed. The top sheet is monogrammed NCL, the N and the C tangling with the tall central L: Nadia and Claude Lemoine. The sheet is so thin and fine it has the quality of lawn but the green satin eiderdown is stained and frayed. Larry has never seen Nadia's bed before. Laid out now in her living room with all its old fashioned and decaying trimmings, it embarrasses him slightly. He wonders if Nadia has ever had a lover in it.

Nadia pours eau-de-vie into a liqueur glass for Larry, returns to her kitchen and makes a mug of Ovaltine for herself. She sits on a chair near the electric fire. Larry notices how tiny her feet are, with flat round nails painted vermilion. His eye travels up from the little feet, up her pink leg, warmed by the bath, half covered by the dressing gown. Her knees look very soft and shiny.

'So my poor old bean is missing Miriam?'

'Oh . . . I'll get used to it.'

'Why you don't write to her and not telephone, Larry?'

'Why?'

'Well, so much distance, you don't know the other one isn't doing her toilet or scraping some carrots when you call.'

Larry smiles, takes a sip of the burning liquor.

'No. That's true.'

'But if you're writing, you know where she's reading you. On the boiled egg or what.'

'Yes.'

'So it's better I think. You don't getting cross in a letter and that fucking Leni doesn't intervene you.'

'You're quite right, Nadia.'

'Not I mind you using the telephone, my dear. Don't think.'

'No. I know.'

'I'm so glad you're coming up in fact. I want to ask you, what do you think for Hervé's new niece. You meet her?'

'Yes. I drove over this morning, mainly out of curiosity.'

'I'm so surprising when I talk with her, Larry. Not you?'

'Surprising?'

'Yes.'

'Well, I thought she was a very pleasant girl. I think Harve's fallen on his feet, if you'll excuse the pun.'

'What's this pun? I don't know about pun, but I am expect some little skunk with a dye head and safety pin on the nostril. Not you?'

'A punk, you mean?'

'Punk, skunk, I don't know. I know these modern young ones. But this is so charming and so thanking me all the time, merci madame and so, and these little English clothes, I believe I am lifting Princess Diana.'

'I liked that. I liked the way she was.'

'And you're not surprising?'

'In a way. I don't think of young people being like that any more. In fact, in my life they never were. I never knew anyone like that.'

'So you like?'

'Yes. I would love to have had a daughter like that.'

Nadia laughs. She sounds relieved when she says: 'So you don't immediately thinking, oh my lost English princess straight from the hockey stick, come to bed with me?'

'What, Nadia?'

'I think all these men in Pomerac when they see this niece are getting these ideas. Even Hervé, when he's so bad to me on my driving, is thinking only of the precious Agnès. So sickening.'

'Harve thinks she's rather old fashioned. He told me she was.'

'But he still loves her, no?'

'Yes. He seems fond of her. She's looking after him very well.'

'But you see there was no need of her coming. Nadia offered. Nadia said, I move in to you, Hervé. I bring the breakfast in bed. I wash you, my dear. I tell him, what is my life you think, Hervé? You don't think I can do this? I have nothing in my life. Empty. Empty. And I am so good for nursing. I nurse Claude. But oh no. This princess is coming. No need of Nadia. Turn me flat. Sickening, you know.'

There is a little wrinkle of skin on Nadia's Ovaltine. She pushes this to the side of the mug and then pops it into her mouth. Larry stares at her. He realises for the first time that this is all she wants to talk about these days: Hervé, the injuries he seems to inflict, some lament for what might be. He feels astonished and yet dim. How have these feelings in Nadia passed unnoticed?

'I think Harve invited the girl as much for her as for him.'

'No. I don't think, my poor old bean. He is asking this princess
to keep Nadia away.'

'Why would he, Nadia?'

Nadia puts down her Ovaltine mug, leans forward and cups
her face in her little nervous hands.

'He is telling Nadia too much. Now he is ashamed.'

'Ashamed?'

'He doesn't know me now. He tells his secrets and then, flit
flit, he slaps me away like a fly.'

'What secrets, Nadia?'

'Well secrets are secrets, you know. I can't tell you. He
trusted me. But then if you trust one, you must also like that
one a little, you don't think?'

'Of course Harve likes you.'

'But not now. Off I go to Thiviers to fetch his bloody mermaid
for him and so now I'm just the chauffeur. He forgets those
secrets and he forgets me.'

'How could he forget you, Nadia?'

'Because I am Pole. He thinks this Pole a ruddy nuisance
because she cry Polish tears when I tell her my secret. No
British stiff lip. Hervé has so much British fucking stiff lip, I
don't know why, but now this girl is coming in her cardigans
from Harrods or what and he thinks, thank God, no more fucking
Polish crying. So, it's okay . . .'

'It's not okay. I'm sorry he's upset you, Nadia.'

'Oh well it's okay. Nadia used. What the difference. All men
upset. And I'm so sorry, my dear . . .'

Nadia's pale eyes look replenished and shining with their
heavy tears. Crying suits her. Larry puts out a slightly nervous
hand and gently strokes her knee.

Mallélou has arrived in Bordeaux with Xavier's bail money. Now
he sits with his son in a warm bar, drinking. He'll get plastered
tonight. Probably the boy will, too. The prison scared old
Mallélou shitless. The dead faces of the men. The freezing grey
brick walls. The shouting. Thank God Xavier was out. Something
must be done to make sure he never gets put back in. But what?
The boy's ashen-faced. More terrified than him. And guilty. It

was a good line, he tells him, nicking stuff from Mme Motte. She let him negotiate with the suppliers and she just signed the chits. A case of wine here, a few vegetables there – it was easy. The offloading, too. Plenty of people would buy cheap and ask no questions. It was an accident he was caught. This old guy running a decrepit waterfront bar found out he worked for Mme Motte, whom he knew. Friend of the dead husband, or some such. Out of some past and idiotic loyalty, he told her to be on her guard. After that, she began counting. The night the police came, he was found with three cases of wine in his room, and on this fragile proof he was arrested.

Mallélou doesn't ask his son why he stole. In the cities, you make out as best you can and you do your best not to get caught. He doesn't blame his son for stealing. What he hates is that the woman, Mme Motte, has now shaped Xavier's future. Her cunning and the pathetic marking and counting of her goods has brought his son to this hell, this terrifying bloody prison. He could cry. His boy, trudging blank-faced round that exercise yard. His boy, carrying a slop bucket from his cell.

'Drink up, Xavier. You're not drinking. Drink while you can.'

'What d'you mean?'

'You never know. With what this country calls Justice . . .'

'I'm not going back inside.'

'No, son.'

'I'll kill her if they put me back.'

'Yes.'

'I'll kill her.'

'Yes. Well, drink up, eh?'

Xavier doesn't know the bar they're in. He doesn't want to take his father to any of his normal haunts. He feels childish, a failure. It enrages him that his father has to be involved at all. Stupid old man, never had any authority, any guts. Used to think he was a big shot because he worked the signals and screwed some leathery old German whore. Used to boast about this to his sons. Boast about that, when it was their mother who ran the family and kept it going. It was their mother, Gervaise, who had all the strength and passed it down to them.

'How's Maman?'

'She's fine. You want to switch to *pastis*?'

'No. Beer's okay. Tell me about Maman. Is she mad at me?'

'I'm switching to *pastis*. Best to drink tonight.'

'Is she angry? What's she said, Papa?'

'Nothing.'

'Go on. I know Maman. I know what she'd say.'

'Why d'you ask me, then? Hey, Xavier let's do some proper bars later on, eh?'

'I don't know. Maybe. I feel tired after those days there. You can't sleep there. People cry in that prison, you know. They cry.'

In one corner of the bar, men still in their working *bleus* are playing cards. Pale youths hang round a pinball machine and a Babyfoot table. The thump-thump of the Babyfoot ball, the ping and grind of the pinball game, these noises are a reassuring day-to-day part of Xavier's life. They reaffirm, in his exhausted skull, his right to a place here, in the heart of the city, a city you know and which knows you. In prison you know no one. The city turns its back. You wind up making pets out of mice or cockroaches, for the comfort of them. You might as well be in Alaska.

Mallélou orders two *pastis*. When they come, he sets one by Xavier's beer glass.

'Drink it lad. You need it.'

'Okay. Tell me about Maman.'

Mallélou sighs. He wipes his mouth with stained fingers, tugs out a cigarette from a crumpled packet and lights it. As he talks, the cigarette stays lodged between his lips, pressed wet and flat.

'She had her little cry. But then she's spent her life blubbing for you boys. What's one cry more? She blames me, of course. Blames the city. If she'd had her way, you and Philippe would have stayed in Pomerac, stayed staring at those cattle till you got simple-minded. That's her idea of a life, that is, staring at cows' arses.'

Mallélou pauses, waits for his son to laugh, but he doesn't; he seems grave and sad. Mallélou coughs, swigs his drink, goes on: 'Pomerac's changing though, did I tell you? Those English people kissed goodbye to their Queen Elizabeth. They're in next door, now. All year round. He looks a confused man. Her you don't often see. I couldn't do that – settle down in some strange bloody place. Perhaps they won't last. I dunno. It's odd them being there, though. You sense things changing.'

'How's the Maréchal?'

'Oh, that one, he'll be around for ever. Your Mother still scuttles round him. Come on, drink up, Xavier.'

'Did he lend us the bail money?'

'Why? D'you think I haven't got it? D'you think I haven't got eight thousand?'

'I don't know . . .'

'I don't borrow, Xavier. Never.'

'Maman does . . .'

'But not me. If my son's in trouble, I bail him out. I *find* the money.'

'Where from?'

'Never you mind where from. I find it. Okay?'

'I'm frightened, Papa.'

'Yes. You look frightened. Frightened to bloody death. Where is it then, this woman's restaurant?'

'Rue St François. Near the station.'

'She's the one who ought to be frightened.'

'Why?'

'Because I'm here, that's why. And I defend my own.'

'What the hell d'you mean, Papa?'

'You think I'm not going to pay her a visit?'

'What?'

'You think I believe in State Justice?'

'Oh, come on . . .'

'State Justice my arse! If you're rich you get justice. I believe in Rich Justice. But not the other kind. Not our kind. No. We just have to find ways of settling things ourselves.'

Xavier shakes his head in disbelief. Big talk. His father always loved this kind of big macho talk. But it remained talk. The nearest he got to 'settling' anything for himself was to go and beat up that German, Marisa. But then, beginning to drink the *pastis*, his fear ebbing a little, Xavier starts to imagine Mme

Motte standing smug and safe by her chip-fryer, wiping her little greasy hands on her apron to take the mushy noodle soup to an early customer, smiling her tight smile, her stubby nose red from the kitchen steam. And this smugness, this safety, oppress him. Why should this ugly widow be so safe in her mucky little café, where the glasses aren't even washed properly but only rinsed, where the ham she serves is slimy, where the oilcloth on the tables is yellow with fat fumes, where her one pathetic notion of decoration is sprigs of plastic oranges? And he, with his whole life in front of him, already on the outside, already destined for Alaska . . .

'She's an old slag. She'd deserve anything she got.'

'So why are you afraid?'

'What?'

'Why are you afraid to take matters into your hands?'

'I'm not. But you could do more harm . . .'

'You said you'd kill her if they send you back.'

'Yeh.' Xavier feels choked, boiling hot. He considers now whether he shouldn't go to some bar where his friends will be, just try to forget the whole business for the time being . . .

'So?'

His father's an ugly man. Even as a child, Xavier Mallélou understood this. He used to search, in the mirror, for his father's squashed features in his own face.

'So I could. I could kill her. But what then? That's my life gone.'

One of the youths putting money into the pinball machine is whistling. This whistling aches in Xavier's head. He wants to shout at the youth to belt up.

'Let's move on, Papa. I know a nice bar.'

'Yes. All right. Get good and pissed, eh? Then we'll think. What time does she finish up, your Mme Motte?'

'Elevenish. I don't know . . .'

'Don't fret, Xavier. That's the thing. Don't fret.'

Mallélou pays for the drinks and he and Xavier walk out of the warm café into the street. A cold rain is falling.

*   *   *

Nadia is alone in her monogrammed sheets. She sleeps with the light on and dreams of Hervé and herself buying lime-coloured tickets for the space shuttle. The astronauts selling these tickets look on her and Hervé approvingly: the man is thin, the woman is small, they will fit in, they won't weigh the shuttle down and stop it lifting off.

Larry is alone in the darkness without Miriam and wide awake. In the rain that drives onto his window is the memory of a night in September 1976 when, after the months of parched weather, with the concrete of his first pool laid that very afternoon and drying by teatime, a storm broke and the dust of summer began to settle back into the clay. He'd woken Miriam and made her listen to the rain. She'd said, good, rain at last, now the willows may survive, and turned back to sleep. But Larry had got up and gone out into his front porch and stared hopelessly at the hurtling weather. In the hot, patient calm of July and August *Aquazure* had begun to grow an order book; now, in this return to dripping and damp and wind, England was pronouncing judgement on his fledgling enterprise: the swimming pool season is over. Around the corner is winter and frost; moss will bubble up in the splits and cracks of tiles; in this country a pool isn't worth the money; this was a freak summer and the pools are simply its legacy. Already, before the first pool was built, Larry had seen the ruin. A swimming pool is only a pit, with plumbing. In time, nature reclaims it as a pond. Later, when *Aquazure* was failing, he'd have dreams of the things you find in swimming pools: dead belly-bloated hedgehogs, blind drowned moles, frogs, newts, water beetles, smashed birds' eggs, blanket-weed, algae, earth. But don't tell the customers. Send in Bill the frogman, in his *Aquazure* blue wetsuit. Clean up. Check the pH and the chlorine levels. Pour in the chemicals . . . He's restless, remembering fears and portents that drove towards one ending. In his survival of that ending he feels cold. The white space in the bed that is Miriam's absence is icy and grave. He wants to turn over into her warmth and feel her arms take him to her and give him hope. Since *Aquazure* he has been deficient in hope. His English doctor suggested a course of vitamin B. Women are trying to ease pre-menstrual tension with these. He wonders if, month after month, women feel this same hope-deficiency. He wants to ask Miriam, but Miriam's periods are erratic, ending. She mourns for this past pain and he's not sure how best to comfort her. Now she's not there to be comforted. Leni the newt, Leni the black beetle, Leni the earth mother, has reclaimed her. Leni's arms blanket her and he's left out in the cold.

He thinks of Hervé, tucked up in his ornate bed with a wire cradle shielding his broken legs from the weight of the blankets and wonders if he can learn to live like that – dry and alone. He thinks of Nadia's hot little bathed body moist in its sudden yearnings for this clean leatherbound man, and wonders if, in the comédie humaine which is his life anyone will ever yearn for him again like this, with tears and fury. He thinks of Agnès. He imagines a nightie of crisp broderie anglaise with a tiny lattice of pink ribbon. In this, she sleeps straight and deep. Hervé's breaths next door don't disturb her. She dreams clean dreams of her fiancé, Luc. Her lips, opening and closing on the dream, are the pink lips of a child, of the daughter he never had. Thinking of this, he tries to forget Miriam and tries to sleep. Yet something in this sweet picture of Agnès disturbs him and keeps his mind beating as the rain beats on and in Nadia's dream she and Hervé Prière hurtle soundlessly in space, strapped to airline seats. Then out of the rainstorm, Larry picks another, frailer sound – the sound of Gervaise's laughter.

Mallélou and Xavier have walked through the rain to one of Xavier's favourite bars. You can eat at one end of it – good, expensive food, not the greasy filth ladled out by Mme Motte – and a group of middle-aged men are ordering oysters.

Xavier has come here hoping to see friends. When any of his crowd are feeling rich, feeling optimistic, they come here. Sometimes they pig out on the seafood, get some good wine opened, and Xavier loves this, this feeling of how wealthy people eat. He decides, eating langoustines, he'll work his arse off to be rich one day.

Mallélou senses the altered clientele in this bar and regrets moving on from the first place, where he felt comfortable. Here he feels shabby. He notices the dirt under his nails, dreads the city people's disdain: he's off the land, he's a shit shoveller. He wants to tell them: I may have married a peasant, but I used to fuck your whores, I used to stub out my fags in a woman's cunt.

'This your kind of place?' he asks Xavier.

Xavier nods, staring at the door. He needs his mates now, not his stupid father. But no one shows. Where are they? Have they forgotten him? Is someone giving a party somewhere?

'You get ripped off in bars like this,' says Mallélou. He's still slurping *pastis*, but without relish now. Xavier stares at him, hating him. It amazes him that he's this man's son. When he was little, he used to invent alternative fathers for himself. One of these was the Maréchal. Occasionally, he still does this: he imagines the day when his mother tells him, you're not Mallélou's son. But it was after the boys left Gervaise that Klaus came. Neither of her sons know that Klaus is always there now, summer and winter.

Xavier drains his glass, feels the burning aniseed fire his stomach. He swallows, then turns to Mallélou.

'If you want to do something about la Motte, it's better you go on your own, you know.'

'Uhn?'

'It's better you go. I'm in enough trouble.'

Mallélou stares at his son. Why in heaven's name did he shed the SNCF uniform for some lousy restaurant job? How could this have been allowed to happen?

'So you want to give me your responsibilities?'

'No. But I don't want to see her again. Her face makes me puke.'

'So why did you ever go and work there?'

'It's all there was.'

'You had a good job, Xavier . . .'

'Good job? You think that's a good job, knocking bits of wood into the ground?'

'You would have got on. If you'd stuck at it.'

'*You* didn't stick at it.'

'I worked my way up.'

'There's no such thing these days.'

'Of course there is.'

'Signalmen. You know what signalmen are now? They're computer operators.'

'You could have trained . . .'

'I didn't have the fucking education!'

'No. But that's not my fault. Don't look at me. If we'd stayed on in the city, you and Philippe could have done okay. They don't give children the right start in the country schools. They don't teach them the right things.'

The door of the bar opens. Three young men, collars turned up against the rain, come in. Xavier's heart lifts. Some of his friends at last. But they're not his friends. They're strangers. They walk past his table to the far end where the oysters are served.

Mallélou is beginning to be drunk. He feels that sliding of his blood which is both exciting and futile. His mind imagines for his body feats it will never manage. He gazes at Xavier. When the drink begins to get to him, other people's faces seem to move and stretch. He feels he could take them apart, like unstitching rags.

'There's a limit to what one man can do.'

He hears himself say this. What he meant was, two men are better than one when it comes to teaching a woman a lesson. But the words echo, as if shouted in a tunnel: there's a limit, limit to what one man can do . . . Dark echoey excuse trapped in a tunnel. The excuse for all the things he will never be, all the women he will never have. He sees Xavier shrug.

'Suit yourself. I don't want to go near her.'

'You fuck her, did you?'

'What?'

'You screw her? I told you not to.'

Xavier makes a disgusted face. 'I'm not so desperate. There're women in this town, you know.'

'I know, son. No one knows better than me.'

'And not just German tarts, either.'

Mallélou looks at his son with the scared eye of a ratty dog. Handsome though Xavier's face always was, he could unstitch it.

'You know nothing about the Germans. You didn't live the war as I did.'

'Thank God.'

'What you hear in France is mostly lies.'

'What lies?'

'About what they did.'

'What the Germans did? Well documented lies, then.'

'They would have run this country well.'

'Oh shut up, Papa.'

'No one likes to admit it, that's all.'

'I'm not interested in your perverted crap. Just because you banged that stinky old woman . . .'

'Beautiful you mean.'

'What?'

'She was beautiful. Marisa. She was beautiful.'

'Go *on*.'

'I used to bugger her. Come in her arse. That's what she liked.'

'So?'

'So it was beautiful.'

'Yeh?'

'Yes. Better than anything you've ever done.'

'You're pathetic.'

Xavier gets up, goes to the bar and asks for change for the telephone. Tired though he feels, he's half decided to ring his friend, Pozzo, and get him to join them. Mallélou suffocates him. His filthy hands. His turgid sex talk. Earlier, he'd resigned himself to giving the old man his bed for the night and sleeping on the floor with a blanket. Now he decides he'll put Mallélou on the floor. After six nights in a cell, he can at least sleep in his own bed. Unless he gets rid of him and he and Pozzo go and look up some girls. One thing feels good anyway: his fear is going. He snatches up the change from the bar counter and orders more *pastis*. Perhaps, if he keeps the drinks coming, he can send his father to 'tidy up' Motte, give her a scare, just enough so that she agrees to drop the case, to tell the police she made a mistake. 'I defend my own,' the old idiot bragged. So let him show that he can. Xavier glances behind him at

Mallélou. His father is looking people over with sad, glassy
eyes.

Now, into Gervaise's mouth, where her songs fly out in the cold
of morning, Klaus pours his red tongue like an eel. Her own
tongue first makes way for it, then curls under it, pushing against
its beautiful weight.

For all his strength, he holds her lightly, carries her aloft on him
to her bed, where they subside onto the featherbed coverlet she
once filled with the down of her own barnyard birds. It amuses and
delights Klaus to make love to Gervaise riding on the bleached
feathers of squabbling geese and ducks that have, in time past,
fed her and kept her alive. The coverlet is noisy with these goose-
ghosts, these duckling-ghosts, and Klaus sets them all squawking,
quacking and gobbling with his rollicking love.

Peeping from his gold-fleeced head, Gervaise sees in the
wardrobe mirror the great happy rump of him butting and
burrowing and her laughter streams out past his eel tongue. Her
legs climb his back. They are the white stems of flowers, she
thinks. He parts them to give in return not some insubstantial
blossom, but the thick, hard root of himself and all the sweet
earth of her being slips and tumbles as it reaches down, further
into her than she knew there was space and feeling.

Out in the dark of Pomerac, widows and wives, and even
Mme de la Brosse shuttered and safe behind her limes, furtively
dream of such a gold embrace and don't dare to imagine with what
royal thrusting and dancing of tongues it's given to Gervaise.
Gervaise, the wife of Mallélou. Gervaise, in her old coarse
scarves. The thin flesh she keeps hidden under clothes that
slumber with age and rinsing and sunshine, how is it woken?
How has it deserved?

The curtains are drawn, tonight, on a private loving. The
grey, greedy stare of Mallélou at the door is blessedly absent
and Gervaise lets tears of happiness and laughter flow onto the
hot skin of her lover's shoulder. And he holds her with such
gladness. His love sings and trembles in him. He lifts her high,
high onto the bleached and noisy pillows. He's on his knees now
and his head is wild and shouting on her bony breast. Love

shivers, love trembles, love bursts in her and pulses to a sweet and blissful end. Rain tears at the darkness, but the bodies of Gervaise and Klaus rock silently in a gentle calm.

Along puddled streets, soaking in sour light, Xavier steers Mallélou towards the rue St François where Mme Motte is wiping tables. The two men are drenched by squalls and Mallélou is cursing: 'Let's find another bar, Xavier. I'm not pissed enough for this business.'

Yet he knows he's drunk too much. His gut feels heavy and sick. If he lay down somewhere warm, he'd pass out. And forget. Forget the prison. Forget what the courts are going to say. Forget this promise to settle things his way. He wants to say to Xavier, I'm too old, son, I was old when you were born. I fought in the war as a stripling. And these days the city's too vast, too freezing. Even with this bellyful of booze, I'm not up to it. But he stumbles on, Xavier's arm pushing him, rain pricking his neck and drenching his collar.

They turn into a long, dead-seeming street. Far down it, a single square of light falls onto the pavement. Above this a boxed sign, strip-lit from within, says *Restaurant les Mimosas. Bonne Table*.

Xavier pulls Mallélou into the shadow of some scaffolding. The older man senses he's being controlled like a kid, tugged here and there, ordered about, when it should be him . . .

'Okay?' hisses Xavier. 'That's her. Where the sign is.' Mallélou stares up and down the street, numb, dumb – too old, too afraid. Xavier wants to hit him, to wake him up. *'Okay?'*

'Sure, sure. But I'm not drunk enough. I need something . . .'

'No you don't. It's a woman. She can't hurt you. Why are you scared?'

'Not scared, Xavier . . .' His speech is slurred. He can hear it. So long since he was pissed like this, he'd forgotten how it makes you weak. Time was when a few *pastis* were good, good and he'd arrive at Marisa's place with a hard heart and a stiff cock, not weak then or afraid or frozen, but ready to do business his way, Mallélou's way . . .

'Allez!'

Xavier pushes him out from the scaffolding and he totters
across the cobbled road. He feels his son's eyes at his back like
a gun and he doesn't turn. He takes breaths of cold air, tries to
send this clean knife of air up into his brain to clear it of muddle
and fear, and ancient thoughts of city days when he was young,
before there were sons, before there was Gervaise, when he
was king of the signal junction. What's one muddling old widow?
What's a place like hers, with a few poor tables and a crammed
yard at the back? He knows this kind of woman, this kind of
place. Rusty boilers, beer crates piled up, stinking tiles like a
public toilet, vermin. There's a sour taste in his throat. Drink is
futile. Sons grow to thugs of men and make you impotent. He
should have stayed in his own cot with his face turned to the
wall. Stayed by Gervaise's fire. Let Xavier weep and rot in that
scum-filled jail, let him find out for himself that in the end
whatever you do you pay, you pay and pay . . .

But he's there now. He's brought himself to the front of the
restaurant. He stares in. The glass is fugged from the hot breath
of the kitchen. Water drips down it inside and out. A sign
dangling on the door says *fermé*. He notes that this is hand-inked
in feeble, illiterate writing. He sways and his forehead knocks
the icy glass. This small sound brings Mme Motte back through
the plastic fly-curtain that separates the restaurant from the
kitchen. Mallélou sees her approach, a small scuttling woman
with a flat mutt's face and black dyed hair. He doesn't move.
He knows that Xavier is still at his back like a revolver, but
distant now, too far to kill, someone shadowy. Mme Motte
stops, one hand holding a soapy dish cloth. She bends and wipes
the plastic cover of one of the tables. Her arms are red and
fleshy, her bosom tight in her floral overall. She looks up, sees
Mallélou still staring at her and points to the *closed* sign.

Mallélou stares and tries to make the right connections: this
woman will put Xavier back inside; this woman has control over
what happens; he's here to alter these things; if he fails to alter
these things, his son will despise him always.

He turns the handle of the door and falls against it as it opens.
Mme Motte, quicker than a rat, comes darting to him waving
her damp cloth and shouting. Mallélou sees her little puckered

mouth, topped with a faint moustache, opening and closing and hears shrill sounds aimed at him. Something damp flicks his face and he feels his legs shudder. She's pushing him now, trying to push him back into the freezing street, but he holds fast to the door, leans all his weight on his arm on the handle and knows that his legs are going, bending, collapsing. He breathes, tries to straighten himself, but the air he breathes is suffocating and hot like the air of a greenhouse. Waves of nausea come. He swims in them, swaying, toppling. At his feet a pattering of lino sends brown and orange whorls into his brain and he follows these down, down, like a dead body chucked in a well and falling miles and miles into darkness.

Waiting by the scaffolding, tiredness robbing his body of its feeble resistance to the rain and cold, Xavier paces and stamps. Light from the restaurant still floods the pavement and he knows Mallélou is in, but he can hear nothing. He expected shouting and the sound of things being broken. He wants a table to come flying through the glass.

He decides to cross the street, to go nearer. He can't wait here all night. He'll die of cold and exhaustion. He remembers an American film where two cops gobble flabby pizza in the street while two rich villains eat lunch in a warm restaurant far into the winter afternoon. He liked this scene. Life is like that, he thought. Unfair. The rich guys ride around in the Cadillacs. They know there are these millions of other guys getting cold in bus queues and this is part of their pleasure. One day, he will be in a Cadillac. One day he will be in the warm, plushy restaurant.

Xavier doesn't cross the street because a police car comes hurtling down it, blue light turning but no siren going. It pulls up in front of the *Mimosas* and two policemen get out, un-hurriedly, and wander in. Xavier presses himself back into the shadows. A red sign slung on the scaffolding says *DANGER. TRAVAUX*. He waits. The rain eases off. Bits of paper and leaves gust round him in the wind. He's dying to go back to his room, to see his own things, to light his gas fire, to smell his own pillow, to sleep. His mind barely questions what is happening when he sees the two policemen come out again carrying the

inert body of his father and then hurling it like a sack of vegetables
into the back of the car. He thinks merely, well, it's over for
now, sees the restaurant sign go out and the car drive off, and
walks quickly away in the direction of his lodgings.

October comes. Larry buys a map of the St Front basilica. He
makes drawings of the ground plan, trying to simplify it and
make a shape that fits his vision of his new pool. When he's
satisfied with the shape, he cuts a template of it out of some
hardboard he finds in Miriam's studio, then calculates the
measurements of this to square with a basic 36' by 18' dimen-
sion. He feels excited. He goes out and stands by the walnut
tree. Through its thinning leaves comes a lovely dappled light.
Larry regrets the need to cut it down but decides that he must
do this now, straight away, before Miriam returns. A tug of love
over a tree strikes him as unnecessarily stupid.

Larry then gets out from the dusty attic his Aquazure Pool
Definition Kit. This consists of a long coil of blue nylon rope, a
bunch of sharp wooden pegs and a forty-foot flexible measure.
With these ordinary tools Larry 'defines', on empty lawns, on
unsightly briar patches, the shape of the miracle to come. He
measures off each angle and inserts a peg till the basic shape is
stitched out in pegs. Then he ties the blue nylon rope to one of
these and winds it on right round all the pegs, thus 'defining' the
pool. At this point, prospective pool buyers tend to pace round
the blue lines, talking to each other: 'Gosh, you get the
impression now don't you, Jessica?' 'Golly, I'm dying to see
Emma's face when we tell her, Edward.' Larry smiles, remembering these long-ago small excitements and sets to work in the
sunshine, hammering pegs into the flinty earth.

Klaus, whose English is non-existent, stares solemnly at this
peculiar endeavour from the low wall separating Larry's garden
from the edge of Gervaise's first meadow and eventually asks,
'Ich help, Larry?'

Larry glances up. *'Nein, danke,'* he says. But he senses
Klaus's continuing large presence and his bewilderment, so
when all the pegs are in and he has led the rope up the south
side of the St Front nave, past the Didron window, round the

vaulted apse where the steps will be, into the apsidal chapel, past the fourth cupola, back along the north wall of the nave and west into the vieille église where the diving board will be, he straightens up and gestures at his handiwork. 'Schwimbad,' he announces.

Klaus stares for a moment at Larry, then smiles a broad disbelieving smile.

'Schwimbad?' Klaus questions. 'In Pomerac?'

'Ja,' says Larry, then struggles with what he thinks may be a German sentence: 'Alles Personnen in Pomerac kann geschwimmen here.'

But Klaus is laughing now, the deafening laugh of a monarch at a banquet: 'Ich kann nicht schwimmen, Larry! Ich kann nicht schwimmen!'

Larry shrugs, joins in the laughter. An image comes to him of the well-fleshed Klaus floundering in the new pool, his legs floating hopelessly down towards the drain. He, Larry, stands by, terrified, doing nothing. It is Gervaise who leaps in and bears Klaus to safety on her sinewy back.

Klaus stops laughing and points in Larry's direction.

'Aber der Baum. Fällen sie den Walnuss Baum?'

'Was?' says Larry.

'L'arbre. Vous allez couper l'arbre?'

'Oui,' says Larry, 'malheureusement.'

'A great damage,' says Klaus.

Larry looks guiltily at the tree. It stands well within his blue perimeter. He wonders how much trouble the roots will be. At Aquazure he had a JCB operator who was a skilled root man, but heaven knows what kind of labour they send with diggers in France.

When he looks up again, Klaus has gone. Oddly, Larry realises that he likes the German. He always seems so healthy and pink and free from any of his native angst. As if he'd come steaming hot like a cake from God's belly, before Eden and sin, before women and toil and Sodom. He wonders if Klaus will stay in Pomerac or whether he'll pack his bags one day and go back to wherever he came from and leave Gervaise weeping and wailing for him in her milking shed. You don't imagine change in

Pomerac. Even the Maréchal shows signs of eternity. Yet change must occur. The swimming pool is change.

Leaving the rope and the pegs in position, Larry gets into the Granada which smells of upholstery shampoo. Since Miriam's leaving he's cleaned it thoroughly inside and out and its tomato body glistens.

At the waterfall, he drives straight past Hervé's drive, denying himself the tempting possibility of lunching in Hervé's dining room with Agnès sweetly smiling over a tidy and delicious meal and heads instead for a café in Périgueux and an afternoon of difficult purchasing from *Ducellier Frères*. He also plans to seek out a tile-maker capable of designing Byzantine tiles. The vision of his pool is strong now. Next summer – on May Day perhaps, when the Pomerac women exchange their little bunches of lilies of the valley – there will be some official opening. Champagne even. And all the people will cluster round and see themselves for the first time reflected in what Nadia has so fortuitously called 'loops of brightness'. Even the Maréchal will come, to see a new chapter added to the English comedy unfolding before his cataracted eyes. And Mme de la Brosse; she will be quietly ashamed that a house in Pomerac other than hers has installed a pool. She will take Larry aside from the marvelling throng of villagers, and ask him to quote for a pool of her own – 'Like this one, Larry, but perhaps a little larger.' And thus *Aquazure France* will begin.

Larry drives fast in his new surge of optimism. Change is certainly coming. Leni will die and Miriam will return, altered and free. Agnès will stay on with Hervé and wear white dresses at the poolside. Klaus will learn to swim.

TWO

LENI

It is the morning of Miriam's fiftieth birthday. A grey rain falls on North Oxford, a heavy autumn rain driving slowly west to the Cotswolds. By Leni's front door, blue hydrangeas, planted by Gary, are dying down; orange puddles lie on the sandy driveway; Gary's Mini sits here uselessly, having failed its MOT test. All is quiet and motionless and wet. Over the front attic bedroom, slates have slipped from the roof and water drips steadily into a variety of bowls set out on a green carpet. No one uses this room now. A faded copy of Empson's *Seven Types of Ambiguity* betrays the past habitation of a literature student. Miriam empties the bowls each evening and remembers that her father, David Ackerman, once had a den up here and wrote his books by the attic window.

Down in Leni's room, an electric fire is on and a Chinese lamp casts yellow light on the pillow. The heavy blue curtains are still drawn. It could be early evening. In her large bed, Leni's body is brittle and thin. It's becoming hollow, she tells herself, like the cuttlefish bones you find on the beach. She drinks cocoa to try to fill it up. Miriam makes her mashed potato. She craves sweet, soft substances – nothing sinewy like celery, nothing sour like apples – paste going through her like porridge, warming the draughty bags of her digestive tract, white, soothing paste in her empty darkness.

In common, she supposes, with most invalids, Leni Ackerman dislikes night-time, wakes early, longs for the household to start opening doors and turning on lights and flushing lavatories. She longs, most of all, to talk. Illness hasn't made her silent, but rather given additional colour to her gritty voice, as if all her dark blood was now gathered at her throat, leaving the rest of her pale and weak.

Since Miriam's arrival, the nurse, Bryony, has left. It is Miriam, now, who comes to Leni in the morning, switches on her fire, brings her *The Times* and a cup of milky tea. She sits on her mother's bed – just as Leni sat on hers to kiss her goodnight as a child – and takes her hands in hers and feels glad that she's there. When Leni dies it will be like this: Miriam will have possession of the fragile fingers. She will lay them down gently. She will close the door and close the eyes. She will sit on the bed, remembering.

'Well,' says Leni, smiling, 'so you're fifty! At fifty, I think one should try to be honourable.'

'What did you do at fifty? Did you celebrate?'

'Oh yes. Your father gave me that parrot we called Aneurin, after Bevan, and we had what he called a Parrot Party, with everyone dressed up in their gayest things. Didn't you and Larry come? Perhaps you weren't gay, Larry's not particularly gay, or should I say jolly, is he? But then all those people made such a deafening noise round the parrot cage, that Aneurin began to peck himself to death that actual night and kept on until he'd done it. Lucky human beings don't have beaks. Or they'd do this, I'm sure. Don't you think? They'd peck themselves. Women would. Men are too vain, perhaps. Woman would peck themselves in moments of heartbreak.'

'I don't remember the Parrot Party.'

'Well then you didn't come, Miriam, because it was very memorable. Your father looked extraordinary, more like a bald eagle than a parrot really. Yellow eyes. He gave himself yellow eyes. I can't remember how he did it. A lot of his students came and they looked so wonderful. I love it when young people look wonderful for a night. And there was a superb parroty scandal on the lawn. Two boys rolling about together near a flood light. They were sent down. It was the fifties after all. No one was permissive except us. I think our Parrot Party started permissiveness in Oxford.'

'And what did you do that was honourable?'

'Well, I decided that morning never to fall in love with anyone again. Except your father. I allowed myself to go on falling in love with him. From time to time, like in the summertime when he'd come out and sit on the lawn and his legs would go brown. I like brown legs, don't you? I always want to touch them. But the question of other men, I thought: that's it now. No more. Not that I didn't have a few of them still drooling round. That medievalist who made such a bad Dean. What was his name? Something extraordinary. I can't remember. He got on your father's nerves. At the Parrot Party he looked like a hen, all goosey skin. Well, I put them behind me, all out of my sight. That was the honourable thing to do.'

'And after Daddy died?'

'After? Nothing important. Nothing that meant anything. Just company sometimes. Another person in the bed. And now look. No one. Leni alone. But I bought you a present for the fiftieth, darling. I got Gary to buy it. If he's awake we'll ask him to bring it in, shall we? You go and see.'

Miriam releases Leni's hands, pats her pillows just as Nurse Bryony used to do. Her day has a simple routine to it now, which begins and ends with the making of hot drinks. In the mornings she often thinks of Larry on the terrace in Pomerac, at night she thinks of the stars above it. Neither thought carries with it any strong emotion. They're just images her mind discovers.

She shuts Leni's door, walks along the passage past the small room she occupied as a child and which, since arriving here, seems to beckon her back, past the guest room she currently occupies, to the end room which, for eight years now, has been Gary's. It's Saturday. Sometimes Gary sleeps late. Miriam waits at the door and listens. She hears music playing softly. Ella Fitzgerald. Gary in love tightens his heartstrings on the strangulating rhymes of Cole Porter: *If a Harris pat, means a Paris hat, okay! But I'm always true to you darling in my fashion* . . .

'Gary . . .'

'Yes. Is Mother awake?'

'Yes. Can I come in?'

'Yes.'

Gary's room, decorated now in his own taste and not Leni's, smells of polish and stationery, like an office. He airs it a lot, even in winter. He puts roses on his mahogany desk. His bed is kept tidy under a Peruvian patchwork quilt. The walls are pale lilac with framed posters announcing poetry readings at which the name Gary Murphy appears small beside large-lettered ones, Ted Hughes, Seamus Heaney, Peter Porter, George Macbeth. Gary is a schoolteacher full-time and a poet on Wednesdays. The boys he teaches play football on Wednesday afternoons. The days between Wednesdays often seem to go very slowly for Gary. He stores words up till he's bursting. Even at weekends he doesn't release them. At weekends, he eats, plays music, has love affairs. His latest volume of poems is called *Wednesday Man*.

Gary in his dressing gown (he sleeps naked, never wearing pyjamas) is lying on his made bed sipping Marmite. He makes the Marmite in a fine bone teacup. This and a plain biscuit are his daily breakfast. He's a slim and pale man with thick, cavorting hair. He has rather long, shiny fingernails. He's thirty-five and an orphan. As long as he can remember, which is back to when he was six and shared a Scoutcub tent with a blond boy called Arthur Wellington, he's been a homosexual. He has never ever touched a woman. The only woman he has ever loved is Leni. He called Leni 'Mother' as a joke. Now, without any effort of will, he thinks of her as his mother and her slow dying is the worst thing that has ever happened to him. Of Miriam, Leni's real child, he's a little jealous. Some evenings he slips in to Leni's room with a mug of cocoa after Miriam's in bed. When Leni dies, Gary thinks he may die too. It will have to depend on how he's feeling that week. The worst eventuality he can imagine is that she dies on a Wednesday morning.

'Leni wanted to know, could you bring the birthday present into her room?'

Gary switches off Ella Fitzgerald and turns with an expansive gesture to Miriam. 'Oh the birthday! What does one say? Commiserations?'

'Yes. I expect so.'

'I told Leni we should have a cake, so I'm going to make one. Butterscotch?'

'Lovely.'

'We'll have a tea party, shall we? Downstairs?'

'Well, it's years since there was a birthday tea . . .'

'So we will. I love treats. We need them more as we grow old, not less. I often think, God, why doesn't someone take me to Peter Pan?'

Miriam smiles. It's the smile of her father, David Ackerman, which Gary cannot recognise and he thinks only, how strange there's so little of Leni's beauty in her. Except the hair. Gary admires Miriam chiefly for her hair. He takes a last sip of his Marmite, lays the little cup down on its saucer. From the bottom drawer of his tidy desk he takes out two parcels, both carefully wrapped.

'I love presents,' says Gary, gently touching them. 'Never mind if there's nothing inside.'

They walk together along the corridor to Leni's room. Gary goes quickly to the bed and places a tender kiss on Leni's forehead.

'How are we, Mother?'

'All right, Gary dear. Still alive for Miriam's birthday. Have you got the present?'

'Of course. *Presents.*' And he places them gently not into Miriam's but into Leni's hands.

'Which one is from me, Gary?'

'Whichever you like. I don't mind a bit giving her the tiara and you can give the Woolies digital.'

Leni smiles a still brilliant smile. Her intimacy with Gary, their unshakeable closeness, is primarily expressed in the humour they share. Miriam is for the moment the onlooker, the outsider. Leni lifts the gifts, feeling their shape and weight. She selects one and holds it out for Miriam to take. There is no card. Miriam dislikes the solemnity in the opening of presents: people tearing off Sellotape with grimly-set mouths: the fear. She unwraps the present quickly – far too quickly for Gary's sense of occasion – and finds an oblong jeweller's box in her hands. She feels checked, off-balance. She hopes the jeweller's box hides something workaday and insubstantial. She eases up the lid. Lying on a velvet pad is a silver and turquoise necklace. Aware of her eager audience, she lifts the necklace and stares at it. It's heavy. She wonders if it comes from South or Central America. She

imagines it circling the olive neck of a Mexican dancer. She looks
at her mother, waiting in the pillows with her mouth gaping.
    'Well?'
    Why? Miriam wants to ask. Why jewellery? You know I never
wear finery.
    'It's very beautiful, Leni darling. Thank you.'
    'Oh put it on,' says Gary.
    'You don't like it, do you?' Leni's smile has gone.
    'Of course I like it. It's the most . . . lovely thing I've had.'
    'Of course she loves it,' says Gary, patting Leni's arm.
    'Yes. I love it,' says Miriam.
    'Gary chose it,' Leni says, hurt.
    'Thank you, Gary,' says Miriam.
    'No. Leni's the one. She said whatever we do, we mustn't
give Miriam anything dull.'
    'No. And it isn't dull. My word, not.'
    'Sky,' says Leni.
    'Sky?' asks Miriam.
    'I told Gary, I think we should find something the colour of
the sky for Miriam because the skies were always the bits you
loved doing, in the watercolours. If you don't like it, you don't
have to wear it.'
    'I do like it. I'll put it on now.'
    Miriam puts the cold metal round her neck. She fumbles with
the clasp. Gary and Leni watch her. The necklace is on. She
knows that this piece of jewellery the colour of a pool must stay
hidden from Larry for ever. When Leni dies, she will give it to
Thomas's Australian girlfriend, Perdita.
    'There.'
    Miriam crosses to her mother. Gary, standing sentinel at the
bedhead, makes way for the women to exchange a relieved
embrace. The little ceremony is over except for the giving of
Gary's present which, in the complicated logic of these three
people's affection for each other, scarcely counts. Miriam opens
this eagerly and is pleased to find a slim volume of poetry:
Wednesday Man by Gary Murphy. Inside it is inscribed, in pencil:
To Miriam Ackerman Kendal. After fifty years.

*   *   *

At teatime, with Leni downstairs on the sofa, Gary's butterscotch cake moist in her mouth and a pale sun breaking through the rainclouds, visitors arrive. Dr Oswald Carlton-Williams, once a student, then a colleague of David Ackerman's, is now a bookshop-owner and known to all who know him as 'Dr O'. He is Miriam's age, or a little older. He prefers the small kingdom of his bookshop to the big echoey palaces of the University. He's a broad, untidy man. Clothes rumple and sag on him. He's shortsighted and an excellent draughtsman. He spends much of his free time in the Bodleian Library making painstaking copies of medieval borders from *bibles moralisées*, of illuminations from Slavonic gospels, and chiefly for this love of his of early manuscripts is he loved by his assistant in the bookshop and his companion of this teatime, Miss Bernice Atwood. Bernice Atwood is the kind of heavily shod, plain girl who fills Leni with boredom. She trudges through life, Leni thinks, when life should be embraced like a lover. Leni longs to teach her dancing, swimming, some grace. She doesn't know how Dr O puts up with Bernice, always at his side, year after year. No doubt they have some kind of silent love affair. Perhaps he seduces her with his Carthusian Breviaries, his Flemish Apocalypses? Decorates her pale plump body with fools and windmills and weaponry and saints? He's a loyal man. So loyal to the memory of David, he comes weekly to visit her. Perhaps loyalty rides in his blood like ancient writing: MS Douce, MS Ashmole, MS Bodley. MS Gough Liturg. – Ms Atwood. This must be the explanation.

Dr O remembers Miriam. He remembers being shown her paintings and admiring what he recognised as careful work. Without knowing Miriam at all, except through her watercolours of Oxford, he once had a dream he'd marry her and come to live with the Ackerman family in the big house in Rothersmere Road, within distant sight of the University Cricket Club pavilion. When he found out she was married to an employee of a Finance Company (in the long days before *Aquazure*, when Larry worked for the Morgan Beatific Trust) he felt cheated and disappointed. The Ackermans had no other daughter. His chance of binding his lonely life to their peopled one was gone for ever. He had never thought about Miriam as Miriam, only as part of that

family in that house. He couldn't, at the time of that dream of
his, have told you whether Miriam's eyes were grey or green,
whether her laughter was loud like Leni's or gentle like David's,
or indeed whether she ever laughed at all.

Since then, Dr O has always suspected his judgement where
women are concerned and he has never married. He doesn't
regret this. Bernice adores him. When he touches Bernice, she
pants like a lion. He suspects most women are like her in bed,
panting and silent with big white thighs like marble, but he's not
particularly curious. Leni he's admired for years. One of his
colleagues, no older than himself, once said to him in a choking
voice: 'Don't sleep with Leni Ackerman. If you do, you'll never
love any other woman.' And after this, until she began to get
old, he often tried to imagine what it could be like to tear off
Leni's clothes and press himself into her. He knew he would
never find out. He preferred to keep her as a friend and spend
large clutches of time in her house, talking, drinking vodka,
reading, even dancing, which he did so badly and she so erotic-
ally, he found it fiercely embarrassing. 'Come on!' she'd shout,
twirling scarves, 'Be the music! *Be* it!' He'd try to obey. He
knew no other house in Oxford where its occupants would
suddenly dance and he felt privileged to be there, as if he were
spending an evening with the Sitwells. He had never danced
with Miriam. Miriam was never there in the dancing days. Or
perhaps she hid. Hid from her Mother's pantomime. For a
pantomime it was really: costumes, shrieking, music, jokes. It
died with David. After that, Leni seemed to get a little smaller,
fade a little. She still had lovers but took them, she told him,
without relish. It seems to Dr O that her life since the death of
David has been like a long convalescence. There was the death
and the grief, then this other time in which she sat still and age
covered her like a shawl to keep her warm. Now, without
knowing it as Miriam knows it, he senses she's dying. He visited
her in hospital and didn't think then she would come back to
Rothersmere Road. But she did and a nurse came. Gary fussed
over her – the adoring son she'd never had. And now, on her
birthday, eating butterscotch cake, Miriam is here. Dr O finds
he's terribly pleased to see her. He wishes in a way that Bernice

hadn't come with him on this visit. Without her there, he would again feel like one of the Ackerman family.

'You remember Oz, Miriam?' (Leni is the only one of Dr O's friends who doesn't call him Dr O. She calls him Oz or sometimes The Wizard.)

'Yes, of course.'

Dr O remembers the auburn hair. In this one feature only was Miriam more striking than her mother. 'Yes, yes,' says Dr O. 'We met very often. But some years ago now.'

'Leni tells me you have a shop.'

'Yes, yes. Nothing as departmental as Blackwell's. Rather small in fact. But yes, yes, a bookshop.'

Bernice Atwood waits, smiling, for Dr O's nervousness to subside and for someone to introduce her to Miriam. Nobody does this, but Gary gets up and offers her simultaneously his chair and a slice of butterscotch cake. She takes the cake and sits. The wide armchair, which her bottom fills, is only a few inches away from Leni's tiny, thin feet on the sofa. Bernice knows little about Leni Ackerman and therefore doesn't know that Leni dislikes and pities her. She decides that Leni is simply one of the 'old type' of dons' wives, eccentric, wealthy enough to run a big house, a mother figure for the male undergraduates. She's glad there aren't many like her. Their dining rooms were like power houses. They had unfair influence. They corrupted the studious mind. And for all their power, they reinforced male supremacy in a closed and competitive world. They are anachronisms. Bernice bites into her cake. No one tells her why there are five candles on the plate.

'I like Oz,' Leni says later to Miriam. Gary is out with a black actor called Gabriel, currently rehearsing *Othello* at the Oxford Playhouse. This is the first evening Leni and Miriam have spent alone together. Leni decides she feels strong enough to sit in the kitchen in a cane chair while Miriam makes soup. 'Do you like him, Miriam?'

'Yes. I remember him from years ago.'

'I always thought you'd marry somebody like that. With a good mind.'

Miriam chops onions, chops parsnips and doesn't answer.

'Oz would have been very right for you. He's an artist in his way. You would have got along well.'

Miriam stirs the chopped vegetables in a heavy pan. She understands both the rightness and the cruelty of what Leni is saying. Miriam feels glad she has no daughter to terrorise with love.

'There's so much, Leni, you've wanted to change in my life. So much you've wanted to be different. I'm sorry you didn't always get your way.'

Leni shifts her small weight in the wicker chair, ignoring this statement with a sniff.

'I think Oz was in love with you years ago. I think that's why he didn't marry.'

'No, Leni,' Miriam says gently. 'He was in love with you.'

Leni smiles, stares at Miriam in surprise. It's the smile of the astounded teacher; against expectations the pupil has the right answer. 'A' will be awarded. A housepoint.

'That was just frivolity,' says Leni. 'I used to teach him to dance, to move his body. He liked this of course. Unless you get them on their feet and dancing, men like Oz spend all their lives sitting down. But he'll never dance again. That Atwood's like an albatross on him.'

'I should think,' ventures Miriam, 'that Dr O is very content – he seems content – without any dancing.'

'But no one gets him laughing. He used to laugh. Before the bookshop. Before Atwood.'

'Where is the shop?'

'Oh, tucked away. Some little alley round the back of Wadham. No one buys anything.'

'Of course they do, Leni, or the shop wouldn't still exist.'

'It scarcely does. When I was last in there no one else came in for half an hour. Not one customer. I think Atwood keeps them away. So she can have Oz to herself.'

'I'll go to the shop on Monday. I want to buy some novels to take home.'

'You're not going home, Miriam. I couldn't manage.'

'Not now. When you're well.'

'I suppose I could be dying. I'm quite old enough. Then you can bury me and go.'

Miriam won't give Leni the satisfaction of a reply. She pours boiling water onto a stock cube in a Pyrex jug. For the swiftest second, she thinks of the chicken broth Gervaise lives on. Bones boiled and boiled. Bread made by Klaus cut up and dipped in the clear liquid. It occurs to her for perhaps the first time, that Larry, in his nearness to the Mallélous' wall, may be lonely. She regrets, partially regrets, her harshness on the telephone and decides she must call through to Nadia, tomorrow or the next day. No card has come from Pomerac for her birthday.

'Of course I'm leaving you this house, Miriam.'

'Yes, Leni.'

'Larry won't want to live in it I shouldn't think, so you'll have to sell it. The problem is Gary. I'd like to make some clause or codicil giving Gary the tenancy, but the solicitors say that isn't fair on you and that it devalues the property. Personally I can't see why. I'd buy a house with a sitting poet. In fact, I think it'd add. But then we live in an age of Philistines. "Monetarism" is the most repellent word they've invented since "bivouacking".'

Miriam smiles. 'You can solve the problem of Gary. Leave him some money to buy a little place of his own.'

'Yes. I could. But it's this house that Gary loves. His room. The garden. He does all the gardening now, you know. We got rid of that girl gardener. Gary said she was too fond of miniatures. He's put in great fat bushes all over the place and it looks much better. You'd see it if the rain would stop.'

'I have seen it, Leni. I walked round it on my first morning.'

'Well. It's better, isn't it? Bolder. You wouldn't think Gary would be a bold gardener, would you, but he is. And he keeps it all so well. Just as if it were his. And then the house. You see, this was really the first home he ever had. He lived with that uncle he hated, then on his own in Earls Court and then here. And he said after all that, Rothersmere Road was paradise. Paradise. He's felt loved, you see. Probably for the first time. You remember how shy he used to be? Crippled. As if he'd just broken the waters of an egg and come floating out. God knows how he survived his first year in that school. I used to wonder

if those loutish boys wouldn't just dismember him. Crunch him
up and eat him, like quail on toast. I dare say they only didn't
out of respect for his poetry. Though, there again, adolescents
don't value the life of the mind. They'd rather have Neanderthals
shouting instructions at them in so-called song. *Hit me with your
rhythm stick*! Baffling. *Come on, Eileen*. I tuned to Jimmy Young
one morning on the hospital earphones. *Come on, Eileen*! I'm
sure Jimmy Young didn't understand that. He's my age without
the topknot, but he was playing it. Perhaps pop is forbidden in
the school and they let Gary speak in peace.'

She talks. Miriam watches the stock cube dissolve, then pours
it on to the vegetables. Leni will talk talk talk till her last moment
on earth. While the soup simmers and Miriam pours herself a
weak scotch and water, Leni starts to talk about David Ackerman. Her remorse when he died. The question that still torments: did her infidelities shorten his life? So many men wanted
a share of what they said she was – beautiful. No age has ever
side-stepped the physical beauty of woman. It was always hard
currency. And if you're rich with it, as she was rich, how can
you bear to hide it and not spend it? But she thinks she might
be wiser now. So much of what we call beauty is fabrication, a
false concept, a conditioning. So it betrays, in the end. Turns
to dust. She envies Miriam her plainness, her lack of natural
riches. Beauty and loyalty conflict. Loyalty and art are a recipe
for the sane mind . . .

Yes, yes, I've heard it all before, Miriam thinks, but doesn't
say. In my love of Leni I'm doubly punished: for my lack of
beauty; for my willingness to preside over the final death of
hers.

Suppertime comes. Miriam blends the parsnip soup and adds
parsley. Leni's chair is pulled up to the table and a bowl of soup
set before her. But she isn't hungry and the soup cools under
her shaky spoon. She can feel the butterscotch cake slowly
drifting down the trickling stream her body has become.

On Sunday morning, after this Saturday of talk and visitors and
cake, Leni sleeps. Miriam brings up tea, turns on the fire and
Leni stares at her with exhausted eyes like sloes. The moment

Miriam leaves the room, she turns over and sleeps again. She dreams a surgeon comes and tells her: your heart is technically dead. Snails have sucked it too small to be viable. The only long-term hope is a transplant, but blood is the problem. Your blood group is HO, which you may recognise as the scientific hieroglyph denoting water. She wakes and tries to drink the cold tea. So much of her wants to be obedient to Miriam's kindness. But the tea is bitter and foul and all Leni longs to do is sleep and sleep. Miriam tiptoes in, removes the tea and turns off the fire.

Gary isn't in his room, nor has been all Saturday night. For the first time since her arrival, Miriam has the house to herself. The rain keeps on and she feels contained in it, a kind of prisoner, like a night-watchman. She stares out at Gary's rusty car. Will Leni insist that this, too, stays when the house is sold? The jealous daughter in her resents Leni's concern for Gary the stray, Gary the outsider. And the woman of fifty resents Gary the man, fifteen years younger than herself, coming and going like a cat. The black boyfriend. The exquisitely satisfied lust. Men ignoring women, except as mothers. A parade of cockerels. Two cocks hard as fists. Men in men. She feels dowdy, lonely and unnecessary.

Without acknowledging what she may be about to do, she searches in Leni's study (a small, downstairs room with a telephone, always referred to by David Ackerman as Leni's library) for the Oxford telephone book and finds Dr O's number. She writes the number down on a piece of paper and stares at this for a while, then picks up the telephone receiver and dials it. Until his voice answers, she has no real idea of what she's going to say.

'Dr O?'

'Yes.'

'Miriam Ackerman here.' Miriam Ackerman. It's years since she called herself Ackerman. She feels astonished, as if by an act of daring.

'Oh yes, yes. Oh indeed. Miriam.'

'Am I disturbing you?'

'No, no. No.'

'I don't know why I'm ringing. I think Leni's going to sleep for most of the day and I suddenly thought it would be nice to talk to someone. I hope you don't think this is very selfish.'

'No, no. No indeed. I'm delighted to talk to you, Miriam.'

'My mother was telling me how very kind you've been, visiting her so often, and I wanted to thank you . . .'

'*De rien. De rien.* Leni is one of my most cherished friends. I'm always very happy to see her.'

There's a sudden silence. Wondering urgently if Bernice Atwood is at Dr O's shoulder, listening in to the conversation, Miriam feels tongue-tied and embarrassed. I've become feeble, she thinks. I let myself feel lonely, instead of working. 'I should be working today . . .' she stammers, 'I really should. But my concentration's bad at the moment, since leaving France . . .'

'Well, Sunday. I don't work Sunday. A little manuscript gravure sometimes, but nothing too engaging.'

'So you have a, well, a more or less free day?'

'Yes, yes. Nothing planned. The weather's too poor for walking which is what I like to do at this time of year.'

'Oh I like this, too. I remember I just used to like walking round the city in the autumn, when I lived here.'

'But in France, in the area where you live, I recall superb walks.'

'Yes. They are. Superb.'

A dog, Miriam thinks suddenly. Perhaps Larry and I should have bought a dog, to give us a better sense of belonging there. And I'd feel better about Larry's loneliness if there was a dog . . .

'I travel to France not infrequently,' Dr O is saying. 'I do what I call my medieval tour. Starting at Fontevraud and Eleanor's tomb. A kind of pilgrimage. I could call your way one year. What did you say your place was named?'

'Pomerac. It's between Périgueux and Angoulême.'

'You must tell me about it. I know Périgueux of course. That Roman-Byzantine cathedral. What's it called?'

'St Front.'

'Oh yes, yes. I have some photographs of it, not good, I'm not good with a camera.'

'I was wondering . . .'

'I'm so sorry. What did you say, Miriam?'

'Oh. Well, I was wondering . . . I'd bought a chicken in the hope Leni would eat some, but I don't think she will today. And it seems a shame to waste it. Would you like to come round for lunch?'

There's a long silence. Miriam feels nervy and silly. She wonders what on earth she's doing. For the first time, she feels sympathetic to Nadia's loneliness, to her need for company. She prays Dr O will accept, out of kindness and pity, as she accepts invitations from Nadia.

'I wouldn't want to intrude, Miriam, if Leni is poorly today . . .'

'No. You won't intrude. She's sleeping. She has days when she just sleeps. But of course I mustn't go out and leave her.'

'No, no. No.'

'So I would be very grateful to have some company . . .'

'How kind of you to think of me. Now I have promised Miss Atwood we shall go to the Ingmar Bergman film at four-ten. This is of course a solemn promise, but yes, I would be very pleased to come to lunch. What time should I arrive?'

'Whenever you like,' says Miriam, calm with relief. 'Say twelve-thirty.'

So for the rest of the morning she prepares. Setting the table in the dining room, she feels for the first time in her life as if this house, whose very skirting creaks in sympathy with Leni's bones, belongs to her and she's quietly happy. 'Give a woman a house,' her father once teased, 'and she'll ask for so very little else you must conclude that all her curiosity has gone up its chimney!' 'I cried,' Leni said, 'when David bought Rothersmere Road. Just the size of it. The garden. I cried for joy!' Leni remained curious however. About the world. About the flesh. About the devil. All that flew out as smoke from the sitting-room fireplace was perhaps her conscience.

Miriam prepares the chicken and makes a tarragon sauce with fresh tarragon she finds in Gary's herb bed. She makes Lyonnaise potatoes, ices a bottle of wine. The rain stops and the brilliant sun shines on her calm endeavours. She feels as purposeful as when she paints. The colours of the roasting chicken, the sauce, the potatoes, the wine, the green-stemmed wine glasses are as obediently pleasing as a successful water-colour of cornfields and grasslands and plough.

Leni sleeps. Her dreaming, empty flesh doesn't disturb or trouble Miriam. She goes up once to stare at it, to listen to the shallow breaths. Since arriving, I love her a little less, she thinks. When the separation comes, I'll be ready. And she closes the door.

Dr O eats with relish. This reminds Miriam of Larry. Swathes of chicken are gobbled. She, suddenly, has no appetite. Now that her guest is here, she knows it must have been wrong to invite him. He's headed for the cinema and Miss Atwood – and Miss Atwood's little pleading hand. Yet he seems happy. Happy and jolly and at ease. He takes long draughts of the wine, wipes his lips, smiling at her over his napkin. 'Delicious, Miriam. I've had many, many meals in this house, but I can't remember any as good.'

'Just a roast chicken, Dr O . . .'

'But the sauce. Excellent. Yes, indeed.'

The silly urge to talk has left her. She can't think now why it was so strong. Far better to have spent the day painting. Only a month or so to the exhibition. So much to start. She is silent then, watching this large, untidy man. One of her mother's lovers, probably. She's had younger than him. He doesn't seem troubled by her stare. He's talking eagerly, eating, talking, eating, talking . . .

'I'll confess, Miriam, years ago – what a confession, my God, I never thought I'd make it! – I wanted to marry you. You mustn't laugh. I was quite serious, and yet not, because I didn't know you. I only admired you very much, you and your painting, and I thought, there she is, my wife. You were married already of course, but in some foolish way, I'd overlooked this. When I found out, I was so put out. I actually thought of it as a betrayal.'

'I've never betrayed anyone,' says Miriam gravely.

'No, no. No, no. Of course you haven't. And of course you didn't. And of course it wasn't. The thing is, what I'm so pleased about, is now I have the chance to get to know you properly. Starting now, as they say.'

'Oh yes,' says Miriam weakly, 'starting now.'

'I was planning yesterday, you see, how to lure you out for one of my Sunday walks. I thought you might come into the shop. Or I'd simply come back here to see Leni, and invite you. And now you've invited me. I'm very, very flattered. Can I help myself to some more of this wonderful potato thing?'

'Yes. Of course.'

She passes the dish. As the wide hand comes out to take it, she has a cruel sense of something done wrongly, too hastily. The hand ladles potato and onion, piles the plate up. Upstairs, Leni is starving and neglected, shoved into sleep, abandoned. Miriam wants to weep.

'You know Leni's dying,' she says and hears her voice quiver. Dr O puts down his fork and looks at her anxiously over his spectacles.

'Yes,' he says. 'I think she may be.'

Utter silence descends. Miriam and Dr O look at each other in dismay.

'Shall we talk about it, Miriam?' Dr O eventually says. 'Or shall we just enjoy each other's company?'

Miriam's tears fall like soft fruit juice, fall and slide. Behind his glasses, Dr O's eyes are petrified with confusion, with his year-in, year-out sense of inadequacy as the kind of man women love. In the film he is about to see, the actor playing this part – his part – gets up and crosses to Miriam. The camera tracks him. He takes Miriam's weeping head in his arms. But Dr O doesn't move. He puts his knife and fork together on his new helping of potato Lyonnaise and stares helplessly across it while Miriam cries. She buries her face in her napkin. Dr O thinks he hears movement upstairs and whispers to Miriam: 'I think Leni's coming down. We mustn't let her see you crying.'

I'm not crying just for Leni, Miriam wants to say. I'm crying because I'm so tired, *tired* of being strong for other people. To be the strong one is so, *so* lonely. No one realises. Least of all Larry. Least of all Thomas. Even Leni, she doesn't realise. They're the tears of years, she thinks. Pent up. Accumulating.

The tears for *Aquazure*. The tears for Pomerac and exile. Tears for being fifty. Tears for this house, full of strangers, empty of David. Tears for the son she never sees. Tears for her own weakness which finally blanketed her strength and caused her to invite an old, untidy friend to lunch.

The footsteps above die out. A door closes. Dr O breathes with relief. And free of his fear of Leni's arrival, he gets up, the actor in the film now, gentle but firm, with the right script in his head, and crosses to Miriam whose whole body is convulsed with sobbing. He squats down by Miriam's chair, gently puts his arms round her shoulders and pulls her head forward onto his green cardigan.

The sobbing continues, but he feels Miriam's hands hold fast to him. The inconsolable child? He doesn't know. He's never held a child. Her lovely hair smells of lemons. She's a gift of fruit in his arms, from the rich French countryside, from orchards and vineyards. Years ago he may have imagined her like this, something bright and scented and large. He rocks her gently, binds her to him more closely. He's no longer the actor playing the part, but himself and marvelling at all the years that have passed between the day when he imagined holding Miriam to him and the day when he did. The kisses he now plants on her burnished head are kisses of pure passion.

For Miriam, to be contained in Dr O's odd embrace is comforting and good. His body smells of fresh baking – of scones or muffins, some homely English invention you enjoy by the fire. I've come home, she thinks. I've come home. Larry and the life she's trying to start in Pomerac have, for this little moment, been removed from her, as if she'd folded them away in a brochure, thinking, that's a place to return to, one day. And loneliness recedes. She's able, after a very few minutes, to pull gently away and blow her nose on the table napkin.

The Bergman film is rather long. Dr O remembers, the moment it begins, that he's seen it, dismembered into three or four parts, on the television. Many sequences have Liv Ullman, dressed in what looks like a cardinal's robe and hat, flitting through the sad chambers of her mind. In one of these she discovers her parents, poor little thin and terrified people. She screams and rages at them, then cries with remorse, then rages again at this pattern they inflict of fury followed by guilt.

At his side, Bernice Atwood is hot and quiet, eating Toblerone. Dr O wonders if Bernice would like to look like Liv Ullman. He looks at her in the flickery darkness. She has a tiny, doggy nose, turned up and pink. Her eyes are small but she opens them as wide as possible all the time, so that she looks both startled and short-sighted, which she is. Her hair is colourless and thick. She clips it back in a slide. She's thirty-three, but there are times, like now, eating her chocolate, when she seems half this age.

Dr O is very used to the white hills and grey hollows of Bernice's body. It's a body quite unblemished by time, untouched by sun, a lapping loving landscape, contentedly heaving. In all his years of knowing it, he has never and she has never admitted desire. Though Dr O and Bernice spend their days toiling over words and ancient meanings, language plays no part whatsoever in their love-making. Neither asks. Neither offers. They give silently. The only sound is the suck of their flesh. Dr O, so easily accommodated and satisfied between Bernice's snowy mountains of hips, has no idea whether the movements he makes give her the pleasure she seems to strive for. He doesn't ask. She doesn't say. Sometimes when he lies still on her, satisfied, heavy and sleepy, he feels her belly continue to move under him, her little mound still thrusting at him. He likes this. He presses down on her as she breathes and pants. He wants to suck her breasts, but she holds him fast in place above her, presses her lips to his. Then she lies still and opens her eyes, and her arms relax and gently stroke his back. Was that good? Is what we do enough? He doesn't ask. She doesn't say. He concludes he satisfies her. She never refuses him. Sometimes in the night, she wakes him and starts fondling him again and he feels her huge soft breasts pouring over his arm. He doesn't like his sleep broken. It's difficult for him to make the gestures of desire. She rubs and rubs his prick. He feels old. But then she kneels and kisses him, her mouth hot with sleep, her tongue lively as an animal. Her hair falls on his face. He is enveloped and borne away. He turns and tumbles into her, rocking in the darkness. He can't deny this gift of her, slippery and silent. I can't deny you, Bernice, says the feeble jet of sperm she wrings from him. And she smiles knowingly. My happiness is his. His is mine.

Now, watching this long, sad film, Dr O trembles with the thought that he may betray her. 'I wish I understood Swedish,' she suddenly whispers to him. He stops looking at her and turns back to the screen. Liv Ullman's grandmother shows her into a little child's room, decorated with pink castles. He forgets to look at the subtitles. The Swedish dialogue goes on like a jaunty train; yoni-oni – yeni-meni – rhude-hude . . . He closes his eyes. The language is beautiful, he thinks, its cadences so gentle, you could prise meaning from it without understanding a word. Yet it journeys at the very edge of his thoughts, thoughts which keep doubling back and doubling back into the five minutes of that very day when he held Miriam's head against his cardigan and found in his sturdy English heart foreign orchards of craving and desire. They invade him and bloom. He's dizzy with their perfume, hard with their fruit. He doesn't recognise himself, the quiet Dr O in his habitual place at Bernice Atwood's side. He wants to lean across to her and confess, I've fallen in love with Miriam Ackerman. I was denied her once. Now I'm going to have her. He has no plan, however. He knows he may let Miriam go back to France without ever telling her that he loves her. So momentous does his desire for her seem that he doesn't know how or when or with what words or gestures to approach her. It's so easy to love Bernice in silence. So easy not to answer what she doesn't ask. But in Miriam's orchard, words will surely be needed. She's Leni's daughter. That family can colour whole rooms, whole houses, whole streets and skies with words. Yet in love-language he's a naif, a pupil, an innocent. Bernice has never taught him. He's never taught her. The embrace was enough. Movement was enough. He craves some manual or dictionary. All his life, he has looked for answers in books. He's not certain if the book exists that can help him now.

Bernice, having eaten almost the whole block of Toblerone without noticing it, pushes the few segments left into Dr O's hands. The chocolate feels warm. Dr O isn't hungry after his lunch with Miriam, but he eats the Toblerone out of simple obedience to Bernice's gifts. Already, he feels frightened for her. If he withdraws his own gift of acceptance, what will she do with all the tender offerings she stores? The warm chocolate slides guiltily into his stomach. He swallows and sighs. Bernice turns momentarily from the film and stares at him.

'What's the matter?' she whispers.

'Nothing,' says Dr O.

Liv Ullman swallows Nembutal, handful after handful, and lies down on the child's bed to wait for death. Bernice Atwood tucks her hand into the warm crease of Dr O's arm.

Miriam tiptoes up to Leni's room. The curtains have been drawn and sunlight falls on Leni's bed. Leni is awake with her glasses perched on her nose and the Sunday papers spread around her. Replenished with sleep, she seems alert and strong.

'Leni. You're awake.'

'Well I heard voices. What are you up to, Miriam?'

Miriam sits down among the papers.

'Up to? I had Dr O for lunch.'

'You mean you *ate* him?'

'No. He gobbled a lot of chicken.'

'Is he still here?'

'He's gone to the Bergman film with Miss Atwood.'

'Silly him. We could have entertained him better. So he asked himself over, did he?'

'No. I invited him.'

Leni peers at Miriam over her glasses.

'And he didn't want to come up and see me?'

'He did. But you were sleeping. We didn't want to wake you.'

'Oh.'

Leni takes off the glasses, which hang on an ugly chain round her neck. Her eyes seem bright, full of curiosity.

'Are you hungry, darling?' asks Miriam, getting up. Leni's stares she has always found discomforting.

'I'd like some of that soup you made yesterday. I'm glad you invited Oz, Miriam. I think that was very clever of you.'

'Clever of me?'

'Yes, you'll have a proper companion, now, for your stay here.'

'I'll go and heat the soup.'

'Was he nice to you?'

'Of course.'

'I don't want much soup. Don't give me too much.'

Miriam is on her way out of the bedroom when the telephone rings. Leni picks it up and stubbornly states a long out-of-date telephone number.

'Oxford 7815.'

Close in her ear, ragged with its pierced hole heavy jewelled earrings have pulled to a slit, she hears Larry's voice, so close that her first thought is the dismayed one: Larry's in England.

'Leni,' says Larry quietly.

In Leni's mind, he's at Dover, standing on the windy front with his baggage. But he's in Nadia's room, tracing a line in the condensation on her window.

'Where are you, Larry?'

Miriam stops, her hand on the door. Not today, she thinks. I'm not ready for Larry today. Yet the France brochure opens. Pomerac sits on its hill in the sunshine. Gervaise stares at her with reproachful eyes, calling her back.

'Where am I?' asks Larry. 'I'm in Pomerac. Can I speak to Miriam, please?'

No courtesies for Leni today. No enquiries after her health. If she's dying, Larry thinks impatiently, let her get on with it.

Leni holds the receiver out to Miriam. 'It's Larry,' she says, 'he's in Pomerac.'

'I'll take it in the study.'

'Yes. Very well.'

Leni says nothing more to Larry, just rests the receiver on her eiderdown. Miriam closes the door on her mother and goes down to the telephone she used only a few hours ago to summon Dr O. Between that moment and this so many emotions have pecked and pulled at Miriam she feels in need of bandaging.

When she lifts the receiver, Larry, puzzled by the silence, is calling her: 'Miriam? Miriam?'

'Hello, Larry,' she says softly.

'Oh, I've got you.'

'You're at Nadia's.'

'Yes. I wanted to ring yesterday, to say happy birthday, but Nadia was out and I didn't feel I could ask Mme de la Brosse.'

'No. Well, how are you?'

Cold, Miriam thinks. I am so cold with him.

'Coping all right, but missing you. I thought of you yesterday. Was it all right?'

'What?'

'Your birthday.'

'Oh yes. All right. Just quiet. Leni got up for a while.'

'She's getting better, then?'

Miriam listens. There's been no click of Leni's receiver going down. Often, when colleagues telephoned David, she'd listen in.

'Yes,' says Miriam wearily, 'she's a lot better.'

'She's not dying then?'

Miriam listens again. Now it comes, like a sniff of disgust, the click. 'She's very weak. I've been trying to get her to eat, but she won't.'

There's a brief and troubled silence before Larry says: 'When are you coming home?'

Home, thinks Miriam. Pomerac. Home?

'I don't know, Larry. I can't possibly leave till Leni's on her feet.'

'How long?'

'I can't say.'

'I thought if someone was dying, they died.'

'They do in the end, Larry.'

'Yes. I'm sorry. It's always been hard for me to understand . . .'

'Understand?'

'Why you love her.'

'She's my mother, Larry.'

'What, the Jewish mother. That?'

'Not only. It's not just duty.'

'What then?'

'A stubborn love that won't go away. And I like it that she . . .'

'What?'

'She needs me. For once. She's never needed me. Now she does.'

'I need you.'

'I know, Larry. How's Nadia?'

'Nadia's here. Do you want to talk to her?'

'Yes. I'll say hello.'

Nadia rather than Larry. *Anyone.* Miriam waits. I must ask him not to call any more, she decides. Letters are better, less painful.

'Hello my darling!' Nadia's high voice flies, unchanged, down the wires.

'Nice to hear you, Nadia. How are you?'

'Well, I'm so sorry, my darling.'

'What, Nadia?'

'I'm not here on your birthday. Larry is coming and coming. Till ten o'clock. He think I am arrested and sent home packing to Poland! But I was at a very good At Home party from some old friends of Claude's. They have some uncle or what in a wine house, so Nadia is absolutely pissing all day and today my God the bloody hangover, you don't know!'

'Oh, I'm sorry, Nadia. But it was a good party?'

'I don't remember! I'm so pissing, Miriam, I don't know what I eat or say or who is kissing me or what, but actually everyone is pissing, even the uncle from the wine house, so we are all not knowing what we're doing. Maybe I dance with someone. I don't know.'

'How's Larry, Nadia?' Miriam says gravely.

'Oh Larry. You want to talk again?'

'No. Just tell me how he is.'

'Well. He is so kind to me, Miriam. I am crying one evening and telling him my bloody life is so and so, and if I was Larry I tell Nadia, look, this so moaning gets out my nose, but he is not telling this and comforting me. So kind, you see?'

Autumn comes. Women getting old start sobbing like children.

'Oh I'm glad, Nadia.'

'But of course he is sad for you.'

'Sad?'

'Yes. And your mother? She isn't kick the bucket?'

'No.'

'So you come back to Pomerac, Miriam?'

'Not yet.'

'I think you leave this old mother and come home.'

'This was my home once.'

'Well so. Poland was mine. Cockroaches on my bloody floor. Some lavatory they make before the First War. My neighbour on the landing with one leg . . . You think I go back there?'

'No. But in my case it's different.'

'But you don't stay so long, my darling, for this Leni.'

'Why?'

'Well if I have some husband so kind as Larry I'm not staying in Poland with my mother and queue for her fucking bread . . .'

'But you know what I feel about Leni, Nadia.'

'I know, my darling, I know. But I say you don't stay there.'

'I have to stay until Leni's well.'

'But you're saying me she was kick the bucket, my dear.'

'She may. I don't know.'

'So if she kick, then you go back for the funeral and so and so and make the white wreath, but you don't forget Larry.'

'Of course I haven't forgotten him, Nadia. Don't be stupid.'

'Well, so I'm stupid. I'm getting pissing yesterday and stupid but today not. I don't know why if I say this of your Leni's death I'm so stupid.'

Miriam sighs. She sits down at Leni's desk which has not been used since her illness. Bills and correspondence are piled up, waiting for Miriam's attention.

'I'm doing my best, that's all,' says Miriam. 'Of course I don't mean you're stupid, Nadia.'

But it's Larry who comes back to the telephone.

'Miriam, I wanted to tell you, I've begun the pool.'

'Good, Larry, good. I'm glad.'

'How fast I can get on depends on the weather. At the moment it's glorious.'

'Is it? Yes, it's fine here this afternoon.'

'Cold, mind you. You've got to stretch the imagination to remember summer.'

After this, there seems little more that either Larry or Miriam want to say. Miriam considers for a moment asking about the walnut tree but decides quickly that it's too late and it will have been felled by now. Larry wants to ask whether Miriam has seen Thomas but her coldness to him cuts the question off before it's uttered. They say a solemn goodbye and leave it at that.

Miriam walks to the kitchen and begins to stir Leni's soup.

In the night she's woken by Gary.

'Mother's had a fall, love. Afraid you've got to get up.'

'A fall?'

'On the landing. She was dizzy, she said. I heard her go. I was reading. Luckily.'

Miriam tugs on the warm dressing gown that has replaced la robe. Gary has carried Leni back to her bed. Her face has the pallor of bone.

'Dr Wordsworth's coming,' Gary whispers.

Miriam sits on Leni's bed, takes one thin hand in hers. There is sweat on Leni's forehead. She draws sharp, shallow breaths.

'I'm so sorry, Miriam . . .' she murmurs.

Gary, his hair wild, his thin body sumptuous in a black quilted gown, rebukes her.

'Ssh, darling. Don't utter.'

Miriam turns to Gary. 'Is there pain, Gary?' To Miriam's irritation, Gary turns straight to Leni and asks her: 'Where's the pain, sweet?' Leni's lips tremble as she answers: 'Foot.'

We're a strange flock of nightbirds, Miriam thinks, a tryptich of pain and devotion talking in whispers round the lamp. Outside the night is starry and cold. Gary crosses to the electric fire and turns it on. Even in his quilt, he's shivering. Tea, Miriam decides. This is an English emergency; we'll drink tea. She strokes her mother's hand and lays it down. 'I'd like tea, Gary,' she says. 'Will you make it or shall I?'

'I,' says Gary and flits like a silky bat out of the room. As he goes down the stairs, he thinks, in seven hours I'll be teaching

Heart of Darkness to IVb. He wonders if this night vigil will help or hinder him. To him, darkness today and yesterday has meant Gabriel. He knows he's in love. He will be as jealous of this black Othello as the character himself is jealous. The way between this night and the winter is strewn with strawberry handkerchiefs.

Gary makes a tray of tea and takes this up. Leni's lips are blue with pain. Miriam offers her tea, but she shakes her head. Gary and Miriam nibble Bourbon biscuits and drink the tea sweet to keep themselves awake. Once, Miriam suggests that Gary goes back to bed and tries to sleep, but he's settled himself on the other side of Leni's bed like her lover and he won't be moved.

He's still there, with his white, shapely legs stretched out beside the invalid, when the doctor arrives. Only the request that he goes out while Leni is examined dislodges him. He mooches back to his room and turns on Ella Fitzgerald: *Miss Otis regrets she's unable to lunch today . . .*

To the accompaniment of this old, old song Dr Wordsworth, a clean and ruddy man of sixty, informs Miriam and Leni that Leni's ankle is broken. She pouts with frustration. 'I'm not going back to hospital, Dr Wordsworth.'

'There's no alternative, Mrs Ackerman. The ankle must be set.'

. . . and from under her velvet gown, she drew a gun and shot her lover down . . .

'I don't want to go back in that hospital, Miriam.'

'Oh, it won't be for long, Leni. Will it, doctor?'

'No. Now I'm going to give you something for the pain.'

'What? What are you giving me?'

Dr Wordsworth is filling a syringe.

'Just a mild painkiller.'

'That means some kind of dope. They give cocaine and heroin all the time in hospitals now. They just call it by some other name, dia-something. Is that what I'm getting, coke and heroin?'

'Just an effective analgesic.'

. . . When her Ma came and got her and dragged her from the jail . . .

'You'd better come with me to the hospital, Miriam. I'll be
spaced out. You must come and make sure they plaster up the
right bit of me.'

'Of course I'll come, Leni. I'll go and dress.'

'No, don't go yet. Let me hold your hand while I get my fix.
Do you remember *Long Day's Journey*? "Caught her in the
act with a hypo!" What a dreadful line! I never admired that
play.'

Leni is turned on her side and her bottom punctured. Streams
of cold anaesthetising poison enter her blood. She looks startled
and her hand holding Miriam's relaxes its grip. Dr Wordsworth,
struggling against the effects of the sleeping pill taken two hours
ago, telephones for the ambulance. Gary tiptoes back to Leni's
door and strains to listen.

Miss Otis regrets she's unable to lunch today . . .

The question of whether, after the Bergman film, Dr O should
spend the night with Bernice is one that begins to torment him
as soon as the film nears its end. It still torments him as he
walks out into the cold, clear night with Bernice at his elbow,
he striding, she taking little running steps to keep up with him.

Dr O inhabits the top floor of a house in Plum Street off the
Woodstock Road, not far from Rothersmere Road; Miss Atwood
has two rooms in Cattle Street, almost within uneasy sight of
Blackwell's. Between these two identically shabby residences
their love affair walks back and forth. Neither has ever suggested
flat-sharing. Bernice has this recurring dream: Dr O buys a
Jacobean hall arranged round a courtyard not dissimilar to that
of the Bodleian Library. On cold flagstones he lays her down.
He places a Book of Hours on her breasts. On this, he swears
to love her for ever, and to make her mistress of his house. She
wakes up satisfied and content. Even if she wakes up to find
herself alone in her Cattle Street bed, this dream seems miraculous and right. She doesn't doubt the bonding and binding of Dr
O to her. One day, they might put their book collections together
in one room. Say some vows, even, though she scorns what
men and women make of marriage. Her love is not domestic.
It's ancient and profound and will not be interred in trivia.

Only a hall or a castle might give it stern enough shelter.

Bernice knows and Dr O suspects that, had they not found each other, they would have led virtually celibate lives. Bernice was a virgin the night Dr O drove her home from the opening of a heraldry exhibition in his Morris Traveller and invited her in for coffee. His rooms smelled of the must and dust of pre-war time. Newspapers and journals in bundles. A ream of blotting paper. Leathery classics from skirting to cornice. A gas fire. A candlewick bedspread. Ink. Parchment shades. Washing on the fireguard. Dr O poured water on Nescafé with a shaking hand, but Bernice was calm. She walked about, touching things. If she had any fear at all it was the thought of conceiving a child. All lay so anciently, so silently in the room, so silently in her small womb, she didn't want it disturbed with new limbs and mewling and milk. She wasn't certain how children were prevented. She'd heard there was a pill. She'd heard there were rubber things you push up. Over the coffee, she said simply: 'The only thing I don't want is a baby,' and saw Dr O nod his agreement. So she trusted him and thought no more about it. When she saw him unroll a little transparent balloon onto his hard prick she thought simply, that must be it, and waited with her legs spread lovingly wide for the first immersion of a man in her blood. The pain is ecstatic, she thought. She mourned the pain the moment it was past. Later she examined the spatter of blood on the sheets. My gift, she thought, given and received. From this night on, her life was entirely happy.

Now, without her knowing it yet, as they walk from the cinema to Dr O's car – the same Morris Traveller that once conveyed the virgin Bernice to Plum Street – this happy life is being taken from her.

'Did you like the film?' asks Bernice. She senses Dr O is grave and distant and wonders if the film depressed him.

'I've seen it before,' is all he says.

They get into the car. The windscreen wipers grind, though there's no rain. Dr O is absentminded about the noises and movements his car makes. He feels sick from the Toblerone and his head aches. He drives to the corner of Cattle Street and stops.

'I'm sorry,' says Bernice, 'I didn't know you'd seen the film before.'

'On television,' he says and she nods.

He waits, afraid and sick, for Bernice to get out of the car. He's no longer tormented by indecision but cruel in his determination to spend the night alone, dreaming of Miriam. Bernice never bullies him. She doesn't need to. Both of them like to be alone from time to time. So, almost tragically unaware of the misfortune about to fall on her, Bernice places a chaste little kiss on Dr O's cheek, gathers up her capacious handbag and leaves him. If she feels a moment's sadness, it quickly leaves her, and when she hears the Morris start up again, she turns and waves.

And as Miriam rides to hospital with Leni, Dr O indulges his dreaming. Leni tells Miriam she's in fairyland after that injection, 'all lighty and flitty, darling,' and Dr O lies in the dark in the fairyland of his future. Throughout the night he hears bells chime the hours. Oxford. His city. Miriam is in Oxford. Safe in Leni's house once more. Where she has always belonged in his mind. Today he held her. When her crying stopped, she said: 'I remember now what a kind person you are. My father was so fond of you.' So the love affair to come will be homage to David Ackerman. David Ackerman, bone under the earth, worn thin in his lifetime with Leni's soirées and parrot parties. Now, his daughter and his former pupil will plant their flowers of love in his departed soul. Leni will die and they will inhabit his very house. In the bed where love was made to the unsurpassably beautiful Leni, and the child, Miriam, began to grow, in this same bed will the wizard spend his magical seed. Not to make children. Not to alter the future, but to alter the past. The years of plain, cumbersome Bernice crumble to nothing. Separately, in separate lives, Dr O and Miriam have waited them out. Now Leni, the witch, near death, her body shedding flesh, paring itself to neat and tidy bone to be with David under a marble book – Jews turned gentiles as the Oxford cloisters cloak them in ancient pieties – Leni, the sorceress, summons them out of separateness and binds them in desire. Before yielding them her bed, she inhabits it, watching, knowing. Death keeps them waiting, wanting. Burning for this death, they wait, still not joined. Leni smiles. Her eyes are wells of soft darkness. 'Wait,' she whispers. They reach out from either side of the deathbed, but their hands don't touch. The bed is too wide. 'Wait,' she instructs again. So they sit as silent as they can with this aching of desire in them, silent as they can, but dying of their longing to drink from mouths, to drown in their own touch. And at last she goes. The eyes stare up, blind. The hands freeze. And together, they lift her aside. Together, they lie down in the softly tumbled sheets her body has kept warm for them and peel away the clothes that still hold them separate from their final joining. Then at last he is in her. Her gold hair streams. History bursts open like a white, decaying peach.

Morning comes. Leni wakes in an iron bed with a drip in her arm. She feels heavy, like colossal stone. Prone, weighted down with oblivion, she can see now that she's in a large ward. Other women, some young, some old, are eating cereal and wearing nighties. She vows she will say not a word to these women. She will say nothing, eat nothing, drink nothing, till she is moved to a private room. She will close like an oyster and they won't dare to knife her open. So they will have to give her her privacy. She curses Miriam for abandoning her to strangers. Miriam, she decides, with that husband of hers who thinks all the wrong thoughts, dreams all the wrong dreams, has become tolerant of stupidity and mediocrity. She's forgotten what life used to be. Even in her work, she's become mediocre, ordinary, giving ordinary empty people the ordinary landscapes they want, the ones without meaning.

A nurse comes and inspects the colourless drip bottle. Leni asks, with a dry mouth, to be moved to a private room. The nurse picks up the arm without the drip and takes Leni's pulse. Leni asks again, unaware that her words are heavy as stone, like the rest of her. The nurse smiles, says nothing and walks away.

Leni sleeps. When she wakes, it's in the same bed in a ward that is now quite noisy with people. Someone is bending over

her and shaking her. She doesn't mind the feel of the soft arms
of nurses. She doesn't feel weighted down any more; she feels
limp and light and yielding, like a baby.

'Mrs Ackerman. Mrs Ackerman . . .'

Leni stares up into a smiling Indian face: wide nostrils, heavy
hair in a knot under the little starched hat.

'Mrs Ackerman, you have a visitor. Let's sit you up, love.'

The Indian nurse lifts Leni's head. Pillows are stuffed behind
it. Her head lolls. They've put me in a pram, she thinks. She's
hauled back onto the pillows. Her covers are straightened. She
feels cold. All around the big ward, little clusters of people are
talking. In the bed next to Leni's a young woman with wild dirty
hair is holding a man's hand and weeping. The man looks
embarrassed. He's brought chocolates.

'Okay, Mrs Ackerman?'

'Cold,' says Leni.

'You're cold, dear?'

'Yes.'

'Do you have a bedjacket, dear?'

Leni can't remember what she has, what she doesn't have.
She remembers her warm, pretty room at home, the way
Miriam sits on the bed holding her hand. Now Miriam has
abandoned her.

'I'll look in your locker, love.'

The nurse searches quickly through Leni's belongings. She
finds a blue crocheted shawl and she wraps Leni in this tightly.

'I'm sorry,' the woman next door is wailing, 'I'm sorry, I'm
sorry, I'm sorry . . .'

Leni, bound in her shawl, looks away in horror from this
spectacle and sees, at the corner of vision, an untidy familiar
figure. He's waiting by the door, quite alone, carrying a parcel.
Leni stares. Thomas. It's Thomas. Leni's heart leaps. So she
isn't abandoned. Thomas has come. She lifts a hand and pats
her hair. She feels hungry. They starve you in hospitals and
your looks go.

'All right, Mrs Ackerman?'

'Could you comb my hair, nurse?'

'Yes. You have a comb, dear?'

'I think so. In my handbag.'

Thomas isn't looking at her, he's staring at the other patients and the groups of visitors. Leni asks for her lipstick. The crying woman is snivelling now. The man has sat down and taken the cellophane off the chocolates. Black Magic. One of David's old nicknames for Leni in the days when she was beautiful and bad.

Her hair is combed and a bright lipstick put on her cracked lips. The Indian nurse stares at her bizarre handiwork with gigantic eyes.

'You look very nice, Mrs Ackerman. I'll bring you some squash, love.'

Degrading, thinks Leni. No privacy, no dignity, no food.

But Thomas comes to her now, holding his parcel high and grinning. Leni fights her arms free of the shawl. He bends and kisses her forehead. He smells of pipe ash. Leni enfolds his bony back.

'Thank heavens you came, darling. I thought you'd all forgotten me.'

Thomas pulls back from this craggy embrace. Leni smells unwashed. Hospitals are the pits, he thinks. Symptoms are treated, not causes. People go home wounded, then sewn together. He wants to carry his grandmother away.

'Forgotten you? Leni Ackerman forgotten? Fat chance!'

'I refuse to die in here.'

'Die?'

'Yes.'

'You're not dying, stupe.'

'Aren't I?'

'No. You broke your foot, Mother said.'

Now she remembers it: Dr Wordsworth, the ambulance, pain, Miriam and Gary at the bedside. She moves each leg experimentally. Thomas laughs at her perplexed face.

'Can't you remember it? You were dancing on this table. Politicians in the audience, ambassadors . . . And you fell. Someone tripped you, goes the rumour.'

Leni smiles. Jokes. Irreverence. Thomas was always like this and she likes it. He's not, she thinks, much like either of the parents. A changeling.

'Anyway,' he goes on, 'the US Ambassador sent you this. Compensation.'

He sits down by her and hands her the big parcel. A few feet away, the man is popping a Hazel Cluster into the runny mouth of the weeping woman. Thomas starts ripping the parcel open. No solemnity with the present, here. He takes out a heavy, polished wood statue and puts it gently in Leni's hands.

'Thomas!' she says, 'What is it?'

'A man,' says Thomas.

'Get my glasses, darling. From the bag. Here.'

Thomas takes out Leni's spectacles and sets them on her nose. Now, in unblurred vision, she sees the statue is of a kneeling figure, sitting back on his heels and hugging in his arms a wooden mast or pole, taller than his head and which rises upwards from his own groin. The top or head of the mast is cloudy crystal. Thomas reaches over Leni and presses a tiny plastic switch located between the man's hands. The crystal lights, Leni stares, marvels, begins to rock with laughter in her dry throat. The chocolate woman stares at her with pink eyes.

'Bedside Man,' Thomas grins.

'Marvellous!' says Leni. 'Where's the flex?'

'No flex,' says Thomas. 'Batteries. He's self-sufficient.'

Leni's head rolls back with laughter. More visitors turn from their visitees and gawp at her. She holds the lamp aloft. 'You're a genius, Thomas.'

'Well I thought you'd like it better than sweets.'

'Here, put it on the locker, and switch it on. Let's scandalise everyone.'

'Well from behind, he's rather chaste. I'll turn him outwards, shall I?'

'Yes. Let's show all these dummies. My grandson's a genius!' shouts Leni to the ward, 'And a genius with a sense of humour, which is rare.'

People turn briefly, but choose to ignore her. 'I'm ever so sorry, honestly,' the chocolate woman is saying again and again. On the opposite wall, a fat woman is being replenished with marzipan. We're just substances, decides Leni suddenly, like nutpaste. My substance is diminished, though. The wind howls in my cuttlefish bones. She craves potato and milk and sweet cake. Thomas tugs out a packet of Gitanes and offers her one. A large sign above the swing doors says ABSOLUTELY NO SMOKING, but Leni takes a cigarette – her first in twenty years – and purses her lips while Thomas lights it for her. She feels hollow and wicked and weightless. She inhales and grins. Thomas pulls a plastic chair near to her and sits down.

'Conspirators,' she whispers down at him. 'With you, I feel like a conspirator.'

'Well you are, Leni. I'm getting you out of here.'

Leni looks at Thomas sharply. 'They've given me nothing to eat, darling.'

'No they don't in these places. It's part of their punishment. I'll cook for you when we get home. What would you like?'

'Where's Miriam?' Leni asks suddenly.

'Talking to a doctor about your fracture. I came on ahead.'

'I'm glad you came, Thomas. How are you going to get me out?'

'Carry you.'

'Now?'

'If you like.'

'You can't carry me.'

'Why?'

'They've done something to me, strapped me down.'

'Rubbish.'

'It feels as if they have. My legs can't hardly move.'

'That's what they want you to think. Let's see.'

The cigarette still in his mouth, Thomas stands up and pulls back Leni's bedclothes. Below her gauzy creased nightdress, one leg is thin and white and still shapely, the other is plastered almost to the knee. Again, other people turn and stare. Thomas bends over the legs and gingerly raises each one in turn. Leni watches him, dazed and dizzy with smoke. There's an ache in her. She feels grey and sick.

The Indian nurse, carrying a jug of squash, returns.

'You're not bolted down,' says Thomas, 'See?'

'My God, what is going on, Mrs Ackerman?' says the nurse. Leni blows smoke and burps. The nurse snatches Leni's fist, removes the cigarette and quickly returns the covers to the thin body. She glowers at Thomas. 'Take your cigarette out, please,' she snaps. Thomas nods, drops the butt, stamps it out on the lino. The wide Indian nostrils flare with irritation. Visitors. They bring the wrong things. They cough and cry. They crease the counterpanes.

'You are very, very inconsiderate,' she hisses.

'Yes. I'm sorry. But we're going now,' says Thomas. 'We won't bother you any more.'

'Yes,' says Leni feebly, 'we're going.'

'You've made this patient ill,' says the nurse. For Leni is retching into her hands. Smoke. Smoke billows and churns in her stomach. Smoke rides in her blood and gathers in her brain. A little puddle of grey spittle sits in her palm. This is all. There's nothing in her but smoke.

'She needs food,' says Thomas.

'Thank you,' says the nurse, wiping Leni's red mouth, 'we shall decide what Mrs Ackerman needs. Now I think you'd better leave.'

The chocolate woman, dry-eyed now, is gaping at Leni. The marzipan woman and her visitors are gaping, gaping at Leni. On their faces is nothing but disgust. They stuff their sweets. Thomas feels like weeping.

Bernice Atwood has had her dream again. This time, the book laid on her breasts is slim: Boccaccio's *Il Filocolo*: MS Canon. Ital. 85. The valuable old paper crumples when Dr O puts his hand on it and starts the familiar swearing of eternal love. She wants to tell him not to press so hard, to show more care. But he doesn't hear what she's saying and goes on. His delivery is liturgical and dull. To Bernice's own amazement, she tells him it's boring. So he stops and, when she reaches out to him, he isn't there.

Gary Murphy has had a dream of darkness. He's sunbathing on a hot Mediterranean beach. Round him, the Italian language bubbles and sings like a hot brew. Then he feels cold and opens his eyes. A front of pitch black cloud is slowly sliding across the sun, a cloud like a continent obliterating all the blue sky, its terrible reflection advancing towards him over the water.

He wakes, glad of morning in his lilac room, glad of normality and Marmite and frost on the oak leaves outside his window. Two days now till Wednesday. Already, he knows he's going to write a love poem to Gabriel, or at least about Gabriel. You don't let the poetry show too much this early in a relationship. It makes you seem squashy. So they keep prodding you to see if you really are. Better to get a few laughs going first, then some trust. Then you can offer the poetry. They know you're quite tough by then. They know you cope with loutish kids all day. Gabriel said, with his impeccable vowels: 'I simply could not do what you do. I don't know how anyone can bear to do that when children are so beastly.'

Gary has a title for his poem: it's called *Walk*.

Bernice has thought of children – unborn, unwanted – and examined her body for signs of swelling. She thinks there's a tight feel to her breasts that isn't normal. As she brushes her hair, they hurt slightly. Bernice knows she would like those secret first months of pregnancy, holding the blind, growing newt in her protecting blood. If she could only have a secret child. Wrap it and put it in the dark like her pots of bulbs. Go and peep at the white limbs, touch them even, like she touches the hyacinth tips and knows her care has made them grow. But it's the infant she doesn't want, the separate squalling person with furious eyes and hungry mouth. Babies depress her. The lolling limbs. The silly pushchairs. The plastic paraphernalia. She couldn't bear this. Her love is too grave, too deep and scarlet and pious to need this lucky, mucky blessing of a child.

She feels strange this morning, overlarge in her small rooms. She makes weak tea, but then doesn't drink it. Instead of going straight to work, she walks to Magdalen Bridge and spends some time staring down into the water. Her own reflection, on this bright autumn day is clear and still. She wishes, as she stares at herself, that for this part of her life she was a beautiful woman.

Thomas leaves the hospital with Miriam, but without Leni carried aloft in his arms, without the prize he wanted.

Thomas is, to Miriam, like one of his fabrications: odd, sometimes beautiful, surprising, vexing and crude. She doesn't know how such a son was fashioned. The grey hair. The sprawling, bony legs, the bright, mad eyes. He was silly at school till he began to understand history. Then he started to read. What he read, he tried to express in drawings and paintings and then in objects and sculptures. He drew Napoleon eating Europe and shitting soiled uniforms: he made a Queen Victoria musical box which played *Night and Day*; he stuffed and stitched a set of Fat King beanbags – Henry VIII, 'Prinny', Edward VII. You sat on them anywhere, on their stomachs, on their heads, on their bums, on their feet. David Ackerman was amused by these and nodded his approval. 'Your lad,' he said to Miriam, 'could do worse than come to Oxford and read History.' Thomas did worse – or better as he saw it. He joined the Communist Party. He founded a squatters organisation in Battersea called SHIT – Squatters Homes in Town. He lived with, loved and left a seventeen-year-old Polish girl called Mima, a sixteen-year-old Battersea girl called Rosalyn and a nineteen-year-old American girl called Philomena. During all this time, he stayed away from Larry and Miriam and Oxfordshire. Only Leni he wrote to. Erotic letters about his love affairs which he thought she'd like. She kept them hidden from the rest of the family and read them on days when she felt old. Larry started *Aquazure* and replumbed his heart to bypass his son. Miriam quietly mourned him. David Ackerman died, never knowing about Leni's letters. Thomas came, for Leni's sake, to the funeral. He wore a black shirt and braces with glitter dust. His wreath was paper daisies, oddly pleasing. When it was over, he told Leni he no longer carried the Party card; the Communists were too cruel on the individual. What now inspired him was the creation of what he called Message Objects or Marxist Thought Things, and thus his business began. He never expected to make money out of it, but he quickly did. This making of money seemed to cure his hatred – which began in the early juvenile days of the Monarch bean bags – for Larry and Larry's commercially-turned mind. The years of father-and-son, son-and-father unwound uneasily on. *Aquazure* crashed. Thomas offered to lend Larry money and was refused. Perdita, the blonde and shiny Australian girl, moved into Thomas's business and eventually to his bed. Perdita broke the last links with SHIT and set them up in a Fulham warehouse – workroom and flat. Now they have a shop in the Wandsworth Bridge Road. They wholesale to Harrods and Heal's. Certain Thomas Kendal one-offs are collectors' items. The shop is called PEE COCKS. Perdita supports her gran in Melbourne with monthly cheques. There is talk of a retail out-let in Brussels. Thomas buys Perdita a Mercedes. With this car to love, she decides to terminate a pregnancy. Then Leni gets ill and Thomas is sent for by Miriam. But he knows Leni will fight a good fight with death and he doesn't hurry. He sands and polishes the Bedside Man. Now, today, he is here.

'How did you think she was?' asks Miriam, driving to Rothersmere Road.

'Starving.'

'It'll set her back.'

'Yes. Why isn't she fed?'

'I mean the broken ankle. It'll be months before she's well now.'

'So what are you going to do?'

'Do you mean, will I stay on?'

'Yes.'

'Till the exhibition. Then I'll have to see.'

'Bet Dad's in a mess without you. Can't order a sandwich in French, can he?'

'Oh, he does very well, really. He's picked a lot up.'

'Does he like it?'

'What?'

'France.'

Miriam brings the car to a stop behind the rusting Mini. With dry lips she says: 'You look pale, Thomas. Why don't you and Perdita come out and stay next summer? Then you can see it all for yourself.'

'You didn't answer my question.'

'I can't.'

'No? Why?'

'If he can get the pool company going again, I think he'll like that.'

'He won't though, will he?'

'Why d'you say that?'

'I don't know. No reason.'

Miriam sighs. 'Time will tell,' she says as they get out of the car. She feels tired. The night was short and the day full of events: Thomas's arrival, the visit to the hospital. She leaves Thomas in the kitchen making tea and tells him she'll rest for an hour. She climbs the stairs and walks, not to the end guestroom where Leni put her, but to the small room next to Leni's which she occupied as a child. The bed isn't made and the room is cold. She draws the soft flowery curtains, takes off all her clothes except her slip and lies on the pink eiderdown under the cotton bedspread. She lies straight and stiff, staring up at the ceiling. The room feels empty. A few child's books remain in a little glass-fronted bookcase, *The Wild White Stallion*, *Lost Endeavour*, *The Snow Goose*, but the Zedbed on which school-friends occasionally slept has gone, the gifts those same friends made or bought – meerschaum ornaments, velvet pigs, balsa-wood mobiles, Knitting Nancy mats, patchwork pillows – have long ago been sorted out into Leni's hatboxes and given to jumble sales. David and Leni were always kind and polite to the schoolfriends. They thought friendship prepared children for love. It was to be respected. Nicknames were given fondly. Outings were arranged – a film at the Gaumont followed by hot chocolate and cakes at the Cadena Coffee House. One evening, as Miriam and Dilys Weston walked home from the Cadena in which they had smoked two Senior Service each, a smog descended on Oxfordshire and Mr and Mrs Weston couldn't drive their Austin into the city to collect Dilys. In Miriam's heart was rapture. The Zedbed was made up. David, who called Dilys Weston 'Dolores', came up and said excitedly, 'Well, Dolores, what larks, eh? And duck for supper.' 'Dolores' and Miriam were given glasses of wine. They floated to bed believing no night of their lives would be as wonderful as this. Dolores chose a nightdress from Miriam's drawer and borrowed her toothbrush. And through the winter night they lay and talked of their lives

to come. Their friendship marched with them into a starry
future. They didn't doubt its everlasting satisfactions. They
shared an orange Miriam had taken from the dining room. They
slept at last just before the alarm woke them, and walked to
school arm in arm.

Miriam turns over and closes her eyes. What a comfy, clean
and precious childhood she had. Music, books, nice clothes,
good food, friendships. It prepared her for nothing – only for life
as it was then, protected, rational and warm – yet she remembers it with joy. Dilys Weston married a hearty banker with a
ruddy neck and clumsy hands. They raise their sons to be
bankers and the sons, too, are hearty, stupid, and cruel. She
says she doesn't remember being called 'Dolores'. 'Your father
would never have called me that, Miriam. It's such a common
name.' Miriam sighs, sleeps. In the dream which follows
she ties a pair of kitchen scales to Dilys Weston's Gucci-shod
foot and drowns her in the Cherwell. Young, bearded punters
shimmer by in brilliant light but they don't stop for the drowned
body.

It's Wednesday. Gary has made himself a tray of food to nibble
at. To get himself in the mood for writing his own poem, he
tugs one or two books from his shelves and reads lines at
random:

> '. . . I am herald to tawny
> warriors, woken from sleep . . .'

'Charles Baudelaire knew that the human heart
Associates with not the whole but part.'

'. . . the round angelic eye
Smashed, mix his heart's blood with the mire of the
    land.'

> 'October is marigold . . .'

'Saint Anthony in the sand saw shapes rising . . .'

Then he puts them all away and sits with his pencil hovering over the blank lines of his Oxford pad. He nervously writes the title: *Walk*. He doesn't know why he's chosen this title, yet he feels it's perfectly right. He suspects it's because the essence of his friend seems to lie not in his smile or his eyes but in his innocent hip movements. As if his soul was tucked in under his pelvis.

Gary hasn't loved a black man before. Gabriel's colour seems to lend seriousness to his feelings. I've tap-danced with love till now, Gary decides. I've done routines. Snickety-pick. Snickety-pick. Then walked away, holding my shoes. He sighs, remembering the vulnerable pale colour of Gabriel's palm, and experiments with a first line:

Love was my dancing partner till . . .

Till? Till what? Poetry is often the art of asking and then answering the right questions. Gary, on Wednesday, strives to be truthful. Poems are not tricks. Wednesday Man is not – must not become – a mountebank.

He sharpens the pencil. A Berol Venus. It couldn't be any sharper. He eats a biscuit spread with cream cheese. Crumbs mess the page. Gabriel is, by this time, in his ten-thirty rehearsal. Piers, the director, wears, says Gabriel, Fair Isle sweaters and neat wool ties, but in contrast to these soft-spoken clothes his voice is Olympian and his arm on your shoulder as weighty as the mountain. Gary's mind makes a tableau of the thunderous Piers leaning on Gabriel as a stone deity leans on a garden fountain and his lovesick body shivers with dread. Jealousy. *Honest Iago, that look'st dead with grieving* . . . Even in his tap-dancing affairs, his flimsy, flickery flirtations, jealousy has kept him wakeful and peevish and silly. He's never fought it. He's not even sure it can be fought. Only edged aside – by trust. But on what insubstantial grounds can he trust Gabriel? His love is ten days old – two Wednesdays old. And Piers the god, Piers the statue, is creating and remaking Gabriel into a future star even as Gary sits with his tray of nibbles and tries to make sense of the title, *Walk*. Betrayal may exist already, at this precise moment as Piers puts his hands on the springy shoulders and moves the actor forward, his huge voice grown intimate in its careful instruction, '. . . to here I think, love, and turn and . . . *I had rather be a toad, And live upon the vapour in a dungeon, Than keep a corner in the thing I love . . .*' Gary sighs, tries to erase the words, erase the tableau. He takes a sip of Marmite and concentrates on his first line, *Love was my dancing partner till*, returns to the image of the darkness that has haunted his week and, pressing so softly on the paper the words look pale, he etches meaning into five more lines. He holds his breath as he writes. (If words came to him in torrents and not in the trickles they do, he'd asphyxiate himself getting them down.) He gasps for breath and reads:

> Love was my dancing partner till
> darkness fell in the pink ballroom
> and my ladies in their salamander heels
> ran chattering to open
> carriages, knowing none of my burning.

He relaxes. It's begun. A direction starts to seep through like a developing picture. Along the landing, in Leni's empty room, the telephone rings. Gary knows that Miriam's in the house somewhere and will answer it. His only dread is that it might be Gabriel, ringing to call off the evening ahead, already spread out in Gary's mind like an exquisite embroidery: birds and dragonflies of love-talk, flowers of fine wine, thickets of touch. On the way to this silken date, he will visit Leni in the hospital. Like Thomas, whose wild and spectre-ish appearance Gary rather admires, he longs to bring Leni home so that everything is once more in place in the house and his fears of her dying quelled by the sound of her presence. He's getting used to Miriam. The thought that, when Leni goes, he will eventually be left absolutely alone in his room and out from his room will stretch only passageways of silence is as awful as anything Gary can contemplate. He imagines the quiet; the stairs getting cold; the boiler going silent.

Gas and electricity cut off. No milk delivery. No post. Just him and a house he doesn't own and has no right to remain in – his home. He gets up and paces round the room, licking the pencil end.

He's there all day. He boils kettles to make fresh hot Marmite. He eats all the food. The hours of Wednesday pass in a sequence absolutely unlike any other day, expanding or contracting with the slow, slow journeying of the poem. The hour for his visit to Leni passes and he lets it go. He hears Miriam and Thomas drive off in Leni's car. The hour of his meeting with Gabriel grows closer. He dreads putting on his evening finery with the poem half-finished. He wants to meet his lover with the gift of his poem wrapped in his head. The telephone rings again and no one answers it. His room heats up as his lilac radiator comes on in the late November afternoon. He switches from Marmite to Earl Grey tea. He unwraps a new packet of Bourbons. Miriam and Thomas come back and he knows it's evening now: Piers lets the cast go and walks with Gabriel to the Randolph for a drink. They drink cocktails? Beer? The sipping of either is torment to Gary's soul. The bedside clock ticks towards seven. One hour left.

At seven-twenty, he slips quietly down the corridor and into the bathroom where he runs a deep bath. And here in the comforting warmth, he at last lowers himself into that slit of time which divides the sombre labours of his day from the embroidery pleasures of his approaching night. In the hot bathroom, the poem sits lightly in him, secret as a child and limb by limb complete. Soaping his legs, he whispers it aloud. There are imperfections, he knows, as in most things: the vaccination scar on his thigh, the jolt in the rhythm of stanza three which he can't seem to correct. But soap and steam cover his yellow scar; the opaque mind of the reader doesn't notice the slight lurch it has to make . . . This, anyway, is Gary's hope. The poem is Gabriel's after all, the first but not the last gift. People don't criticise gifts. Even Miriam, who clearly hated the turquoise necklace, accepted it smiling. So here you are, Gabriel. Put down your cocktail. Tell Piers to leave. Listen:

Walk
Love was my dancing partner till
darkness fell in the pink ballroom
and my ladies in their salamander heels
ran chattering to open
carriages, knowing none of my burning.

I took my shoe-shuffle heart
to a high tenement,
and hung up my crimson laces.
I thought of my gauzy ladies only
when I heard
cuckoo-blues or alley-jazz:
a number.

Now love walks like a panther up
my stair.
There is no accompaniment, no beat
and I try my best to make
no sudden movement, no
safari smile
to scare the animal away.

Timidly, I offer food: yesterday's
bones.
But my panther disdains them
and with a proud impatience treads
down my bed, tearing fresh red
meat from the wall:
my dancing shoes.

At ten to eight, Gary in a lambswool rollneck and a blue velvet jacket, calls goodnight to Miriam and Thomas in the kitchen and walks past his dead car into the spangly night. A big, ochre moon is up.

Dr O has bought *The Joy of Sex* from Smith's. It sits white and unopened on his bedside table – an Aladdin's lamp he's far too

frightened to rub. Listening to the shipping forecast at five-to-six
(there is a certain quiet comfort in shipping forecasts, a few
moments of gentle reassurance before the terrible bombardment
of the News), he keeps glancing at it, knowing that this is the
evening he promised himself he would read it. He has structured
the whole day round this promise, heard himself refuse to go
with Bernice to hear madrigals in St Mary's on the grounds that
he's feeling ill, acted out the suffering man all day, blowing his
nose, sighing, leaving uneaten the cheese sandwich Bernice
buys him for lunch, complaining of heartburn (a malady not
unconnected with his actual state) and chest pains. All this so
he can read a sex manual. He's fifty-three. He feels terribly
ashamed. He doesn't know where, since the days of Leni's
dancing lessons, his life has kept him. He's sure some long-stay
prisoners have had more experience of women than he has.
Pert, tight-waisted, dolled-up women with names like Tina.
Women who shout and swear and teach you what their bodies
like. Then, when you come out after all the years of your
sentence, you haven't forgotten what to do. Tina waits for you
with her hair in a new style. She knows you'll be all right because
you learned it all properly when you were young.

'Viking, Forties, Chromety, Forth, Tyne, Dogger,
Fisher . . .' In her Cattle Street room Bernice Atwood listens
to this same repetition of places she will never see. She brushes
her hair, preparing to walk alone to St Mary's Church. It's been
a hurting week. Bernice feels a pain like a bruise in the area of
her breasts. She's certain Dr O is ill. Since the night of the
Bergman film, he's been so silent, like a dumb dog in pain. Now,
today, he doesn't eat, he describes certain symptoms, he's
vague and distant with the customers. He needs, he *needs* my
care, says the pain in Bernice's chest. I would make him well,
if he would only let me. Bernice's aunt is a nurse. Bernice knows
how caring should be done. You must never pester a person
to get well. Healing has its own time-span. Not for nothing
are nurses called angels; patience is the first lesson you
learn.

In her mind, as she switches off her heavy old radio and puts
her coat on, Bernice rearranges Dr O's bedroom as a sickroom,

making space on the bedside table, putting weights on the scattered papers, drawing the dusty curtains, warming the bed with a bottle, bringing disinfectant and water, a thermometer and oranges. Then she sits – not on the bed as Miriam sits in Leni's room – but in an armchair, near enough to the patient for him to reach out and touch her if he wants to, and reads to him quietly till he sleeps.

Dr O also switches off his radio. As Bernice starts to walk alone to her madrigals, he sits with a sigh of trepidation on the bed so recently prepared in Bernice's mind for his illness and opens The Book. He stares dumbly at the pictures. The men and women depicted are young and muscular and serene. His hands are trembling. He turns again to the front, where there are no pictures and reads, deliberately at random: 'Orgasm is the most religious moment of our lives, of which all other mystical kicks are a mere translation. Men are apt to growl like bears, or utter aggressive monosyllables like "In, In, In!" The wife of the Leopard in the novel used to yell out "Gesumaria!"' So already the learning has begun: Dr O understands from the very first lines he reads that he and Bernice have failed each other in bed by their silences. Why couldn't she have taught him to whinny or trumpet or snort? What prevented her alabaster throat from choking out a saint's name? He makes himself more comfortable on the bed, removing his shoes and propping his heavy innocent's head with cushions. He tries – and fails – to quell the anxious beating of his heart.

In vaulted St Mary's, a single tear rolls down the cheek of Bernice who sits with her hands and heart folded on the music. The little group of singers – so serious the faces, straining for their complex counterpoints – moves her as much, if not more than the ancient lovesick songs given this Church-dignity. She would like to take the madrigal singers home to Cattle Street, make them mugs of cocoa, tell them how greatly she admires their singing and ask them to sign their names in her favourite books of love poetry. She would make them as comfy as she could on her floor and in the morning they could sing, just for her:

'Love in my bosom like a bee
Doth suck his sweet:
Now with his wings he plays with me,
Now with his feet . . .'

She invents humble ordinary names for them: Sidney, Mary,
Alan, Roger, Kathleen. And she presses her tummy with her
little quiet hands. If a child is growing inside her, let it grow up
to be a singer of madrigals.

She looks about her at the rest of the audience. The middle-
aged couple on her left sit arm in arm, their heads held high at
identical angles. In front of her two students with thick tangled
hair lean gently towards each other. On her right is an empty
seat. She wonders tenderly whether Dr O is eating his supper
in bed.

He has in fact, reached a section of the manual called *Main
Courses* and reads distractedly: 'If you haven't at least kissed
her mouth, shoulders, neck, breasts, armpits, fingers, palms,
toes, soles, navel, genitals and earlobes, you haven't really
kissed her,' sighs and puts the book down. He feels exactly like
a schoolboy, horny, excited, full of longing, knowing nothing.
How much learning stands between him and the taking of Miriam
in his bed? Will he practise his newly learnt techniques on the
accommodating body of Bernice? He doesn't think he can make
love to Bernice any more; Miriam's large bones and radiant hair
have eclipsed her swoony whiteness, her little-girl nails, her
dimpled knees. These things repel him and invite him to set
aside as a foolish mistake his years of loving her.

So in the dark, she leaves St Mary's and walks home by
herself. So in the dark, Dr O stares at the yellowy moon, envying
Larry Kendal his summers and winters of Miriam's palms and
navel and earlobes. *You haven't really kissed her. Now with his
wings he plays with me.* Each in a separate language, Dr O and
Bernice Atwood examine the past and toy with the uncertain
time ahead.

Thomas leaves for London, promising to stay in touch. With his
departure, Miriam seeks the shelter of her old room and makes

up the narrow bed where once she lay awake with the house wrapped in the fortunate silence of the winter fog and Dilys Weston's vacant future whispered to her from the Zedbed.

Leni, stern in her plaster cast, is wheeled on a trolley to a private room which Gary, in the full blossoming of his love affair with Gabriel, has ostentatiously filled with flowers: carnations, though it's October, asters and chrysanthemums and little pots of African violets. Miriam is instructed to fill in more BUPA forms. Leni, in her bower, fed with fish pie and sponge pudding, seems to rally. In her commandments to the tireless nurses, Miriam detects some returning strength. The Leni of years ago, with all her beauty hurtling in her blood, begins to shimmer back.

Her child's bed smooth and tidy, her possessions in place on the old chest-of-drawers smelling of mothballs, Miriam now approaches her father's attic, turns on his radiator and here begins at last to work. She feels suspended, closed in and safe. Here, neither Leni nor Larry can touch her. She stares straight at her fifty years of life and sees the survivor she has become, the castaway who stayed sensible among the island cruelties that came after the shipwreck. There's a look of exhaustion and of triumph. It's time, she says to the dead surfaces of her father's study, to do something for yourself – without the reproaches of Leni, without the weeping of Larry. Something which is outside them both – a deliberate exclusion.

And so when she paints, it isn't Pomerac or the wooded hills behind Ste Catherine, it isn't Oxford or the rolling downland where she once lived; it's herself. In the space of a morning, a pastel portrait is finished. She signs it but decides pastel is the wrong medium: she looks too young, too soft and indistinct. She wants to capture the hard edges of her own stare. She begins an ink drawing – simple, purposeful lines like black thread. Now she feels excitement come. What she boldly reveals is a face pared of its craven compassion. The eyes have a proud set like the eyes of an ancient Indian chief. She ties a bandana round her thick hair, starts the drawing again with her brow bound. The afternoon arrives and darkens. Leni is unvisited. When she thinks of Larry, as she does when the evening comes on, it is to imagine him alone for ever in Pomerac, watching the walnut tree being carted away, digging out his hopeless loss of her from his mind with the making of a swimming pool. He is, the fierce Indian decides, a futile man. Yet she's waiting, she knows, for something to happen. Or someone. Someone to give her permission not to go back to France. A sudden absence of love, though it has invaded her utterly, isn't sufficient, she senses, to set her free. She and Larry have given, taken, shaped side by side so many years.

Larry was – and remains – her one defiance of Leni. With this stranger from outside the charmed Oxford circle, she decided to grow up. It was Larry's sturdy health that attracted her. He was uncloistered, energetic and free. He kicked life like a ball. With him in the Oxfordshire summers she *ran*. She knew he wasn't clever or even wise. She knew he had a small man's dreams. She knew Leni would pout and scold. *Intellectually he's very weak. He's too physical for you, Miriam.* David Ackerman kept quiet. Leni's disapproval was enough. And when Miriam married Larry in secret in the year of Suez, her father merely recognised that the world did, and would ever, behave in ways inimicable to him and returned to the sanctuary of the room where Miriam now stands staring at the new severity of her face. She remembers David always with quiet pleasure, with a sense of loss so familiar, it has become comfortable. As for Larry's courtship of her and their wedding, these, too are precious memories. What she feels now doesn't corrupt or destroy what she felt then. Larry was a passionate and brave bridegroom. Having won her love, he began his long fight to make himself worthy of her. Now, it's precisely this struggle that she's weary of. She knows, as she finishes her drawing, that the sun has gone from the Pomerac garden, that Gervaise is leading her cows past their door to the milking barn, and that in this rural twilight Larry is bitterly alone. But she feels no guilt or pain. She refuses to feel these. He'll come to accept it, is what she whispers aloud.

She hurries late to the hospital. A don and his wife, friends of Leni's she doesn't know, are with her. So she stays only long enough to note the dabs of healthy colour in Leni's face and to admire Gary's flowers. When she returns to the empty house (Gary is not seen these nights, even though today is Wednesday) she sees an unfamiliar car parked behind the Mini. At the wheel, patiently waiting, is Dr O.

As soon as she and Dr O are out of their cars, she hears herself apologising: 'Dr O. I should have telephoned you. I'm so sorry about what happened the other day. I feel so stupid . . .'

'Oh no,' Dr O says hastily, 'don't say that.'

'I actually seldom cry,' Miriam explains, 'and I don't really know why I did except that I seemed to feel so tired all of a sudden . . .'

'I don't *want* you to apologise, Miriam,' says Dr O with emphasis. 'The incident allowed me . . . to get to know you better, and I'm so grateful that it did . . .'

'Come in, Dr O,' says Miriam, opening the front door. The moon is up and the air is very cold. She wonders if the first frost is coming. 'If you've got time, I'd like to show you the work I've done today. You can tell me if it's good or if I'm wrong in thinking it is.'

In the yellowy light of the hall, she turns and smiles at Dr O. She notices that under his familiar overcoat he's put on a dark, well-cut suit. In this, he seems leaner and younger. The thought flits across Miriam's mind: he's wearing a corset.

She leads him up to the attic without asking him why he's called on her. She assumes he wants news of Leni. He follows her up, a little breathless by the time they reach the attic door. She remembers Leni's instruction: *You have to get these men up and dancing*!

The ink drawing is shown to Dr O, who holds it with awe, as if it were a Carthusian Breviary.

'Yes,' he says. 'Yes, yes, yes.'

'I don't often do portraits,' says Miriam, 'and I'm not sure my technique is right for them. What do you think?'

'Oh *yes*,' says Dr O.

'You like it?'

'Yes, yes, yes, yes.'

'I look stern, I think. This is what I'm pleased about.'

'Superb.'

'Oh, I'm glad.'

'One can't take one's eyes from it.'

'Well. Would you like tea, or a drink perhaps?'

'Is this the face . . . ?'

'What, Dr O?'

'You're very beautiful, Miriam.'

'You're very kind. It isn't true of course, but you're kind to say it.'

'I say it because I believe it. I would very much like to buy this portrait.'

'Would you? I think I might do others of myself and they may turn out better.'

'I'd like to buy this one.'

'Well. Come and have some tea.'

'And I'd very much like . . .' Dr O lays down the Breviary with shaking hands, 'to take you out for dinner tonight . . . if you're not otherwise committed.'

He swallows. Miriam stares at him. Her thought is, he put the corset on for *me*! She feels embarrassment and shame but chooses to set these feelings aside in favour of a quiet tableau her mind makes up: she sits with Dr O in a warm and pretty restaurant. They talk about David and Oxford and books, and the coming exhibition. All is comfortable and civilised and easy. And there is no ambiguity. They're old friends. Dr O was like a son to the Ackermans in his youth. They're brother and sister.

'Are you sure,' she asks calmly, 'that you want the expense? You don't have to pay me back for the lunch, you know.'

'No, no. It's not that at all.'

'Well. I don't know what to say, Dr O.'

'Say you'll accept. I've booked a table at a rather pleasant French restaurant.'

'You've booked a table?'

'Yes. I took the liberty . . .'

The restaurant is not unlike the imagined tableau. The table-cloths are pink and the lighting warm. Dr O's wide face gazes serenely at her over a red candle. He seems anxiously happy – like a boy out on a treat. The food is excellent and the restaurant busy and cheerful. Miriam feels rewarded for her day of good work – spoiled and fortunate. She wants to talk about the

recovery she has spied in Leni, the death postponed, but Dr
O seems for the first time almost uninterested in Leni and
uncharacteristically concerned to tell her about his own life.

'I expect,' he says, looking away from her and rearranging
the napkin his large hands have already creased, 'I expect word
has got around Oxford that Miss Atwood and I have been, how
shall I put it, "fellow travellers".'

There is silence. Again Miriam thinks of Leni: *Atwood keeps
the customers away so she can have Oz to herself.*

'I don't belong to Oxford any more,' says Miriam, 'so I don't
know what people say or think about each other.'

'No, quite,' says Dr O. Momentarily, he seems filled with
melancholy.

'I wouldn't care a jot about the gossip,' says Miriam, gently.
'It's your life. Oxford was always gossipy. You just have to
ignore it and get on.'

'I agree, I agree.'

'And you and Miss Atwood have so much in common. I used
to think – at the time when I married – that this wasn't very
important, but of course it is, and sharing your shop the way
you do . . .'

'No, no. What I wanted to explain, Miriam, is that anything
at all that might have existed between myself and Miss Atwood
is now in the past. I confess I hád thought this relationship would
be lasting, but I want you to know that nothing more will now,
er, take place between us . . .'

Miriam wants to smile at the old fashioned cadences of this
speech. Dr O would have belonged very well in Barchester. She
looks at him fondly. He's agitated and red.

'I'm sure Miss Atwood must be very sad,' she says.

'Well . . .' Dr O takes a grateful sip of wine. 'I think she must
come to realise it's all for the best, that we are not, in certain
respects, completely compatible. I hope I'm not offending your
sensibilities, Miriam, when I tell you that in the, er, privacy of
the, er, bedroom, Miss Atwood is utterly silent. Now of course
I'm not a man of the world, but on this one very personal
question, I do feel that true sexual congress cannot take place
when there is, well, silence. Wouldn't you agree?'

Miriam stares at Dr O in disbelief. Today she had felt free of the ancient intimacies binding her to Larry. She's not in the mood to discuss Dr O's closet secrets. She marvels at his sudden insensitivity and sighs deeply.

'How we each behave,' she offers, 'in our private moments is luckily not a matter for legislation. Now, Dr O. I don't want to pry into your life. Please. Let's talk about something else.'

Dr O now looks totally confused and begins gulping wine. 'Have I offended you, Miriam?'

'No. Let's talk about my father, shall we? I was so happy working in his room today.'

'I have offended you.'

'No, Dr O.'

'I have. Oh dear. It was only my anxiousness to make you understand . . .'

'Understand what?'

'How deeply I love you.'

Bernice Atwood is listening to a radio programme entitled *Vanishing Fire* about the disappearance of the red squirrel from English woods. A Norfolk gamekeeper recalls: 'There want no shortage a' them. You saw plenty a' them when I were a bor. An' we had thisere game. Squiggie-stooning, we named it. Cruel, I reckon. But we did that. A bor's game. Harmless, we thought . . .'

Bernice enjoys programmes which tell her about nature, vanishing or not. She likes to imagine, on her infrequent excursions to the countryside, the tens of thousands of creatures she can't see, invisible to her yet at this very moment burrowing, building, gathering, spinning, fornicating, fleeing, flying. If nature was still, it wouldn't interest her. If nature showed her all of itself, it wouldn't interest her. It's the boundlessness of its hidden world that makes her stand still in the forest and say breathlessly to Dr O, 'Listen!' Now, sitting silently by her fire, she imagines seeing a red squirrel one day. Then in old age saying on the radio, 'I remember the last days of the red squirrels. I saw one not far from Oxford.'

Yet even as Bernice listens to the programme, she knows

that something terrible is happening in the quiet, primeval forest of Dr O's love for her. Something has crept in under cover of darkness and turned the soil. All the roots of trees more ancient than buildings are cold and dying. She knows that the chief protector of this love was time, settling gently year by year on the quiet arrangement of her limbs with Dr O's, on their minds, on their identical responses to the labours of long-dead monks for the glory of the illustrated word. And now, time has unsettled them. Why? Why, she wants to wail. Her love is unchanged. Her love is as fiery, as swiftly-leaping as the vanishing squirrel. For Bernice, future and past are one, unchanging. Time held them safe, she thought. She even imagined them old, side by side in the shop, side by side in their tumbled bed. On the night of the madrigals, she felt sad. Now, days have passed, days in which, with a mortifying clumsiness, Dr O has, like St Peter, denied her. *Why?* Bernice's mouth sits in a little straight line of pain. *Why?* She knows – but this is small comfort – that she isn't guilty of even the briefest moment's withdrawal of love. She is as constant as the mayfly to its single day. Her only transgression is to be sick in the bookshop lavatory one morning, causing Dr O to stare at her accusingly and ask: 'No connection with maternity, I trust, Bernice?' and her to answer as stylishly as the dying Nelson: 'None. Would you kiss me, Dr O?' He pecked her hot cheek and withdrew. The smell of him near her made Bernice reach out her white arms and bring him to her and lay her face on his neck. Again, he withdrew and she let him go, afraid. She smelled of sick and disgusted him. And so for the rest of the day he showed her no kindness. That night, in need of his comfort and finding herself alone, she began to feel afraid.

The programme on the squirrels ends. Someone informs her that these creatures are still plentiful in France, especially in the densely wooded area of the Dordogne. So Bernice, who has never travelled to this region, tries to calm her helplessly anxious heart with imaginings of these distant-seeming forests.

Leni is alone in the mauvish light of her private hospital room. Books and magazines have been brought to her by her visitors, but tonight she isn't reading. She lies propped up and dreaming of her life.

Leni, the witch, stares at the brew she has made.

Age, she decides, hasn't quelled her love of mischief. Merely, the people she knows are too old or too dry or too lazy to practise it any more. The Oxford of her younger days has vanished from sight. In rooms she doesn't visit, where she isn't invited, she imagines that something which passes for mischief goes on quietly. (In the old, quiet world it was daring to be noisy, to dance and cavort and yell; now in the modern scream-bombarded world, it might seem bold to be silent and secretive.)

A night nurse, her eyes puffy with daylight sleeping, comes in and gives Leni the two pills she has taken each night for sleep since the death of David, and Leni thanks her. The first night she took the capsules, she dreamt they contained a tiny powdering of ash from David's burnt body. He was a man who, all his life, slept well. Sleep is like thanks, she decided, for the strength of the day. David's contentedly snoring face reaffirmed this. Now all her days are weak and her brain won't give her this blissful gratitude. She mourns it guiltily, swallows her pills, lies like a cat in the dark, seeing the edges and outlines of her past.

She had a nickname at one time, the 'Duchess of Oxford'. There was some venom in it, from which David tried to protect her. She laughed at his protection then, knew there were a hundred women in Oxford jealous of her beauty and more jealous still of her wit. So few people she meets now are witty. For all that it allows, this age is bleak. As if all the big juicy brains had shrivelled and dried like her own womb which is so small now in her small body it couldn't push out a bird. She'd like David's protection from this drying up of life. With age, he would have grown in girth, as she has shrunk. In his bulky warmth she would have felt less arid.

The night nurse removes Gary's flowers, some of which have begun to wilt. Seeing the flowers go, she remembers today was Wednesday and wonders what bits of love-blinded thought he's struggled with. She thinks of him tenderly, his head close to the desklight, the night coming on in his lilac room. 'Mother . . .' he calls her softly, 'I'm going to miss you, lovely.' And Leni sighs, remembering his future homelessness. 'I must do something about that,' she says aloud.

'What did you say, dear?' asks the nurse.

'I must remind myself to do something about the house. Or Gary will be chucked out – by my son-in-law.'

The nurse, whose morning this violet-lit darkness is, looks reproachfully at Leni. The old suffer from disconnected thought. You have to yank them back to reality and pin them down.

'Time for sleep,' she says firmly, snatching one pillow from the pile where Leni's head is lodged like a precious vase padded out for packing. 'Now, I'm going to pop you on the pan, Mrs Ackerman, ready for the night.'

THREE

THE SLEEPWALKERS

Word that Larry's swimming pool is begun travels on frosty breath round the lanes of Pomerac. Children come and throw stones into the big yellow-clay pit. A dog falls into it and breaks its neck and lies in the rain for a day, unnoticed. Up from his tobaccoey room comes the Maréchal and pauses at Larry's wall and stares with his bird eyes at the hole and the felled walnut tree and the mountain of mud. By Gervaise's kitchen fire he sits nodding his disbelief: 'Swimming pools! This isn't America.'

But Gervaise feels as emotional as on her Saint's day at the thought of this apparition slowly forming behind her south wall. As if worlds she will never see have been brought to her doorstep. As if her love of Pomerac, deeper by fathoms than any pit sunk in Larry's garden, is now nevertheless shared by this stranger who has chosen to spend his money not in Paris or Hollywood but here, right under her nose. So she feels protective of Larry. The more because he's alone now and sometimes helpless-seeming. She's taken to calling on him, bringing leeks and parsnips from a vegetable patch so fertile with the rich cow-muck that her beet comes shouldering out of the earth and her summer peas climb waist-high. He seems rather grateful for her care of him. His struggles with her language have lessened. He finds words now, to thank her with dignity and to offer tobacco for Mallélou who, since he returned from Bordeaux, behaves more and more like a very old man, sucking a vacant pipe in the cold yard, standing still.

Larry and Gervaise even talk of the pool and he has explained to her how he found inspiration in St Front. She thinks this is clever. Life is often the art of seeing in one artefact or idea the embryo of another. Klaus, too, admires this vision of a pool and has negotiated with Larry a small fee for helping him do the pipework and concreting. Only Mallélou and the Maréchal have in common their disdain. Their old men's bones distrust shiny, treacherous surfaces.

'You would have thought,' grumbles the Maréchal to Gervaise, 'Pomerac was safe from this kind of comedy.'

But Gervaise is stern with this moaning: 'They say swimming strengthens the heart, Maréchal.'

'The heart? It's going to break mine.'

'Why?'

'You ask me why, Gervaise?'

'Yes.'

'Because it's a madness come to a place that was sane.'

'But a small madness. It's not hurting anyone.'

'It's hurting me.' And he taps his ancient chest. 'It's going to finish me off.'

Gervaise leans over and presses her lips to the Maréchal's head. As winter nears, he wraps this head up in a muffler. He smells of oily wool. 'No one understands,' he's fond of saying, 'the cold gets in through the skull. Small wonder people die young.'

Mme de la Brosse has closed her house and gone to Paris for the winter. She will open it briefly for Christmas, then leave again till spring. Pomerac in November, petrified by the first frosts, shedding its leaves, held in the sighing of the wind, bleated to by the high rooks, only reaffirms the passage of her own life into a dead season. In Paris, in busy restaurants, in warm shops smelling of leather and perfume, this season is partially obscured. She still has one or two old admirers. They take her to the theatre and to dinner at the *Mediterranée*. In her small, smart flat she is comfortable and safe. Catherine Deneuve lives in the same block.

No one misses her in Pomerac. Her limes are clipped. Behind the worn shutters, her furniture is shrouded. Chickens and guineafowl and goats stray into her garden. She could be dead. The Maréchal stares at the closed house and remembers her old father-in-law, the Colonel, a jumpy, well-tailored man with an old-world sense of grandeur. The house was done up with velvet and brocade. There was champagne on the lawn on family birth-days. At Easter the village children brought posies of wild flowers and were given history books and pencil boxes. The Colonel believed in education for the peasants and sent his wife to Périgueux to buy these gifts with care. Over the years the Ste Catherine school library was virtually restocked by Colonel de la Brosse and, though the headmaster was a man who hated the military, he was forced, year after year, to thank this man for his patronage. When the Colonel died, this teacher felt profound relief, as if a heretic had been burned. The Colonel's son, Anatole, was a man too shy and reserved to give pencil boxes to shabby children. For a year or two, the Easter posies came and the little girls and boys who had made them waited awkwardly for their presents. The old widow was absent. Anatole and his wife took in the flowers and gave beakers of lemonade, round which the children's hands grew cold, waiting. They could tell all the zeal had gone from the house. Easters came and went and not one book nor one mathematical instrument ever came out of it again. These same children, now grown into mothers and fathers of the stone-throwers in Larry's garden, remember Colonel de la Brosse with wary affection. They conclude he may have been corrupt. Stories are told of a bribery scandal. But at least he was colourful and kind and had seemed to be as brave in his charity as he had been in the war. No collaborator, he. Escaping from prison, he walked two hundred miles to Paris and on forged papers made his way to London where he joined de Gaulle's Free French. He returned a hero and in Pomerac he was garlanded with wild roses. All his life, he was given flowers. Now, he lies at Ste Catherine but his marble grave is visited only once a year, in March, by the Maréchal, who brings mimosa for all the old soldiers buried there.

With his garden in ruins and all Miriam's flowers covered in clay, Larry is trying to dig out the future. The eagle he hopes plaintively to see doesn't visit him any more. The bulldozer has frightened it off. The future looks like a rubble pit. Larry's old knack of seeing the finished pool just under this pit seems to have left him. He feels frightened of the scar he's made. He cleans and polishes the Granada, hiding it and his bulgy reflection out of sight of his excavations. His hand, fretting over the body of his car, seems a lunatic limb, making silly little motions. Yet what is there in him so easily comforted by shine? He should be a car salesman. Cars come mirror-bright from someone else's labours. All the salesman does is try to love them, to slap their boots and bonnets with familiarity and pride, to show them off looking their best. Pools are so complex by comparison. Even finished, they're temperamental. Larry stares at the rumpled earth and knows he's lost faith. The future refuses to appear in any guise but the chopped-up present. He digs and digs and still he can't see it. He wonders if, by leaving him, Miriam has snatched it away.

For a few days he thought Miriam's absence would be short. He trusted Leni to die. Now, he senses he's been abandoned. Miriam's voice (so cold, he shivered by Nadia's fire) on the telephone first told him this. It also told him that she didn't know why she'd done it or even how it had happened. 'It was an accident,' her flat voice seemed to say, 'an accident that just happened.' All the digging he does and the ordering of pipework is, of course, for her return: the pool will be finished; Miriam will come home to Pomerac. But Larry can't see either of these things. His loss of faith extends suddenly to his marriage and he gasps with fear at the thought of being alone through the winter. When Gervaise comes round bringing turnips, he feels grateful relief: he's not forgotten by everyone and everything. He keeps an anxious watch out for the eagle. 'My friend, the eagle,' he says to himself boastfully. But it doesn't come. More and more as darkness creeps on in the afternoons, he scuttles up to Nadia's. Between them, she and Gervaise, by giving him food and warmth and their bizarre companionship, seem to keep him from despair.

These days, Nadia's longing to be loved by Hervé is no secret from Larry. This pent-up love of hers is catching at her smile and carving channels of hurt from her fine little nose to her crab-apple chin. 'What,' she asks, as the dark settles round Pomerac and the children are called in to the blackened ranges, 'is this old bean to do?'

Larry is doggy-dumb. Life, at present, refuses to provide him with answers. Nadia gets cross: 'I don't know what is the English heart made of? Waste I'm thinking. You live in the constipated heart!'

Larry nods, feeling the lead-weight of his own chest. 'I'm sure you're right, Nadia. But there's no logic in love, you know, and as a nation we tend to be rather good at logic. What you lose on the swings . . . you see?'

'Swings? What is this swings, Larry? You mean *balançoires*?'

'Yes. But never mind. Shall I go and talk to Harve for you?'

'Oh no. This is a lost cause, my friend. To Hervé what I am but an old Pole? He has this clean Agnès, so what he need some old Gulashka for? I am only some dirty fly he swats away with his handkerchief from Simpsons of Piccadilly, no?'

'No. He's very fond of you, Nadia.'

'Fond? Fond? So he treat me like some sister or mother! I don't want his fond, Larry. I want his desire of me.'

Desire of her. With her fluff of dyed hair and her pink, stubby, restless hands, Larry can't imagine she stirs the gentlest whisper of blood in Hervé's aristocratic groin. His body seems fitted out for tall fashionable women with the cool smiles of cats. This week his plaster casts were cut and fell open like conker husks, revealing his mended legs within, still shapely, hairless and at the ankles royally tinged with blue. He walks on them fearfully, as if they were stilts he hadn't got the hang of. This revealing of his new legs increases Nadia's sighings.

'How I am a fool for elegance, Larry! My Claude is once so elegant a man. We order all his shirts at Sulka in the rue Royale. And when I walk with Claude on his arm, in the Champs Elysées, I'm thinking, my God Nadia, you would be back in Warszawa now this minute with some one-legged neighbour on the landing snitching or snimping food, and, I know what a lucky woman I'm being with my beautiful Claude in his neckties. And how could I imagine his rocker would go? I ask you. If you had seen my Claude at the Tour d'Argent, at Laperouse, you would never have guessed, this man is getting bananas . . .'

'It's very sad, Nadia. I'm so sorry about Claude.'

'But destiny, no? First I'm getting a madman. Then it's my fate to lose my stupid Polish heart to a man of stone. You know this fashionable Polish director, Wajda, is making movies about men of stone and this is my Hervé.'

'No, I don't think so, Nadia. His men are factory workers or shipyard people.'

'Well, what it matter? All the men in Nadia's life are notty or iron.'

'Notty?'

'Notty, nutty, nitty. I don't know what's the difference? Or men of ice, like my poor Hervé with his precious little niece. Look at his legs! When he fell down, they packed his legs in ice.'

She's drinking a lot, these cold nights. Mme Carcanet who owns the épicerie at Ste Catherine, gets the vodka she orders, but Nadia's too poor to buy the crate all at once. She saves on electricity and nail varnish and butter to buy the bottles one by one. She's generous with the liquor, seeming to forget what it costs. Larry drinks gratefully and notices the way Nadia has begun to fling her small, plump body round the flat, throwing it onto chairs like a dancer, gathering cushions into her short arms and pressing them into her face, sending her shoes hurtling to the ceiling, then kneeling and weeping against her Japanese screen. He's uncomfortable with these performances and yet grateful for them. She doesn't often ask him about himself. In her pink-faced lamentations, he forgets the hole he's making in his garden and the void around which his self-respect now seems to be constructed. One night, he dreams he's become a swimming pool, become this cold, empty space. Someone has filled him not with chemically treated water, but with vodka. In Nadia's warm flat he feels protected from dreams like this. Her grief shields him from his. He feels an affection for her which now and again surprises him. He longs to comfort her, yet knows he never will. On and on goes her little tragedy. On and on goes his listening.

On a mild morning, when a soft rain has chased away the cold front, with a vodka hangover pressing on his forehead, Larry climbs wearily into the Granada and drives past the waterfall to Hervé's mansion. The wistaria leaves are gone. Even the Michaelmas daisies he remembers Agnès picking are dying down and all the summer grandeur of the garden has disappeared. Larry gets out of the car and breathes the wet air. He's come determined to do or say whatever he can, as inconspicuously as he can, for Nadia. Agnès sees him standing in the drive and comes out. Over her neat little skirt she wears an apron. She's laying fires, she says, and smiles. Then she puts a hand on Larry's arm and says, 'Luc, my fiancé, is here. I would like to introduce you,' and leads Larry down the armoured hallway to the sitting room. There is no sign of Hervé. He's not in the house, is Larry's immediate thought, when he sees the boy, Luc, lounging on one of Hervé's expensively covered sofas, reading a magazine. The doctor, on his newly knit legs, has gone back to his surgery. Agnès and her young soldier have the house to themselves.

The conversation is brief. Luc isn't interested in Larry, looks at him insolently through long dark lashes and barely tilts up off the sofa to shake his hand. Silence hangs in the big room. Larry moves to leave. To his surprise, Agnès sounds flustered when she says: 'Don't go. Stay for some coffee, or tea. I could make Lipton's tea.' Luc stares at her. The boy's body is leggy and soft, like a colt's. Of this soft sinew, the army is trying to fashion red muscle. It's to annoy Luc that Larry agrees to the tea. To find a disdainful, lazy animal in possession of Agnès is vexing. He wants to say to this obedient girl, don't marry yet. And with these words almost on his lips he follows Agnès to the kitchen, abandoning the soldier to his magazine.

She fills a heavy kettle and lights the gas. Larry imagines her grown old, making these identical movements from sink to stove. And in between, time slips and vanishes. It's as if she has no life through thirty years. Larry wants to catch her arm and shake her, but he just stands still, watching her. He's aware that this is what he does these days when he comes here: he watches Agnès. It doesn't seem to bother her at all. It's as if she expects it. Like the protecting regard of a parent. She doesn't shrug off his watching of her or push him away but rather brings his look closer by treating him fondly and seeming to share with him thoughts she keeps from her Uncle Hervé. Reaching for a tray, which she begins to set with pink and white cups and saucers, Agnès says quietly and without self-consciousness: 'Luc wants me to sleep with him. Today. He wants me to do it today. Do you think I should?'

Larry stares at her over the teacups. Her green eyes address him calmly. She's not nervous, only perplexed. Larry aches for

summer and the finished pool. By this, he would find Agnès a
protected little corner in the sun. Say to Gervaise and Klaus,
this is my adopted daughter.

'Do you want to? If you want to, then it's all right.'

'I'd like it if . . .'

'What?'

'If it was going to be right.'

'Why wouldn't it be right?'

'Because he knows nothing. He's never had a woman. Only
whores.'

'You'll learn together.'

'No.' She says this with force, then looks down at her hands,
setting out the tea tray.

'Why not, Agnès?'

'Because I know what this means. You learn the man's way,
just the selfish way, and later you have to find out what's right
for you. So you betray your marriage. But I love Luc. I don't
want to betray our marriage. You see?'

Larry feels astonished not so much at the dilemma but that
Agnès, with her strange old-fashioned ways, should understand
it so well. Momentarily, he's sorry for Luc. What twenty-year-
old boy understands that he, the best of lovers, can be, for his
first woman, the worst lover she will ever have? His pride, his
youth, his potency all deny this. He laughs and struts away. His
woman runs crying, following, begging him not to go. She loves
him. Yet in time she'll betray him. He understands neither the
quality of her love nor her reason for betraying it.

Before Larry can find in himself anything by way of advice for
his wise-child, he discovers Luc standing silently in the kitchen
doorway. Agnès flicks her soldier a look of sudden sorrow and
turns away to the kettle. Larry stares helplessly at the back of
her sweet head that he wants to protect with his hands.

Since Bordeaux, Mallélou sleeps with a light burning in his
narrow room and his hands tucked between his legs. He feels
so cold and defeated in his head, he thinks his brain's becoming
dry like a tuber. He's grown forgetful. His legs are weak.
Measuring barbed wire, setting posts, shovelling leaf-swamp

from the ditches – soundlessly through these November tasks creeps a certainty of death. He stands in Gervaise's fields and feels afraid. He hopes God is a German, his rightful master, and will forgive him his cowardly life. He weeps hot tears that fly in the harsh wind for his leaving of Marisa. 'I loved you, Marisa!' he bleats across time. 'With you I was a man.'

Gervaise discovers him crying like a baby in an empty corner of the meadow and asks him again, 'What happened in Bordeaux?' But he's told her everything that happened: his visit to the prison, his round of Xavier's sad bars, his arrest at Mme Motte's, his night in a police cell, his release. What he can't admit is his old-man's terror. When he was kicked out of his cell at dawn, grey with sleeplessness and smelling of puke, he sat in an empty café and watched life wake up and pass him by with disgust. He wanted to cry then. He saw he was finished. Irrelevant. They tore down the old signal hut and built a concrete palace of flashing squares and digits. He had been superseded. He warmed and warmed his shaking hands on a bowl of coffee. Buses clinked and hissed outside the café. People got on and were whisked off to city jobs his own sons had never been educated to do. There was nothing left for him but to go back to Pomerac and wait to roll over dead one night like a sick sow. Winter's coming, say the hunched backs of the city workers clambering on their buses. Keep the light burning, says Mallélou. Keep the frost from turning your balls to ice.

One mid-November day is Gervaise's birthday. It's become her custom, over the years, to receive very little, but to give the kind of feast that warms up the blood and sets Klaus singing German lullabies far into the night. The Maréchal is invited and normally eats so much he falls asleep by Gervaise's fire. They cover him with a rug and leave him to dream his dreams of the old days of the pike fishing or the days of his April chivvying of women. This year, the heads fly off four ducks and their livers are mashed with bacon and garlic and sweet wine into a rich pâté before they're scented with dried tarragon and fresh bay and roasted in their own fat. Trout are brought up from Ste Catherine and poached with fennel. Bottles of apricots and damsons come down from the larder shelves and are arranged by Klaus in two flans as big as bicycle wheels. Cheeses are unwrapped from their muslin. There is food enough for eight or ten (all the more because Mallélou only picks at meat these days) and Gervaise decides, scraping turnips and carrots for a vegetable compote, to break with custom and invite Larry. Mallélou complains: the English don't know how to enjoy themselves; you can't feel at home with a stranger. But no one listens. Larry is invited and readily accepts. He drives to Périgueux in search of a gift for Gervaise and comes back with a tree.

Setting her table with linen, Gervaise feels as happy as a child. Let Mallélou sit down and die if he wants to. Through her hard soles of feet, Gervaise feels her plantedness on the earth. She is strong. Her cows are healthy. Her lover shows no wish to leave her but rather on this very morning has tossed forty-nine kisses into her hair, one for each year of her life. If her sons are absent, this is only because she's never tried to keep them by her at Pomerac, knowing this was vain. She believes they love her. Even Xavier with his petty thieving will remember this is her day and pause in his city life to think of her. She smiles, folding her best napkins. Her kitchen smells of roasting and wine. She thanks her Maker for this gift of life.

At six in the evening, Klaus walks the lanes to the Maréchal's house. The old man has shaved and put on a tie the colour of a bilberry. He's as hungry as a lion, he tells Klaus. Klaus guides him gently through the dark farmyard to the warm kitchen lit now with twenty candles, the table decorated with ivy and fir, six bottles of wine open on the sideboard. He shakes Mallélou's hand, then pulls Gervaise to his nightfrosted cheeks and holds her face against his. Then he tugs a crumpled little parcel from one of his many pockets and presses it into Gervaise's hand. It's a brooch he gave his wife when she was fifty. Mme Foch used to wear it on Sundays clipped to a velvet hat. Gervaise recognises it at once and feels it should never belong to her, but the Maréchal anticipates her protests and says sternly: 'If I had a daughter, Gervaise, she would have it. You're the nearest damn thing I've got to a daughter, so you take it, and if I don't see it on you at Christmas, there'll be hell to pay.'

So she takes off her cooking overall and pins it on her skimpy chest and Klaus and Mallélou and the Maréchal all stare at her, each knowing in his own heart his private quantity of love for her.

'Forty-nine,' she says quietly to her audience, 'I don't think it's a bad age to be.'

Larry arrives then, carrying his tree, a wiry blue spruce. Gervaise, who sees in the spruce the friendly ghost of the lavish lawns she suspects still roll across England, lawns sloping down to pools or up to rockeries and summer-houses, insists that the tree is brought in and stood in a corner of the room. Larry, smart in a brown suit he used to wear at *Aquazure*, is congratulated on his gift. He knows they expected him to bring something inappropriate, like a shop-bought cake. But the tree has delighted Gervaise, so even the old Maréchal offers his hand to the Englishman to shake and Klaus slaps him on the back and smiles, *'Das ist schön, Larry, sehr schön,'* and Mallélou hands him a glass of wine and Gervaise gives him two insubstantial kisses like moths on his face.

In the months to come, Larry will remember this night of Gervaise's birthday many times. It's like a safe place, kindly lit, to which he will often return. The feast is mountainous and good. After the rich pots of pâté, the trout come steaming to the table smelling of caraway and wine. It grows hot in the kitchen. Klaus fills and refills the glasses. Bright blood comes to all the faces, even to Mallélou's. The Maréchal sucks and chomps on his false teeth, Klaus tells a fable about a Lutheran monk roasted and eaten with watercress by one of the Popes, Larry is asked to sing *God Save the Queen* and all but Mallélou laughingly join in: 'Zenne er vee-tauriouse, a-pie an gloriouse, Go say ar Cuine!' Before the main course, the Maréchal staggers to the door and pisses in a bright arc into the yard where the hens and geese are settling for the night. He returns as the four crispy ducks, surrounded by the vegetable compote and served with a frothy cider sauce, are carved by Mallélou. Larry wants to applaud the sight of these. He gets to his feet and begins a round of toasts to Gervaise who looks young in the candlelight, so young and happy that Klaus wants to gobble her bright lips with his meal. After Larry's toast 'To my good neighbour and superlative cook,' it's the turn of the Maréchal to stagger up with a trembling full glass and bless, not for the first nor the last time, this day he remembers so well, Gervaise's birthday. Klaus, comfortable with his well-fed belly, his hair like an angel's hair in the golden room, asks that forty-nine more of these special days, forty-nine more Novembers be given to Gervaise. She laughs in mock protest and, before the little company can turn to Mallélou, who hasn't proposed his toast, thanks each of them in turn for remembering her and sharing her food.

More wine is opened. The duck bones are shovelled away and the cheese and the flans come on to the table. Larry loosens his tie. Klaus rolls up the sleeves of his clean white shirt and fetches his mandolin from its nail on the wall. In the sad songs that come warbling out from this happy giant of a man, Larry senses that the heart he has hardened so bitterly since the failure of his pool company is gently being forced open to take in this tiny particle of France. He feels his shoulders comfortably settled in his chair. He knows he's smiling. Gervaise passes him a big wedge of apricot flan. His gift of a tree sits proudly in its tub. All that he touches, tastes, sees, is simple, uncomplicated and good. He marvels that Miriam could choose Leni's corrupting world. In this hot candlelight he thinks of Oxford's monotonous chimes, and shudders. Then he takes up his glass, forgets England and Miriam, and leans back to listen contentedly to a lovesong he can't understand.

The singing makes the guests pause in their joviality and sit silent for a while, wrapt in memory or hope, or, in the case of Mallélou, in the language he has since the war associated with bravery and love. He's never questioned, nor found anything strange in his admiration of the German race. I'm a ragged dog, is what he believes; I hoped for a fine, clean master. That Klaus is king of his household saves him from his failures and satisfies his ache to see his peasant wife possessed and mastered, her skinny little arse bunched like dough in the breadmaker's hands. That she's in love with Klaus, and that between these two is a passionate affection, he seems not to notice. When he watches their love-making, he sees a tableau: Gervaise his dark, mucky, ignorant, stewed, pig-proud French *paysanne* screwed to hell and back by all the anger and longing locked up in his soul. No feeling is sweeter than this. If Klaus leaves, Mallélou knows that, to find the same terrible relief, he will have to beat his wife to death.

How superb the songs are! In this music, in the wine that soothes his blood, Mallélou sleepily forgets his fear of dying:

> *Und immer weht der Wind, und immer wieder*
> *Vernehmen wir und reden viele Worte*
> *Und spüren Lust und Müdigkeit der Glieder . . .*

He forgets the cold night outside and the nearness of winter and the trial of Xavier still to come. He lights a cigarette and remembers, with a feeling of breathlessness, his days in the signal hut and his nights in Marisa's scented bed. These memories reassure him that even if his life is now imprisoned by this silent village, by this one room, where the candles begin to gutter out and the Maréchal starts to snore with his head on the wine-stained damask, he once lived like a man.

Hervé Prière, back in his mahogany surgery chair, recognises very quickly that all his weeks away from his practice have made him lazy. His patients toil in and out of his consulting room, with their colds and sprains, with their colic and boils and bleeding, and all he longs for is for the last one to leave and to be left in peace.

He sleeps fitfully. He doesn't trust his new legs not to lead him back to the abyss. He longs to put a nursery gate at the top of the stairs, yet he feels too ashamed to do this. Called out sometimes in the middle of the night, he goes shivering and exhausted to his car, drives badly, wakes as if from sleep to find himself at the bedside of a stranger. He prods soft flesh with anxious, freezing fingers, colder to the chest or abdomen than his stethoscope. He feels the sufferers recoil from him and doesn't blame them. He thinks of giving up medicine for good and travelling first class to some Pacific island to examine the remainder of his life under a parasol.

Now that he's working again and his nights are disturbed, he realises what comfort there was in the days of the slithering round an absolutely eventless life on his bottom. Not only was he entirely happy, he was polishing his floors. (Polished surfaces

have always given Hervé Prière great pleasure and satisfaction.)
Though he doesn't want the pain or the shame of legs re-broken,
he ponders nostalgically his time as an invalid and longs distractedly for silence and peace and summer flowers in a bowl and a
morning cassis in his bureau.

One Sunday – a morning of colossal sunshine, the morning on
which Agnès has driven her soldier-fiancé to the Paris train –
Hervé is enjoying just such a cassis and listening to a Mozart
piano concerto on his rather antiquated record player. His
thoughts are of his sister-in-law, Agnès's mother, a woman of
reassuring elegance and quiet integrity. She is the right person,
Hervé decides, to tell him whether he should cease to be a
doctor. He considers telephoning her, decides he will and is on
his way to turn down the music when Larry's voice calls him
from the hall.

Hervé is glad to see Larry. Since the departure of Miriam,
Larry seems more reflective, wiser even. His Englishman's chatter about England has almost ceased. In his solitude, embarked
on his ridiculous pool, he seems admirable where before he was
absurd, brave where before he was only stubborn. Perhaps he,
decides Hervé on impulse, is the person to confide in.

'Come in, come in, Larry. You're not disturbing me.'

They shake hands. Hervé pours Larry a drink. The sun glints
on the regimental box.

'How are you, Harve?'

'Tired. I seem to be very tired. Tell me about the pool. How's
it coming?'

'Slowly. The digging down's about done.'

'The frosts may slow you down.'

'Yes.'

'I admire you, Larry.'

'*Admire* me?'

'Yes. Your perseverance.'

Larry sits opposite Hervé and sips at his cassis.

'It's limited, my perseverance. If I fail this time . . .'

'I don't think you'll fail.'

'No. I've lost touch with the future, anyway. It seems blank
these days.'

'And mine is too full.'

'What, Harve?'

'Too full of people. I've decided, I want to give up. I want to hand over – to someone young.'

'Why?'

Why. This is the one question Hervé didn't expect to be asked. He thought it was obvious. His heart wasn't in medicine any more. His heart was in sitting still.

'I'd like to go away for the winter, Larry. Spoil myself. A doctor's life is too rigorous for me now. The time away from it was so pleasant.'

Slightly to his own surprise Larry hears himself become stern with Hervé. People who exchange work for idleness are courting misery. Life without work is hopeless. Life without hope isn't hope, but death. Hervé laughs, calls him old-fashioned, an old Victorian. And knows his choice of confessor is wrong. Larry Kendal is the kind of man who will die working on some new blueprint, just slump forward, worn out, onto a batch of drawings of rustless cars, finger-light chairs that snap open like umbrellas, portable toilets, recipes for insomnia . . .

'Ah, well,' sighs Hervé, 'I see you think I'm a shirker. I shall probably carry on, anyway. My sense of duty has always been strong. Let's talk of something else. How's Nadia? She doesn't visit me any more.'

Larry asks for another cassis. He takes his refilled glass to the window and stares out at Hervé's lawn. He wonders, but doesn't ask, whether Agnès is in the garden. Now that he's here in Hervé's tidily arranged room, he's aware how completely Nadia would disturb the man's peace. He wants to apologise to Hervé for what he's about to say. He feels idiotic. There's no hope here for Nadia. He must help her to stop drinking. To stop dreaming. It's not fair to expect anything from Hervé.

'You know,' Larry says without turning, 'that Nadia believes she loves you.'

There is silence behind him. Hervé's hand alights quickly onto the box lid and begins its stroking: Patrice Armoutier, Guy de Rocheville . . .

'Loves me?' he says quiveringly.

'Yes.'

Larry turns and looks at his friend. Hervé is grave, as if a death had been announced.

'Poor Nadia,' says Hervé. 'My poor little Nadia.'

'Yes,' says Larry.

'My poor, poor Nadia . . .'

'She says she's loved you for a long time, Harve.'

'This is terrible,' says Hervé.

'Yes,' agrees Larry.

'A tragedy.'

'I thought it probably was.'

'You must comfort her, Larry.'

'Comfort her?'

'Tell her she must not come and see me again. Tell her this house is out of bounds to her.'

'That isn't comfort, Harve.'

'You must help her to understand.'

'That you don't love her? She suspects you don't. It doesn't stop her loving you.'

'What a catastrophe. I must leave France, Larry. I must go to the South Seas.'

'There's no need for that . . .'

'It's so absurd! She's already locked up Claude.'

'That wasn't her fault.'

'Not her fault? I'm not so sure. He was a very respectable man, Claude Lemoine.'

'Respectable, maybe . . .'

'He couldn't live with Nadia, that's all. Who could live with her? No man could live with Nadia and stay sane. Oh my God, this is terrible. You must persuade her to leave Pomerac.'

'She has no money, Harve. The little flat's all she's got.'

'Then I must leave. We must never see each other again.'

'But you were fond of her.'

'Fond? But only so far, my friend. *Copains*. You know the word? And she should never have presumed otherwise.'

'She doesn't "presume". She loves you. She doesn't imagine you love her.'

'Oh Larry, Larry, what a misfortune.'

'You had to know.'

'Did I? Why must one always know the bitter things?'

Hervé has left the silver box and begun to pace about the room, or rather to take mincing little steps back and forth across it on his brittle legs.

'Women!' he says despairingly, 'I swore I was exempt. I swore I'd never love one of them and I never have. So how have I deserved this? By being kind to Nadia? By writing prescriptions when she's ill? It isn't fair, you know. If you'd seen what she did to Claude . . .'

'Love is seldom "fair", Harve.'

'Well don't play the philosopher, Larry. Why are you involved in this at all?'

'I spend a lot of time with Nadia . . .'

'*You* love her, then. Let her send *you* mad.'

'Don't get angry. All she talks about, night after night, is you. I couldn't go on listening to this and saying nothing.'

'Why not? Why did I have to know about this?'

'Because Nadia has to know what you feel. She has to be sure.'

'You tell her then. And tell her I never want to see her again. Never.'

'This is very harsh, Harve.'

'Yes, it's very harsh. This is the only way.'

Hervé sits down, tired. Larry feels like the Egyptian messenger, beaten for bringing bad news. Ahead of him stretches vainly an evening with Nadia. She's cooking a Polish meal. More vodka has been ordered from Mme Carcanet.

'I'm sorry, Harve,' he says hopelessly. 'She'll get over it, I suppose.'

'I can't bear tragedies.'

'She will get over it.'

'And this is tragic.'

A car sounds on the magnificent gravel. Agnès returning.

'Say nothing to Agnès,' Hervé says quickly.

'I must be going,' says Larry.

'No. Don't go. Agnès likes to see you.'

Yet he does leave. He feels punished and sad. His friendship with Hervé may have been jeopardised. In the dark hall, Agnès runs up to him and kisses him fondly like a dear parent, but he leaves her grimly, with scarcely a word to her.

Nadia is making what she calls her *snotty gulashnova*. Pork is boiled to silver shreds in a sauce of garlic, white wine, rosemary and prunes. She says it's a recipe she got from the wife of her one-legged neighbour on Wielkopolski Street. It's always looked disgusting, she admits. Everything that came out of those Wielkopolski Street kitchens looked disgusting but this stew always tasted good. You eat it with mashed potato.

While the *snotty gulashnova* simmers, Nadia re-tints her hair with a new bottle of Nice n' Easy. Blueish paste runs out of the cling-film, in which it is suggested she binds her head, and trickles down her neck. She shivers, wiping this away. She wonders how grey or even white her hair is by now.

She has a bath and drinks tea. She enjoys preparations. Her hair looks yellow and clean. She tries on a new lipstick, makes an orange and chicory salad. I'm behaving, she thinks, as if a lover was coming to dinner, as if Hervé were coming. She changes from her candlewick dressing gown to a tweedy dress and from tea to vodka. She murmurs, badly, a sad Polish song: '*A girl came with a branch of whitebeam and lay her leaves in my true love's arms . . .*'

The Pomerac clock has just struck seven when Larry arrives. Though he still feels choked by his conversation with Hervé, he bounds cheerfully into Nadia's room, determined, somehow, to be gentle with his hurting news, to make the unbearable bearable. One thing Larry has always been is kind.

'Oh,' says Nadia as soon as she sees him, 'you are looking quite handsome tonight, you know. I don't know what you are living – on Gervaise's old beetroot or something – but you are getting so thin since Miriam leaves you. You know this, my darling?'

'Thin? Well that's good. I'm a middle-aged man . . .'

'But looking younger now. I think all this digging out your pool is good for your brawn.'

Larry smiles. It seems years since anyone paid him a compliment. Nadia's compliments, though they come out so peculiarly, are agreeable because he knows they're truthful.

'Thank you, Nadia,' he says gently.

'Well don't thank me, my dear. I'm saying true. Now I shall pour you some little vodka. Can you smell the *snotty gulashnova*? Not bad, no? You like it?'

'Yes. It smells delicious.'

Nadia hands Larry his vodka. He looks at her small, smiling face with its new-blonde hair and feels terror. She sees his look and asks anxiously: 'You don't like my hair?'

'Your hair?'

'I'm doing my new preparation on my hair today, in honour of this dinner.'

'Oh, it looks very nice, Nadia.'

'I don't know how much is grey underneath. If I stop my preparation, maybe I am an old white Saint Niklaus – Santa Nadia!'

Larry laughs. Nadia smiles, but sits patting her hair anxiously.

'How time is our enemy, you don't think?'

'Yes. I suppose.'

'Though men aren't suffering so from beauty. You know that story, *La Belle et le Bête*? Every woman reading this story is loving this beast, no matter how he is so grizzly, you know. They feel his sorrow. They want to put this ugly head in their lap and be so gentle and reviving. But you think of this table turning round! Another question altogether, my friend! If you take some handsome young stripple and he meets in the rose garden this grey hag, no matter how she is kind and loving of him he won't cradle her poor head and say don't worry I am loving you anyway in spite of warts. You think he will? I don't think. Never in stories. Never in life.'

'You're probably right. But I don't think I've ever been really impressed by beautiful women.'

'Well, your wife is beautiful, no?'

'Miriam? No. Not beautiful. Striking. Proud-seeming, a bit like an animal, but not beautiful. Her mother was, of course, and traded on it for years.'

'That bloody Leni?'

'Yes.'

'And she put you off the beauties?'

'Maybe.'

'Yes, I think. Because most men are so greedy of this. You are some exemption, Larry.'

'Exception?'

'Even Claude, when he's starting to go, I can see how he sighs in the cafés, you know. He sees some thigh or a young bosom and he looks to me to say your thigh is not so-and-so any more, Nadia, and your breasts are not so-and-so and I think out there in the Pas de Calais poor old Claude is still sighing for some young tits. So stupid, no? Like in Poland where I am a girl and hungry and my Uncle Leopold tells me, you eat the moon then, Nadia, the moon is good cheese. And I believe him, you know? I look up at this winter moon and I see the blue holes where the worms go in.'

After two glasses of vodka, Nadia lights red candles on her little table and serves her gulash. She tucks a monogrammed napkin into Larry's shirt collar. The draping of things round him, as at the barbers', makes him feel helpless and he quickly pulls it away. Nadia reprimands him like a child: 'You will spoil your very nice jacket, you know.' He avoids answering by complimenting her on the meal. She's made a great quantity of potato. The dish sits between them like a hillock. Larry can't climb this sticky white mountain to reach her and tell her to stop loving Hervé. Tonight her smiles, her little flushed laughs, guard and hide her sadder feelings. She's playing hostess. Her table is immaculately set. She's put out her best wine-glasses. Larry feels grateful for these attentions, just as he felt grateful to Gervaise for inviting him to her birthday feast, for taking him in. As the meal progresses and the mountain of potato diminishes a little, Larry feels more, not less, unwilling to spoil Nadia's evening by talking about Hervé. Another day, he thinks. On some cold morning, when there's no comfort of vodka and wine and this Polish meal. When there's nothing to spoil . . .

'So you're not infatuating the niece?' Nadia says suddenly.

'What, Nadia?' says Larry.

'This Agnès. You don't falling in love with this young beauty while Miriam is back to her mother?'

'No. Of course not.'

'You don't seeing her, even?'

'Well, I've seen her, yes. I met her fiancé the other day.'

'Ah, so she has some handsome young prince already?'

'Not a prince. A soldier.'

'A soldier. Well, is this suit her? She make love to his uniform?'

'No. She says she doesn't want to. Not yet.'

'And so she tells you this, my darling? You are acting so confidential?'

'Not really. I don't know why she told me. I was just there, I suppose.'

'Oh my dear, you don't be so modest.'

'It's not modesty, Nadia . . .'

'You English are so pretending this and this.'

'What d'you mean?'

'Pretending so bloody innocent, you know?'

'Nadia . . .'

'But you don't know this old game? I think you do.'

'What old game?'

'So, the innocent again! But you don't pull the yarn to Nadia. I do this in my time when I am young. I go to my Uncle Leopold, the one who is telling me so lies about the moon. And I tell him my troubles, how I am virgin and so afraid for my first time. But you know what I hope? Of course you do. He is so handsome man, my Uncle Leopold, and I hope he says okay, just don't worry about nothing, Nadia. You can come to my bed and I teach you.'

Larry stares at Nadia, who is laughing. He has never seen her dimpled pink face so happy or amused. She should be grey, he thinks, with her memories of Poland, grey with sadness for the lost Claude, grey in her hopeless love, yet she's golden and plump as a little partridge and rosy and hot.

'Oh, don't look so scolding!' she laughs, 'You think some girls aren't doing this since time is beginning? You don't think some students don't go to their favourite teacher and tell this and this and cry in his handkerchief. Me, I was student in Paris and I know these girls are doing this, just as I was doing to Uncle Leopold and this niece Agnès is do to you.'

'She's done nothing to me, Nadia. She asked my advice, that's all.'

'Oh, you dear English! Never suspecting. Never understanding. I don't know how Britannia rules the bloody waves when she is so stupid.'

'She doesn't any more.'

'But how is she ever doing this, I don't know. You were never invaded I think. Not since some Norman days. If a people are invaded and oppressed as in Poland, they don't stay so innocent. I think this is why.'

'What happened with Uncle Leopold?' asks Larry without interest. He feels uncomfortable with Nadia's teasing and his first thought is to protect Agnès from it. Solemnly he remembers Hervé's instruction; *this house must be out of bounds to Nadia.*

'What happened? Well, he is not so stupid. He sees what I ask. But he is so generous man. He takes me alone to some teashop and buys all plates of cakes and chocolate and I'm gobbling these up because in my home we don't have any fancy pastry or what. So he says to me, look at you, Nadia, you are still a little girl, eating her cakes. You see? You are my niece and still a child in your heart even if you have some beautiful breasts, and your uncle is not touching a child, only to give a little kiss on her head or give his arm on the walk to the tearoom. So I feel a little ashamed, you know. I start crying, I think I see he was honourable and Nadia dishonourable. So I try not to think of him no more. And when I lose my virgin, I forget him.'

'Is he still alive, Nadia?'

'Uncle Leopold? I don't know. He was a banking man and never so for the Communists. I don't know what happen when I leave and go to Paris. I just forget that sad Wielkopolski Street and all the cold streets and doorways and one doorway I forget is Uncle Leopold's. But it was painted blue. I remember this blue. Some cousin is given a big consignment of blue paint, so all the whole family is painting everything blue, even my bed and the meat cupboard or what. I think maybe this lasts them all out till they die and they paint the Poniatowski mausoleum blue. So funny, no?'

The gulash is pressed on Larry until the large dish is almost empty. As Nadia serves fruit – tangerines and dried figs and chocolate-covered nuts – his belly feels cramped and he's glad to sit still at the table, sip his wine, watch the candles burn down and talk quietly of Nadia's past – of Paris, of Claude, of her children. The weight of the unasked question about Hervé lies as heavily in him as the food. Slowly, with a subtlety he didn't imagine her capable of, Nadia steers the conversation towards those icy shores and Larry feels himself shiver.

'So Hervé's going away?' she asks finally.

Larry takes a tangerine from a glass dish and begins peeling it. 'Why do you ask this, Nadia?'

'Because, my old bean, you are avoiding this subject of Hervé like in Russia they avoid to talk of Stalin. So I suspect something– some bad news.'

'Why would he go away?'

'I think he is.'

'Did somebody tell you this?'

'So it's true, no?'

'He's thinking of it.'

'Well, I knew. Running from his nightmares and now running from Nadia.'

'No. He just says he's tired. He wants some kind of a break.'

'But you talk to him of Nadia. I see this in your face, my friend.'

'Nadia,' says Larry solemnly, 'you have been such a good friend to me. I feel so grateful for how you've kept inviting me here, cooking meals . . .'

'Well, you think it's so difficult?'

'I'm not saying it is. What I'm saying is I'm very fond of you and I wish everything in your life could be what you wanted . . .'

'So there's nothing for Nadia, uhm? No hope?'

'Oh Christ, Nadia, I don't know if there's hope or not . . .'

'It's all right, my dear, you can tell me. I'm not crying tonight.'

'I'm very fond of Harve . . .'

'So. Fond, fond. Fond of me. Fond of Hervé. Just tell me, no?'

'He doesn't love you. He doesn't love anyone, not in a romantic way.'

She sits bolt upright at the table. Her eyes are bright like a kitten's.

'You're not saying he's pederastic?'

'No. I'm just saying he's a very . . . unemotional man. He believes love complicates life . . .'

'So? Of course it does, no?'

'And he doesn't like that kind of complication. It wouldn't matter who you were, Nadia.'

'If I am young, you mean?'

'Young or old, it wouldn't matter. Harve has sworn never to get involved.'

'So he asks for his dreams, then.'

'What dreams?'

'This dreaming and sleepwalking and so afraid of what life shall maybe bring.'

'I don't know. He doesn't talk about this to me.'

'You know he's breaking those legs in his sleep. Running away.'

'I didn't know . . .'

'From *life*, Larry. But he says to me, Nadia, Nadia, I can't do this for ever, run and run from all I'm not finding out. But who would teach him? Not his niece, I know. *I* would teach him. I would say okay you go on a journey but you go with Nadia. Nadia has seen persecutions and deprivations and is not being afraid. I want to say I love you, my dear Hervé, and all with love is so possible. But now he never learns, you know. He goes on his journey away, always running, always dreaming and taking with him some silver box to caress. What is in this bloody box? Not warm kindness, not some touching hand, not any passion . . .'

She is near to tears but for once fights them back. She drinks a deep glass of wine, wipes her lips with a fretful little hand.

'He is so stupid,' she says at last, 'to think life is lasting for ever. I don't know how old he is. Fifty. Maybe fifty-two. Not so young to imagine he can waste so many years, staying so safe, never seeing outside his nose or what. You don't think this is waste?'

'It's what he wants.'

The wine, the *gulashnova*, the chocolate nuts, filled with these and with a tender pity for Nadia, Larry staggers through the silent darkness to his house. He lies in his cold bed and tries to think up enough inventions to make himself drowsy. He finds himself remembering Thomas's Monarch bean bags. In his mind, Thomas sits sprawled in one of these, staring accusingly at him. Somewhere behind his son, in shadow, is Miriam. The looks on these faces say, you're about to betray us.

Larry covers his face. More than with the meal, more than with pity for Nadia, Larry now aches with the new thoughts about Agnès which Nadia has planted in his mind, and which the vain pursuit of inventions and even the near presence of Thomas and Miriam can't seem to chase away. He feels invaded. He longs for the morning, hoping that in the sensible light of a grey autumn day the invader will return to the shadowy place it came from and cease to bother him. But in the dark his mind reconstructs. Conversations. Little sly smiles. The sweet kindness she gives. And Nadia's laughter at what she called his English innocence. He wraps his poor frenzied head with a bandage of uncertainty. Sleep tilts way out of sight. The trees hiss as the wind gets up. Mice fidget in the floorspace above his head. The night seems to scratch itself.

He dozes and is woken by Gervaise crooning to the cows. It's still dark. In darkness these mornings Gervaise puts on her old coat and leaves her men sleeping. The wind is stronger now, carrying bits of her song away. Larry looks for the invader and feels it planted boldly inside him, its presence in his head more firmly established. Again, he covers his face. He's glad Miriam is away and can't see him cowering like this. And with a surge of loneliness he remembers his wife – her hair on the pillow, her breathing, her hand touching his neck. He's survived her absence, but now, to save him from his new and treacherous thoughts, he plaintively calls her back.

He remembers – as if it was something done by someone else, not him – the night years ago when he got in his car to drive halfway across England to join Susan, the pert, dark-haired girl who had worked for him at *Aquazure* and become his mistress. Half-an-hour out of Miriam's life and he'd known he wasn't capable of leaving her. Not for this girl. Not for anyone. He and the car, a Renault 16, journeyed in circles round Oxford-

shire till dawn came. They were of one mind. He couldn't leave.
The car wouldn't take him. They cruised, happy as homebound
fliers, towards the sunrise. Courteous, they let Miriam sleep,
and took themselves to breakfast at a Post House. Larry had
bacon and mushrooms and coffee, the car was given a pint of oil
and eight gallons of 4-star. They sang home, the engine making
poetry of the miles. And Miriam took them in.

Larry sleeps again and is woken by the post van turning round
by Gervaise's yard. There's a hint of sun beyond the curtains.
He feels quite calm in his certainty that downstairs is a letter
from Miriam. He hears children playing on his earthmound.
These days, his life is cornered by trespassers. He longs for
Miriam's familiar, calming prose.

Dear Larry, he reads,
   *Each time we talk on the telephone we seem to say hurtful
things, or misunderstand each other, so I thought it was better
to write to you, even though the post from here to Pomerac takes
ages, as we know.*
   *I hope you're all right. I hope you don't feel too lonely. I'm
sure you will be seeing a lot of Hervé and Nadia. Perhaps
Madame de la Brosse even invites you up for dinner? And now
you have the pool to occupy you. This is good news of course
and I hope it is the beginning of a new start for you in France.
Please write and tell me how it's all going.*
   *I'm working very hard now for the exhibition. I would suggest
you came over for it, but I know if you do, you'll want me to
come back to Pomerac with you afterwards and part of the
reason I'm writing is to tell you that I don't think I can come
back yet. All my instincts tell me to stay in England, to make
something of my time here, so that when I do come back I can
do so joyfully and with energy for your new pool company, and
so on. I think, after the Aquazure fiasco, I was your nurse for
too long and I hope you will understand and not think me selfish
if I take some time away from you – for myself. We've never,
you and I, been apart for any length of time, and I don't suppose,
without the SOS from Leni, I would have thought of leaving.
But now that I'm here in Oxford, I feel it must be right to stay*

— not for ever, of course, only until I've rediscovered some purpose in myself, outside of you, outside of Thomas, outside of Leni. Then we might be able to make the kind of new start Pomerac was meant to be and yet never really was. I felt too tired. Too worried about you. Too anxious that you'd repeat the Aquazure mistakes in France. Perhaps I'm being bossy or presumptuous when I suggest it may be a good thing for you, too, to be on your own for a while. You can ask yourself, as I keep asking, what can we make of the next years, the years when we shall gradually be old? Is Pomerac right for us or will we feel too lonely, too much the exiles? I don't know the answers to these questions yet, but I feel determined to find them and not let our lives drift into bitterness or regret.

This all sounds very high-handed, very preposterous. Forgive me for this. I find it hard to express what I feel.

Now for some news: Thomas was here for a while, but can't leave the business for long. He seems happy in his life and I think he may get married to Perdita. I love him deeply, the more because he is such fun to be with these days.

Leni is still in hospital after breaking her ankle on the landing. They're going to keep her there till she can walk with crutches. In herself, she seems much better. I don't know if this is some lull before the real storm, or if she has recovered. It's lovely and peaceful here without her, anyway! I've turned David's attic into a studio and sleep in my old room, the little room next to Leni's. Nothing disturbs me in these two places.

It's getting very cold here in Oxford. The students are all wrapped up in their scarves. I hate the thought of winter and Christmas in particular. I wish the seasons, along with everything else, would stop changing.

With my loving thoughts.
Miriam

The sadness Larry feels after reading this letter has perhaps less to do with Miriam's delayed return (he predicted this, after all) than with his awareness that his wife — in all her actions — from the simple choosing of furnishing or clothes through to her loving forgiveness of unfaithfulness and failure — has tended to be right and admirable, whereas he has tended to be clumsy and base. Must she be wise till they die? Will he, dying before her, croak out yet one more, yet one last apology before putting her to the inconvenience and expense of burying him at Ste Catherine? Briefly, he envies men who have married women in whom, beauty aside or notwithstanding, there's nothing to admire. All these years, he's tried to live up to Miriam and still he's found wanting. He's nearer than he's ever been to understanding Harve's misogamy. Only his armoured ancestors reproach Harve with their clunking weight of bravery and renown. For the rest, he is what he is – himself. No one reproaches him. No one saves him from his plummet down the stairs. He's the doctor after all and heals himself.

Larry folds the letter and puts it tidily back into its envelope. He then sticks the envelope among the books, just shoving it in where he will forget it. Let Miriam be right once more. Let her profit from her time without him. But she mustn't imagine, because she's chosen to set him aside, that he'll cease to exist.

On this windy day, with the last chestnut leaves flying, Xavier Mallélou arrives in Pomerac. He gets a lift from the Thiviers train as far as Ste Catherine. He doesn't stop to glance at the graves or at the children in the schoolyard where he learned clapping songs and the spongy feel of girls' thighs under their overalls and the art of swopping and dodging and lying. He walks the familiar walk along the Ste Catherine road, past the sewage plant, past fields of the de la Brosse vines, past the sandy track that once led to the pike river and up the stony road to Pomerac on its hill.

He carries a plastic suitcase, bound with string like a parcel. He feels shame for this broken case and shame for this melancholy, droop-shouldered self sidling home to his mother. In the wind slapping his face, he feels like crying. He's full of trouble. The dogs sit and bark at him as he comes into Pomerac. He hurries past the Maréchal's door, dreading the old man's stare: *Xavier? Is it? What's happened to you, boy?* He's in the lane leading to the cowshed, the lane which skirts Larry's boundary. He turns a blank face to the yellow crater and the vast heaps of mud and imagines fretfully a tall building going up and dwarfing Gervaise's house. Fear for his unannounced homecoming mixes with a more cruel fear of unexpected change. In Xavier's mind, not one stone is turned, not one bough is felled in Pomerac except in obedience to the seasons. In the city, businesses opened, prospered, fell back, went bankrupt, closed. Signs came and went. Everything moved, shifted, altered, stopped and started, as if pushed by perpetual tides. But here in Pomerac you heard the quiet of the land. Even dawn and dusk came slowly. Light or darkness didn't overtake you. You had time to cross the field and close the gate and take off your boots after the moon was up . . .

Xavier is resting the broken suitcase, and still staring at a row of white lengths of pipe stacked by the pit, when Gervaise comes out of the milking barn, pushing a handcart of muck, and sees her son. What she sees first are his troubled eyes. She runs in her torn working coat calling, calling his name, her fists tight with her protecting love, and flings her hard chest against him and circles him with her grateful arms. 'Xavier! Xavier! Oh this is something! This is *something*!'

He can smell the farm on her, the milk, the cowshit, the earth. From a perfume counter he's brought her toilet-water and soap, to make her smell like a woman. He chokes with love for her. So brave she seems in her headscarf and rubber boots. He knows in that instant that he and his brother, Philippe, have none of this bravery. Gervaise has always humbled him and here was his principal reason for escaping her and her timeless landscape. Though he towers over her, he feels small.

She doesn't ask why he's come. She pulls back and stares at him. Under his eye is a blemish of raw skin, an eczema he rubs and fidgets with. She touches this sore place and he winces.

'Don't touch it, Maman.'

'You're not ill, Xavier?'

'No.'

'You're skinny. Mallélou said you were skinny.'

'Well, I used to eat okay, but now . . .'

'I'll take care of you.'

'It's cold . . .'

She feels him shivering. She feels the sobbing he keeps buried

in his ribcage. Her boy. Her baby. Beautiful from the day they
tugged him from her.

'Oh Xavier . . .'

'It's cold, eh, Maman?'

'Well, it's November.'

'I remembered your birthday. I got something . . .'

'Come in and get warm. It's warm by the fire. Then we'll see
to a room.'

She picks up the tied-together suitcase. Where they turn in to
the yard the wind drops suddenly and the noisy hens and
guineafowl peck as idly as on a June morning. Xavier stares. In
their midst, plumper even than the birds, is a bright-fleshed,
golden-haired man he has never seen. In his huge hands is a basket
of eggs and his body is draped in a rain-cape. He sees Gervaise
and Xavier and smiles. All maliciousness seems absent from his
face. Behind him, Xavier senses his mother hesitate before she
tells him quietly, 'This is Klaus, Xavier. Klaus lives with us now.'

Immediately, Xavier's mind accuses this man of beginning,
next door, the building that will blot out this farm. When he
holds a hand out to shake his, his look is uneasy.

The little room Xavier had here as a boy is used by Mallélou
now. On one of its walls is a faded poster of Jean-Claude
Killy, the skier, put up by Xavier when, in the hot snows of
adolescence, he had dreams of mountains and fame. Mallélou
likes the poster, yellowy though it is. It reminds him not only
of his son but of the grace and daring the human body is capable
of expressing in certain seasons of his mind. He sleeps facing
it, his back to the room, his back to the barnyard noises.

It is here, still sleeping, that Mallélou is to be found on
the morning of his son's arrival. Xavier shivers by the stove
downstairs while Gervaise boils milk for coffee. She remembers
Mallélou snoring up there with his light burning and feels
ashamed that Xavier should discover his father like this. 'Your
father's not well,' she tells him. 'So I let him sleep these
mornings. He's not well at all.'

'What's the matter with him?'

'He won't say.'

'So he's skiving. As usual.'

'No, no.'

'Letting you do all the work.'

'I like the work. You know that.'

'But Papa should help you.'

'He does what he can. He's put in a new fence on the top meadow since the summer.'

'What's that mess next door, Maman?'

'What mess?' Gervaise is uncritical of Larry's excavations. She can see in her mind only the finished St Front pool.

'What are they doing? Building a tower block?'

'A *tower* block?'

'Or what?'

'Where?'

'In Lemoine's house.'

'Ah. Lemoine's long gone, you know. The house was sold to some English people.'

'Lemoine's dead?'

'No. Put away. He was put away.'

Change. Xavier huddles near the stove where Gervaise watches the milk. Change has crept here, right to his mother's frayed hem. Xavier feels so sickly and troubled, he knows his whole body is shaking. Gervaise, moving quietly, trying not to be agitated, makes a bowl of milky coffee and puts this gently into Xavier's hands.

'I'd like a drop of cognac in it, Maman.'

'I don't keep cognac, Xavier. Only eau-de-vie.'

'Eau-de-vie, then.'

They sit at the table in the kitchen where Gervaise had her birthday feast. Outside, Klaus leaves his basket of eggs by the door and walks away, up to the barn, where he continues the shovelling and hauling of manure begun by Gervaise. Upstairs, Mallélou sleeps on, dreams of the railways, never imagines his son has come home.

'I feel a failure, Maman.'

'Get away. You did a stupid thing, that's all.'

'I won't last in prison. I'll be one of the ones who can't take it.'

'Who says it'll come to prison?'

'It will. Or a fine we can't pay.'

'We'll pay.'

'What with? The Maréchal's savings?'

Gervaise feels herself blushing. Stupid, she thinks, to blush when no one knows better than Xavier the debts she owes to the old man. Yet, at almost fifty, she's a proud woman. She doesn't like to imagine a debt so large it can never be repaid.

'We'll find a way.'

He's glad to be with her. He's always felt pride in belonging to her. From the broken suitcase he tugs out the toilet-water and the soap, gift-wrapped by the shop, and gives them to her – a present from his city life. She smiles and thanks him, but they distress her. In the days of the signal hut, Mallélou would often come home reeking of this same scent. In her mind, it's the smell of city-death.

'Put some on, Maman.'

'What now? In these clothes?'

'Yes. Why not.'

'No, no.'

'Why not?'

'I'd like to save it.'

'Save it what for?'

She doesn't know. Some ceremony perhaps. A funeral. Mallélou's funeral.

'I'll just save it.'

At her table, drinking the good coffee, Xavier is calmed. He thinks of the room he's left behind in Bordeaux, his few possessions there, and knows he was right to leave it. He was going mad in there while his neighbours, two students his own age, tormented him with their laughter, with their serious music and with their tender ways. He felt too melancholy even to drink with his friends. The lives of those students on the other side of his wall were full of hope and his own was devoid of it. At night he'd hear them talking about the books they were reading and feel astonished that they could do this in and out of their love-making which was like some novel, full of expressions of fidelity and joy. He wanted to thump the wall to shut them up. One night he brought a whore to his room and screamed at her to keep the students awake. Then, lying by her side, her old puckered mouth snoring, he felt a sorrow for himself so profound he began to cry. He sensed the students listening in silence – holding tight to each other probably – to his pathetic sobbing and found himself wishing they'd come and comfort him. For the first time in his life he longed to have a wife, some woman he could admire, some clean girl with a mind. Women fell for him, that had never been a problem. Corinne, the brunette who worked in a babyshop opposite Mme Motte's restaurant was dying of love for him, so she said, literally dying of it. But he was indifferent to her. Not even flattered. Indifferent to them all. Perhaps the woman did not exist who could move him.

He was having perpetual nightmares of the prison, and waking tired, as if he'd really been there in his sleep. He kept imagining himself old and prison-tainted, an old lag, all his good looks gone for ever. Why had he bothered to steal wine and potatoes? Even his mates laughed at the potatoes. He was getting stupid like his father. He began searching for a new job. He applied for posts as a biscuit packer, a florist's van driver, a station newspaper kiosk attendant, and a demonstrator of electrical goods. He got none of them. For the demonstrator's job he was expected to have Bac Part II – just to switch on switches, plug in hoses, assemble food processors . . .

His money was low and he saw the winter coming. Already his room was cold. The students started to discuss Marxist and non-Marxist interpretations of the English Revolution. Xavier, unaware that there had ever been an English revolution, lay buried in misery like a dog and began to long for the comfort of his mother.

One morning, he knocked on the students' door. They were pale, dark-eyed people who slightly resembled each other. Xavier told them they could use his room over the winter – 'If you have a colleague to put up, or if you want to give a party' – and asked them only to take care of his things. 'Where are you going?' they asked, and Xavier looked blank, unprepared for this question, 'I have a friend . . .' he stammered and waved his hand hopelessly, 'I have a friend . . .'

On the train to Thiviers, he imagined the students going

through his magazines, and saying: 'Look what he reads. He's thick. Look at this muck he buys.' He envied his brother Philippe his life in Paris. His job wasn't much – he worked for a cigarette company – but he'd stayed right with the law, he was engaged to the daughter of a chemist, there was hope in his future. It was freezing in the train. When Thiviers station came he didn't remember it and almost let it go by. Then he got out and felt the bellowing of the wind in the brilliant air. The chestnut leaves and the oak leaves were streaming off. Everything was flying and thudding and whooshing in the huge wind. Well, he thought, let it carry me off. Let it blow me up to hell.

But now the wind's settled, and, hugging his bowl, he's calm. Loving this frightened child, glad to be his protector, Gervaise nevertheless begins to wonder how the presence of her son in her house may alter the ways and affections of her lover.

The only resident of Pomerac to have noticed the arrival of Xavier Mallélou is Nadia. Since the evening of the *snotty gulashnova*, she's spent a lot of time standing at her window rehearsing what she'll say to Hervé when he arrives – as she's certain he will – to scold her for falling in love with him. As she rehearses, she strains anxiously for the sight of his car, even pressing her cheek against the glass. It's with her face at this peculiar angle that she sights the stranger with his sullen head and his clapped-out suitcase and recognises in this sad-seeming person Gervaise's son.

With her eye for beauty, her worshipping of straight-limbed, elegant men, Nadia had long ago been fascinated by Xavier Mallélou. His brother Philippe was an ordinary-looking boy, wiry like Gervaise, untidy like Mallélou, but Xavier was different, a changeling, an imposter, illegitimate surely, with the body of a god.

She knows the saga of Mme Motte and the stolen wine. All was explained to an impatient-sounding lawyer over her telephone. She didn't expect Xavier to turn up in Pomerac. She stares at him, stares with a feeling of hope she can't account for. If forced to express it, she might simply say that with Xavier's arrival, life in Pomerac – she can't say how or why or when – will be subtly altered. She trusts him to alter it. Her heart cheers him home like a runner.

Larry, arriving soon afterwards at her flat to tell her about the letter from Miriam, is informed immediately. 'Come up, Larry. You know that Mallélou boy is arriving, my dear?'

Larry closes Nadia's door and sits down on her colourful sofa. 'The one who got into trouble?'

'Yes. And he looks you know like the dog coming home, the tail under the legs.'

'You mean he's arrived?'

'Oh yes. Just one hour ago. I see him come up the hill so bent, you know, like that Prodigal Son. You learn that bloody story? The fatted-up cow is given to this one who is away and fucking, and the good brother who is minding the sheep is getting Matzo balls or what. When I learn this paraphrase I think my God this Christian religion is like Claude sometimes, round its rocker! Anyway, you want tea, my darling?'

Larry laughs, then on impulse says: 'Let's visit Claude. I'll come with you. Let's go to Calais or wherever he is and make sure he's all right.'

Nadia stops her preparation of tea and stares at Larry over the Japanese screen. 'You don't know what you say, Larry. There's no sense to Claude. And to see this notty man breaks my heart.'

'But he must wonder why you never come, Nadia.'

'No, I don't think. He forgets me. If I come, he's saying who is this woman?'

'You don't know that. Perhaps he's very lonely and missing you.'

'Oh no, Larry! Don't *talk*! My heart is breaking enough . . .'

'But you can't leave Claude there for ever and never visit him.'

'So, you reproach?'

'No. I'm not scolding you. I'm just thinking how it might be for him. It might make him very happy to see you, Nadia.'

'Well I don't know if I could do this. We Poles, we know of the institution, you know. We know what is liberty and what is the trouble of the soul in prison. And what am I remembering if I see my Claude? Oh my God I am remembering how he was strong and takes me to an open-air restaurant in the Bois and

I'm crying for what is gone. So how is this help Claude, my dear? You tell.'

The kettle is boiling. She pours water on the tea and sighs heavily. Her face is flushed. Larry looks away from her out of the window where the trees are buffeted by the wind. This hurtling of leaves reminds him painfully that winter is almost here. In that instant, waiting for the tea, he feels old.

'I'm sorry, my dear,' says Nadia, bringing in the tea tray, 'perhaps you are so right. Perhaps one day I must go to this institution, but I know it's giving me some nightmares and I don't want to fly out of the window, you know, or down the stairs like poor Hervé. I have a little root now in Pomerac. I am like some shallow heather or what with a small poor root in the soil and I don't want you just tear me up, you see?'

'Yes. I see, Nadia.'

"*Compris*? Okay?'

'Yes.'

'So now you tell me, you want to telephone?'

'To Miriam? No. I had a letter this morning.'

'Bad news, so?'

'She wants a kind of rest from me.'

'Rest? So are you so exhausting, my dear? Are you biting her in your loving and so?'

Larry smiles. Nadia pours tea.

'She helped me so well when I was down. Now she needs a break from me.'

'So this is all? Poff! She leaves you in a puff of steam?'

'Yes. For a while.'

'So what you *do*, my darling? I don't know what she expects you do in Pomerac. You have no friends, no? Only Nadia and Hervé and those old Mallélous . . . You make your pool all alone? I think Miriam's going a little mad. I think she don't see what hurting she makes. I am really surprise.'

They sip the tea. The last two biscuits from an expensive packet are set out on a plate but sit there uneaten. The room is hot, as usual, and very tidy, with Nadia's bed folded into the wall. Sitting silently in this small protecting space, they hear a car begin to climb the Pomerac hill. Nadia gets up and goes to

the window, squashing her cheek against it to see along the
road. It is Hervé's car. She turns to Larry with the fear of a
startled rabbit in her face.

'So, he's coming.'

'Hervé.'

'Of course Hervé.'

'I'll be on my way then, Nadia.'

Larry gets up but Nadia flurries to his side and grabs his
hands.

'Don't go! Oh tell Nadia what to do, what to say! I'm so
beating in my heart, Larry. Please stay . . .'

'You'll be all right, Nadia.'

'Oh my God, my God . . .'

'He's a kind man, Nadia, he's fond of you . . .'

'Listen!'

'What?'

'Listen, Listen.'

They're quiet. The car engine now sounds fainter.

'Oh my God . . .'

'What, Nadia?'

'He's not coming. He's not stopping.'

She rushes back to the window. She can't see the car. Despair
and confusion shimmy in her body as she turns helplessly back
to Larry.

'It's going . . .'

'The car?'

'He's not coming to Nadia.'

'Perhaps he's turning round.'

'Ssh!'

They listen again. They can't hear the car now.

'He's gone to *you*, Larry.'

'Okay. It's okay, Nadia. I'll go and find him. I'll ask him to
come and see you.'

'But not to scold! Oh I'm dying if he tells me you are so foolish
Nadia, so stupid Pole. Oh my God, what trouble!'

'Try to be calm, Nadia. Harve's a good man, a kind man. He
won't hurt you.'

'But he won't love me neither! Never! I know it. He's wasting

his life and Nadia's life and now I think, is poor Claude seeing
all this in his padded room or what? All is *confusion*.'

Nadia is crying now and Larry's reluctant to leave her. He
gives her his handkerchief and gently pats her yellow hair.

'Let me go and find him, Nadia.'

'I don't know why I am ever fall in love with any man. Better
to be lesbian! Women are kind, you know . . .'

'Not all are.'

'Oh so not that fucking Leni, but most are feeling and won't
make you suffer.'

'Try to stop crying, Nadia.'

'Yes. I will. You go, Larry. You go.'

He can still hear her sobbing as he goes down the stairs, but
he finds himself hurrying away from the sound, a feeling of
excitement beginning to beat in him as he tells himself with
sudden certainty that his visitor isn't Hervé after all but Agnès.

He runs out into the wind. Colossal white clouds chase over
the village, coming west from the sea and billowing towards the
south. It's a day in which Pomerac feels small and Larry minute
within it, hurrying like a dot to its little i among countless reams
of writing.

The car is parked right outside his door, almost blocking the
lane. Agnès is standing by it, wearing a woollen beret. When
she sees Larry, she waves and calls: 'I've come to see the pool!'

Larry's out of breath quickly these days and arrives at her
side panting. He apologises. 'I'm sorry Agnès. I was up at
Nadia's. Luckily, she heard the car.'

'Oh, it's okay. What a terrible windy day, hmn? So. Will you
show me the pool?'

'Yes. If you like. It's looking its worst now, though. Just a big
pit.'

'Well, I think it's exciting. I expect these Pomerac people are
scandalised, *non*?'

'No. They aren't. They seem rather pleased.'

'I don't think many can swim.'

'No? Well, they'll be able to learn then.'

He hates her snobbery. All snobberies he hates. Even
Oxford's self-pride was repellent to him. He's stern with Agnès.

He makes her move the car and park it carefully behind the Granada before he leads her round to the pool site. And he offers no helpful comment. Just lets her stare at the hole and the mounds of rubble and earth.

'It's so funny,' she says, 'when I see a swimming pool, I never imagine all this happening. I imagine the work is very tidy.'

'No. It's not tidy. It's foul work at this stage.'

'So when does it become like a pool?'

'Oh, eventually.'

She looks at him sadly. She knows he's cross with her, yet doesn't know why. She wants to say to him, I needed courage to come here. Don't hurt me.

'What colour will it be? Blue?' she asks.

'All pools look blue. It's the volume of water – provided it's clean.'

'But you won't make it blue?'

'The floor will be a very pale blue. The sides will be white and the mosaic trim black and white like the St Front cupolas.'

'Like St Front? How *wonderful!*'

She smiles – the approving child – and he feels gratified. His anger begins to go.

'In the summer, if you're still here, it will all be finished – and tidy.'

'In the summer? So long? I don't think I shall stay so long. I may get married in the summer.'

'To Luc?'

'Yes, of course.'

She turns suddenly and walks towards the house. Larry wants urgently to say, don't get married yet. Stay here. I'll make you a little place by the pool . . .

Inside his house, she hesitates. The cautious careful Agnès wants to walk quickly away, get in the car and fly. But the purpose that brought her here still whinnies in her for attention. She's like a restless pony jangling its bells, tossing its head this way and that. Larry watches her. This feeling of her precious-ness to him gathers again in his chest. His caring for her weighs him down. He feels heavy and breathless. They stand, fixed apart from each other, unspeaking.

But the pony in Agnès is so proud, it won't be denied its favour. It's decked for the circus and must strut, must shake its plumes and flash its tail. It leads her stubbornly to Larry, then stands waiting, waiting with its head bowed.

Larry is as still as granite. I won't be the one, he wants to say, I won't be the one. But the pony is still, too, now. *Help me. I've come as far as I can.* Moments pass. The wind drums on the stone and sings down the chimney. Next door Mallélou wakes and hears as if in a dream the voice of his son in his own house. *Help me.* But Larry moves away. *I won't be the one.* Sensing that the moment which has just passed was of the greatest, saddest significance and that a similar moment may never ever occur again, Larry takes Agnès gently but firmly by the hand and leads her to her car. Without a word to him she drives away.

In the dark, Xavier Mallélou tiptoes to his mother's door and listens. Wrapped in a cold mist which settles on the village as the wind drops at dusk, the house is silent as the mind within the skull.

Down the passage, Mallélou's light burns. Next to his small room, Klaus sleeps in a carved bed – his only possession apart from his clothes – that he had expensively transported by truck from his mother's house near Heidelberg.

Xavier had forgotten this Pomerac silence. He had forgotten there were silent places at all. He wears his coat over his underwear. In the city he sleeps naked, but the bed that's made for him here is freezing, as if the sheets were stored in the damp barn. He can't sleep in this cold and silence. He feels like getting drunk and bleating out all his sorrows, to be rid of them once and for all. He wants to wake Gervaise, but takes pity on her and lets her sleep. He knows she's up before it's light, tugging at her cows, blowing on her fingers to warm them for the teats. She sleeps like a child, a grateful and rejuvenating sleep. Even thoughts of her son with his eczema face, even thoughts of Klaus lying in his painted bed, don't keep Gervaise from sleep. Time will heal the eczema. Time will bring her lover back to her chicken-down pillows. What matters in this silence is rest.

Xavier goes down to the kitchen and turns on the light above the oilcloth-covered table. This shiny cloth reminds him of Mme

Motte's restaurant and he shudders. He wonders, but won't ask, what happened when his father went in that night. Did he insult her? Did he throw up on her floor? It was all vain, anyway, vain and spiteful, the reaction of clodding myopic idiots. If he survives prison, he promises himself he'll fight his way into a college and get an education at last. If he survives. If it's not too late. If colleges take people like him with no experience of anything but petty jobs, petty ways and petty theft. *Je suis petit*, he repeats helplessly. *Je suis trop petit* . . .

When he looks up at last from this pessimistic mumbling, he sees Klaus standing on the stairs. The German wears a mighty quilted robe, stained at the cuffs and elbows. His hair is wild from tumbled sleep, his wide feet stuck into sabots. Xavier wants to laugh. He's like some monarch out of ancient time. You can imagine a courtful of retainers following him from the banquet to the closet to the royal bed, applauding his appetite, his blue-blooded stools, his possessing of a courtesan. Yet Xavier has also found him admirable. At supper, he was courteous and full of gaiety. Mallélou, diffident and quiet even on this day of his son's return, clearly liked and respected him and Gervaise sat contentedly in his wide shadow and showed him an unobtrusive tenderness. He'd become important to this family. His presence coloured the room like Christmas boughs.

'I'm not disturbing you? You like some drink with me. *Ja*?'

'Yes,' says Xavier, 'I'd like some drink with you.'

'Well I keep in the cupboard here some schnaps, out of a little sentimental reason. I think it's getting stale because I am not a very sentimental man, so I don't often drink it.'

He laughs his big laugh. Upstairs, Mallélou wakes and hears it and envies this man his big chest and lungs that can make such a joyous sound.

Klaus finds the dusty bottle and two little fine cut glasses left to Gervaise by Eulalie, the Maréchal's wife. (The Maréchal alone, she had decided, would have absolutely no need of cut glass.) He pours the schnaps and holds the drinks up to the light.

'Fine glass.'

Xavier stares at Klaus and wonders about his age. He could be forty. He could be a lot older.

'To our friendship!' says Klaus.

'Yes,' says Xavier, 'to friendship.'

The schnaps is bitter and warming. Xavier is glad of it and glad he isn't alone.

Klaus seats himself, pushing up the sleeves of his robe on his fleecy arms. He turns to Xavier, looks at him steadily and quietly begins: 'I was working in Thiviers. My trade was the bread and patisserie. I learn this from a master-baker in Heidelberg, then I am apprenticed to a patissier in Périgueux and finally I am a partner in a little business in Thiviers. You know the shop, perhaps. Your mother and father both came in from time to time. We bought honey from them, honey from the flowers and clover of Pomerac.

'These people, your parents, are good friends to me. I am invited here and I think to myself, these are true friends where I have not met true friends in all my life. You know what this is, to meet with affection? You know what the soul says when it finds this relief? Stay. *Bleib. Bleib.* And I could not do otherwise. So I sell my half share of business and I don't mourn this, not for an hour, not for a minute.

'Now you are a young man. You may not understand how I could give up this business to settle here. But I wasn't so young. My skill had become a routine. I had no feeling for anyone. My life was dry, you know, without any love. Dry as ashes. Like I am an urn and all I hold is the burnt bones of people, not their smiling or their giving or even their tears.

'Well, I had lived long in this condition. So long. You see how I am – so big a man. So loud. I can't help this. And if you cut my heart out I tell you it's the size of a watermelon! So I need love. I need what these people, your parents, give to me and I will not leave them.'

He stops talking and drains his glass of schnaps. 'So this I tell you. You are the son and should know what this stranger, this foreigner is doing in your house.'

Temporarily, Xavier feels set aside from his own miseries. Change has indeed come to Pomerac, but change of a fortunate kind. All the dark spaces he remembers from his adolescence in this house seem to have been filled, obliterated by this smiling man. If his father is declining, his mother has been made stronger than he remembers, and when she looks at Klaus, ladling his soup and passing it to him, her face is luminous with happiness.

'You're her lover, Klaus.'

'Yes. Of course.'

'Does my father know?'

'Again, of course. He's an old man. I do his work for him. He's not ungrateful.'

'She loves you, doesn't she?'

'Yes.'

'Very much?'

'Yes.'

'And you?'

'She's my woman. Gervaise is my woman.'

He pours more schnaps. His smile is wide, with no hint of apology in it. Xavier, too, finds himself smiling, happy in Klaus's company and content with the deep silence beyond.

Agnès Prière lies in her narrow bed and examines her life. It's like a cluttered room; nothing in its place. Her marriage to Luc lies in a corner of it, a garment of sequin and shimmer she's flung down impatiently, waiting for the right time, the right occasion to take it up again and put it on. The trouble with Luc is he shows her no gratitude. He's like an enemy come to pillage, not a lover come to woo. With this enemy she will be safe – from poverty, from other, sadder worlds, from change. But the ground she gives – her body smelling of clean wool, of roses and sunshine, her virgin self solemn as incense – he scorches it with his soldier's fire. His kisses burn.

There's a cupboard in this untidy room. In there hidden away in darkness, is the gift of herself she wants Larry to discover. She won't marry the soldier till the older, wiser man has loved her gratefully, with tenderness, and shown her her own inner fire. She's a child in love and Luc is the handsome classroom bully-boy, shining up his buckles and his boots and letting all his understanding go dull. She's tired of the boy's firecrackers and wants the quiet teacher. All this, to Agnès, is perfectly logical and wise. Yet what she can't do is invite the teacher in. He must

come to her. So she waits, and her life meanwhile is confused.
She thinks sadly of leaving and going back to Paris, to its stately
black winter. Today she's almost resigned: the teacher won't
accept what she offers. Yet Agnès is stubborn in defence of the
orderly patterns her mind makes. She refuses to imagine her
sumptuous summer wedding till she's understood the rites she'll
be dressed up for. Rites and rights. Her own. Not just the
groom's.

So she'll try once more. A last time. Then her room can be
put in order. She doesn't doubt that, a year from now, she'll be
Luc's wife.

One morning, soon after Xavier's arrival in Pomerac, the Maréchal wakes with the notion that sewage from the Ste Catherine
sewage plant is seeping into Eulalie's grave. To think of the
clean woman his wife was lying with her bones in muck troubles
him so badly he can't eat his habitual breakfast of coffee and
bread. He sits in his grey room, repentant for the small care he
takes of Eulalie's plot. He wants to find flowers to sweeten her
earth. He wants to talk to her through the marble chippings.

Raising his stick in greeting to the villagers he meets on his
way, he shuffles up to Gervaise's door, watched by Nadia from
her window, seen eventually by Klaus and Larry who are down
in the pool pit laying pipes to and from the central drain, received
at last by Mallélou in his morning idleness, unshaven, pale and
smelling of sleep.

'Mallélou? It's me. Come for a favour.'

'Yes. Come in, Maréchal, come in.'

All decisions, all rejoicings, all rows, prayers, repentances
and family arithmetic take place, in Gervaise's house, round the
oilcloth table. It's here, then, that the Maréchal sits and brings
out his pipe.

'Wine, Maréchal?'

'Well, all right. Just a glass.'

'Nothing bad happened, I hope?'

'To me? What more can happen this side of death?'

Mallélou pours the harsh red wine he likes to drink on and off
all day. 'Plenty, Maréchal.'

'Well, I could lose my speech or my wits, I suppose. I could get dumped in a rabbit hutch like Lemoine . . .'

'Your house could burn.'

'I could get the English as neighbours!'

He slaps the table and laughs. Mallélou joins in. Mocking Larry and his pool is a bond of a kind – one of the few – uniting these two men. But the Maréchal looks solemn.

'I need a lift to Ste Catherine. I can't walk that far anymore.'

'Today you want to go?'

'Before too long. I need to spend an hour with Eulalie.'

'Eulalie. God rest her.'

'I think they're disturbing her.'

'Who?'

'Those sewage lines.'

'Disturbing her? Best go today then. Tell you what, Xavier will take you.'

'Xavier? He's here?'

'Yes.'

'No one told me.'

'Well, he's here. Come back to his mother.'

'I'm glad for her, Mallélou.'

'Yes, yes, glad for *her*. But what about the boy? So skinny he is. Where's his youth? Where's his energy? If it comes to prison, God save him. He's not up to it.'

'I'd like to talk to him. We were all fond of Xavier.'

'Well you talk to him, Maréchal. You try to put some pep into him.'

The Mallélou family own an old Renault *fourgon*, empty of rear seats, smelling of pipe ash and cornseed. Calves, goats, guineafowl, hens have at one time or other been bumped down the Pomerac lanes in this rusty car. Now Xavier drives the Maréchal in it, holding fast to his stick, his owl's eyes watery in a day of strong sunlight, to visit Eulalie's grave. The wind which howled at Xavier's arrival has gone, the brittle leaves and bright berries of the hedgerows are still and the sky is clear. It's the last of autumn before the winter drizzles, the last warmth dredged from the sun.

The Maréchal, his mind on Eulalie's bones, talks to Xavier of

mighty things, of the evanescence of youth, of the *ennui* of old
age. Xavier drives and says little, scratching his sore face. The
journey by car is very short. They arrive quickly at the church
of Ste Catherine les Adieux and its crowded burial ground, past
which the road to Thiviers thunders.

Xavier is glad to get out of the car and away from the Maréchal's
wisdom. The old man wanders off towards the tall headstone that
reads: *Eulalie Marguerite Foch, 1899–1971. 'Quand j'ai traversé
la vallée/Un oiseau chantait sur son nid.'* He stands in silence,
holding the chrysanthemums he's brought and remembering the
warts which buttoned out on Eulalie's chin as she passed sixty and
began to be flustered by premonitions of death.

Xavier, who has been told by Gervaise to let the Maréchal
'be alone with Eulalie', decides to go into the church, where, as
a boy, he heard his mother pray repeatedly for rain or sunshine,
for healthy cows and a good crop of apples and give thanks when
these blessings came about. The God inhabiting this church
seemed always very obedient to Gervaise. In Xavier's mind the
Christ who watched over the labour of her animals and sent his
sunshine to ripen her tomatoes was the plaster-of-Paris Christ
propped up on the Ste Catherine altar. There was nothing
universal about him. He only heard you if you lived near Ste
Catherine. He was a CB God, a short-wave deity.

He's still there on the gaudy altar. The hand raised in blessing
has a chipped thumb. The eyes are painted a fierce blue. If the
statue were dropped, it would smash to smithereens. Xavier
walks down the nave towards it wondering, now that he's back
within the orbit of its power, whether he can ask to be spared
prison and be heard. He makes his genuflection and slips into a
pew. There's only one other person in the church, a woman
kneeling in the front row, praying, her head covered by a silk
scarf. Xavier wonders whether this hunched figure isn't Mme.
de la Brosse.

He says his prayer: 'God save me from jail. Please save me
from that. Save me from jail, please God,' and crosses himself.
The church is cold. He fears that his prayer is as cold, as empty of
poetry as it. The plaster Jesus with the mutilated thumb stares,
unseeing, past him towards the font where, when he was eight

Gervaise insisted he and Philippe be rebaptised, knowing in her soul and in her liver that the holy water of cities is polluted, hoping that the holy water of Ste Catherine, despite its nearness to the sewage farm, would wash away the childhood of the tyre dumps and the wall slogans. Xavier can't enter this church without remembering the embarrassments of that baptism. Mallélou got up like a bridegroom or a mourner in a suit of shiny black. The priest ladling water on their heads like soup, the Maréchal coughing into a handkerchief, a cluster of Ste Catherine children at the door, laughing. After it, they walked in a little formal troupe up the Pomerac hill, their hair still wet. And he and Philippe kicked stones, missing the city litter.

Xavier watches as the woman in the scarf gets up, stands staring for a moment at the sentimental window behind the altar, then turns and walks towards him. The woman is Agnès Prière. Expecting the dejected, resigned, life-is-bitter countenance of Mme. de la Brosse, Xavier finds his knees on the hassock shivering with the greengage beauty of pale Agnès. Quickly covering his eczema patch with his hand, he sends to her hazel eyes a stare of absolute longing. She falters in her smooth walk and is for the briefest second face to face with his young man's desire. Then she walks on, passing him, setting her face towards the open door. She wants to look back at him. She resists and resists till her feet touch the slab of sunlight at the doorway, then she turns quickly and sees him standing now, as if preparing to follow her, and she knows from his open mouth that this touching of each other with their eyes has made him breathless. Sadly she walks away to Hervé's car and gets in and drives off. She wonders whether, in an average life – in the life of the kiosk woman on the corner of her Paris street, in the life of her piano teacher with his fathomless spectacles – there are many moments like this one, moments when what is suddenly glimpsed is as suddenly and as swiftly lost.

At Eulalie's graveside, the Maréchal's eyes weep from strong sunshine and remembered days when his wife was living, smelling of lavender. He remembers her linen drawer and all her home-stitched camisoles and petticoats and knickers. So neat and flying was Eulalie with her sewing machine, that women tramped to her from five villages with their paper patterns, their cards of lace and their cotton remnants. She could have made ballgowns. When the Maréchal's hands undid the ribbons at her breast, his lust sometimes faltered at her woman's artistry and all he then asked of her was to lay his head on her ruches and pleats and gathers and let her hands gently caress his back. She died thin, in the same size bodice she'd worn on her wedding day, and was boxed up in a white smock she'd made especially for death. Now she's bone and even her children are bone in their Paris graves and only the Maréchal has any memory of her body in its camisoles, its little accommodating movements under his belly, its more knowledgeable ways with the crimping iron. 'Eulalie,' he says soundlessly, 'I hope they're not disturbing you with muck.'

Xavier stays in the church. He walks to the Ste Catherine Roll of Honour for the two wars and starts to read off the names. I would like, he finds himself thinking, to do something brave and be remembered in carved letters. I would like there to be some honour in my life. The face of the girl stays with him like a presence. So clean. Her breath would be innocent. He would take her to the pike river and let his love for her spring up. After loving her, he would ask her to wash him with freezing water. They would stumble about, splashing, laughing. There would be blood on her thigh. And they would be lovers very often after that. For years. It breaks Xavier's heart to know this will never happen.

Riding home without his chrysanthemums, reassured that all seems peaceful at Eulalie's resting place, the Maréchal says to Xavier: 'It's a very precious thing, a wife. I shouldn't neglect her like I do.'

'Well,' says Xavier, 'it's of no significance. She's not there to notice whether you neglect her or not.'

'You don't believe in an after-life, Xavier?' says the Maréchal.

'No,' says Xavier.

'Neither do I,' says the Maréchal, 'neither do I,' and shakes his head. Then, as they near the Pomerac hill he says suddenly: 'I believe in this one, though. It's no good neglecting that. Eh, Xavier?'

'No,' says Xavier.

*   *   *

Nadia Poniatowski still finds herself spending some part of each day at her window, craning for the sight of Hervé's car. Sometimes her watching is overtaken by the darkness and she becomes suddenly aware that she can't any longer see the lane on which her eyes are fixed. When this happens, she draws her curtains and renounces her vigil as pointless, promising herself not to waste another minute of her life in this way. She busies herself then, writing letters to her children, doing her *gros point* cushion covers, polishing silver. She knows her love is hopeless. She knows it's harming her like an illness. Yet it refuses to leave her. November goes slowly to its end. She tries to save on electricity to afford her vodka and her room is often cold. She shivers and dreams through her days, arriving very often in her mind at Hervé's bedroom door: two sleepwalkers meeting at last. 'So stupid, *stupid*!' She screams at Larry, her only confessor, her only visitor. 'Why am I so suffering from this stupidity?'

But since the morning of Agnès's visit to him, Larry has less patience with Nadia's infatuation. Her talk of Hervé doesn't help him in his own forgetting of Agnès, tempts him, in fact, to consider himself wildly fortunate as the unlikely altar of Agnès's sacrifice, tempts him to get into his Granada and go flying past the waterfall, up Harve's drive and on, on into the cool white tower where his child sits and waits . . . 'Stop it, Nadia!' he hears himself shout. 'We'll both go mad with this thing. Stop dreaming!'

Together they sit down and talk of Miriam. There is sanity in Nadia's dislike of Leni; there is sanity in Larry's missing of his wife. Another letter has come, informing him that the exhibition opens on December 1st, that Leni is out of hospital, that a man called Dr O has taken Miriam to the theatre to see *The Rivals*. In Miriam's life, all seems to perch serenely, even Leni the macaw. Or so she wishes Larry to believe. She makes no mention of an end to the separation, won't say what she plans. Nor does she mention the pool. Laying breeze blocks, Klaus says one morning: 'Such a surprise for Miriam. Not?' And Larry's heart thuds. 'Not,' he says wryly. He's stopped building it for Miriam. He's building it for Agnès.

So, towards the end of November, a feeling that he must see

Agnès steals on Larry and sends him hurrying off to Périgueux
one morning to buy a gift for her, something to offer, something
to reassure her she's not spurned, only protected. He wanders
the market, staring blankly at birds and rabbits and overalls and
flan tins. He stops at a flower stall and nearly decides to repeat
his gift of a tree, but this doesn't satisfy him. The tree would
become Harve's. He's in search of something Agnès will keep.
He goes back to the rabbits, remembering tenderly her soft
jerseys, then realises that these rabbits are sold for breeding
and eating, not as pets. He feels muddled – 'stupid' in Nadia's
vocabulary – and English and heavy with wearying lust. He goes
to the busy café where the dominoes players are just starting a
threes and fives and orders a beer. Sternly in this busy bar, he
reminds himself that Agnès is younger than his own son and
once again makes a solemn promise to forget her.

The lines of love or longing, if you drew them, they'd criss-cross
Pomerac like a tangle of wool. Up in the de la Brosse garden,
the old man paid to keep the edges tidy is dreaming of the bosom
of Mme Carcanet in the Ste Catherine épicerie. Down at
the school, the elderly headmaster says prayers in the library
donated by a Colonel he despised and adds one for himself: 'God
punish my wife for the lovers she takes each spring.' From the
Maréchal's foetid room, lines travel not only to Eulalie in her
smock but half across France to his dead sons and all the
grandchildren who year by year expect news of his death and
never come to visit him. And down into Pomerac, deep into the
very centre of the village, comes the cold, black line of the
longings of Claude Lemoine. This is the cruellest line. It's
threaded not merely to Nadia but to the land on which he once
owned two houses. It touches every stone and every season.
    From the Mallélou house, a tattered thread winds back through
time from the room where Mallélou lies and stares at the wall to a
room in Bordeaux where Marisa once lay in her cream satin
sheets. From Gervaise, a patient line travels to Paris and encircles
her eldest son, Philippe. To and from Heidelberg go the confectioner's lines of love for his mother and her missing of him. Yet in
the embrace of Klaus and Gervaise all longing is forgotten and all

desire satisfied. Their lovelines weave a basket which holds them together. But from Xavier a web is spun, reaching vainly from house to house, from hamlet to hamlet, in search of Agnès, whose name he doesn't know, whose own longings he can't guess at. Larry knows where she is, his irresistible child. As winter nears, the springtime man he sometimes is sends his green foliage of desire. And Agnès sits in her castle, writing love letters to her soldier, waiting, waiting, as Nadia waits at her window for life to alter, for the future to become clear . . .

Freezing winds sigh over the Pas de Calais ploughlands and in these Claude Lemoine hears the eternity of his own exile. In the complicated patterning of Pomerac's affections, the sharp and wounding line his heart sends is never noticed.

Certain lines, however, are about to be redrawn. While Larry sits in the Périgueux café listening to the shouts of the dominoes players, Hervé Prière sends Agnès down to Larry's house with an invitation to dinner. In a month's time, Hervé is going on holiday to Florida; Agnès will then return to Paris; the dinner is a little farewell to his neighbours. Hervé's old-fashioned courtesy dictates that he invite Nadia, but the coward in him declines to do this. He asks Agnès to ask Larry not to mention the dinner to Nadia, only the departure.

It's another bright and tranquil day: November going gently. That morning, the de la Brosse maid, Lisette, arrives to collect rugs and bedspreads for dry-cleaning, picking her way among the goat droppings in the garden. The Maréchal, seeing Lisette pass, thinks of Christmas and the sorrows reborn each year with it. 'How many more?' he asks aloud.

Xavier and Klaus, grown quickly fond of each other's company, are working together on the swimming pool, laying the breeze-block base and walls onto which the concrete will be moulded. Amateurs both, they work painstakingly with plumblines and levels, strange guardians of Larry's vision. Sometimes in Klaus's ample imagination, the pool takes on the form of an actual cathedral, a work of magnitude and grandeur. He longs to be entrusted with the mosaic steps. He forgets that he's neither a masterbuilder nor a swimmer. He's boisterously happy. And a little of his optimism passes, at first imperceptibly, from him to Xavier. The eczema is healing. His idea of starting some late education seems less a mirage, more a possibility. It's as if the German was pouring into Xavier's dark skull some of his own peculiar light.

Getting no answer at Larry's door, Agnès walks round to the back of the house. Standing at the pool edge, she looks down on the blond curly head of Klaus and the dark straight head of Xavier. Xavier looks up and sees her and in his surprise absentmindedly wipes his eyes with his trowel, thus banding his face with mortar. Under his breath, not to her, but to his dreaming of her by the river he's gasped, *'Ah mon dieu, c'est toi!'*

Seeing him, she's dumb. As if she doesn't want to reveal the self she's been until now, neat and clean Agnès with her careful nails, fiancée of a boy from a good family. She blushes, in fact, at the very thought of the person she is. Xavier's stare, his sweet confusion, only add to her feelings of wanting to conceal herself, to become, in this instant, someone entirely different.

Wiping the mortar from his face with a rag, Xavier climbs out of the pool pit and is, before she's fully aware of it, at Agnès's side. He rubs his hands on his overalls and rashly reaches for her white little wrist. Like one of those meddling elders, Juliet's nurse, Pandarus, Klaus stares in wonderment at the antics of these two young people and rightly concludes, as they walk hand in hand away from him, that the same benign God who brought Gervaise to his patisserie with her honeycombs has thrown a thunderbolt at them. He shrugs and smiles and goes back to the contented building of his cathedral walls.

Thoughts of England start to trouble Larry half way through his second beer.

Since the night of Gervaise's birthday he's felt a bit more comfortable with his life in Pomerac, less sorry for himself, less afraid of winter and language, happier with the ancient ways of the village. Klaus has become a kind of friend. Even Xavier is courteous to him and pleased to work on the pool. And then there is Agnès. He'd like to kidnap her. Dress and undress her like a doll. Make her room beautiful. He knows these are the fantasies of his middle years. Though they feel like love, they're base. Yet they make him happy. He's happy with his fictions.

Then in the noisy café, where the air is full of greeting, he remembers the blue telephone and the white telephone on his desk at *Aquazure* and the Year Planner above them and his Golfer's Desk Diary signed by Tony Jacklin, and he feels a stab of misery.

The *Aquazure* offices were sited on the boundary of an industrial estate, on a road called Edith Cavell Way. The buildings on it seemed uniformly made of painted tin but were in fact built rather soundly and only clad in this corrugated substance as a measure against the damp. The Cavell family had once owned a cottage on this piece of lowland but the damp had been the eventual cause of its demolition. Whether Edith had ever stepped inside this cottage no one knew, but the new estate stuck her name up proudly and it was on the whole a conglomeration of rather proud, self-making people, like Larry Kendal, who traded here. Next to *Aquazure* was a fitted kitchen business called *Amora Kitchens* and on the other side a glazing company called *Aviemore* Ltd. Three A's in a line. At lunch, if he wasn't seeing a client, Larry would join John Aviemore and Mick Williams of *Amora* for a ploughman's at the estate pub, *The Ferryman*. Like the Frenchmen now absorbed in their dominoes, Larry and his friends were reassured by their own routines. The barman knew their names and their preferred drinks. They discussed the sport they watched on TV – golf, football and snooker. And all three, at one time, seemed like people on the up. People who would, in due time, shake hands with members of the Royal Family, or at the very least with the Secretary of State for Trade and Industry. Their respective ambitions had been set into patio doors, melamine worktops and heat exchangers and if one of them had suggested, over a Guinness, that in less than seven years Larry would be crumpling his Year Planner and scribbling 'Shit!' in his Tony Jacklin diary and abandoning *The Ferryman* for a foreign café, the others wouldn't have believed him.

He thinks of Mick Williams and John Aviemore now and wonders who rented the space between them. They'd had a farewell drink with him. That morning Aviemore had clinched an order for two acres of greenhousing and Larry saw the lesson he should have learned: in England all life is creeping inside shelter, like pictures back inside frames. He was working on domed plastic covers for his pools but they were too vulnerable to gales and punctures, not reassuring enough. John would prosper with his glass and Mick with his kitchens because this was where life had paused. The grandiose experiment, the bold essay, these weren't happening any more. England seemed to be learning only from the Dutch. Covering vegetables while they grew. Larry got sick-drunk on these late realisations and Mick Williams drove him home, lighting Rothmans for him with the car lighter and sticking them in his mouth like a thermometer. And this is what he became from then on: the patient.

Larry finishes the second beer and orders a third. The dominoes players are drinking red wine in small glasses, like Mallélou does all day. Larry has a longing he can't classify to be discussing Steve Davis and Hurricane Higgins with John Aviemore and spreading Branston pickle on dense white bread in *The Ferryman*'s saloon bar. Those were optimistic days. The news beleaguered you, but then in the mornings your office carpet had been hoovered and you knew that on Edith Cavell Way there was order and sense and everyone going about their business. Susan of the dark hair and quick-batting Leeds voice made excellent coffee on the Cona and brought in the first cup of the day, smiling, and you knew that a day might come when you'd go not to *The Ferryman* at lunchtime but to the downs with Susan and fuck her in your car. You bought the Renault 16, with its reclining seats with this act in mind. And Larry can't see a cherry coloured 16 now without remembering the way Susan's white feet had pounded the dashboard. Odd that it was the same car who refused to let him leave Miriam. Odd too, how easily Susan was forgotten.

Forgetting England needs practice, he knows. Surprisingly, he's doing better on his own than when Miriam was there; he's hardened his heart. Then, without warning, nostalgia – for the Today Programme, for Match of the Day, for Blackwell's Bookshop, for Marks and Spencer, for his Oxfordshire kitchen, for milk deliveries, for the voice of Sir John Gielgud, for Wimbledon, for the smell of post offices, for the double ring of a telephone, for his

Aquazure desk, for *The Ferryman* and for the sound, the unmistakable cadences of his own language – invades him like a fierce pain, and all he wants then is for things to be as they were. At moments like this, he longs to ask more famous exiles than himself what they miss most. The trivial things, he decides. The smell of London buses. Cheap tea. The Test Match . . .

He stares at the men banging down their dominoes and envies them their place in their own culture. He drains the third beer and goes to piss in a foul smelling open urinal before driving home without a gift for Agnès. Klaus is still in the pit laying blocks. When he sees Larry, he calls him down to tell him the morning's news, his huge body pleased with what it relates.

'Good. Not? Not? Thunderboulders whizzing!'

Hervé Prière is very pleased with his decision to go to America. In Florida, they understand the terrors people get not just of death or violence but of their own shortcomings. They've got ways to soothe you. The hotels have storm windows. The cars are like portable rooms. French food is reverenced. The women have shiny hair. The elevators are large. Money is a friendly not a devious God. It's not difficult, there, to go through a day without smelling any uncomfortable smells, aside from exhaust clouds. Even the toilets are air-conditioned with lavender air. You feel like an ancient Roman. Pampered. Clean. An elite. The bathwater is hot. The hotel supplies soft white bathrobes, like togas.

Hervé has been a doctor for thirty years. His mind makes a terrible collage of all the wounds, the tumours, the warts, the faeces, the rashes, the shaven hair, the burns, the bleeding and the dead souls he's examined over this great stretch of time and an exhausted voice inside him bleats, 'Enough!' The sight of his own toenails flaking off makes him shiver these days.

His memories of America, where he's been three or four times in his life, are of clean teeth and white roller-skates and charcoaled T-bone and oldsters' jokes. He feels superior to his hosts in their Bermuda shorts, yet comforted by them, reassured, separated from his own (European?) mournfulness. He quickly acquires the taste for the whisky camaraderie, the back slapping, the hand pumping. 'Hair-*vay*!' they call him, accenting the second syllable and his liking of their country makes them hurrah like children. He prefers speaking American to English and likes to put zest into his favourite expressions, 'Sonofabitch!' and 'Yip, yip, yip!' He's not certain what 'Yip, yip, yip' actually means, but he says it often: 'Freshen your drink, Hairvay?' 'Yessir! Yip, yip, yip!' 'Ever met Brigitte Bardot, Hairvay?' 'No *sir*. Yip, yip.' America makes him feel like a celebrity. Celebrities are cushioned from their own consciences because their least actions are thought worthy of attention. In America he becomes a man of substance. People take care of all his needs. They make sure he's comfortable on his lavender-scented toilet. His ancestors are centuries older than the country and deference is paid. Someone makes certain he has practically no need of the regimental box.

So it's with enormous relief that Hervé informs his colleagues he will be retiring before Christmas. He lets thirty years of knowledge slip from him like a shirt due for the laundry. He sits in his bureau and thinks, very pleasurably, of the idle days and months ahead, his reward at fifty-one for the dedicated medical man he's been since his youth. He feels serene and calm, freed of an unbearable weight. His suite at the Demi Paradise Hotel, Boca Raton, is booked, as is his flight to Miami, first class. He plans his farewell dinner: his partners, Dr Roger Jolivet and Dr Jacques Albert and their wives, Larry, Agnès, Mme de la Brosse, a distinguished solicitor from Thiviers and his wife, an undistinguished but charming writer, Georges Agnelli, also a bachelor, an old friend of Claude Lemoine's. Ten is an excellent number round his mahogany dining table. His maid, Chantal, is back from Paris and will take care, with Agnès, of the dinner. Before the sweet course, Hervé will make a speech – an au revoir. Champagne will be served.

The date set for Hervé's dinner is December 14th. The following day, the 15th, it is planned that Agnès will catch the train back to Paris.

These two events are less than three weeks ahead on the day when Xavier Mallélou and Agnès Prière make, at the river edge, a bed of wild pampas grasses.

It's a still mid-day, cold but motionless. The dark water, empty of pike now, meanders on towards the Gironde. The willows are leafless and black. Agnès feels this hard winter earth at her back and knows that only lovers make of it anything but a cradle and a tomb. And Xavier, looking down at this pale face turned up to the sky, remembers the students on the other side of his wall in Bordeaux, his jealousy of their tenderness, and feels choked with love. So hurtingly in love with Agnès does he feel, he can't stifle a grateful crying when he feels himself push past her little reproaching membrane and tear like a hurricane into her blood. It's a crying he can't still. He kisses her and both their triumphing faces are wet. And he moves her more than anything in her life. She who is so obedient to beauty, finds in Xavier a lover her enfolding arms want to possess for ever. She wants to shout with him. Hurl rocks. Climb the sky.

'You're beautiful, Xavier!'

'So are you. I love you, Agnès.'

'So strong in me, so hard.'

'More than I thought I could love . . .'

'I love the hardness of you.'

'Marry me. I want you to marry me.'

'Marry you?'

'Yes.'

She laughs a delighted laugh, then silences her own laughter by kissing his mouth hungrily. From the overcast sky, rain falls on the empty trees over their pampas bed and drips onto their heads, a peculiar third baptism in the life of Xavier Mallélou. Though they begin to feel very cold, neither can bear to break away from the other. They just hold each other more tightly and Xavier covers them with his coat.

This place by the river is some way from the window where Nadia stares out at the rain. For the time being, then, the love affair of Xavier and Agnès remains hidden from Nadia and it is Larry who says to her that morning: 'Something's happening in Pomerac.'

She turns from the window and looks at Larry with bright beady eyes. 'Something happens? Oh at last is something! Well, you tell Nadia and we'll have some little vodka to toast.'

But then to Nadia's irritation he sits silent. He's hunched up in an old green cardigan. He looks miserable. Nadia gets out the vodka glasses and the last two inches of vodka in what she's promised herself must be her last bottle till Christmas when a cheque is sent to her from Claude Lemoine's estate. She's broke on vodka. She's eaten no butter or cheese for three weeks. Her meals are boiled vegetables and cheap sausages. This state of affairs is getting bad. Her nails are becoming brittle. When she climbs her stairs, she feels weak. She's begun having a dream that she's put herself in a concentration camp.

Larry watches her pour the vodka and feels grateful for its impending warmth. Life, on this day, seems to Larry Kendal as sad as an English hymn.

'So? So? You tell me what, old bean!'

Smiling, Nadia hands Larry his glass of vodka. He sighs. Her irritation increases.

'Well, come on! What's this so terrible thing you're sitting like a shivering dog in the veterinary waiting to put away? Is someone threat? your life, or what?'

'No, no. Of course not.'

'Then what, my dear? They fill your pool in again?'

'No. The snows will do that. But not until.'

'Well I don't know? you're so pessimistical! We're not live in Siberia, you know!'

'No. But it'll be a hard winter. I feel it.'

'How you can feel it, my darling? So you become a snail making the deep burrow?'

Larry's silent. Yes, he wants to say, I'd like that: carve out something under the earth and stay there till spring, or till Miriam decides to come back.

'Well, I don't mock,' says Nadia gently and comes and sits by Larry and pats his hand. 'I'm sorry, my bean, if I'm so impatient, but Nadia is pass so much time waiting, always waiting and always I'm so glad if they tell me, something happens. You don't mind. Okay?'

'Well, I'll tell you, Nadia,' says Larry slowly. 'Something's happening to Agnès.'

'Oh, to the fairy princess? You don't say she is turn into a frog?'

'No. She's fallen in love with Xavier Mallélou.'

A look of astonishment crosses Nadia's pink face. She takes a hasty sip of vodka.

'Well, I'm telling you, when I see this boy come up to Pomerac, I am think, now he puts some firecracker under all the bums! No, truly, I am decide this. I think, now the dead bones wake up in the earth! But how you know this for sure?'

'Klaus told me. He described to me how they met. He said he's never seen this before, two people just struck dumb by each other.'

'So that is what, then. Well, I like this, you know. Like *Wuthering Height*, no? The girl of so perfect family and in her silk bodices loves the wild boy. But I don't know what Hervé is saying! My God. I think he's not approve at all! My God. I think he's having to stroke his bloody box now!'

'Perhaps they'll keep it a secret.'

'Well, in Pomerac, it's not so easy, you know. Every person stick their necks into your onions. You think it doesn't go, the story of those Mallélou's and Klaus König? Believe me, people are learn there what is what.'

'Maybe, maybe,' says Larry dejectedly. 'I'm not really bothered by any of it.'

'So I don't know why you're so sad, my dear.'

'I'm not sad.'

'But you *seem*. I think it's not Nadia crying today, but you.'

'I'm sorry, Nadia.'

'No, no, you don't sorry. You tell Nadia what. Is this fucking Leni send you some poison-letter?'

'No.'

'And you don't get a word from Miriam? You don't know when she's coming?'

'No.'

'So no wonder you get sad.'

'Yes. But it's not only Miriam.'

Nadia walks to the window and stares out for a moment, then turns and looks reproachfully at Larry.

'So I think I was right,' she says, 'I think ever since you're

putting eyes on this Agnès, you're think of the bed, Larry. I'm
not right? No? You deny? I don't think you deny.'

'I do deny. It was she who came to *me*.'

'And after?'

'What?'

'After she is putting this thought in your mind, you don't
thinking how wonderful, how fantastical I'm making love with a
virgin, I'm taking her maidenform?'

Larry shrugs. 'I don't know what I thought, Nadia. All I know
is that now I can't stop thinking about her, I'm so jealous of
Xavier, I could kill him.'

Nadia's silent. She looks dismayed and disappointed.

'Well I tell you my old bean,' she says at last, 'every man in
Nadia's life is sighing after these little princesses. But what
madness, you know. What stupidness. I just don't know why
they are doing this. Why is youth so wonderful? Just for the
buds of tits and the flat belly? Perhaps this is all you're wanting
in the end. Not companionship. Not any intellectual conver-
sationing. Not any loyalty and familiar person. Just tits and
maidenforms. I am so amaze. When I am young and in the
teashop with my Uncle Leopold, I don't know what I *have*, this
so precious thing, this youth you're all strive after. I don't
appreciate. I long for growing up and experience of life. But no
one of you *wants* my experience of life! You want maidenforms.
I tell you, my darling, this world is so badly arrange, better to
be like Claude and shut out or shut up, I don't know which or
what. I am just confuse. It's like we are all sleepwanderers.
Even me. Why am I wait at the window? I don't know. I know
Hervé is leaving. I knew he's leave without one word to Nadia.
And still I wait. Stupidness no? Sleepwanderers. You, me,
Hervé, even these young lovers. So what will happen? You tell
me, my dear. What is come next? Winter, we know, that's all.
And perhaps you're right: all the animals are burrow down and
down and snow is coming from Siberia.'

Larry says nothing. Outside, the drizzle is steady now and
the trees are still and shiny. Nadia takes up the vodka bottle
and empties its contents into their waiting glasses.

FOUR

WINTER

One December Wednesday, two days before the opening of Miriam's exhibition, Gary Murphy abandons his lilac room and the unwritten poems that sit in it like bored guests, and takes himself walking in the Cherwell meadows. He feels the piercing cold of the day most keenly in his neck, from which all his jutting hair has been shaved. His new hairstyle makes him look younger and more cruel. The front is kept long and falls over his eyebrows. Piers, whom he's forced to meet very often these days, informs him he's 'bang in with the new mood' and Leni tells him the beaux of her youth cultivated this look under broad-brimmed velvet hats. Gabriel, who's decided to play Othello as shavenheaded as Kojak, has dreams about Gary's hair. The altered face of his friend disturbs him. He's superstitious about touching the shorn neck. He wishes that Gary had no modern vanity.

Leni has equipped Gary with a pair of green wellingtons, attaching to which is a little history that still creases a smile in her once matchless cheeks. The wellingtons belonged to a lover of hers, a Gloucestershire farmer called Roddy and always known to her and David as 'our dear Philistine'. David never once imagined that Roddy was Leni's lover and indeed never knew. Leni wanted to punish David for his presumption and punish Roddy for being the kind of man he was. She sent Roddy away. But only after she'd exchanged, in their respective cars, David's wellingtons for his, identical green wellingtons, different only in size. If David ever noticed, he never admitted the discovery. Leni would watch him walking on the downs in boots one size too big for him, the innocent, his feet tucked up in warm socks, not knowing the flip-flap of the rubber was Roddy's. And she'd imagine Roddy on his farm, staring at pigs, fingering grain, becoming aware that his boots pinched him, thinking he'd got off scot free, thinking, men can come and take what they like – own the land, own the women – but punished day after day in his hurting feet. Petty. She knew it was. Yet she didn't like events that had no consequences. Both these men had to pay a small price for what had happened. Otherwise, what did any of it signify – the words of love on Roddy's hayseed breath; David lying like a boy in her arms and sleeping? She made fools of them to tell them both: nothing is ours *as of right*; in the least action, we are responsible.

Gary's feet are the same size as Roddy's, so the wellingtons fit him very well. He wraps his bare nape in a crimson scarf and trudges with his hands in his pockets through a landscape shorn, too, of all its foliage. A heron on the river stares at him and flaps off. A skirt of mist sits on the further fields. Nature is pared down, quiet, pale, waiting. The sky is a flat white. Ahead are the January storms, the snow blizzards, the sleet, the winds. Ahead, too, is Gabriel's *Othello*. Far into each night, now, this *Othello* is being made. Like the getting of coal, it seems to be hard, back-breaking, heart-straining work. Gabriel's eyes are red with exhaustion and excitement and fever. When he looks at Gary, it's with a miner's contempt for one who's never been near a coalface. Gary shivers with fascination and dread. The more hectic, the more savage Gabriel seems, the more he craves his wild embrace. The performance itself waits to catch him – the gazelle in the lion-trap – and wound him with too-strong emotion. He practises sitting quietly. He persuades Leni to come with him to the first night. He warns her he may have to sob. She promises to bring chocolate truffles to pop into his child's mouth and scented hankies for his tears. A special space is reserved for Leni's wheelchair. Filled with vanity and longing and strangely empty of poetry, Gary orders himself a new Italian suit made of dark green velour. And the days pass.

Here, on this cold morning, unaware of Gary walking towards her in the mist, is Bernice Atwood, wrapped in a threadbare coat and staring at the water. She doesn't own any wellingtons, nor has anyone lent her a pair, and her strong brown shoes are very damp. Her toes in nylon tights inside these shoes, curl and uncurl in time to a tiny swaying rhythm her body has set up.

She's singing to the baby inside her. No words or notes come out of her, but just as, without consciously offering food to her baby, it takes what it needs from her body, so when she sings in her head she knows the baby is calmed in its waters and rewarding her by its silent growing. She likes to sing to her baby several times a day in this way. Its existence is unknown to anyone but her. The child is her secret and only she can sing it secret songs.

These walks she takes in the damp December countryside are in obedience to her child, who seems to ask that she fill her lungs with freezing air and get her feet wet in the sodden grass, but who then lets her come home to her flat, deciding not to go into the bookshop, deciding to put off for yet another day the questions for Dr O with which her heart feels squeezed, lets her come home and light the gas fire and eat a buttered scone and rest and wait for the future. Lying down on a rug, she can sleep away the whole day after her walk by the river, so tired is she from the air and the walking and from the invisible giving of her blood into her baby's buds of limbs. She wakes up at a teatime and thinks of Dr O turning on the lights in the shop and putting on the kettle in the stockroom. In the fading teatime light, she longs to tell him about the child which, though hers, is part of him. If the sunset is golden and green and brilliant at her window, she thinks of her pregnancy as a thing of splendour and imagines Dr O filled with admiration for her, embracing her stomach, humbled at her womanhood, saying sonorously: 'My task was a small one, Bernice, but yours is mighty.' The fact is Dr O is absenting himself from her life. Going. Day after day. Slipping off. Not since the Sunday of the Bergman film has she been alone with him, except in the shop. In the shop, he's silent, withheld, preoccupied. Even the lunches she makes he eats in silence. A voice in Bernice – the voice of the child? – tells her to be patient. By nature, she's a patient woman. Her work, her life, is lived painstakingly out. Now, at the river, she patiently sings her song and curls and uncurls her feet and reminds herself that people's lives have had the strangest shapes, that the most famous lovers endured seasons of separation, and prays to the earth of Oxfordshire to let Dr O come back to her. When she looks up and sees Gary walking towards her, she feels afraid.

In all its minute detail, Bernice remembers the teatime visit to Leni Ackerman. She remembers the colour of the cake and the colour of Miriam Ackerman's hair. She remembers the way Leni screeched and how Gary fussed over her. More acutely than the fact that no one introduced her to Gary or Miriam does she remember what happened to Dr O in that room, in that company. He became awkward. His hands looked too big for the teacup they gave him. His clothes looked shabby. He was a man who never apologised for the way he was, yet in the Ackermans' room all his gestures were apologetic. This grieved her. Immediately, she'd seen Leni as the cause and thought not much more about it. But now, as she sees Gary, she realises with a stab of pain like a quill going through her abdomen, that it was on this day and in the presence of Miriam, yes, Miriam, not Leni, that Dr O began to change. In the time it takes for Gary to raise his arm to her in a muted greeting, in these scant seconds, has Bernice understood her fate.

Gary stops a little way from Bernice and rubs his hands. He doesn't want to have to spend time with this dowdy girl and offers a gesture which says, it's too cold to stop. Bernice stares at him with a pasty and terrified face. Her song has vanished with her stab of fear and her body has stopped its rocking.

'Not too cold for you, Miss Atwood?'

She doesn't know Gary's name and is surprised that he's remembered hers. Perhaps, in that household now they talk about her: 'That poor faithful Miss Atwood! What on earth will become of someone like that?'

'Hello,' she says slowly. She hopes Gary can't hear the fear inside her. A coot bobs at the water's edge and Gary looks from her face to it.

'One gets fond of the river, don't you think?'

'How's Mrs Ackerman?' says Bernice bitterly.

'Much better,' says Gary. 'Thank you. I'm taking her to the theatre next week.'

'Oh, what are you going to see?'

'*Othello*. A friend at the playhouse has the lead.'

'Oh, *Othello*, gosh. It makes me so jumpy, that play. Why does he kill her? *Why*? If he'd only believed her . . .'

Gary smiles. 'Then there'd be no play.'

And he starts to walk away from her, tugging slightly at his red scarf. To Bernice's own surprise, and to his, she begins to follow him. They walk side by side in silence for a few steps until Bernice stops suddenly and hears herself say:

'Does Dr O come to your house?'

Gary stops and looks at Bernice. Her coat is literally worn out. Her fists are clenched. For a moment he feels deep sorrow for her.

'Dr O?'

'From the bookshop. Dr Carlton-Williams.'

'The man Leni calls Oz. Yes, of course. Yes he visits from time to time.'

'To see Mrs Ackerman, or . . .'

'Yes. To see Mrs Ackerman. They're old friends.'

And he walks on. Bernice follows for a moment then decides she will cross the river and cut back through to the city. In her realisation that Dr O may be in love with another woman, she feels swoony and sick. She and her baby must sleep, must renew their strength before they see him and find out.

'I'm going this way,' she says to Gary, indicating her direction with her still-clenched small fist. He says goodbye to her and watches her go. She seems to be hurrying – to the bookshop perhaps, or is Wednesday her day off, as it is his? Just to my room, she could explain, to turn on the fire and lie on my bed covered by the bedcover, to try to sleep, which is good for my baby and good for me, and try not to imagine my life is changed, my life is finished . . . She's begun to cry at this point, but by now she's walking fast on the other side of the river and to Gary she's no more than a tiny brown shape, a sparrow. In her coat pocket, she discovers a used mauve Kleenex and she struggles to stem her abundant tears with this.

To forget her, Gary turns his attention to the struggles IVb are having with *Heart of Darkness*. Yesterday, a blond freckly boy called Billy Skipper said he thought Conrad must have been a manic depressive like Billy's Aunty Rose who was sacked from

her job at the Wimpy for eating fudge while writing down the
orders. She took this sacking badly, he told Gary and the class,
so badly she started to see black spaces in the TV and even in
the bedroom walls. He bet Conrad saw black things. Else, why
would he go on and on up that river? Though writing the actual
book could have made him better. He'd heard, if you wrote
things down, it got them out of your system and you cheered
up. Gary wanders on, his restyled head bound in the scarf and
four lines of a new but hopeless poem settling obstinately into
his brain. (If you write things down, you get them out of your
system.) Aloud, to the winter meadows he recites:

> 'Any news
> of the famous Hughes
> stops
> my heart with envy.'

His voice, in the cold air, lingers for a split second, like an echo.

In the crush of people and the hot spotlights of the gallery, Dr
O feels giddy and light. It's not a terribly large space and Dr O
is the biggest person in it. He sips the sparkling wine the gallery
owner has served and thinks, in this push of admirers, *I am
outnumbered.* From the walls, Miriam's face watches him. That
fabulous face! His belly feels empty of all but worship. *She has
surrounded me.* He doesn't see the Pomerac paintings, even
though red 'sold' tags are going up on some of these; he sees
only the portraits. Every one of these, in his hectic brain
belongs to him. *I am privy.* She asked his advice about the first
self-portrait and all the rest followed from there, from that day.
He has made her promise, promise on Leni's life, on David's
memory, not to sell the bandana drawing which is, in the end,
the only one of all these pictures he can afford. There's no 'sold'
disc on it and he doesn't know why. He wants to corner the
gallery owner, an upright and silky man with a soft voice like a
woman's, and tell him: This one is mine. But Miriam told him
not to do this. 'Don't be silly, Dr O,' she scolded, 'you don't
want to pay the gallery price. You can have the drawing direct

from me when the exhibition comes down.' And she was off into the push and gabble of the people, her cheeks red, in a coral dress that made playful fire with her hair, wearing Leni's turquoise necklace, telling the people about her life in France, letting him fend for himself. *She loses me.* His darting eyes follow her everywhere. They can't get enough, enough of the sight of her. Any day that he doesn't see her is featureless and dark.

Leni is there. Thomas stands guard by her wheelchair. Leni's forgotten how screechy and silly people sound at cocktail parties. Her eyes sting. The bubbly wine inside her is acid. She's glad of Thomas, her sentinel, and won't let him move. And together they watch Miriam, magnificent tonight, they both recognise, a success. The French watercolours are much admired. The gallery owner is cooing like a hand-reared pigeon over his catalogue: 'Oh quite clearly, France is an inspiration to her. Quite clearly! Dramatic shift of colour emphasis. So much more radiance in them . . .' He moves from person to person, wearing his matching grey silk shirt and tie, ruffling his neck feathers, a neat and springy man, flattered to find 'so much of the University' in his tiny space, his face charmingly smiling, his hand laying on Miriam's coral shoulder a gentle, congratulatory caress.

'Look at Oz!' Leni whispers to Thomas. 'She's got him bowled over you know.' And they watch Dr O's struggles with the crowd and with his scarlet infatuation. Though he moves about the room, his eyes perpetually follow Miriam. He makes a circular kind of progress, talking to no one, knocking into people without meaning to and spilling their wine. They glower at him and he doesn't notice. 'Just look at him!' hisses Leni, taking Thomas's hand. 'Men in love are helpless, you know. Just like toddlers! Well I think that Atwood's done for, but what now?'

'What does Miriam feel?' says Thomas.

'Oh, she's not saying. Not to me. I suppose she's being honourable.'

'Honourable?'

'Yes. She said to me, what should one be at fifty and I said, honourable. So she's being it.'

Perdita is there. In the shiny skin of Perdita with its down of blonde hairs Leni has glimpsed gigantic sands and skies of

fathomless blue and decided to approve of these for her grandson. Also, Perdita is witty. Wit and the gift of a continent seem,
to Leni, more than adequate for Thomas, and she tells him
sharply, 'Marry her.' But no one is obedient now to Leni's
commands. Miriam's success, the crackling wit of Perdita, both
these things reaffirm that Leni's days of power are over. Only
Oz, in falling in love with her daughter, has obeyed her, yet his
helplessness maddens her. 'Look at him, look at him,' she says,
tugging at Thomas's arm. 'Call him over, Thomas. Let's try to
do something for him.'

Leni's right: he is helpless. Day after day, Miriam refuses
him. He doesn't know why. He prepares his room for her arrival
in his bed, tidying up some of his papers, sending his curtains
to the dry cleaners, removing his washing from the fireguard.
Why is my love refused? Bernice never once refused him. She
was silent, admittedly, but silently accepting. And her body,
even now, keeps seeking him out. He knows that in her Cattle
Street room she lies and dreams of him and cries, probably, and
feels hungry in her woman's emptiness. While he lies uselessly
in Plum Street with his prick so full of ache he has to keep
milking it himself and holding it in the dark to comfort it. He
thinks his longing will, if many more nights pass in this way,
drive him mad. When he takes Miriam out to dinner or to the
theatre – neither of which he can really afford – he sees her
looking at him so kindly, so fondly and his heart vaults with hope
and he starts to tell her for the thirtieth time: 'Miriam, Miriam,
I'm so much in love with you. Let me kiss you, Miriam. Please.
Just kiss you. I can't go on like this . . .' But all she does is
smile her orchard smile and stroke his hand and even laugh and
say: 'It mustn't be like that, Dr O. It can only be friendship.'
Why? He keeps asking her, *Why can it only be friendship?* Then
he won't let her answer. He knows the answer: *It's all I want.*
Yet how can this be? When he wants, wants, wants her night
after night. His wanting's like an animal in him, a jungle male in
its spring season sounding its hullabaloo over all the acres of
veldt and forest and brimming river. *Primitive. Man, in love, is
primitive.* His books and manuscripts, all his careful work he
neglects. The nourishment has gone from them. He's amazed

they satisfied him for so long. They and Bernice. He's sorry for his neglect of Bernice. He can't bear to think what she's feeling, but he won't let her talk to him about any of it. He just walks away. 'I'm sorry, Bernice,' he says and walks away from her. *She is not Miriam's equal.*

'Come and talk to Leni, Oz.' Thomas is at Dr O's side. He lets himself be led over to the corner, near a potted palm, where Leni sits in her throne. He stoops and kisses her hand flamboyantly. She looks up at him. This heavy, loyal, intelligent man. What's Miriam up to, making him suffer like this? Like Roddy in his hurting wellingtons. He suffered. He wrote letters saying, boorishly, *I can't bang my wife any more.* Silly Roddy. Silly Oz, acting like a toddler.

'What are we going to do about you, Oz?' she says with her witch's smile.

'Do, Leni?'

'Yes. About you and Miriam.'

Dr O blushes like a child and straightens up. *Help me Leni,* he wants to say. He wishes Thomas would go so that he could talk to her privately.

'I'm very pleased,' he stammers, gesturing at the crowded room, 'it's such a success. I don't think Miriam dreamed it would go so well.'

Leni passes Thomas her glass and asks him to refill it for her. In the thicket of heads, he can spy Perdita's corn-coloured hair and he walks towards her. Though he doesn't admire watercolours, he feels delighted for Miriam and suddenly radiantly happy in his life. Only the image of his father, alone in the fields Miriam has sketched, troubles him slightly and he wonders if he won't take Perdita out to Pomerac to see him.

'Sit down, Oz,' says Leni and gestures to a black plastic chair. He tumbles into it with a sigh and it creaks under his weight. 'Stop *toddling!*' she says. And he casts her a look of real agony.

'Yes, I know, Oz,' she says, gently for Leni, a tender, chiding voice. 'What you have to realise, darling, is that Miriam's learning to be obstinate. She refuses to obey anyone any more. Certainly not me. She looks after me wonderfully, but she absolutely won't do what I say. I'm beginning to admire her.'

'I admire her, Leni,' Dr O says, casting a look in the direction of Miriam's coral frock, 'too much, I suppose. I admire her too much . . .'

'And of course she's loving it. She pretends she's indifferent, but at fifty one can't be indifferent, n'est ce pas?'

'I don't know Leni. Heavens, I don't know what to think, what to hope . . .'

'Just be sensible, Oz. Play the game.'

'What game?'

'Be mercurial, Oz! Be fantastical! Do some disappearing tricks. Stop all this constancy.'

'I can't stop what I feel.'

'Of course you can't. But you can stop *showing* it. You're not three years old, are you? You're not still *teething*.'

'That's where you're wrong, Leni. In love I am like this. My experience is . . .'

'What about Atwood?'

'What?'

'Use Atwood.'

'What, Leni?'

'Make Miriam jealous. Let her know you're still involved with Atwood.'

'But I've told her I'm not.'

'Well, how silly of you. Why did you do that?'

'Because it's the truth.'

'Yes, but this is love, Oz. You've got to practise a little deceit.'

'But I don't seem able . . .'

'What? Don't seem able to what?'

'To lie. I can't.'

'Then try.'

'I can't, Leni.'

'Then you don't deserve her, Oz.'

'Well, I probably don't "deserve" her.'

'Oh, don't be silly.'

'I'm not up to all this. I'm going crazy.'

'So, be the magician. It's your only hope.'

'You mean, go back to Bernice?'

'Or *seem* to. It's the seeming that's important. And stop paying for dinners out. You can't afford it.'

Leni says this with finality. *The conjurer snaps the box shut.* Dr O's heart is thumping like a lion's tail. Leni holds out a white, frail hand and her fingers touch his tweed jacket: a soft butterfly landing there.

'You've got time, Oz,' she says. 'She won't go back to France.'

'Ever?'

'I don't know about ever. She won't go back yet. Whether she goes back eventually is up to you.'

'I'd like to marry her,' says Dr O and swallows, as if this admission chokes him.

'Of course you would,' says Leni, 'but I can't imagine why you thought it'd be easy. Perhaps you don't understand women, Oz?'

'No, I don't,' says Dr O. 'I've never needed to till now.'

Leni looks at him sadly. Takes away her butterfly hand. She's made it clear, *I'm on your side*, but more for him she can't do. She feels an arm on her shoulder and turns to see Gary, very splendid tonight in a magenta shirt, smiling down at her.

'Okay, Mother sweet?'

'Yes, Gary. Where are you off to, darling, you look so wonderful.'

'Oh, you know. Out.'

'Is Gabriel here?'

'No, alas. He wasn't able.'

'But you're meeting him later on?'

'Yes. After his rehearsal.'

'You know Oz of course.'

Gary and Dr O look up and each nods an awkward greeting. They're like two different species, Leni notes with a secret smile. If only Oz could acquire some of Gary's dazzle . . .

'I met your colleague on Wednesday,' Gary says to Dr O. 'By the river.'

'My colleague?'

'Yes. Miss Atwood. She and I seem to enjoy the same bit of river.'

Dr O looks petrified, as if news of a rail disaster or a tenement fire had suddenly reached him.

'Ah,' he says. 'Yes. Yes, yes.'

He didn't know Bernice took herself off to the river. The river and Bernice seem quite alien to each other and immediately he's frightened for her. His confused and embattled mind dresses her in Ophelia's white skirts: Ophelia gathering her rue.

On this same evening, as the red 'sold' stickers go up on Miriam's watercolours of Pomerac, Mme de la Brosse arrives in her house and her maid, Lisette, draws the heavy, timeworn drapes of the salon across the winter night.

'I'm afraid it's very cold, Madame.'

'Yes. I'll have my supper in here, by the fire.'

She sits in the armchair Anatole used to favour, still wearing her Paris suit and a silk scarf at her neck. They're burning applewood this year – one of the old, tired orchards cut down at last.

'Shall we replant, Madame?' her manager had asked, and she'd hesitated. Her heart isn't in this land any more. She doesn't want to spend money on hundreds of new young trees which will all outlast her. Better to redecorate the bedroom of her Paris flat, plant 'orchards' there, where at least she'll see them. So she remains undecided. The old trees are torn out and some of them saved and stacked for burning, but the field where they grew is left to seed itself with thistles.

When she looks round at the room, lit with yellowy light from the fire and from two table lamps in the shape of cannons, she feels weary with its familiarity and tired in its shabbiness. She remembers her father-in-law in it, pouring port from his boxed decanters, his leather boots creaking, his slicked hair smelling of almond oil. He loved Pomerac. He planted the trees she's just cut down. He was an expert in soil analysis and worked hard to improve his vineyards. His military mind drilled the land into obedience. Now she lets it go. The morale of her manager is low and production is down, year after year. She stares at the dancing fire and decides, I've got to be rid of it.

Lisette puts up a gate-legged table in front of Madame's

armchair and lays it with the heavy old de la Brosse knives and forks and beige lace mats for her plate and glass. Outside, the stumps of limes stand guard on a clear, star-laden night and frost glimmers in the furrows of the Pomerac lanes. *Douce Nuit. Sainte Nuit.* With the arrival of Mme de la Brosse, Christmas isn't far off. The children are dreaming of pencil boxes, the wooden swivel kind their parents told them they once got. Gervaise is sizing up her geese, deciding which one to fatten. And the maid, Lisette, can't refrain from asking: 'We're giving wine after midnight mass as usual, Madame?' Because she senses in Mme de la Brosse her weariness of the place. I'm a Parisian now, say her clothes, her subdued smile, her lack of appetite for the big meal Lisette has prepared.

'Wine at Christmas?' says Mme de la Brosse, 'Yes I suppose it'll be expected. I suppose we must carry on the tradition.' But then she thinks, this will have to be the last year. I can't keep on and on. In the spring, I'll sell.

Few people write to her at the Pomerac house. Invoices have come, for gutters repaired, from the stonemason who has rebuilt a section of the garden wall. Among these is an invitation from Hervé Prière to a dinner party, enclosing a note which explains: *I'm spending three months of the winter in Florida – a retirement present I have looked forward to for some time. So this is a farewell dinner. Please do accept.* And she thinks with envy of Hervé getting out of an aeroplane onto warm tarmac and feeling in the hot wind no trace of winter. The cycle of her year, with these lonely visits to this once-fine, once-grand house has begun to irritate her. Better far to abandon it and spend the cold months travelling. Better to see London and New York with their streets lit up and their hotels warm than the hard, simple, earth-reared, toil-blinded faces of the people of Pomerac.

Lisette takes away her half-eaten meal and brings her coffee in a silver pot. She sits back and stares into the burning apple logs. That's it, she thinks. It's decided. Years of obedience to Anatole's memory fall away. She lights a cigarette and feels herself relax. At least in that high bed upstairs she will sleep well.

'Goodnight, Madame,' says Lisette at the door and Mme de

la Brosse turns in the tall chair and smiles at her maid. Lisette's eyes are bright and nervous when she says: 'Oh I forgot to tell you, Madame. We have something new in Pomerac since your last visit.'

Mme de la Brosse inserts her cigarette into her Dupont holder and inquires without any interest: 'Something new?'

'Yes,' says Lisette, 'down at the English house. A swimming pool.'

'A *swimming pool*?'

'Yes. Quite a few of the village people are helping to build it.'

How strange, she thinks. Just when I'm giving it up, someone is starting something here, someone is building. How perverse. And a pool, *mon dieu*. A desecration. A vulgarity.

'Was permission granted from the Mairie for the pool?'

'I don't know, Madame.'

'You don't know? Well we must find out. Nothing can be built here without permission. Good night, Lisette.'

Dismissed, the maid retreats into the big, draughty kitchen and begins to wash up the crockery. She's just old enough to remember a time when five-course banquets were prepared here and thirty bottles of wine were drunk in one night.

While Mme de la Brosse lies and dreams of a life reduced and simplified to the small, pleasant trafficking she does to and from the Place St Sulpice, the Maréchal wakes in the frosty quiet and finds on his lips the words: *So it's here, then*. His head is burning hot. He moves it and sees at the window the impish faces of his sons, grinning and laughing and moving their spread hands backwards and forwards like shoe-shufflers, a little cheeky dance. They're eight or nine. They wear their lives like bobble hats, easily, jauntily. The Maréchal stares. 'You don't take me in,' he says to his children, 'you don't convince me.' So they back off, still grinning and showing their pink palms. 'What boys!' he mutters into his damp pillow and curses the need these ghosts have woken in him to pee. Though his head burns, his body in its ancient bedding feels cold and weak. Without lighting his lamp, he leans over and reaches for the chipped china pot he keeps under his cot and slides it out. He looks at it. For years and years Eulalie used to hitch up her pinch-pleated nightgowns and settle down on this potty like a nesting hen. So sweet and white. So modest in her little performance. She never let you see her yellow streams. He crawls out of the bed, and the pyjamas smelling of earth, smelling of his damp habitation, fall round his knees and he kneels in front of the pot as if before his Maker, with his pale legs shivering and his hands cupping what he calls these days 'my old bunch of figs'. A luminous fat half-moon etches the pot. As he pees, he silently admires: I'm pissing streams of light! But in the fire that binds his head flickers the truth that woke him: *It's here then: this is the beginning of the road down: Ste Catherine is waiting* . . .

Though he manages to pull up his pyjamas and tumble back into his bed, he feels trembly in the dark as if he'd shed his strength like a carapace. *Cover me*, he whispers. Tears of helplessness start in his owl's eyes. Deep in his throat the prairie grass sings with the dry souls of Eulalie and his dead sons, beckoning him out.

At sunrise he's still strong enough to get to his door and poke his shaggy head out into the frosty lane and call to one of the children setting out for school, 'Fetch Gervaise. Go quickly.' When she comes, wearing a worried frown, he's lying on his back and remembering the day of her grandfather's funeral and the snow that fell in the churchyard, but these memories are as insubstantial as snow. They fall and vanish and, when Gervaise bends over him, the Maréchal believes for a brief second that it's Eulalie on her way to Ste Catherine with her sewing box, and to the mortification of Gervaise he mumbles forlornly, 'Goodbye, my chicken. Take care of yourself.'

'Maréchal!' Gervaise strokes his cheek gently but her voice is stern. She's come running to him with her shallow chest full of fear. 'Maréchal! It's me, Gervaise. Tell me what's happened.'

He focuses on her face. Eulalie with her bindings and her broderies vanishes.

'Oh Gervaise . . .'

'What's the matter, Maréchal? Aren't you well?'

'It's got me, Gervaise . . .'

'What has? Try to make sense, Maréchal.'

'They've got me.'

'Who?'

'Those boxmakers at Ste Catherine.'

So her fear grows. She feels her fear not just in her loudly beating heart but gathering in her sinuses so that her nose twitches like a rabbit's.

'Can't you get up, Maréchal?'

'I'm too weak, Gervaise. I'm as weak as a new lamb.'

His face is very hot under her hand.

'Are you in pain?'

He smiles his bird's smile.

'Pain? We're all in agony from the day we're born!'

'Special pain. In your chest? In your stomach?'

'Everywhere. I tell you, they've got me.'

'I'll call the doctor.'

'Stay with me, Gervaise.'

'Yes, yes. I'll stay. We'll get you up to my house.'

'That's good. I don't want to die in the hospital with those gawpers.'

Gervaise finds clean rugs in an upstairs blanket box and she spreads these over the Maréchal's cot. The schoolchildren, the message-carriers of Pomerac, are told to call at the Ste Catherine surgery, where Hervé Prière is toiling out his final week of duty. Gervaise empties the Maréchal's pot, boils a kettle and brings him a drink of hot honey and water.

Up at her own house, Mallélou is still sleeping with his face turned to the ski-ing poster, but Xavier has been awake since first light, waking in surprise to another day of his infatuation, already aching for his meeting with Agnès. 'Xavier!' Gervaise has called on her way to the Maréchal's room. 'You and Klaus see to the cows this morning.' So his city hands, so swift at the Babyfoot table, so deft with bar change and fag-rolling and card playing and the eating of oysters, now tug at the leathery teats of the cows while Klaus makes coffee and sets out bread and ham and warms his rump at the stove.

Gervaise and the Maréchal wait. The Maréchal remembers his children's impish faces at his window and tells Gervaise, 'I saw ghosts this morning. Who'd have thought ghosts would come here? I think it's that swimming pool.'

'What's that got to do with the pool?'

'Disturbing the earth. We do too much of that in this time of ours.'

'I didn't know you were superstitious.'

'I'm not Gervaise. I'm just old. Old men understand certain things.'

'But not how to look after yourself.'

'Well I've done it for twenty years.'

'But you've let yourself catch a chill.'

'That's not a chill, my poor Gervaise. That's death.'

Sitting tall and pale, driving his heavy car, Hervé Prière arrives at the Maréchal's house, anxiously scanning the lane for any sign of Nadia. These days, he dislikes coming to Pomerac. The smell and the cold of the Maréchal's decrepit room enter his body and go round in his veins. When he looks at the old man and listens to his shallow breaths, he feels only the weight of their impending obliteration, the marble that will lie on them. Stone, at least, is clean, though. Even France's horrendous wars are, thank God, remembered in smooth granite and lead and gold. Frailty and decay are, finally, too much for Dr Prière.

'Swelling?' he asks coldly.

'Eh?' says the Maréchal.

'Any swelling in the groin or neck?'

'I don't know, Monsieur.'

'We'll feel, then.'

His long, cold fingers press the Maréchal's stubbly neck and his almost hairless groin. There is some swelling. Hervé nods his head at his own diagnosis, knowing as he pronounces it that the old man's life is numbered in weeks or even days.

'He has mumps,' he tells Gervaise, '*la parotidite*. There's an epidemic at the school.'

'Oh,' says the Maréchal, as Hervé begins to pack away his things, 'that's why the boys came to the window. To give me their diseases.'

An hour later, the Maréchal is carried up to Gervaise's house in Klaus's arms and laid gently in the hand-painted bed from

Heidelberg. With a three-day beard on him, Mallélou shuffles in
and stares at him. We're paying him back finally, he thinks, for
all the years of borrowing. He'll have the last word by dying in
our house. But the ghosts have gone. The Maréchal's sleeping.
Gervaise has taken charge. The German bed is soft and large
and the clean sheets smell of lavender, reminding him of Eulalie's
petticoats. He doesn't see Mallélou staring. He sleeps in the
knowledge that when he wakes, he'll only have to lie still and
listen to hear, not far away, the sound of Gervaise's voice.

When two o'clock sounds on the Pomerac hill Xavier is driving
furiously in Mallélou's old *fourgon* down a silent, sandy track in
the heart of Ste Catherine's woods. A plantation of pines bends
and sighs in the slight wind. Where the track turns left, these
give way to oaks and chestnuts and beeches, and it's here in
the belly of the forest, where only the woodmen come, that he
expects to see Agnès waiting for him at the wheel of Hervé's
car. She isn't there. Xavier's first thought is, she came and went
and didn't wait for me, and his next thought is, she's decided
against me. She's gone back to Paris and her soldier-boy.
    He drives the *fourgon* off the track and the dead beechleaves
fly up round the wheels. He switches off the engine, gets out
of the car and stands anxiously listening for the sound of Agnès's
approach. He lights a cigarette. He can still hear the sighing
of the pines, though the larger trees are motionless, damp,
exhausted in their year's leafcrop that now lies all around them,
waiting sternly for spring. In Xavier's own heart is a similar
extraordinary expectation. Like them, he waits. His Bordeaux
life, the pettiness, the hopelessness, he treads these down,
kicks them into the past. Even his prison-dread falls away, as if
the crime was years ago, already forgotten and forgiven, a thing
he did as a boy. His eczema is healed. His work in the fields and
on Larry's pool has brought back his strength. If Nadia at her
window saw him coming up the Pomerac hill she would see, in
these days of his passion, a fine and proud face, the pretty colt
grown to a handsome and sharp-eyed man, a lover to make her
little foreign heart stop as it stopped in the pastry shop when
Uncle Leopold laid his big paw on her head. But what does

Agnès see as she bounds in Hervé's car towards Xavier, waiting under the silent trees? She's running to him fast, wildly. Her eyes aren't lowered in their usual obedience to orderly things, they're wide-open, pleading eyes. *Devour me*, they say. *Break me.* They see a fleeting grandeur of love, a feast to snatch and swallow. *Kill me with love. Kill me before the future comes!*

He's at her car door. He helps her out and binds her to him. The smell of her steals away his breath. No woman he's ever held has had this sweet, irresistible smell. *I want it forever*, says his entranced mind. *Marry me.* She kisses him so hard, his lip is bruised. Her body hurries him. Her desire and not his love, which is a slower thing, a marvelling spectator, hauls him swiftly to his male buck's antics, butting up into her, the pushing, braying, blunt-snouted animal while her legs flail his back, while she screams and bites and twists her head on its bed of earth and yells to heaven in her pleasure and tears his seed from him like an explosion of flowers.

He stays in her but his head falls. He wants to love her more slowly than this, love her with words and small caresses, with his humanity. He's not her stud, her buck, her bull. He adores her with the core of his being. He cups her head in his arms and holds it in the hollow of his shoulder. *Marry me.* The air is freezing on his naked bottom and legs. *The wind at my back.* This phrase and the cold December ground fill him with a longing for spring and a house of his own and Agnès with him in a high bed.

'Marry me, Agnès.'

'Don't talk, Xavier.'

'Why, "don't talk"?'

'Because.'

'Tell me why. I want to talk to you.'

'But I just want to hold you.'

Obediently he lies down again and she begins to nibble at his neck and lick it and he laughs. Hearing no answering laugh from her, he looks down at her face and it's serious and frantic as she says, 'I want to come again. I need to come.'

He kisses her gently and asks, 'Do you love me, Agnès?'

'Don't I show it?' she says.

'I can't live without you.'

'Yes. I think about it all the time.'

'Think about what?'

'This. Fucking.'

'Am I good? Am I a good lover?'

'Yes. Make me come, Xavier. It's so fantastic.'

'Why won't you marry me?'

'I didn't say I wouldn't.'

'Will you?'

'I don't know. Please make me come.'

'You won't marry your soldier, will you?'

'I don't know.'

'Agnès . . .'

'Oh, hurry. I need to come. I have to.'

'Just tell me there's some future, Agnès . . .'

'Of course there is.'

'You're not lying?'

'No.'

So slowly and tenderly and with an anxious kind of hope Xavier gets onto his knees and buries his worshipping head between her spread legs.

No more than an hour passes before she's back in the car and driving away from him. He watches her till she's out of sight, then stares at the track that's taken her away. This is all we have, he thinks, this hurried ritual. And suddenly, he's no longer content with these brief, wild meetings. He wants more than anything he's ever wanted, to be with her in her bedroom in Hervé's house and hold her in his arms all night, easy and intimate and slow, like the student couple to whom he gave the key to his cast-off room. Strange how they've become his model. He suspects it's because they, with their books and their difficult music and their odd knowledge of other countries' wars, understood in private what each was giving and what, in the easy logic of their particular love, each took.

He drives, without hurrying, wrapped in his plans for his future with Agnès, back to Pomerac. Half way there, he notices that his lip is bleeding.

She's home by this time, running in, preparing tea for Hervé before the evening surgery. She feels dizzy and tired from her own pleasure. She sits gratefully by the fire in the bureau and takes up the letter from Luc that has arrived that morning. She learns from it that her mother has invited him to stay for Christmas.

Foot by foot, the big sunken box that the pool now is, is growing. Klaus and Larry, wearing baggy *bleus* from the Périgueux market, seem to be fighting back the descending winter, fighting back each afternoon's earlier and earlier sunset with their busy mixing and shovelling and pouring and smoothing of concrete. Gervaise, hurrying from the Maréchal's bedside, chivvying Mallélou to dress himself and not shame her by flopping round the house all day in pyjamas, scuttles over the earth mounds with bowls of coffee and looks fondly at the new straight walls and the high colour in Klaus's cheeks:
'Mon dieu, c'est formidable, quand même!'
'We're not far from the mosaic, Gervaise,' says Klaus with huge pride. His confectioner's soul and his easy love of God make him long for this magnificent challenge. The thousands of black and white facets waiting for his attention in cardboard boxes mesmerise him and urge him on. He works as hard as two men. Larry is amazed at the speed now being achieved and senses that the German has brought to his vision a kind of superstitious luck. Larry's no longer building the pool for Miriam, not even for Agnès though his mind still seats her at its edge, but for the thing itself, for Pomerac. On certain days, he hears the water already in it, sees its satisfying reflections, Nadia's 'loops of brightness' made even more dazzling by the cathedral colours under the surface. Though darkness breaks further into each day, and up and down the village families are making Christmas garlands, Larry no longer feels cold. His house is dusty and neglected. He's stopped imitating the way Miriam used to care for it. Let it sit and wait for her. Let it bear the burden of her neglect, not him. He's forging *Aquazure France*. He's doing what was asked of him: beginning again.
Only his nights are sad. Miriam. Agnès. Neither of them are with him, nor even thinking of him. This suspicion that he's been

let go even from the thoughts of his wife makes him feel small.
You can hold people as tenderly in your head as in your arms. He
tries his sleep trick, the inventions. But the anxious, commercial,
opportunistic Larry of the *Aquazure* days is going; and gone,
with the moderating of his ambitions, is the old knack of inventing
that bludgeoned his brain to sleep for so many years. Instead
he finds himself remembering Miriam's habits and gestures. The
stern way she looked at herself in the mirror. The old fashioned
daily brushing of her hair. Her peculiar wearing of la robe. The
way she drove the Granada, sitting bolt upright. The hardness
of her chest as if, under her breasts, she was made of steel.
Her fat tears. Her unfussy way of waking. Her Ackerman pride.
Her eyes in the landscape. The feel of her tongue in his mouth.

In the direction of Agnès he tries not to glance. But there she
is at his mind's edge: her soft clothes, her skin of an English
schoolgirl, her plump hands folding, straightening, gathering,
arranging, polishing, patting, smoothing, touching. He's caught
between Miriam's familiar mouth and Agnès's unfamiliar caressing hand. What heaven to take both these women in his arms.
What peace.

He's up as early as Gervaise now, keen to shrug off the
hopeless nights. He makes coffee the French way, very strong,
with boiled milk, and eats hungrily from the loaves Klaus brings
him every second day. He sees the sun come up and the cows
come bumping up the lane. He puts on his *bleus* and feels
impatient to start work. Some mornings the frost is so hard he's
afraid he'll find cracks in the new concrete but the sides are
holding. He pats the pool walls like the neck of a faithful horse.
Good girl. Keep going. Keep going. The lean-to he's made for the
filter plant is topped out with a smart little roof of coral tiles. As
he sits up there, putting them on, he remembers Miriam had a
favourite dress of this exact colour.

Then, one afternoon, the concreting is finished. Klaus looks
at the smooth walls, the two sets of perfect, gently curving
steps (one set under the main cupola, one in the apsidal chapel)
and throws his trowel in the air with joy. *'Ich liebe dich, Larry!
Ich liebe dich!'*

'Tomorrow we start the mosaic, Klaus.'

'Oh, my God, this is so wonderful!'

'We could finish by Christmas.'

'Look at this! All with our hands!'

It's almost dark. Only the faces of the two men stand out palely. With the blue dusk falling on them in their pit, they feel acutely both the ridiculousness and the wonder of their achievement. They sit down at the deep end wall and laugh.

That evening, after drinking a celebratory schnaps with Klaus, while Mallélou sits and watches the television and ignores them and Gervaise spoons broth into the Maréchal's fever-cracked mouth, Larry drives down to Mme Carcanet's and buys two bottles of vodka. Tonight, a landmark night in the rebirth of *Aquazure*, he has decided he and Nadia will for once drown their sorrows in style.

There's no *snotty gulashnova* simmering behind the Japanese screen when Larry arrives and Nadia apologises.

'If you had tell me, my darling, we were celebrating, I could have make you some blinis with salmon eggs.'

'Oh, it doesn't matter, Nadia.'

'But you know all I have is a little saucisson.'

'I didn't come for a meal.'

'Well, I tell you, I'll put out the saucisson and we can nobble it.'

'Nibble, Nadia.'

'Nibble, nobble, I don't know you're so pedantical . . . Now you pour the bloody vodka and I'm tell you some important decision I make.'

As Larry pours the drinks he remembers that until he met Nadia he'd never even tried vodka. Now, because it's her one luxury, he's come to reverence the taste of it. He passes Nadia her glass and raises his own.

'To us!'

She looks at him quizzically. 'To *us*, Larry? You think we are coupling?'

'Well, to you and me, perhaps I should have said. Because we're the ones here.'

'And we don't drink to our absent friends?'

'If you like.'

'Well, I think.'

'To them, then.'

'Yes. To them. Though I tell you what I'm think this morning when I wake up: I think we never see them again, and you know I feel so desolated I just hug in my bed and not get up.'

'We will see them again, Nadia.'

'No. I don't think.'

'You mean Hervé and Miriam?'

'Yes. And not only these two.'

'You believe Hervé won't come back from America?'

'Well, not for Nadia. No one comes back for Nadia, so you know what I decide?'

'Wait a minute, Nadia. You said you don't think Miriam's coming back either?'

'Oh how can I know, my dear? What's my feeling? Right or wrong?'

Larry sits down, takes a sip of vodka, and looks apprehensively at Nadia. She pats her hair and looks away from him out of the uncurtained window. He feels chill, tired suddenly from his day's labours on the pool.

'I don't know why you say that about Miriam, Nadia.'

'I don't say. I *feel*. Maybe that fucking Leni kicks her can and she comes back after all. But I wonder. Because what is take so long, you know?'

'Her exhibition.'

'Yes. But this is over now, no?'

'I can't remember which night it opened.'

'So you are forgetting her a little too, Larry. You see? We live for all these days and years with this one person and saying all the time, my dear one, the companion of my life's trip, and so, and chosing so nice foulards or the favourite confectionery at Christmas and for the birthday, and then what? They are leaving us for the loony bowl or the bed of the mother. And I think when we're old we're remembering them and not feeling so happy. We're finding some old foulard we gave in the bottom drawer and some moths have come and eating holes in the foulard and the so beautiful colours of it are gone . . .'

'Oh stop it, Nadia!'

'Well, I just say what is true.'

'No you don't. As long as I've known you, you've hardly given Claude a thought.'

'But today I find this foulard.'

'What?'

'Yes. I find it. I can show you.'

'Claude's?'

'Of course. I don't have so many men's things in my drawers.'

Larry sips to hide his smile.

'And the scarf had the moth in it?'

'No. But it's so thin, you know. Like a moth wing. And so I decide.'

'Decide what?'

'That you are right, my friend. On all matters I don't say, but for this one thing, you are right.'

'Well, that's a relief. What am I right about, Nadia?'

'I must go to see Claude.'

Larry looks up at her. Her little foxy eyes seem clouded and grave. It's as if she's announced her own death.

'When?' he asks gently.

'At Christmas. I can buy a new foulard to take. No? But I don't know if let him wear these things or if they're so suspicious he hangs himself with it and they take it away. What you think?'

'I don't know.'

'I never go there because I have such the fear of the institution, you know. Even in my school, I'm writing my name on my desk and on my peg and every little place that is mine. Nadia Poniatowski. Nadia Poniatowski. Everywhere I can write it. So I won't lose myself.'

'Would you like me to come with you, Nadia?'

'Well, you know, my bean, I would feel so grateful. I don't persuade. Don't think.'

'No. I'll gladly come with you.'

'But you don't imagine we're on a pic-nic, you know.'

'What, Nadia?'

'These adjustment places, they're so bad, you know.'

'If they're so bad, Nadia, why's Claude left in there?'

'Oh he's not knowing, Larry. You ask Claude, is it summer, is it winter and he's telling you, summer in my ears, winter in my arse, or some nonsense like this. So what's this place to him? His home, you see. Like Pomerac is yours.'

Home. Larry picks up the vodka bottle. Home. The only warm light he's sat in for weeks was the candlelight of Gervaise's birthday feast. He's always thought of home as a place kindly lit. His house here is lit like a workshop with cheap strip lights. When they bought it, they never imagined winters in it.

The theatre is filling up. At the edge of the second row, with Leni's wheelchair drawn up next to him, Gary keeps glancing behind him to see whether people are still coming in. He wants a good audience and hopes all the press are there, yet inside his green velour suit feels cavernous with apprehension. He wonders if Gabriel's first speech won't be too momentous for him: . . . *but that I love the gentle Desdemona* . . . He fusses with the programme, staring at the director's name: Piers Duckworth. Piers and Gabriel. Gabriel and Piers. A winged couple. Stars. A spangled future leaving the Wednesday Man behind . . .

'All right, Gary dear?'

Leni is pale in her chair. Wrapped in an old fur stole, she reminds Gary of decrepit royalty. Pushing her in, he felt very protective of her, like a loyal equerry. People made way. They were glanced at like celebrities.

'Yes. Will you be comfortable, do you think?'

'I like this little theatre, even though the heating's so poor. What are the costumes like, d'you know?'

'Oh, basic drapery. Nothing wonderful.'

'I saw a performance of this play here years ago where they all seemed to be wearing yellow rugs. It was most peculiar.'

'Designers like to make their marks.'

'Quite, but what a silly mark to make. Perhaps the thing was sponsored by Colman's Mustard.'

'Well, or Bird's!'

'Oh yes, Bird's! I adore custard, you know.'

The lights begin to go from the auditorium. Leni takes off her gloves and settles them in her lap. She glances anxiously at Gary and slips a parchment hand through his arm.

'I think, darling,' she whispers to him, 'you ought to take off your hat. Or they'll be prodding you from the row behind.'

In his nervousness, Gary had forgotten Leni's 'first night present' to him, bought by Miriam, a thirties'-style trilby, pale grey with a broad brim, the hat to compliment his new haircut. He snatches it off and rests it carefully on his knee. He's aware of looking modish and fine. The lights are gone now, the darkness settling down round them like a soft bird. Unseen, Gabriel waits, the whole play in his head. Gary marvels. Actors know plays like musicians know symphonies. Every move. Every rill. Today, Billy Skipper had to recite eight lines of Coleridge in assembly and got stuck at line 4. Gabriel's taken it all into him, to the last syllable. The coal's mined. Now the fire . . .

Gary gasps as the fierce lights come up and Roderigo and Iago come on. He's aware of the actors' feet very near him. Vulnerable. Actors are flesh. Yet there are flames to go through. Leni's hand tightens on his velvet arm. He feels boiling hot, slightly sick. Thank heaven Leni's there. She was the right choice because she's seen it, she knows it can be got through – *Othello* in yellow rugs – he must have faith . . .

He's glad the first scene's quite long, preparing him for Othello's entrance. During it, barely taking in what's being said, he tries to calm himself with sensible breathing. The actor playing Iago is young, playing him kittenish, spiteful, petty. He moves himself about like a little dark Puck. Yes, Gary thinks, this could be right. It's the young who show us our worst selves. And he sees himself old, still teaching Conrad, taunted by younger and younger seeming boys.

But Gabriel's on now. Beside the puckish Iago he looks huge. His gestures are slow. He's like a big gold and ebony statue. Gary fears for this slowness. Was it Piers's idea? Express his slowness to realise he's being fooled in lazy body movement? The muscle-bound soldier? The gullible Moor? He risks to push out the play's length. Gary coughs with irritation and looks sadly at Gabriel's feet, where the pink colour of the soles curves round the toes. Leni takes her hand from his arm and Gary

wonders if this isn't a sign of disapproval, if she won't say at the
interval, 'Well, it's a shame they've understood it all wrong.'

Then Desdemona is sent for. Small and blonde, with earnest
pale hands seeking out the touch of Othello constantly, she
starts to bring his slow, deliberate gestures into another focus.
You feel the Moor's heat. He's the dark, bountiful earth where
this little fritillary of a woman has planted herself. Already, you
weep at his coming rejection of her. They play their present
need of each other to perfection: *I have but an hour of love* . . .
You don't doubt what kind of love this is. Gary starts to marvel
at the ease with which his lover can seem to be this woman's
husband. The tenderness, the eyes caressing, the constant
touching and holding. The audience are settled now, concentrat-
ing. Leni holds herself still and taut. You feel the play begin to
catch hold.

There's no muddling or stumbling. Piers has moved his actors
cleanly through the verse. Meanings appear. Buds of meaning
fatten to revelation. Cassio is a curly-headed beauty. Puck
buzzes his venomous aside like a mosquito . . . *as little a web
as this will ensnare as great a fly as Cassio*. And when at last
Iago comes to Othello with his first but terrible: *Look to your
wife, observe her well with Cassio*, Gary is so moved by Gabriel's
look of pain, is so certain that all the weeks spent mining this
performance are at last yielding something memorable, that he
turns to Leni to retake possession of her hand.

It's not very dark in Row B. Light from the stage is reflected
in the line of faces looking up. And it's in this half-light, as of a
coming dusk, that Gary sees Leni's head fallen sideways onto
the shoulders of her fur stole, her mouth wide and her tongue
gaping, her eyes staring, blind as glass into the empty space
above them. The sight of this tears from him a peculiar scream
and he's next aware of what seems to him like a minute of
absolute silence. Have the actors stopped talking? There's a
soundless shuffling and turning of heads. A long strand of saliva
falls from the corner of Leni's mouth down onto her fur. Her
face is terrible: the witch in the lap of her demon. Gary observes
himself lift up his grey hat and cover the face with it. He knows
he must get to his feet. *Get her out. Ger her out*, he instructs

himself. Sound returns. He can hear someone running down one
of the aisles. On the stage he can hear the cadences of Gabriel's
voice, but not the words. People have left their seats. A posse
of heads is staring down at him and at Leni's dead face covered
by his hat. Still he can't stand up. He's clinging frantically to the
arm of his seat. He thinks he may be going to vomit. The saliva
strand . . . the witch in her trance . . . The running stops. A
man he doesn't know asks the posse to go back to their seats.
This man's hands are on Leni's chair. He seems to have taken
charge. Gary can hear his own breathing has a peculiar note to
it and breath comes hard. Death suffocates. The witch dies in
the dark at the edge of the stage . . . He's wailing. He can hear
it. Leni is wheeled round away from him. A man leans in from
the space where the chair was and gently takes his arm, helping
him up. So he's standing now, so tall above all the seated people,
it's as if his legs were six feet long. They gape at him. At his
back he hears Gabriel throw himself into his first jealous agonies:
She's gone, I am abused, and my relief must be to loathe her . . .
'Let's go out,' says the stranger holding his arm. Ahead of him,
Leni's being pushed through a door and he sees the hat fall off
into her lap. 'Mother!' he wails, but she's gone through the door
and the stranger's grip tightens on his arm. 'Come on, sir.
You're all right . . .'

Leni. Leni Ackerman. In the foyer they lift her onto the
ambulance stretcher. Gary sits on a step and cries and watches
them. She's covered up with a red blanket. Leni. Mother. They
bring him tea in a mug saying *I love NY*. Someone points him
out to the ambulancemen who are fastening straps round Leni's
body. They turn and look at him and nod. They carry her away.
Beyond reach. Beyond sight. Where will they take her? Where
do bodies go? In Russia they're laid out in open coffins but their
mouths and eyes are shut before the people trudge past. The
tea's foul, far too thick. He sets the mug down. He's never been
in a morgue. Will they put her in a drawer?

He looks up. The ambulancemen have come back and are
walking towards him. Why couldn't she have died in her bed, in
the kind light of the Chinese lamp? She died without a sound.
None. Just the mouth dropping and the head falling, sideways.

Bundled away by strangers. 'I'm her son,' he says indistinctly to the ambulancemen. Both are middle-aged men with clean, tightly buttoned uniforms. Their breath smells faintly of pepper. They say, with quiet dignity, 'We're very, very sorry, sir.' They help Gary up and he's led like a prisoner between them out into the waiting night. The first snow is falling.

'This snow,' says Miriam the next day, standing at the kitchen window, 'this snow is most peculiar, Gary.'

She means the quiet. She means the way it's come when in the house there's the silence of Leni's death. It wraps them and isolates them. All life except their little kitchen huddle feels miles away, out of reach.

Unshaven and tired, Gary's wrapped in his quilted dressing gown. He's sitting at the table, quietly waiting.

'The trouble about the snow,' says Miriam, 'is there are so many people to be told and lots of them will want to come here and I suppose travelling's going to be impossible.'

Gary nods. In his lilac room, he heard the early morning weather forecast. More snow is coming from Scotland. In Ayrshire sheep are marooned on high ground.

'I'll go to the study and do some telephoning,' Miriam says.

'Yes,' says Gary, absentmindedly.

'What are you going to do, Gary?'

His hands are folded, wrist-on-wrist, inside the arms of his gown. With each thumb and forefinger, he circles the bone of his arm.

'I'll just sit, Miriam.'

She goes out of the kitchen and he hears her open and close the study door. Now he thinks, she'll call them all to her, her family. In this silence of the snow he envies her the blood ties she's forged. So easy, when you're loved, to put on independence. What Leni's absence wakes in him is a longing for certainty, for a trusting love. Waiting for the black, brocaded actor, Gabriel, ransacks his equilibrium, makes the days too cruel. Let him climb his starry ladder with Piers Duckworth. Gary must find a gentler man. And it's strange, too, how in the wake of this death, his curiosity about the play has vanished.

He doesn't even feel like reading the reviews, or telephoning to say why he missed the party. No one has inquired, of course. No message has come. He feels like a drab sparrow in need of kind behaviour. Other people's scraps aren't enough.

Miriam is dialling Pomerac. Nadia's number has sat, perfectly remembered – a code she might need again one day – in her head for weeks. Now she dials it and hears at last the familiar one-tone ring. It's ten o'clock in the morning. Nadia will have finished her breakfast of coffee and pastries and will be folding her bed away into the wall. In moments Miriam will be talking to Larry. The one tone sounds on and on. Around its ringing, Miriam imaginés Pomerac sitting in strong sunshine, its real winter still far off. She replaces her receiver with a slight unease. Nadia's usually home at this time. She dials the number again, making sure of every digit. No one answers. Miriam hugs her shoulders. She can't bury Leni without Larry to be strong for her. In his mocking of Leni and her world, there's a future. Without it, all seems to be silence. Quickly, she dials the number of Thomas's shop. Perdita answers and tells her Thomas is in Brussels.

'We must get him home, Perdita, I'm afraid.'

'He'll be back next week.'

'Can you contact him?'

'Yes.'

'His grandmother died last night.'

There's a long silence before Perdita says, sorrowfully, 'Gee.'

'I'd like him home,' says Miriam.

'Sure you would,' says Perdita, 'and you know he's going to be sad?'

'Yes.'

'He's going to be broken up.'

'Yes.'

'He loved Leni so much.'

'I know.'

'God. It's awful. You know?'

'Yes. I do.'

It's snowing again. The sky's lead-coloured. You can see the sticky flakes settling. When she was a child, Miriam used to long for snow to pile up against the windows of this house, sealing them off. The Ackermans. Safe in their moated life. Now, she's the last of them. Leni's Crow Dress lies in tissue paper in a drawer. David's papers were long ago dispersed into libraries. Already the house, empty forever of Leni, feels different, as if it's entering a fallow season. It yielded what it could. Now it sighs and rests. Its future will appear after a certain time has passed.

Perdita promises to contact Thomas and she and Miriam say goodbye. Carefully, Miriam dials Nadia's number and lets it ring for a full minute before she puts the receiver down. To talk to Larry has become a matter of urgency. She needs his indifference. Those close to her here – Gary, Thomas, even Dr O – will simply show her their own grief. She dreads, in particular, Dr O's sadness. The man's sorrowing feverish voice wails at her across centuries, shows her the wounds she's made, like a *flagellant* showing you his slashed shoulders. I've heard enough, she wants to say. Take your bleeding flesh away. But to Larry she wants to plead, don't punish me for my indifference. We all need some time outside our most binding affections. The silence in Pomerac fills her with foreboding. She imagines their house deserted, the wind starting to pull at its tiles and chimney pots. And Larry and Nadia gone. Gone where? And why? To punish her?

She goes back to the kitchen, where Gary is still sitting as if he's afraid to move. She suggests a cup of tea.

'I'll have Marmite, love,' he says.

Putting the kettle on, she feels a surge of friendliness for this old-fashioned kitchen, the heavy table, the warm, scratched, scorched, time-stained Rayburn, Leni's favourite teacups on hooks. The house is hers. It holds her, as it's always held her, safe and she doesn't want to part with it. Merely, she wants Larry in it with her – a desire, with Leni gone, to gather her own people, her own things round her, to breathe easily, sensing her life's complete. She's surprised at how very little grief for Leni she's actually feeling. As if she'd left all the mourning to others.

'Will she be buried beside David?' Gary asks suddenly.

'Yes. This is what she asked for. They were so close, really, when he was alive.'

'A marvellous "pair". How I envy the ones who get this right, this *pairing*.'

'It always has its problems.'

'Yes. Yet it's what we all ache for. Like lemmings, you might say. Lemmings who learned how to swim!'

Miriam smiles. 'How do you want the Marmite, Gary?' she asks.

He looks up and his eyes are brimming. 'Black, dear,' he says.

As the telephone rings and rings unanswered, in Nadia's flat, Larry and Nadia drive north into the vast, treeless plains of the world war battlefields. It's sad country, Larry always feels, like Lincolnshire and Norfolk without their hedges or oaks. The big patchwork of prairies is only here and there green, mostly a dark empty ploughscape with only the church spires recalling its old dignity.

They've been driving since dawn, taking turns at the wheel of the Granada, stopping for coffee and sandwiches near Tours, and again near Orléans, both feeling content in the hard, bright morning that replaces the five o'clock dark, warmed from the sun on the car windows, talkative, glad to be going somewhere, away for a time from Pomerac. Larry's impressed at how well Nadia drives, like a strong, venturing soul, not like the confused, mistake-prone person she actually is. And in her liking for the Granada, he feels grateful. The car, in its turn, is behaving very well. The journey's peculiarity is its joyfulness.

Claude's institution lies in the triangle formed by Arras, Bapaume and Cambrai in a place called Rouigny, a landmark either so insignificant or so willingly forgotten, it appears on almost no map. 'You know why?' says Nadia. 'Because they don't want, if there is some loony getting loose, they don't want him to find himself.'

The home, Larry learns in the course of the long drive, is run mainly by monks and the director is a certain Father le Sueur, hairy in Nadia's memory and talkative about the planets and stars. 'He has a telescope on the roof,' she tells him, 'but I don't

know what some monk is being an astronomer for. Maybe he's
looking for heaven?'

It's dark afternoon when they enter Bapaume. They plan to
stay the night here or in Arras and visit Claude the following
day.

Now that they're near him, Nadia feels her dread of the
meeting return and she's glad not to be alone. In her small
suitcase are presents for Claude: Périgord pâté ('I don't think
those monks cook so well, you know, and Claude had so fine
taste organs') and a paisley foulard bought in Périgueux ('a
neckchief or a weapon, I don't know. If he wants to hang himself,
better with my rope, no?') They go on in silence through
Bapaume, but when, in Arras, they pull up in the central cobbled
square and Larry gets stiffly out of the car, he stands in this
formal and oddly silent place and sniffs his nearness to England
and feels, as deep as a wound, his loss of Miriam. Nadia senses
her companion falter and asks anxiously, 'You're okay, my
darling?'

'Yes,' says Larry, quickly.

'I think we're tired, you know. I think we just see our rooms
and then go to the bar, no?'

'Yes. I agree.'

'So beautiful *place*, no?' says Nadia looking round at the
tall-shouldered houses. 'You don't imagine how it was so
destroyed.'

'No,' says Larry. Yet he feels its quietness is peculiar, as if
the town had long ago lost its spirit.

The hotel manager gives them a churlish reception, eyeing
them with suspicion. As they sign the cards he sets out for
them, they can see that the small, dimly lit bar on their left is
empty, except for a large Alsatian which lies sleeping under one
of the tables. A radio is on in the bar, news bulletins followed
by old pop songs. 'I think,' says Nadia, as they go up in the tin
lift, 'we're the sole guests.' Larry smiles. He is proud of Nadia
today. Proud of her bravery. Both of them feel a vodka-longing.

Their rooms are side by side, both with tall, thinly-curtained
windows looking out onto the square. The floors are lino, the
only heating squat, rusting radiators of the kind that always

remind Larry of his parents' house and of Miriam's hair. Sad places, he thinks. Rooms you could die in. They scuttle down to the empty bar and order their vodkas.

When Larry dreams, that night, about Miriam, it's not to see Leni lying in the hospital morgue or to hear, in Nadia's flat, the vain ringing of the telephone, it's a dream in which, in the cabin of a huge luxury liner, he's saying goodbye to his wife. She's seen him onto the ship and even brought him flowers for the journey, an old-fashioned courtesy. He's trying to persuade her to sail with him. Where to? No one says where the ship's bound. The rest of the passengers seem like holidaymakers, carrying children, wearing sun-visors. Miriam's restless, scared she'll be trapped aboard, and she leaves without touching him. 'Don't worry,' she says as she goes, 'there's plenty of recreation.' When Larry wakes it's still dark and a lone drunk in the Grand Place is hurling bottles at the sky.

No more than ten kilometres away from here, where Larry lies thinking of Miriam and next door Nadia lies dreaming of a ride she once took in the Bois de Boulogne, Claude Lemoine curls his body into a womb shape and repeats, cold as three glittering icicles in his brain, the three syllables of his wife's name: Na-di-a. It's without form. It's just the cruel, satisfying wound his mind must constantly make. Na-di-a. Naa-di-*aa* . . . The woman his wife was stands not in but outside this saying of her name. Like a ghost at the edge of this word. The pain is in the word, not in the insubstantial woman who lingers to one side of it. He's forgotten what she looked like except that she was small and that she was once, at dawn, in a high bed, in clear light, beautiful. Claude presses his pale chin to his fustian knees and rocks to keep the pain of his word bearable. Na-di-a. Na-di-aa!

'Lemoine!' shrieks a voice near to him. 'If you don't shut up, I'll kill you!'

All three, Claude, Nadia, Larry, are glad of morning when it comes, Claude unaware of the visit that's about to happen, Nadia washing her fluffy hair and painting her eyelids blue to look clean and feminine for this exiled man, Larry keen to forget Miriam in his protective care of Nadia.

Breakfast is brought to them in the bar at nine. Outside in
the square, since first light a fair has been setting up, the convoy
of trucks hissing and grinding through Nadia's dreams of the
Bois and Larry's dreams of the ocean liner. It's Saturday. Down
the buried chambers of the channel bed an urgent summons
from Miriam is moving towards Pomerac. It arrives at the Ste
Catherine post office and is being driven, on blue paper in a
yellow van, up the Pomerac slope just as Larry and Nadia climb,
full of apprehension into the Granada and take the road to
Rouigny.

Like the monks, the patients in the Rouigny Maison d'Ajuste-
ment breakfast after six o'clock vespers. The cook's keen on
junket. Lines of dull faces, growing old under Father le Sueur's
heaven, suck bowls of this white wet substance in the cold early
dark, then shuffle off to their 'classes' in groups of twenty.
Claude Lemoine is making baskets. Down the furrowed drug-
washed track of his memory the Maréchal comes out into the
Pomerac lanes and sits on a chair in the sunshine and places on
his knee an identical basket to the one Claude is weaving, a tall
bread pannier. My fingers, thinks Claude, winding this cane, will
get as old as his. 'As old as whose?' someone asks. Quite often,
Claude says out loud by mistake his private thoughts. Or else
the people in here are mind readers. Father le Sueur sometimes
says, 'We know what's in your head, son.'

One thing Claude has worked out. Father le Sueur, by virtue
of his communication with God and his observation of the stars,
will be the first person on earth to know about the end of the
world. He, Claude, therefore, will be the fifth or sixth person
to know or at worst the sixty-seventh. He imagines how it will
be. It will happen during basket-making. Like now, for instance.
Father le Sueur will come in and announce – privately to Claude,
because most of the others couldn't be trusted not to vomit or
fall down at this news – 'The world's ending today, Lemoine!
Spring hawthorn, church spires, the laughter of girls at café
tables, all the works of God and man and the Devil are turning
to lava. Heaven will be crowded. The early birds will get the
pardoner's worm. Know what I mean?'

Claude looks up over the rim of his basket as Father le Sueur,

looking grave in his grizzled face, comes in. Conversation stops
as the twenty faces are turned up like potatoes and watch their
chief protector out of their sprouts of eyes. Claude's heart begins
to beat frantically, 'Spring hawthorn, cathedral towers . . .'

'You have a visitor, Claude.'

'You mean –?' God? he wants to say, but is afraid to show off
in front of the class.

'Your wife.'

Claude gazes at the kindly, hair-pocked face. 'Me?' he asks,
'Mine?'

'Yes.'

'Now?'

'Yes, Claude. Leave your work and come with me.'

It could be code, he thinks, as he follows Father le Sueur
down the disinfected corridors, code for some universal catastrophe. He knows I'm one not to panic, not to let him down . . .

But then he's led into the quiet, comfy room smelling of carpet
that's reserved for visitors and he sees, waiting at the window,
clutching her handbag and some parcels, the woman he knows
embodies the three freezing, tormenting syllables to which, each
day as darkness comes down, his mind returns: Na-di-a.

She's smiling. Her hair is a halo of light at the window. Father
le Sueur touches Claude's arm. There's a new smell in the room,
a smell of musty flowers. Claude wants to get out of it and go
back to his pannier and remember the old man in the sunshine.

'You can sit down, Claude,' Father le Sueur says. 'I will ask
for some tea to be brought.'

So Claude sinks into a chair and Nadia at the window doesn't
move. The door closes, at Claude's back, on Father le Sueur
and Claude knows he's alone with his piece of ice. 'Girls' hawthorn, spring spires,' he whispers, 'all turned to laughter . . .'

The appearance of Xavier Mallélou in court is set for the coming
Monday morning.

In his obsession with Agnès, he's pushed to the very remotest
corner of his mind the idea that prison will one day separate him
from her – a separation he knows his love but not hers will
endure. Now, the summons comes. Gervaise pulls his petty-

thief's head to her breast and scolds, 'Why potatoes, Xavier? The silliness! The waste!' Mallélou stares at his son and remembers, like a bitter taste in his mouth, his own failure to avenge him. 'The stupidity,' he says morosely, 'was going to work for a woman.'

This time Klaus is going with Mallélou and Xavier to Bordeaux – a kind of talisman in Gervaise's mind, a protector of her son's fate. She'd go herself, go down on her knees to the magistrate if necessary, promise to keep Xavier on the right side of the law, but she can't leave the cows and she can't leave the Maréchal. Enthroned in the Heidelberg bed, the old man is doing brave battle with his infantile disease. He knows, however, and has told her as much, that without Gervaise he would die. In his increasingly confused and fevered brain, Gervaise is actually, with her woman's strength, with her knowledge of animals' ailments, fighting the poisons in his blood. He can't spare her, not even for her son.

The thought that Xavier may leave tomorrow for Bordeaux and not return is like a ghost in the household, the ghost they all see and none admit to. Only the Maréchal mumbles from his pillows, 'Say goodbye to him, Gervaise, and hope for nothing. Our idiocies are punished the hardest. That's a thing I've learnt.'

On Saturday, Xavier's head is filled, *bloated*, with a single idea: he wants one night – the whole night, not just one hour of it – with Agnès, a memory of normality and tenderness and passion with dignity to sustain him through his months of shambling round the prison yard, of listening to those no-hopers crying.

After supper, while Mallélou and Klaus settle down to the television and Gervaise is upstairs collecting the Maréchal's tray, he says casually, 'I'm going to see someone. I'm taking the car,' and before Mallélou can turn his attention to him, he's out into the yard, running past the inquisitive necks of the Christmas geese and reversing the *fourgon* very fast up the lane past Larry's house which lies in darkness.

He drives past the waterfall with his fear and nervousness increasing. Will Agnès be alone in the house? Was it yesterday Dr Prière left for Florida? Instead of loving him, will she simply say, 'I'm sorry, Xavier. We can't meet here.' Will he, before he leaves her, be forced to tell her where he's going? The pale drive comes into view. The car swings. The yellow headlights bound up on the laurels that border the drive. Xavier feels invaded with longing and with fear. How easy, how sweet life was for those two students in their room full of books . . .

A light is on in a downstairs room as Xavier draws up on the gravel. When he gets out and stands listening in the dark, he can hear, faintly, piano music. Agnès once talked about her playing, told him she might have had a career. He stays listening, shivering by the front door, before he reaches out and rings the bell. Below him, Hervé's garden seems to fall away off the hill. The night snatches at shapes and bears them away.

More lights come on. Now Xavier can see, in the dim hall, the suits of armour worn by the ancestors of Agnès. These cruel, visored generations of men seem to announce to him: 'She's not for the likes of you. Never.' He's hunched against the cold and against the spectre of his love flying away into these hollow bodies of soldiers when the door is opened and Hervé stands above him.

'Yes?'

The piano music goes on, louder now.

'I'm sorry to disturb you.' Xavier's voice is hopeless, faltering.

Hervé crushes him. 'Who are you?'

'A friend of Agnès's. Can I see her please?'

'No. You can't. She's gone. Who are you? Don't I recognise you? Aren't you Mallélou's boy?'

'Yes. That's Agnès playing, isn't it?'

'I told you. Agnès isn't here. She returned to Paris yesterday. Sooner than planned.'

'But that's her playing . . . I can *hear* her.'

'No that is not her playing. She doesn't, alas, play that well. That is the very fine Mexican pianist, Murray Perahia, playing Mozart's Piano Concerto No. 12, Opus No. K414. Agnès is with her family in Paris.'

Hervé interprets Xavier's dumb expression of pain as a look of disbelief and offers politely but coldly: 'Come in and see for yourself,' and holds the door open for him. But Xavier shakes his head. He doesn't want to smell the polish and the dust and the old varnish of her dead relations. She's his girl. She belongs in his arms. The smell of her is his.

'Is she . . .'

'What?'

'Is she . . .' he knows the answer but he asks the question anyway – the peasant in him hoping the poor dying calf won't die – '. . . coming back?'

Hervé, sensing his distress perhaps, smiles his practised doctor's smile: 'No, no. I shouldn't think so. She's getting married in the New Year.'

'Ah,' says Xavier, 'ah.' And, still staring at the row of metal breastplates, he stumbles backwards into the night.

When Mallélou has turned off the television, while Gervaise boils milk for their night drinks, Klaus tugs on his bulky anorak and tells Gervaise, 'Just going to have a look at the mosaic,' and goes out past the animals settling in their warm straw, past Larry's silent walls and round his garden to the pool.

The clouds have drifted away and a brilliant three-quarter moon is up. Klaus's huge shadow is just visible on the pool floor. He stares at his work. More than any loaf or extravagant patisserie he's ever made, this confection with the shimmery black and white and silver pieces of mosaic makes him feel proud. He's completed one set of steps and is halfway round to the second set.

'*Meine Kathedrale,*' he murmurs, '*meine wunderliche Kathedrale!*'

He turns and is about to walk back into the house when he notices the old *fourgon* parked at the top of the lane and sees, in the bright moonlight, Xavier resting his head on the wheel. He hesitates before deciding to go to the car. Xavier has kept his love affair with Agnès secret from Gervaise and Mallélou, but Klaus saw it begin and it's to him that Xavier has confided, 'This is the only girl I've met I feel love for.' That this message has passed, in the warm darkness of the featherbed, from Klaus to Gervaise is something only they know. Day by day Gervaise has watched her son and said nothing.

'Xavier,' Klaus calls softly in the lane.

Xavier looks up, startled. He waits without moving for Klaus to come to the car. The German bends slightly and his big face fills the small side window like a portrait in a frame. Xavier's staring straight ahead. He seems abstracted, ghostly in the peculiar light, filled with his trouble.

'Open the window, Xavier.'

'She's gone, Klaus. Without telling me. Without saying good-bye. She's gone back to Paris.'

'Can't you open the window?'

'I suppose I should have known. I'm so stupid. I don't seem to know a thing. Why does everything go wrong?'

Hearing this indistinctly, Klaus opens the opposite door of the *fourgon* and crouches by Xavier in the manner of an athlete limbering up. Xavier's face is white and his thumbs are repetitively moving up and down the inside rim of the steering wheel.

'Are you telling me this great love is finished?'

'Not in me it isn't. It never will be . . .'

'Yet she's gone? Back to the army boy?'

'Yes. I wanted to marry her, Klaus. She could have saved me.'

The squatting position isn't comfortable for Klaus who, in his meaty legs, has the beginnings of varicose veins. He straightens up. He looks behind him at the mosaic rim of the pool so glorious under the night sky and feels a tremor of fear that this work of his could, like Xavier's affair, be suddenly and brutally ended. He sighs and looks back at Xavier.

'I'm so sad for this thing,' he says, shaking his head. 'Love is few.'

For Nadia and Larry, it's been a strange day. After Rouigny, they drove north-west to Montreuil in silence, Nadia's fluffy head turned stubbornly away from Larry, the brown of her sorrow for Claude in close harmony with the flat, brown fields going past her. Larry took her to a good restaurant he remembered from his years of journeying to and from the Boulogne hoverport. They sat down in a comfortable, crowded room and Larry ordered *kir* and chose a rich meal for her, and she tried to coax the brown in her head into warmer colours and her little short hand reached past the vase of flowers on the table and touched his and she said in a voice full of gratitude, 'I don't know you are so caring of me, my bean, but now you teach me.' Yet the colours in her head wouldn't change.

After lunch, they drove to Boulogne beach and stared into the wind and heard the sea thunderous on the shingle and he thought of England and Miriam but didn't speak of either. They drove back to Arras in the dark and the fair, when they got there, had started up and the empty square was hectic with light and machinery and music and shouting and even the hotel bar was full of people.

They retreated to their rooms, neither hungry after the Montreuil lunch, and lay on their beds and tried to read. But the noise of the fair and its thumping multicoloured lights invaded their small, side-by-side spaces and the silences of the day seemed to Nadia wrong, hostile, a travesty of friendship. If strangers could make such a din, right there in her room, surely it was better to talk through it or under it, to shout with it, even, to let herself go. Larry would understand and forgive her. She couldn't keep the visit to Claude locked in her for ever.

So now, towards eight o'clock in the evening, Nadia puts down her book, pats her hair, steps into her shoes, takes her key and goes out into the passage and knocks on Larry's door. He's not surprised she's come. He's been down to the bar and bought a bottle of vodka. When he hears her knock, he's glad.

He pours the vodka into tooth-glasses. Outside, numbers are being announced through a microphone – a lottery. There's a sad, mischievous gremlin in Larry that wants to laugh till he cries. Today he stood and stared at the flat, dull grey horizon which, further off, was England. The gulls shrieked of their journeys there. Larry threw stones into the sea. One stone for each thing he'd lost.

There's only one chair in the room. When Larry has poured the vodka, Nadia sits down on this and he goes back to the bed. Nadia caresses the rim of the tumbler, staring down into it.

'Nadia,' says Larry gently, 'what happened today is between you and Claude. You don't have to tell me, or anyone.'

'No,' says Nadia, 'I want.'

Larry sips his drink, waits. After a moment, Nadia says: 'I think I was imagine he's not remembering me. You know? I think I was *hoping*. Because I am the one who must decide, after he has so many years of depression and therapy, I am the one who's signing the paper for Rouigny. The guilty one. The jail-maker. The "screw" you're calling this. Me. Nadia the screw.

'But of course he is remember. Nadia, he says. So many times over. Nadia, Nadia, Nadia, like in the language laboratory you repeat what the voice is asking: *voulez-vous des tomates, voulez-vous des tomates* . . . You know? Till you think these fucking *tomates*, I can't never eat one again!

'I gave him those presents – my pâté and my foulard. I put the foulard round his neck but it's looking so silly, you know, with this baggy clothes they put on him, I don't think this was so good a present. And he's starting to cry then and asking me, how's Pomerac, how is my houses, how is the old man making baskets? Imagine these *questions*! I'm so amaze. All these years I think, oh well so Claude's forgetting everything. Forgetting what is Christmas or who was his mother, forgetting to tie the tie or what is the colour of a post box or where is America. But I'm so wrong. He's not just remembering Nadia, Nadia, Nadia, but Pomerac too and asks me, do you taking care of my houses! And all this time he's getting these tears in his eyes and so staring at me, I just pray this Father astrologer is coming back with the tea. But he doesn't come. We're just alone. I don't know what I do, my dear, I'm so sorrowful for him and I feel so bad I'm signing those papers and my God, you should see what he's look like in these terrible clothes and this hair so white and standing there in my foulard, I want to cry and cry. I try to ask him, how you are Claude, and what do these monks teach you, but then all he tells me is, Nadia, Nadia, I'm going to be the first one to be told when it's over. So I ask, what is over because I think he's meaning when he can come out and go back into this life, but he's not mean this, he's explaining me, I'm going to be the first one or the second one to know about the end of the world. So then I can't help it. Though I'm try so hard, I just cry for him, my bean, I can't help. I'm try and try but I'm so full of sadness, I can't stop these tears, so he's coming to me and wiping my face with the bloody foulard and really I think, my God, this fucking human race is so sad disaster . . .'

Nadia wipes her eyes with her sleeve and gulps her drink. Larry watches her, nodding silently, and feels the only way to blanket his own grief is to give her as much as he can in the way of comfort, to let his understanding touch her, stroke her, caress her, calm her. We're like a little tribe of two, he thinks. The jungle savages us. We lick each others' wounds.

'Come here, Nadia,' he says softly. And he opens his arms to her. She looks up in surprise, but she doesn't pause to question what he's asking. Wiping the smudged blue mascara from her eyes, she moves to the bed and lies down and feels Larry's warmth and his arms bring her to a kind of shelter.

'My bean,' she says with laughter. 'You are so wonderful!'

The following morning, Sunday, Mallélou dresses himself with the shutters closed on a damp, misty day and shivers as he thinks of the journey to come and the courtroom and the lawyers' jargon designed to confuse the likes of him and the terrible future lurking in the city for his son. He fumbles with the stiff buttonholes of his fly. All this agony seems to lie there, in his balls, this one, vulnerable part of him taking the pain of the whole. And why can't he ever get warm these days? Stupidly, he envies the Maréchal his body's fever. His own bones are as freezing as railway iron.

Klaus and Xavier are tired. After the nightly ritual of Gervaise's hot drinks, they stayed at the table and the 'sentimental' schnaps was poured on Xavier's heart and he was forced to be content with this and with Klaus's kitchen-wisdom because this was all, on this night of betrayal, there was to cling to. They talked till one or two in the morning. Upstairs, the Maréchal coughed and wheezed. Klaus said there was often more learning in the actions of others than in our own *bêtises*. Watching these, you became a better judge of character. 'Next time, Xavier, you'll see what a girl wants of you when you screw her. You'll see it in her eyes.'

'I don't want any more girls,' Xavier said bleakly. 'I can't love the others.'

There was no real comfort in the talk, but it helped Xavier through the night. He snatched at sleep, afraid to dream of his lost girl. Now, it's the morning of departure and he knows that Pomerac will go from his life yet again, only taking him back in some distant, obscure future. 'It's over,' he says silently as he stares at the cold, shrouded day. 'It's over.' This time, Pomerac was Agnès. His love. He tells Gervaise as they sit down to breakfast: 'Even if they let me off, Maman, I'm not coming back.'

'Not for Christmas?' she asks.

'No, Maman. I can't this year. I can't.'

'Well,' she says sadly, 'we'll miss you.'

He wants to say goodbye to the Maréchal, but the old man is sleeping when he goes in. Xavier stands at the door and stares at him. La Comédie Humaine, Larry Kendal calls him. In his parchment cheeks is the faint dimpling of a smile. Dead bodies smile, someone told him during a game of Babyfoot; it's the fixing of the facial muscles. But the Maréchal isn't gone yet. His ancient chest rises and falls. The white stubble on his chin is as lively as mustard-seed.

'Wish me luck, old man,' Xavier mutters, 'and if your luck holds, then lend us the fine.'

He chooses to see in the Maréchal's tranquil-seeming sleep a hopeful sign. He was a prisoner-of-war. He survived.

Gervaise with her peasant's pride, with a strange reserve, has never chosen to make a fuss over departures. Time and nature take things, animals, people from you. If you learn nothing else from the seasons, you learn about change. Though she's planned her Christmas dinner and this year saw, in her mind's eye, Xavier on one side of her, Klaus on the other, she lets her son go with two light kisses, saying only, as he picks up the tied-together suitcase, 'God be with you, Xavier.' He will never, in the days to come, be far from her thoughts. But he knows this. She doesn't have to tell him. If he needed proof of her love, it's in the sending of Klaus, her big golden angel, to watch over him. And when her thin arms go round Klaus's neck to kiss him goodbye, she whispers urgently to him, 'Pray for him, Klaus.'

With breakfast over and Xavier's suitcase packed, there's no point in lingering. Mallélou says to Xavier, 'You drive the car, boy. It's too far for me.' And the tired man climbs into the back of the *fourgon* and sits on his bony arse among the chaff. He wears his ancient railwayman's winter coat. Xavier and Klaus get in. Gervaise stands at the yard gate, with her chickens pecking near her legs, and takes out her handkerchief and waves bravely, cheering them away.

It's in the course of this day – while Miriam's cable lies on the mat by Nadia's front door and in England flowers are arriving for Leni's funeral – that Nadia and Larry make the long drive back to Pomerac.

They arrive after dark, Nadia so filled with her memories of Claude and with the sweet comforts of the night that followed her visit to Rouigny, she feels that days and days have passed since she left her flat. She almost expects to find dust on all the surfaces and mould on the tangerines in their glass bowl.

As they take the Pomerac lane, Nadia reaches out and touches Larry's face. 'I like if you spend one night in my flat, my darling. You want?'

'Yes, I want,' says Larry.

His loving of Nadia has distanced him from his miseries. He feels strong today and at peace. He acknowledges a peculiar gratitude towards Claude.

Nadia picks up the letters on her mat and puts them down on her table while she switches on her fire, draws the curtains, searches her fridge and her cupboard for the ingredients of a little meal.

'I have a small jar of salmon eggs. You like this, my dear? And then I can make some omelette. Okay for you?'

'Excellent, Nadia.'

'Now, where is the vodka you are bringing the other night? I think we drink to our friendship which is a little altered. No?'

It's while searching for the vodka that she notices the blue cablegram. She considers, for the briefest second, just to make sure Larry stays with her tonight, hiding it, letting tomorrow take care of it, but she doesn't do this. She passes it to him in silence. He stares at his name on it in disbelief, then with mingled fear and hope.

'So,' Nadia says quietly, 'Miriam sends you at last.'

He opens it quickly, not wanting to give the moment too much reverence. Joltingly, he reads: *Leni died last night. Have been trying to telephone. Please come at once. I love you and need you. Miriam.*

Nadia stares at him, holding her breath. Last night she thought as she lay with him in the funfair flickering light, at last someone comes to me. At last I'm not alone. Now, as Larry looks up from the cable, his face slightly flushed, she knows he's about to be taken from her.

'It's Miriam coming back, my dear?'

'No. Leni's dead. She wants me to go to England.'

Not tonight, not tonight, my dear bean, thinks Nadia . . .

'You won't go tonight?'

'Of course not. Tomorrow or Tuesday.'

'Well . . . I'm so happy for you, my darling. What an upturn! At last she's pushing up the sod, this fucking woman. But how silly, you know. Yesterday, we were at Boulogne. You could have took the ferry and now be with Miriam.'

'Yes, it is strange. The way things occur is often peculiar.'

'Can I read your cable?'

'Of course.'

Larry hands Nadia the torn blue paper.

The words *I love you* stare out at her, yet her mind is still warmed, soothed with Larry's tendernesses towards herself. Her life has in it, she decides, the cruelties of Eden.

'So she is loving you again, Larry. You deserve this. How you deserve! Let me kiss you, my darling, because I think you are so kind a man, so helping and redeeming of Nadia. Whatever happen, I will be grateful. You know?'

'I've done nothing, Nadia. Only what I wanted to do. You're lovely.'

She sits on his knee and he presses a long kiss on her fine little mouth. In bed, she's like a doll, a painting, so round and smooth and small. But even as he holds her and feels her tongue

come probing his, he's remembering the big bony body of his
wife. Miriam, Miriam, say these gestures of love, says the
hardening of his cock under Nadia's perky bottom, Miriam wait
for me!

On Tuesday afternoon, near to the time that Larry's boarding
the Bordeaux flight to London, Mme de la Brosse walks up the
lane to his house and knocks on his door. Getting no reply, she
picks her way round to the back and stands still as a ghost
looking down at the swimming pool.

No, she thinks, no, no, no. The effrontery. The presumption.
To live in Pomerac, you must obey its old ways, not invent new.
'The English,' she mutters: 'No taste.' She's a strong Gaullist.
She liked the way de Gaulle kept humiliating Wilson. *'Non, alors
non,'* she repeats.

She's heard the Maréchal is ill. Her sense of herself as 'head'
of the village dictates that she visit him. She goes round to
Gervaise's gate and calls above the noise of the birds, 'Madame
Mallélou!'

Gervaise is in her kitchen, resting by sitting still in a straight-
backed chair, waiting for one more day to pass, waiting for news
of Xavier and for the return of Klaus. Hearing the call, she
straightens her apron and goes out into her yard.

'Ah,' says Mme de la Brosse, 'I was told our poor Maréchal
is with you. I wanted to call. I've brought him a little Turkish
Delight – from my bonbonnier in Paris – for when he's
well.'

'Come in, Madame,' says Gervaise, 'and please forgive my
untidiness. My family have gone to Bordeaux.'

'Oh yes? And it seems Mr Kendal's away too, is he?'

'Yes. Today, he went. His wife's mother's passed on. I don't
know when they'll be back.'

'Ah. I see.'

'Have you seen the pool, Madame?'

'Yes, I have.'

'So courageous, we think he is.'

'Courageous, you think?'

'Yes.'

'Well, that's a point of view. Now let's see our old soldier and give him these sweets.'

Gervaise feels anxious as she goes in front of Mme de la Brosse up the stairs, hating the smell of perfume at her back. Outside the Maréchal's door, she says firmly, 'Let me go in first, Madame. He likes me to tidy him up before visitors see him.'

'Oh naturally. I'll wait outside.'

He's asleep and dreaming of Eulalie. She squats in a mustard field, her plaited hair loose and starting out strangely from her head. She smiles and waves a pale hand at the acres of nodding yellow flowers. 'Piss!' she announces. 'Fields of piss.' She's young. In his dreams and in his wandering mind, Eulalie gets younger and younger. 'I am her bridegroom,' he sometimes says out loud.

Gervaise bends over him. Since the early morning, his temperature has been high. His face on the pillows is falling back, sucked inwards towards the skull, and Gervaise blames herself for this sudden deterioration: too much of her strength has fled to Bordeaux with Xavier and Klaus; the little that's left may not be enough to keep the old man alive.

Snoring there, he looks so deeply asleep she doesn't want to wake him. Not for Mme de la Brosse and her futile sweets. Yet gently, she does. Obedience to Pomerac's hierarchy comes as easily, as naturally to Gervaise as the opening phrase of the *Our Father*. She puts out a hand to the Maréchal's face and says: 'Forgive me, Maréchal. Forgive me this once for waking you . . .'

But he's glad to leave his peculiar dream of Eulalie in the mustard field, to see Gervaise and the calm white walls of the room.

'*Mon dieu* . . .' he says.

'Let's sit you up a little.'

'They torment you, dreams.'

'Come on, *mon vieux*, let's sit you up.'

'What's happened, Gervaise?'

'Nothing. Madame de la Brosse has come to see you. She's brought you something.'

The stretched face collapses into a smile. 'Not a pencil box!'
'No, no . . .'
'That's what they used to give – books and pencil boxes.'
'I know, Maréchal.'
'But I never had much learning. Not me.'
'All right, are you? Shall I show her in?'
'My breath stinks, Gervaise. That's death for you.'
'Ssh . . .'
'You stay, Gervaise.'
'No. She wants to talk to you.'
'Why?'
'I don't know. I don't ask.'

She doesn't stay very long. When Gervaise goes up to the room again, the gift-wrapped box of candy has been placed on his feet. He's staring at it, moving it up and down like a little pink boat.

'Why's the house so quiet, Gervaise?'
'Well, Klaus and Mallélou aren't back.'
'Something's happening, Gervaise. I don't trust this quiet.'
'Nothing's happening here, Maréchal. And Xavier –'
'Keep a watch out, Gervaise.'
'What?'
'I feel it.'
'You must sleep, Maréchal. I'm sorry to have woken you.'
'Don't blame me, Gervaise.'
'*Blame* you?'
'If something happens. Don't think I caused it.'
'You're safe here. Quite safe.'
'It's not me I'm afraid for.'

She removes the sweet box from his feet and sets it by him on a table. At this moment Xavier could be riding to prison with the police light turning.

'Is it . . .' she asks as she straightens the Maréchal's blankets, 'is it Xavier?'

But he only stares at her helplessly, his eyes glassy with fever and through his pale lips repeats: 'It's not me who's to blame.'

She goes back to the kitchen, feeling cold, and banks up the fire. Tired from her worries, she makes a soup for her supper and stands over it, hugging the kitchen-warmth to her.

At five, she forces herself out into the freezing dark to milk the cows, disliking this task, on this day, more than she's ever done and promising herself, in some kindly future, the modern milking parlour she's so often imagined. If a pool can come to Pomerac, then any miracle can occur. Though Mallélou is useless now, old long before his time, she and Klaus will work and save for the milking parlour. Then, in her old age, there won't be this ritual. 'I will,' she says to the warm udders, 'have earned the rest.'

When she comes in, the milking done, the churns lugged to the bottom of the hill for collection by the de la Brosse milk pasteurising company, she goes up again to the Maréchal's room, listens for a moment to his snores, then returns to the kitchen, eats her soup, parks her body in its straight chair and is lulled quickly to an exhausted sleep by the warmth of the soup in her belly and the grey, flickering coming and going of subtitles on an American TV movie. It's a movie about truckers. A vast convoy of juggernauts rolls in to a mid-western town. In a grinding of gears and a scream of engines the trucks smash up the town to set free a prisoner. The noise fills Gervaise's head and wakes her. She opens her eyes, stares at the screen. The revving trucks remind her of the huge sewage tankers thundering down the Ste Catherine road and of her time on the edge of the city. 'God save my son,' she thinks and closes her eyes again and sleeps and the noise of trucks goes on in her head.

Upstairs, the Maréchal wakes and hears the convoy and feels relieved, for a moment or two, that the house is filled with noise and no longer with silence. But then, outside his window, he sees a light. This room looks out onto the edge of Larry's garden, not onto the lane and the Maréchal questions the existence of this light beyond the thin curtains. Unless, they've moved me, he thinks. But the room with the painted bed is familiar in all its detail. Even the pink box of Turkish Delight is there on the table. He stares at it, remembering the tight features of Mme de la Brosse as she sat tidily on a chair, out

of reach of his breath, talking about community responsibility
and her friend the Mayor . . .

'Gervaise!' he calls urgently, 'Gervaise!'

He waits. He knows the noise is too loud and she hasn't heard
him. He looks back at the window. The light jolts, recedes,
returns. He measures the distance from his bed to the window:
three metres perhaps. He can't walk three metres. For his
feeble excretions Gervaise brings a flat pan and sits him on it.
He'll never leave his bed.

'*Gervaise!*'

He wants to pummel the floor. Though he tries to call loudly,
he knows his voice is feeble. But then he hears her coming, her
sabots on the wooden stairs, a galumphing tread for this thin
woman. She flies in to the room, one side of her face red where
it's rested against the chair, her eyes wide and startled.

'What is it, Maréchal? You need the pan?'

'Look, Gervaise!'

He points a frail finger at the window.

'What?'

'Lights. Something happening. I told you . . .'

'What is it?'

'Go and look. I can't tell what it is.'

She's at the window. Its panes are icy, frost forming at the
edges. Out in the night she sees two lamps like searchlights
moving close to the ground. They shine towards her, moving
forwards at first then stopping. Downstairs the television is still
noisy but now she can hear, outside where the lights are, what
sounds like tractor engines. Her breath frosts the glass. She
rubs impatiently at it. She thinks, Pray to God I'm dreaming.
Pray to God it's part of the television dream – Robert X, the
man even Klaus admires, altering lives . . .

But she's out of the Maréchal's room and down the stairs in
her clogs and snatching up her coat before the Maréchal, his
heart full of fear, has time to implore her one more time, 'Don't
blame me, Gervaise!' He twists in the bed and stares helplessly
at his door left ajar. His feverish brain remembers with shame
the blue spruce tree.

Run, Gervaise urges herself, as the night cold fastens itself round her . . . up the lane, turn left past Larry's house, over the rubble-strewn garden round to the back . . . run and it will still be there, smooth, pale, silent, its mosaic shimmery even in the darkness, waiting for summer, waiting for the water . . . But she knows she's too late. She knows, of course, as she stands and watches the digger moving backwards and forwards and the vast mounds of earth go tumbling in, that all the months of Larry's work are brought to nothing – the reward (yes, the same one they gave her in the city) the reward for his struggle to belong – and that within seconds, as she scrambles in her clogs over the frosty mud, Klaus's foolish vision of a black and white cathedral will be obliterated by the terrible tireless clay of Pomerac – earth returning to earth, a burial.

She stands and weeps. Upstairs in his agony, the Maréchal picks up the box of Turkish Delight and hurls it with all his strength at the window.

Larry lies in his wife's arms and pretends to sleep.

I have missed, Miriam thinks as she holds him, the weight of Larry. Leni's element was air while she breathed: words fluttering off, like paper or leaves. Dr O's is fire: his scarlet longing spilling over like lava. But Larry's is earth: his close-packed legs, his patient ploughing of his dreams. With Leni gone – a speck now, Leni's life like a kite miles up in the blank white sky – she's felt a longing to be taken back by Larry, to be held down as he holds her now, his woolly heavy head on her breast and shoulder. What had made her long for him in recent days was not merely Leni's going, but a sudden fear that the vain ringing and ringing of Nadia's telephone somehow signalled a withdrawal of his love for her. No less than you deserve, she told herself. You withdrew your love for a time. Now he's punishing you. When, finally, she had heard his voice on the telephone, she had wanted to say to him, Please try to forgive me.

Carefully and with a quiet feeling of excitement, she had moved herself out of the child's bedroom and spread her things round the guest room as if in a hotel, enjoying its luxury. Larry was on his way. She was free to love him generously now, no part of her withheld in obedience to Leni. She expected to feel old at Leni's death. Instead she felt free. The snow ceased and began to thaw. Flowers and cards started arriving. Gary stayed in his room and cried silently to Ella Fitzgerald. And eventually, inevitably, Dr O turned up.

Looking grave, he came into the hall, stood staring not at Miriam but at the three-quarter moon face on the grandfather clock and started to say how he felt, at this death, empty handed.

'What do you mean, Dr O?' said Miriam. He was wearing a dark suit. He held himself apart from her, stiff and formal. His poor pasty face seemed painted with sadness.

'I wanted,' he said forlornly, 'to offer something to Leni. She seemed to ask it. The thing I wanted to offer most was my love for you . . .'

'Please don't say that, Dr O,' said Miriam more brusquely than she intended, 'I've told you very often this isn't possible.'

'Yes. I know. I know. Don't worry. I'm not going to pester you any more. It's just that, without this, I do . . . well . . . feel I can't come to the funeral because I have nothing to *offer*. Do you understand?'

'No,' said Miriam. 'Not really. Because offering anything isn't important now. Send flowers if you like. But even that . . . She won't see them, will she?'

'I admired her so,' he said with despair.

'Yes, I know you did,' Miriam said more gently.

'She once taught me to dance, you know,' said Dr O and stared forlornly down at his weighty pelvis. 'I should have kept on with dancing.'

'As an *offering*?' Miriam said spitefully and Dr O looked up, hearing the acid in her voice.

'Yes,' he said, 'as something.'

Now Larry opens his eyes and finds, very close to them, a hank of Miriam's hair. He gazes at it, counting the grey threads. His mind travels to Nadia's blonde head, a head so tiny he seemed able to hold it to him with his palm. She'll be alone now in Pomerac, poor Nadia, making tea, turning on the little fire, remembering Claude, remembering Arras and the fair outside the window and him . . .

This thought makes him feel suffocated, slightly breathless.

He props himself up and watches Miriam's face. She smiles at him – the smile he thought he'd lost. I want to be strong for her, he thinks. He flicks away the spectre of Nadia to the furthest corner of his mind. Nadia's so light and insubstantial, it's not difficult to push her away. Larry's finger touches Miriam's brow, still hot after his hungry, celebratory embraces, a love-feast so abundant it reminded them both of their first years together. It was their passion which defied Leni then, just as now, on the day before her funeral, it's their passion which buries her.

'Bitch!' he says suddenly. 'Why did you stay away so long?'

'Well, it was good I did.'

'Why?'

'Because look at you – you're well again.'

'It was the pool that did that.'

'And you wouldn't have started the pool if I hadn't gone.'

'Maybe. But you didn't stay away for me, Miriam. You stayed away for you.'

'Yes. Mainly.'

'And you had a lover, did you? One of Leni's courtiers?'

'No. There was an offer. I declined.'

'Why?'

'I don't know. Isn't that odd? He was so kind to me. Bought me expensive suppers. But I didn't want him.'

Larry lowers his head and kisses Miriam's face. He wants, after this odd confession of hers, to tell her about Nadia, but the smell of his wife's body is too heady and he can't find the words.

That evening Thomas and Perdita arrive. Thomas's grief for Leni has given him a startled look. Trying not to shed tears, his eyes look bulgy and blue, like a rabbit's. *Bright Eyes*, Larry privately christens him; Leni's last mourner. Yet Thomas, with his flaxen girl to smooth his starting troubled hair, seems a more gentle, a more manageable son to Larry than he's been for years. When they walk in, Larry feels moved to embrace them both and wants to say to the corn-coloured Perdita, Stay with Thomas. Have his children. Give me, one day, a granddaughter.

And it's very quickly clear to Larry that his son's glad to see him. This is surprising and Larry feels an unexpected gratitude. Perhaps it was Leni's witch's spell that kept them apart. He imagines her forging it with her rouges and her wrinkle cream, vulgar little pots they'll bury with her like the balms and unguents of the old Egyptians, all the power gone out of them.

Red-eyed and peculiarly resembling a Mosleyite with his short hair and his black shirt, Gary is persuaded out of his room by Miriam and sits quietly with the family through a meal of chicken casserole and jacket potatoes, Larry's first taste of bland English food. The question of Gary's future lurks anxiously in Miriam's mind but she won't discuss it yet, just as she's decided to postpone discussion of her own plans. Since inhabiting David's attic, she's reattached herself to the house of her childhood so completely, it's almost as if she'd never left it. Now, with Leni gone, it's hers and she inhabits it gratefully, letting a little pride into the smile she gives the diners at her table. All – except Larry – are here for Leni, yet it's in Leni's chair that Miriam chooses to sit. Half way through the meal, she thinks, when will I start to miss Leni? When will I shed some of my famous tears?

After supper, Gary, with ghostly quietness, goes back to his lilac room. He bathes his eyes with Optrex. Downstairs, he hears Larry laugh and thinks, it's over. I must move on, whatever they decide, whatever Leni has put in her will. And he starts to imagine, as he tugs on his coat and wraps his empty neck in his red scarf, the little flat he will buy, the lovers he will receive there. As he's about to leave his room, he sees, on a peg, the grey hat that was Leni's gift and with which he covered her face. To defy death, to defy his own predicament, he snatches it up and sets it carefully on his head. He creeps silently downstairs and lets himself out into the cold night. The walk from here to the Playhouse stage door takes exactly eight minutes. He knows because he's timed it.

Perdita goes early to bed. She lies and listens to the chimes and traffic of Oxford and feels her Australian soul has travelled to the heart of something, though she's not sure what. She just knows she's glad to have come this far. Outside in the drive, her new Mercedes is parked next to Gary's rusting Mini and the juxtaposition of these two cars is slightly vexing to her. For the first time, she wonders if the Mercedes isn't rather vulgar.

Miriam, Larry and Thomas drink red wine and hold a kind of unspoken wake for Leni. They don't talk about the future. Thomas describes his trip to Brussels. Miriam talks about the exhibition. Success is what they're showing me, Larry thinks, and with a pang of sadness he sees, robed in flat winter light, his swimming pool. This, he wants to say to his wife, to his son, is all I've got to offer. I designed it along the lines of a cathedral. Klaus understood my vision and has started to make it beautiful with his mosaic. It's a work of art, or at least that's what I want it to be. Long after I'm gone, the people of Pomerac will be proud of it: the St Front pool. An Englishman built it, they'll say. He had this wonderful idea.

On the morning of Leni's funeral, which is at ten o'clock, Dr O hurries to the bookshop to make sure Miss Atwood will cope sensibly with the customers and won't – as she's taken to doing – hide away in the stockroom drinking Bovril and reading *Jane Eyre*.

He waits for her until 9.45, but there's no sign of her and no answer from her Cattle Street number. Exasperated and uneasy and with a dread of the ordeal to come, he writes a polite note of apology, sticks it up on the door, double-locks it and hurries, feeling a kind of vertigo, to St Mary's Church. In his haste to get the note written he's left out the word 'closed' and it reads rather strangely for a man so meticulous with language: *The Management apologises to customers and regrets that the shop will be all day today*.

Dr O expects to find St Mary's crammed full with Leni's mourners. If she'd died at forty, the whole of the University would have flocked to pay her homage. But apart from Miriam, with her family in a close, protecting group shouldering her off from his glance, there are perhaps a dozen people in the church, mostly old colleagues of David's and their wives, couples whom he knows slightly and who went once to Leni's parties in fancy dress. They all seem old. Leni once said to him: 'When I die, bring all the young men to my funeral, Oz! Let's have some frolicking on my bones!' But apart from Thomas and Gary, there isn't one young man. Just a couple of rows of lined faces, wrapped up in fur collars. Well at least, thinks Dr O, as he slips into a back pew, the church is burying her. Leni, born a Jewess, had courted the Church of England not for its God but for its respectability and for the splendour of its architecture. In time, it had forgotten she didn't really belong. It certainly didn't question her burial rites. But, as the service begins, Dr O finds himself shivering with anxiety about the fate of Leni's soul. Why hadn't he gathered in the young undergraduates as she'd once instructed? She is Babylon, he thinks fretfully, and the voice of St John the Divine undoes his concentration. Poor fallen Leni! *And the light of a candle shall shine no more at all in thee and the voice of the bridegroom and of the bride shall be heard no more at all in thee* . . . I wanted to be a bridegroom for you, Leni, he hears himself protest. Now, nothing remains even of that intention. I let you down, Leni. *So much torment and sorrow give her: for she saith in her heart, I sit a queen, and am no widow, and shall see no sorrow* . . .

Dr O's eyes fill with tears. He's glad he's at the back. No one notices him or turns round. He remembers the lunchtime Miriam cried in his arms. What made him so bold with his courtship: this one moment of weakness in her? Now it seems futile. Bernice has suffered terribly in her silence with her peculiar making of Bovril and the hiding of her body in a little corner of the stockroom and sometimes humming over her reading of *Jane Eyre* a tuneless kind of song and rocking herself backwards and forwards. He thought it was eccentricity in Bernice, this rocking. Now he sees it was suffering and he feels ashamed. She once gave him so much. He left her for a woman he never possessed. How stupid mankind is. *The fruits that thy soul lusted after are departed from thee* . . . *and thou shalt find them no more at all.* Dr O blows his nose and is touched by loneliness in the marrow of his wide bones.

The vicar of St Mary's is recalling David's contribution to the life and thought of the University. Miriam, whose hands are held tightly, one by Larry, the other one by Thomas, is aware that the legacy, in her, of David and Leni is a kind of stubborn strength. She refuses to let life cast her down. Even the artist in her – never great, never fantastic – kept struggling on. She turns and looks at Larry and finds he's looking at her. She feels a sudden happiness she can't account for.

The service isn't long – no magnificent hymn singing for Leni – and its ordinariness seems quite inappropriate to the way she was. Only Gary, in a black cape he's borrowed from Wardrobe at the Playhouse, lends a touch of drama. His eyes stream. Perdita finds in her pocket a cotton scarf with *Beautiful Sydney* written on it and passes this to Gary who remembers, just after Leni's death, being handed a mug with *I love NY* on it. Relics, Gary thinks. In time to come, Leni will be bone – a relic. In his mind Leni's soul, black as a tadpole, is already nosing its way into darkness, into the heart of nothing. Not even IVb, attentive in the Bilge lab, see it pass. Leni, once his mother, is nothing. She is less than the almost invisible morsel of life under IVb's microscope. And though it's not Wednesday, the first few lines of a poem start to intrude themselves into his head:

> You
> were the one who
> in the album of my love
> was chiefly photographed . . .

He's agreed, though he hates the macabre of it, to be a pall-bearer. The other bearers are Thomas, Larry and an elderly don called Professor Whitburn, a collaborator with David Ackerman on a book about Richard Cromwell, son of the Protector. Gary has to put one caped and trembling arm on this Professor's shoulder. He senses, as the unsteady procession moves off with Leni held high, that there is dandruff under his fingers. She feels heavy. The four men breathe hard. Thomas, taller than the rest, has to hold himself at a tilt. Gary longs now for it to be over, to deposit her in the ground and turn away, orphaned for the second time. His cape smells faintly of stage make-up, reminding him that life is not perpetual bereavement. Tonight, he's going to *Othello* again. He thinks he will keep the scarf saying *Beautiful Sydney* and in the fretful triangle of himself, Gabriel and Piers try to let it play some part – his strawberry handkerchief – to reassure himself that Leni hasn't stolen all his cunning.

As they move out from the draughty porch and load Leni back into the hearse (St Mary's has no burial space left; Leni will lie with David under a windswept hill north of the town) Larry starts to wonder whether Leni, her old powers lingering for a few days, hasn't ushered in a season of dying. He imagines the procession they will make in Pomerac for the Maréchal: every man, woman and child in the village following, the sewage tankers slowed by the mourners on the Ste Catherine road, Gervaise leading bravely, behind her, Mallélou and Klaus and behind them, in her Paris black Mme de la Brosse. He sighs. La Comédie Humaine – ended. He looks anxiously at his son for his few remaining signs of youthfulness.

Dr O hovers while Leni is shoved back into the hearse and Miriam, Larry and Thomas climb into their limousine. He's forgotten to bring his car. He imagined, wrongly, they'd find a space for Leni at St Mary's and now he can't follow to wherever they're going to put her. Miriam sees him waiting, but quickly turns away and in another moment is driven off, her husband's arm around her. Dr O is touched by how white her skin seems above her dark coat. He can't break the habit of finding her beautiful.

Bernice Atwood is packing. She has written a letter to Dr O expressing regret that she's not able to work for him any more and asking him to forward her final salary cheque to her aunt's house in Newbury. The letter doesn't mention love or betrayal or her unborn child. It ends with the peculiar line: *Yours sincerely in my hope for your future happiness, BA.*

She hasn't got many possessions aside from her books, which she has decided to put into storage. She has one frock, a loose kind of smock, girlish yet sombre. She thinks this will do, soon, as a maternity dress. Though she's taken to wearing heavy, baggy jerseys, the mound of her baby is now clearly visible to her. Her skirts won't fasten and her big breasts feel cramped in her size 38 bra. The day is approaching when Bernice is going to have to TELL. She's not afraid of doctors, but dislikes the touch of them. Her aunt is a widow and a nurse and childless and very fond of Bernice. She's inclined to put her trust in this quiet woman. Also, her aunt keeps pets – two dogs and a cat. She's read somewhere that pets are helpful in developing a child's capacity to love. Bernice wants her baby to love her.

As she fills her two suitcases, she thinks, It's been the unhappiest time of my life. She can remember so clearly what she calls 'the time before', the hundred or more nights in Dr O's bed, the way she could, just by kissing him, get him to fuck her in the middle of the night, his breath and his body hot with sleep and lazy and very beautiful to her in the darkness. It was at these times that she often wanted to shout out 'I love you, Dr O!', scream at him as she came and tear at his back with her little white nails. She folds and pats her two nightdresses. In summer, she had liked to sleep naked in that Plum Street room, fold her arms behind her head and admire the breasts Dr O had once described as 'remarkable'. Why hadn't she ever screamed it out? 'I love you, Dr O!' Do men expect to be told this in order to carry on loving you? Is the fact that she never said it in some way to blame? Did Miriam Ackerman, that day at tea, whisper it to him behind her slice of cake: 'I'm in love with you, Oz.' She never heard it. Miriam didn't seem to pay him a lot of attention. It's all, thinks Bernice, beyond my understanding.

She stares at her empty room. She never owned the furniture in it, so none of it is going, yet the room has a deserted feel. It's a question of time, she decides. If you're in a place long enough, you fill it up with yourself. Now, she's leaving it. Her travelling alarm clock is already closed. Her radio is packed, her brass rubbing (done one Saturday afternoon with Dr O) torn down and crumpled into the bin, her set of Samuel Palmer postcards tucked in between her spongebag and her Complete Shakespeare. She sits down on the tidy bed and stares at what she's leaving. Not much, Bernice. You never had much. But the *time*, though. All those hours in the Bodleian Library. Those millions of strokes of the Rötring pen, of the fine squirrel brush. Books of Hours. Hours and hours and hours and hours . . . Time, in Oxford, was full. You filled it up. Now it spills. The future's a spilt wasteland. Yet *why*? She still asks the question. Why?

Her train to Newbury is at one o'clock. She still has an hour or more to wait. She wonders whether she won't unpack her radio and turn on Radio 4. She doesn't feel like reading. *Jane Eyre*'s in the case, too. She decides, though it's cold, to go for a last walk round the city. She knows her walks are good for her baby because her own colour is healthy and this means the blood in her is fresh, not stale and full of poisons. She puts on her coat which is tight across her belly and very frayed at the cuffs, she notices. You're an evacuee, Bernice, she informs herself. A 'vaccy'. They're throwing you out.

Then, as she's buttoning the coat, she feels it: a little push inside her, a little wriggle or kick, a movement. 'So it's alive!' Bernice says out loud and bumps back down onto the bed and takes up her rocking position, but this time marvelling. Her baby moved. She's not afraid of the child any more, of the milk and paraphernalia. In fact she's begun to look forward to holding it, not inside her, but in her arms. No one can snatch her child from her at a Sunday tea party. It's hers, hers and beating its soft little limbs in her comfy womb. She'll protect it from all cruelty. She'll sing it madrigals, or even old nostalgic country songs:

> 'Take me back,
> To the black hills,
> The black hills of Dakota . . .'

She has no firm notion of where Dakota is, nor which range of hills this song is actually talking about. But this is a good rocking song. Her baby seems to stop moving and listen.

Then her doorbell is rung. The taxi she ordered to take her to the station. Now, with the thought that it's here, she feels the finality of her departure. Tonight, she'll lie in an unfamiliar room in Newbury. Oxford is over. Finished. She gets up. She puts on her woollen gloves, picks up the two cases, gives her room one last caressing glance and goes awkwardly down the stairs, leaving her door ajar. As she lets the cases drop to open the front door, she feels another impudent small kicking inside her. When the child comes, she thinks, I won't be so lonely.

Dr O is standing at the door. He's dressed very formally in a dark suit with a plain black tie. When he sees Bernice with her suitcases, he knows at once that she's leaving him and will never come back.

'Words,' he says helplessly. 'I don't know what to say.'

'What?' says Bernice, her heart racing like an engine under her thin coat. 'What, Dr O?'

'Can I come in, Bernice, or are you . . . ?'

'Come in, please.'

She holds the door for him, pushing her luggage out of his way. She closes the door. She didn't expect to see him ever again. Her face is flushed. Though she tries to force them back, tears prickle in her grey eyes.

'You're leaving,' says Dr O.

'Yes,' says Bernice. 'I did write you a letter. I said I hoped you'd be happy . . .'

The tears fall. She can't stop them. She had more control before she was pregnant. She's read pregnant mothers often cry . . .

'I'm going . . .' she says with her face buried in her woollen gloves, 'I'm going . . . to have your baby.'

So it's gone from her. Her secret. It's out of her. For weeks she rocked it and held it in. Now it's out and she can't stop her crying. She lets herself tilt towards him. One of her suitcases stands between them and, as she moves, it falls against Dr O's legs. But he's not bothered by this bruising of his shins. If this is the worst pain there is, he thinks, then I've been let off lightly. Carefully he rights the suitcase and puts his arms round Bernice like protecting wings.

'Bernice,' he mumbles in a voice thick with sorrow, 'marry me.'

It's a bright mid-day in Pomerac but the air is bitter and Gervaise stares up at the sky and sniffs. Snow, she thinks. Snow is on the way.

She's standing at her gate, saying goodbye to Dr Prière whose last visit this is. Tomorrow he leaves for Florida. He's offered to arrange to move the Maréchal to the hospital in Thiviers, but Gervaise has given the old man her word: she won't let him die among strangers.

'If he goes in the night, I'm afraid it's no use calling me, Madame Mallélou. You must call the surgery number and you will be put through to the doctor on duty.'

'I can't call anyone, Dr Prière,' says Gervaise. 'We don't have the telephone.'

'The more reason to let him go to Thiviers. He's so weak, Madame. He can't last very long.'

'I buried my parents, Dr Prière. I'm not afraid of death.'

'No. Well, it's your decision.'

'So you're going to America?'

'Yes. Florida. A fine climate there.'

'My sons talk about America.'

'Do they?'

'So I tell them, go if you can. It's a country for the young, from what I can tell.'

'Ah, well. I'm not young, Madame Mallélou.'

'No. But I expect you have acquaintances there.'

'Yes. A few.'

'We don't understand America – not from Pomerac. I don't think we can, do you?'

Hervé Prière shrugs and opens his car door. 'I expect we understand them as well as they understand us. Good bye, Madame Mallélou.'

'Good bye, doctor. Enjoy Florida. We'll think of you, by your pool . . .'

He drives away. Nothing, of course, has been said about Agnès and Xavier. This interlude, in Dr Prière's mind, doesn't seem to have existed.

Gervaise turns back into the house. She's baking today – bread and cakes and flans for the return of Klaus. Her kitchen smells of flour and cloves and sugar. Into her baking she's putting prayers for her son. Upstairs, the Maréchal dreams of the pike fishing, a six o'clock mist sitting on the river, his sons wearing sou'westers and eating cinnamon biscuits, the stink of the bait in his hands, the clusters of grey snouts coming silently to the shallows . . .

Her baking done, Gervaise goes up and tiptoes to the bed. The Maréchal sleeps on, his mouth wide. The room is acquiring a sour, musty smell. Gervaise wants to open the window but the wind is too keen and the snow is coming. 'Let me die in my own stink, Gervaise!' the Maréchal asked. 'It's the least you can do.'

There's a commotion downstairs. Gervaise whips off her apron and hurries to the landing. At the foot of the stairs is Klaus, smiling his huge smile. You could, Gervaise thinks, dam up the Gironde with Klaus's face! She hesitates before going down to him. In her brief hesitation is her first question: Xavier?

'He's free, Gervaise.'

'No? You're not lying?'

'He's free. A fine, that's all. No sentence.'

'Oh mon dieu. Oh, mon dieu, Klaus!'

'He bought you these.'

Klaus is holding a bunch of limp, hothouse daffodils, wrapped in florists' paper. Gervaise runs down the stairs and throws her skinny arms round Klaus's neck.

'You did it, Klaus! You looked after him. You and my prayers . . .'

'Not me, Gervaise. The judge was very fair . . .'

'It was you. I know it was you! If you hadn't gone with him . . .'

'Well, it's over.'

'Thank God. Oh Mother of God, thank you!'

Mallélou's at the door, his head sunk down into his overcoat. He's staring at his wife and Klaus with the impartial, freezing stare of the executioner.

'It's gone then!' he blurts out.

Klaus turns. 'What's gone?'

'You mean you didn't see?'

'See what?'

Slowly and almost soundlessly, Mallélou begins to laugh.

'You saw, didn't you, Gervaise? Eh? You saw what they've

done. Damn me if they haven't ruined it! All that work, hah! All that work!'

'What's he talking about, Gervaise?' asks Klaus.

Gervaise pulls away gently from Klaus, then reaches out to him again and strokes his cheek like a child. Mallélou's laughter has turned to coughing and he spits with relish onto the lino.

'The pool . . .' says Gervaise, '. . . Madame de la Brosse got a demolition paper out of the Mayor. Illegal, they pretended it was. They said Larry needed official permission . . .'

'So?' The great valley of Klaus's smile has gone. His cheek, under Gervaise's caressing hand, is white.

'Diggers came. It's ruined. They filled it in.'

'No . . .'

'Last night.'

'Nein. Nein! Das ist nicht möglich . . .'

'I couldn't stop them, Klaus. I ran out as soon as I heard them . . .'

'Nein. Nein. Meine Mosaiken! Meine Kathedrale . . .'

Klaus thrusts the bunch of daffodils into Gervaise's hands and pushes past Mallélou out into the yard. They hear him start to run up the lane.

'Go on, then,' says Mallélou, still coughing, 'run after him, scamper after him. Neither of you can change it. The whole damn thing's buggered!'

But Gervaise doesn't go out. She holds the bunch of daffodils to her face and smells their unfamiliar scent of spring. At least Xavier's safe. Her prayers were answered. No prison. No cell. He's safe. Now he must try to start again. Gervaise walks to the dresser and reaches down an ugly glass vase which she fills with water. She unwraps the flowers and sticks them in.

The table is set for lunch. Mallélou sits down, still wearing his coat, and pours himself a glass of red wine. Gervaise goes to the stove where a *pot au feu* is simmering.

'How's the old man?' Mallélou asks after a while.

'Very weak. I sent one of the children for Dr Prière.'

'He's going to croak, Gervaise. He should be in the hospital.'

'No. He's staying.'

'I don't want death in my house!'

'It's not your house. It's mine.'

He looks away. These days, he hasn't got the strength to argue with her. At least someone did for that swimming pool. That's taken the grin off all their faces! Someone showed a bit of sense. He must remember to mention it to Mme de la Brosse at Christmas, mention it to the Mayor, if he should ever happen to see the Mayor . . .

Kneeling by the pool, Klaus is scraping at the hard clay where it touches but doesn't completely obscure his mosaic work. The digger drivers, in their hurry to do the job and be gone, didn't fill the pool quite to its rim and some of the black and white mosaic trim is still visible, a weird patterned band sunk in the earth, like a gigantic game of dominoes. As he feebly scratches at the soil, a memory comes to him of being taken one summer by his mother to stay with his cousins who lived in a small chalet in the mountains, near a lake. She had bought him red bathing trunks. 'In this lake,' she told him, 'all children learn to swim like eels.' His cousins *were* eels, or so they seemed to him, their thin bodies twisting, flicking, gracefully darting through the water. His mother held him up, his bottom sticking out of the water like a cherry. She held him and held him and he can remember the feel of her hands under his chest and tummy. But the longer she held him there and screamed at him to paddle, to kick, the deeper grew his fear of the lake. His cousins swam out to a raft and dived like sticklebacks. They yelled at him to watch and then mocked, 'Klausie-wausie can't swim! He's too fatty-watty!' And so he was. He was landlocked.

Now he hears footsteps coming over the garden and looks up, expecting to see Gervaise. But it isn't Gervaise, it's Nadia. She stands a little way from Klaus, nervous of him, nervous of his anger and loss.

'So I see your returning car,' she says, 'and I must come to tell you what a stupid sad business I think. You are working so well on this black and white. Larry is so proud of you. He tells me, Klaus is so good a worker and so driving of inspiration.'

'I must telephone Larry,' says Klaus, still prodding at the earth and touching the little shiny ceramics with his thumb. 'Perhaps I can use your telephone?'

'Well,' says Nadia, 'of course you are welcome to use. But I must say to you I am awake all the night after these bulldozers are coming and by morning I am deciding no, I think we don't telephone to Larry yet.'

'Larry must know. Then I will work to get this order revoked. And we shall clear all this away.'

'But not yet, my dear. Please. You don't tell Larry yet.'

'Why?'

'Because this will spoil the return to his wife. You know if you are loving a person so much as Larry is loving Miriam you want, after the separation, to take a gift. You understand me? You want to bring the chocolates or the flowers or even some foulard. Something to say, "I love you, my dear person, and I am so missing you." But this is all Larry is taking. You understand? This is all the precious gift he has to take to his wife, this swimming pool. You appreciate? He goes so in a hurry, you see. He says to me, my God Nadia, I've got nothing for Miriam, no chocolate, no basket of sugar-almonds. But I say no, you just think sensibly, my friend, and you will see you have a gift. You have made this pool for Miriam and this is it. So what I ask is we don't telephone Larry for some few days. Just some few days. Okay? We give him a little time till the gift is not so the important thing. Like if you bring flowers, so after some days they die but you don't bother. You remember how it was nice to give them. You do understand? Please. We wait a little.'

Klaus straightens up and brushes the yellowish earth off his hands. He feels tired in all his heavy flesh, tired, tired. But he smiles affectionately at Nadia.

'You are right,' he says.

'So,' says Mme de la Brosse to Hervé in his candlelit dining-room, 'how long will you be away?'

Hervé glances down the table at his guests. They're all, he thinks, growing old with ease, getting comfortably through the years, untroubled by dreams of violence and confrontation, harbouring no guilt for what they don't know, passing without despair from the eating of *foie gras* to the tomb. It's how it should be, he decides. Life should be pleasant. In Florida, he imagines, life will be very pleasant. See Miami and die? 'You know something, Hair-vay?' whispers the ghost of his friend, Howard J. Mills, 'guilt's right out of fashion here. Vietnam, Watergate, it's all gone through us and out and we've flushed it down the john. And we're bringing back Fun.'

'Sorry?' says Hervé to Mme de la Brosse. 'What did you say?' say?'

'Oh it's not important. I wondered how long you'd be in America?'

'Until the spring, I think,' says Hervé. 'My niece is getting married in January and she wants me to come back for this, but I don't think I will. I've told her, if she wants me at the wedding, she'll have to postpone it.'

'Ah yes. Agnès. I heard she stayed with you here. An absolutely charming girl, I remember. Do you approve of the young man?'

Hervé's concentration seems to be bad tonight. He hears the question, but sees in his mind not Luc but Xavier Mallélou standing in his porch late at night. He hears, in the distance, the Mozart concerto. The young man's face is thin and fine, like the face of a filmstar.

'Yes,' he says, 'yes, very much. I only feel . . .'

'Yes?'

'That she's too young.'

'Oh, I think the young know their own minds these days, Hervé. They have to learn so much so fast.'

'True. But Agnès has had a sheltered upbringing. Very correct. I thought there might be a little rebellion.'

'Ah well,' says Mme de la Brosse, taking up her glass and looking admiringly at its crystal in the light of the candles, 'if I were you, I'd just be grateful there wasn't.'

'Yes,' says Hervé, but still the image of Xavier Mallélou remains. That night, he understood Agnès's sudden departure. But the young man's distress had, in Hervé's mind, made his niece seem cruel. They go hand in hand, he thought, obsessive domestic order and indifference. He doesn't know what's become of the Mallélou boy. Nadia would know, of course, but Nadia is out of bounds and must remain so.

'What about you, Madame?' he says to Mme de la Brosse.
'How long are you staying in Pomerac this time?'

'Oh, just for Christmas. I don't want this generally known,
Hervé, but I have decided to sell up.'

'Ah.'

It's not really yours to sell, Hervé thinks. It was Anatole's
family home. In the old days of the Colonel they passed it
forward in their minds from son to son, from generation to
generation.

'I can't run two homes any more. It's too great a burden. And
I find Pomerac very changed. Certain liberties are taken now.
It's not the community it once was.'

She means Larry, thinks Hervé. And the pool. Her boldness
in upholding the bylaws of the commune are the talk of this
dinner party. She expects – and receives praise. Hervé, alone,
finds her high-handedness distasteful. There was something
fantastical in Larry's project, something comfortingly mad. Now
order has been reimposed. Xavier's white face in the moonlight,
the shimmer of Larry's cathedral – both have been obliterated.
Though he smiles at his guests, Hervé is feeling a silent,
deepening unease. He pours wine and notices his hand is trembling. He wishes he'd put the regimental box on the dining-table,
within reach of his fingers.

As Hervé plays host at his farewell party, Nadia lies in her
monogrammed frayed linen and listens to the silence all around
her. There's something eternal, tonight, about the quiet, as if,
far away on his roof at Rouigny, Father le Sueur had stared
through his telescope and seen, in their clusters and shoals, the
stars wink out and all the universe blanketed in darkness.

I'm alone. Finally.

Je suis seule. Finalement.

Ich bin alleine. Letztens.

Jestem sama. Nareszcie.

She doesn't feel afraid. She's remembering, with a little laugh
inside her, her passion for Uncle Leopold, how she'd lie in the
dark of her Wielkopolski Street room and hear the night choked
with sounds of neighbouring lives and make a secret pathway

through all this rumpus to Uncle Leopold's blue door and imagine him holding out his hefty arms to her and taking her in. 'Nadia,' she used to pretend she heard him say, 'you are my princess!'

She wonders if Uncle Leopold is still alive, if his door is still blue, if the teashop exists where he bought her pastries, if, in his ancient eyes, he sometimes imagines the moon is cheese. She's led so many lives since then. Now, all of them have brought her here, to this stillness.

Under the soft bedcoverings, she lays her stubby-fingered hands on her breasts, which are still round and full with mauvish nipples the colour of plums. Claude, when he felt fretful, liked to suck her breasts like a baby. 'Your sad Polish milk is good,' he'd say and at one time in her life with Claude she began to lactate a little and Claude's lips would pull and pull at her nipples, drinking the last drop out of her and she'd start to feel the tug of him in her womb. She wonders if, in his dormitory, he remembers the taste of her body.

Since her visit to Rouigny, she's thought about Claude almost constantly. Claude Lemoine. The handsome man she met as a poor student in Paris. Claude in his fine neckties. The father of her children. Claude locked up, making baskets, gabbling about the end of the world, remembering he once owned two houses, repeating and repeating the three syllables of her name: Na-di-a, Na-di-a . . .

Like Gervaise, she senses, in this colossal silence, the nearness of the first winter snows. Winter, in Wielkopolski Street *was* snow. You lived with it piled up against the basement steps from November to February. Here, it snows and thaws, snows again, freezes for a week or two, crystallising the forests, then slowly melts. She likes its obliterating cleanness. She likes the sound of the children laughing in their snowball games. She puts on her ancient fur-lined boots and walks down to the Ste Catherine woods. And now, this year, it's coming before Christmas. Claude, she asks soundlessly, do you remember Christmas, my dear?

She's made a plan. Tonight, in this final aloneness, she's made it. She will telephone Father le Sueur and ask that this year Claude be allowed home for Christmas. *Home*. To the small flat she will decorate with fir and the mistletoe that grew in all the ancient apple trees torn out by the de la Brosse manager. Home. She will make the flat into a home for Claude, just for a time. She'll cut his hair and tidy him up. She'll roast a goose with apricots. She'll bargain with Mme Carcanet for some good claret. She'll set a place for Claude with his own family silver . . .

'Look,' she will say, as they come up the stairs and into this room he's never seen, 'how my life is small now, Claude. You see? No bigger than yours, my dear. Just one small place and my small bed I fold into the wall. Some small kitchen space here where I shall cook your goose, and this little Japanese screen you remember from our bedroom in Paris?

'Now, sit down, my darling, and take some breath after this so long journey and Nadia will make tea and put on the fire. You think I forget what you like, Claude? Well, I don't. I am breaking myself to buy you some delicacies – truffles you see here and some rillettes with armagnac and of course one pot of salmon eggs for Nadia's famous blinis. So please relax, my dear, and we won't be sad or regretting for this short time. N'est ce pas? I think you are so long with those monks and with your baskets, you're forgetting what is in the world. So I will show you. I will show you the forest, Claude, and the frozen river where the pike fishing men used to go. I will show you the old lanes of Pomerac and the clock which still chimes and the Mallélou yard and tell you the story of all what happens in our old house we sold to the English couple, the Kendals. This is a long story, my dear, so you must be patient and not intervene me with your talk of the world's end or the astronomical thoughts of Father le Sueur. In fact this story is too long for now, Claude. I shall tell it to you later, when I unfold my bed from the wall and I undress you, my darling, and you put your head here, where I think you used to like to be, on Nadia's breast . . .'

She's busy in her head with her preparations, like a small-snouted animal slowly gathering its solitary winter hoard. Near morning, it starts to snow and she sleeps and dreams of Claude's white head beside hers on the pillow. When she wakes, late, and sees the bright and dazzling landscape, she catches her breath with wonder. 'So you don't be some gloomy Pole today,' she instructs herself, 'the world is beautiful, Nadia.'

Xavier Mallélou is back in his old room in the city. The students next door have gone to their families for Christmas and he finds on his table an envelope containing two keys – the key to his own room and the key to theirs. A note in clear, energetic handwriting reads: *Thanks for the loan of your room. We had a party one night and several of your glasses got broken. As recompense, please use our room till Jan 3rd if you want, but make sure no books or records are taken.*

It's cold in the building. He goes down to the communal telephone in the hall and calls Pozzo's number. He must get out to one of the warm bars, order some oysters, start tapping the grapevine for some work, any kind of work, something to keep him fed while he tries to sort out his life. Pozzo doesn't answer. Xavier fingers the cash in his pocket, almost a thousand francs – money he's earned working on the pool. He must try to make it last. It'll soon go if he starts treating Pozzo and his friends. But he needs their company. In the bar-talk, he'll start to forget Agnès. Crazy-headed virgin. Cunt of a debutante. Love is for the middle classes. Romantic crap. Forget it. Get yourself laid, Xavier. Get a piece of hardworking city arse. Ride that till it doesn't hurt any more. Forget the river. Forget that time you first saw her in the church. Forget your pathetic high-and-mighty notions of dignity. Dignity. Humanity. They're just *words*. Life's about making it through. Get a job. Get a woman. Forget her.

He can't manage it yet, though. There and then in the dark hallway by the pay-phone, he remembers the sweet smell of her, that beautiful, sad sweet scent of her hair, her breasts, her breath, her cunt. He closes his eyes. Above them is the drip-drip of the winter forest. Her skin, lit by pale sunlight, is as fine as the skin of a child.

He goes back to his room and lies down on his bed which the students have left made and tidy. How can he forget her? Just the smell of her will haunt him all his life. He'd give his future for a night in her bed. Go and find her, says his terrible longing. Get on the Paris train. Kidnap her. Snatch her out of her society

wedding. Marry her. But then he remembers the suits of
armour, her ancestors staring at him from Hervé Prière's hall,
they in the warm house, polished and oiled and tended, he with
the night at his back, out in the cold. To go to Paris would be
futile. Just a waste of his precious money. When he got there,
if he even found where she lived, there'd be some grand stairway
to climb, some smart brass bell to ring. She'd stare at him coldly,
like she'd stare at a florist's driver come to bring her flowers.
'Go away, Xavier,' she'd say. 'It's over. Can't you understand?'

With the students gone, it's silent in the sooty apartment
block, as if he's the only person left in it. Perhaps even Pozzo
and his other friends have gone away for Christmas. Christmas
is in all the shops – big, lighted displays of chocolates and
wristwatches and leathergoods and toys. Tinsel and trees and
dyed greenery outside the flowershops and in the markets.
Everyone shoving and spending. Old women pushing home jars
of expensive liquor-soaked fruit, whole cheeses, tins of pâté in
plastic wheeled baskets. Carol music through megaphones tied
to the lamp-posts. A one-legged man selling wrapping paper
from a clothes horse on a street corner. Christmas all around.
In Xavier's cruel imagining, Agnès puts on her coat and her
gloves and goes shopping for expensive presents for Luc.
'You've left me nothing,' he wants to say to her, 'not even my
strength. Just a memory. A feeling of pain.'

Though he's heard them, so close to him on the other side of
the wall, he's never been inside the students' room. For something to do, something to take his mind off his hopeless yearnings, he takes the key they've left him and, with a slight sense
of being an intruder, a voyeur, opens their door. In size, the
room is almost identical to his, but it faces out to the street and
has a tall balcony window curtained in rough-weave, brightly
coloured fabric. Similar fabric covers the bed. Shiny cushions
are bunched against the wall and make the bed seem like a wide
couch. A desk with a worklamp has been placed in front of the
window and by the desk an umbrella stand has been filled with
tall dried flowers. On all the available wallspace – even above
the bed – bookshelves have gone up and these are crammed
with books and papers and records and a Japanese stereo

system. The kitchen corner – in his room greasy and dirty – is clean and tidy. More dried flowers have been hung up here. There's a spice rack and a vegetarian calendar and a shelf of pretty china jars. Xavier stares at it. Compared to this, his own room is a dingy hole. And just as he used to envy the students their contented love, so now he envies them their ability to transform their room. There are ten days till they come back. He walks to their bed and sits down on it, fingering the satin cushions. I'll move in, he decides.

There's no point in fetching his things. He hasn't got much, anyway. His clothes can stay where they are. He turns on all the lamps and lights the gas fire and the room seems cosier and warmer than any room he's ever slept in. He thumps the bed. He feels happy. For ten minutes, in his pleasure at the room, he hasn't thought about Agnès. He sits down at the desk. Papers and notepads are arranged tidily on it. Pencils and pens are stuck into a glass jar. He takes up a biro, the only kind of pen he's familiar with, and writes on a blank, lined sheet the word *Begin*. He underlines it.

He goes to bed without his oysters, without phoning Pozzo again. He goes to bed hungry and light in his head with relief that he's here in this peculiar room that smells of paper and joss sticks and not, thank Jesus, thank Mary, thank the plaster-of-Paris Christ at Ste Catherine, in a cell, covered with a grey blanket, shitting his prison-issue pyjamas with fear at all the hopeless days to come. The pain of Agnès is sharp, a deep wound. In prison, though, it'd be ten times worse. Here, he won't die of it; there, he might have died.

Near sleep, he thinks of his mother, Gervaise. Her trust in him. Her loyalty. Her refusal to criticise or condemn. She'd be proud of me, he decides, if she came to visit me in a room like this. She'd see I was getting on, making something of my life. I'd make her a nice meal in that clean kitchen space and explain to her very patiently all the things I'm studying: the rise of the Third Reich in Germany, the fall of the Tsar in Russia, the conduct of the English Revolution I never knew existed till a short while ago . . .

He dreams, of course, of his lost girl. He's brought her to

Bordeaux and they're walking arm in arm in the smart middle of the city. I'm hungry, she tells him, so he steers her towards an expensive restaurant where, in its soft light, she will say to him: 'Take your shoe off, Xavier, and make me come with your foot, under the table.' They start to run. He can feel, at his shoulder, her desire for him. They run and run, but the restaurant recedes. When they get there, it's Mme Motte's greasy place and she starts to bray at them: 'Pigs! Animals! Scum!' And he wakes, full of tribulation.

It's the middle of the night. The streetlights are on outside the curtains he's forgotten to draw, the ugly sodium lights they don't put in the posh boulevards. Above him, the spines of the books stare out at him. Knowledge. The power of knowledge. The thought he could acquire it teases and torments him. Does learning make people happy? He doesn't know. The students seemed happy, but then they had each other. With Agnès, he would have been happy. Or would he? How long could he have loved this spoilt child of a dry and dusty aristocratic past? Would she have changed or does class and custom prevail even against passion? Do these books contain the answer to this? He suspects, if he could once understand them, they would.

In the morning, with snow falling hard on the scurrying Christmas crowds, he stares at the word *Begin* he wrote on the pad and takes up the biro again. Underneath *Begin* he writes:

1. *Enrol college. Jan. Semester.*
   2nd Phase. Bac.
2. *Find part-time work*
   or
3. *Use Corinne.*

He sits back. His heart's beating very fast. Corinne was the dark-haired girl who worked in the babyshop opposite the *Mimosas*. She was dying, she said, of her infatuation for Xavier. For the touch of him, she'd do anything he asked. Women. They 'die' for the touch of you, or they destroy you. It's all enigmatic, stupid, hopeless. But fleetingly, in the quiet of this borrowed room, with the books and papers hedging him round, he sees the faint flicker of a chance for his future: he'll make use of Corinne. Make her crazy with that feeling he once described, lying by the river with Agnès in his arms, lying with his bare bum butting the sky, as love. Then get Corinne to support him. Let her earn, with her no-hope job selling prams and matinée jackets and plastic bibs, enough money to see him through college.

He likes the cruel logic of his plan. Agnès tricked him. He'll trick Corinne. Love's a fairytale. The big con. You have to get dignity by other means.

For a long time, Xavier sits and stares at what he has written. Already, the word 'college' frightens him, and when he tries to imagine himself buying books and pens and walking one cold morning through its high doors, his mind pauses in dismay, refusing to construct the picture.

In France, the snow keeps on. In England, on Christmas Day, there's no sign of it, only a hard, beautiful frost.

At three o'clock, with darkness already settling down over Oxford, Miriam, Gary and Perdita walk arm in arm to St Mary's for a carol service. A few rows in front of her, Miriam sees the close-together heads of Dr O and Bernice Atwood. Neither of them turn and look at her. Gary notices them too and remembers his meeting with Bernice by the river. He sees now that she's wearing a new coat.

Larry and Thomas, both indifferent to carols, stay behind in the house. Though Larry wants to talk to his son, the old unease between them seems to return the minute they're alone together and Larry soon retreats from the hot kitchen, tugs on a coat and goes out into the frosty dusk. He walks quite fast, enjoying the silence of the city.

He's barely out of earshot of the house when the telephone rings and Thomas hurries to Leni's study to answer it. Entering Leni's 'own' rooms – her bedroom, her bathroom and this room from which she used to write to him – brings the loss of her back to him. It's with a subdued voice that he gives the Oxford number.

There's a lot of crackling and whooshing on the line. Thomas waits. Clear and high out of these peculiar noises comes a voice which says, 'My bean?'

'Who is this?' asks Thomas.

'Nadia. It's Nadia. It's not you, my bean?'

'This is Thomas Kendal,' says Thomas.

There's a long silence, save for the whooshing on the line which is like the sound of a sea gale.

'I'm sorry,' says Nadia, 'I must speak to Larry. You can fetch him, please?'

'He's not here,' says Thomas.

There's another burst of sea noise before Nadia says urgently, 'I must speak to him, you know. I promised I would telephone today.'

'Can he call you back?' says Thomas, absentmindedly. His long fingers are gently touching the leather corners of Leni's blotter. On the blotting paper itself are imprinted one or two pale, indecipherable ghosts of her stylish handwriting.

'I think,' says Nadia, 'this news must not wait any longer. I think you must tell him. You tell so kindly, please. I think it's better you tell him. Okay?'

'Sure,' says Thomas, 'tell him what?'

'Well . . .'

Thomas waits, impatient as Leni would have been impatient with this anxious-sounding person. When next she speaks, it's a rush of words, a wave breaking: 'Please, you tell him I am so ashame, that this whole village is so ashame for so cruel a thing. You must tell him Klaus is not to blame, nor these Mallélous. Please say we could do nothing. None of us. In the night is coming two bulldozers. And we are told afterwards Mme de la Brosse has given them some paper from the Mayor . . . just a piece of *paper*, you know, and with this piece of paper they are falling all the earth in, you understand? All the earth back into the swimming pool. And for so many days I am keeping this thing from Larry, but now I have to tell him. So you tell him please the pool is destroyed and I am so sorry, my poor bean. Say him Nadia is sorry . . .'

When the wave has receded, an awkward goodbye is said and Thomas is alone with his father's tragedy. He sits down at Leni's desk and stares at her pens in their tray, her gold-handled scissors, her Japanese inkwell. So deliciously cruel she always was about Larry. Now, in her study, Thomas hears her empty laughter and feels afraid.

It's completely dark when Larry comes in. In the December sky, over the worshippers in St Mary's hangs the same full moon Uncle Leopold once told his gullible niece to eat. Larry's nose is red and icy. He's grateful for the warmth of the house as it takes him in. And he feels clear-headed from the walk, calm inside himself, full of hope.

Thomas comes out of the kitchen. He's made tea, he says. His blanket face is grave, his eyes over-bright, as they were at Leni's funeral. Strange boy, thinks Larry. Too like his grandmother for my comfort. Yet, he puts a friendly hand on Thomas's shoulder. 'Let's start old Gary's Christmas cake, shall we?' he says.

So the beautiful iced cake is cut and plates laid and the tea poured, and over this modest, very English meal, Thomas gently tells his father what has happened in Pomerac.

The moment Thomas starts talking, Larry gets up. He has to move away from Thomas's look. When the full realisation of what has happened comes to him, Larry's first thought is, I want to hurt him, I want to throw my fist in his face, I want to kill him – for his *pity*! Instead, he brings his hand crashing down onto the burning hot enamel of the Rayburn. Above it, some tin mugs of Leni's jigger on their hooks. Larry takes them one by one and hurls them across the room. They don't break. They're hardly dented. Like Leni herself, he thinks. Indestructible! Except at the end. Everything, in the end, goes back into the earth. Maggots fiddle with her now. There's a thought! Where she was caressed, now she's eaten. But she cast this one last spell. The old 'Duchess of Oxford' came whispering in the ear of Mme de la Brosse as she sat by her fire in her empty house. Together, they laughed and laughed. They cackled like hags in the night, and then she fled. Leni the cat. Leni the ghost of beautiful women. And the plan was formed . . .

Thomas moves to pick up the mugs, but Larry stops him. 'Don't touch them!' And Thomas understands. 'If you're blaming Leni . . .' he begins, 'you're idiotic.'

'I *am* idiotic, Thomas! Didn't you know that? Has it taken you twenty-seven years to realise your father was an idiot?'

'Please don't, Dad. Don't start blaming me. I had nothing to do with it.'

'No? But you all understood, didn't you? He'll do what we tell him. Larry the lamb! He'll trot off to France when we tell him to. He'll get well when we tell him to. He'll start building his silly little swimming pool. Well, you were wrong about the swimming pool. You were all wrong. I wasn't building a swimming pool. It never *was* one!'

'What was it, then?'

'It was a bloody cathedral! That's what it was. It was a *cathedral*!'

'I thought you were indifferent to God.'

'God? Who mentioned God? I am totally and absolutely indifferent to God. I wasn't building it for Him. It wasn't a church monument. It was a monument to *me*!'

Larry bangs his barrel chest with his helpless fists. I'm like a child, he thinks. I've got a child's trust in the world. And he lets his hands drop.

He moves from the Rayburn to the window. On the sill is a line of Leni's cacti Miriam has neglected. They seem shrivelled and light. He hates the look of them. He closes his eyes.

'I would like to have seen it,' says Thomas quietly.

'Seen what?' Larry's voice is steady now. He feels the first weight of his anger begin to lift.

'The French pool.'

'You were never interested in the pools.'

'Not in the old days, not much. They all looked the same.'

Larry shrugs. 'This one wasn't that different.'

'What was the cathedral thing, then?'

Larry turns and looks at his son. In the boy's face is real sadness. Go to Australia, he wants to say. Go with my blessing, with my love even, but go and leave me with my failures. But he doesn't say this. He rubs his eyes and says: 'It was just a kind of inspiration I had. New colours. Black and white instead of blue, and in the shape . . .'

'What did you use, tile or mosaic?'

'Both. Tiles on the sides, mosaic on the trim. Some silver bits which would have shone under the water . . .'

'Sounds good.'

Larry shrugs again. 'Probably not.'

He sits down then. He pours himself some tea. With the pain of his anger easing, his mind travels to Pomerac. It's early morning, cold and clear. With his ladder propped against the deep-end wall, Klaus is working with the mosaic pieces. The sun is up, the whole place gloriously lit. Larry stands, holding a bowl of Gervaise's coffee in his hands, and watches. The scene is fine, yet at the very edge of it there's a speck, a shadow, something he can't describe that gives him a small sense of unease.

'Do you know,' he says suddenly to Thomas, 'that while I was working on the pool I saw an eagle? I saw it twice. The second time, it was so near me I could almost have touched it. And they look at you, you know. They look you in the eye. I thought about it a heck of a lot. I wanted it to come back and it never did. But I knew why. It despised me. I was much too tame.'

Larry hears the front door open then and Miriam, Perdita and Gary come into the hall. They're laughing and singing snatches of carols.

'Larry!' Miriam calls above the laughter. 'We're home.'

More snow falls on Pomerac. Behind her draughty windows, Mme de la Brosse looks out at the silent lane and wonders anxiously, will the roads be passable, will I be able to get back to Paris? Last night, after midnight mass at Ste Catherine, she and Lisette waited with the mulled wine and the cakes and the sugar angels for the children, but no one came. She sent Lisette out with a torch to see if families were waiting at her gate but there was no sign of anyone and up and down the lanes of the village all the lights were on and the fires burning and the doors closed.

'Ah well, so much the better,' Mme de la Brosse said to Lisette. 'It's an out-dated custom. I only kept it on for Anatole's sake. Take the cakes and the other rubbish home to your family, dear.'

'Thank you, Madame. But I still don't understand. Why did no one turn up?'

Mme de la Brosse shrugged. 'They've forgotten the old ways. It's not my fault. We live in a disrespectful time.'

Mallélou didn't go to the mass. He hated snow and was growing, in these last months of his decline, to hate God. Why had God sent His son among ignorant Jewish fishermen who needed everything explaining to them in crass anecdotes about virgins and weddings? Why had he not arrived among the sensible burghers of Bremen, made them his apostles and baptised them in the Weser? That plaster-of-Paris Jesus at Ste Catherine had started to seem stupid to Mallélou, anyway. Jesus with a broken thumb: typical French peasant ineptitude.

'I'll stay with the old man,' he told Gervaise, as she and Klaus put on their coats. 'Someone has to stay with him. We can't all go rushing off to get our sins forgiven.'

'What sins?' asked Gervaise curtly.

Mallélou looked from her to Klaus and grinned. 'Plenty, Gervaise!'

'And you? You don't think you've got any?'

'I didn't say that.'

'I'm happy to stay with the Maréchal, you know. You go to the Mass.'

But Mallélou started to push them out into the yard. 'Go on, off you go. You leave me in peace . . .'

Wearily, then, he climbed the stairs to the Maréchal's room, went in without knocking and sat down by the old man's bed. The room was cold, with the snow pressing and mounting up against the window, but the smell in it was foetid and Mallélou tugged out a grimy handkerchief and sat with this pressed to his nose. Half asleep and dreaming of his dead sons, the Maréchal felt the presence of Mallélou near him and opened his eyes and said: 'Not long, eh, Mallélou?'

Mallélou stared at him over the handkerchief.

'For me or for you, Maréchal?'

'You, you're young compared to me. But you're tired of it, Mallélou. I can see that. In your eyes. Life's hard. It's no good being tired. You've got to have the stomach for it.'

'Eat. Sleep. Shovel some shit. Have a nip of wine. There's
no point to it, is there? Even my cock's limp as a dead bloody
sparrow. Not like in the old days. I was chipper then. Horny as
shit then. In that signal hut where I worked, we had this ashtray
the shape of a woman . . .'

'You've told me, Mallélou.'

'. . . I used to put the fag-end right *there*. Burn her right in
her black pussy every damn morning! Fantastic, non?'

Mallélou stared down at his feet and noticed that his sabots
were worn and scratched and that there was a hole in one of his
socks. He sat staring at these familiar things for a long time,
remembering the long-ago days of the signal hut and repeating
in an almost inaudible whisper 'Fantastic, non? Fantastic, non?'
A choking and gurgling sound from the bed disturbed his reverie
and he looked up. With his owl's eyes wide open on the falling
snow and his snowy hair flying like flax across the pillow, the
Maréchal had died.

Now it's morning. The sun's brilliance on the white landscape
is startling. Gervaise sleeps. Upstairs, the body of the Maréchal,
washed and dressed by Gervaise and Klaus in the silence of
one o'clock on Christmas morning, waits for the undertakers,
covered with a clean white sheet. Gervaise dreams of the party
she gave the week Klaus became her lover. It was high summer
and they set up a long table in the yard and got pissed as lords
in the sunshine and danced to accordion music on the dry, flinty
earth of the barnyard with the hens pecking at their skipping
legs and the guineafowl flapping and screeching on all the roofs.

Mallélou wakes and stares at the ski-ing poster. The snow's
here now. If he were young, he'd like to dress up in a stretchy
yellow suit with a number on his back and go tearing down
mountains, hearing the ice under his feet. He blows his nose.
The smell of his handkerchief reminds him of the old man lying
and waiting for his coffin and he shudders. 'Let me,' he asks the
Aryan God of his imaginings, 'have the stomach for spring.'

Klaus wakes in Gervaise's bed. He can feel, in the weight of
her deep sleep, her sadness. She was, in her heart and even
sometimes in her head, the Maréchal's child. Her care of him
was daily proof of her love. To her land, to her animals, to her

sons, to the Maréchal, she was as steadfast as the seasons. Let no one and nothing else, thinks Klaus, desert her.

He gets up without waking her and goes out to the cows, lodging himself against their warm bodies to milk them. Christmas Day. In Heidelberg, his mother will be opening the present he sent her, a set of wicker canisters for the storing of angelica and peel and vanilla pod. And here, later in the day, they will sit, the three of them, Klaus, Gervaise and Mallélou, as they always sit round the Christmas table, decorated with ivy and paper roses, and eat rich goose, and the fumes of their heavy meal will waft upstairs and creep into the Maréchal's cold room under the door. Gervaise will be solemn and silent. Mallélou will drink to distance himself from the body above his head. He, Klaus, will note that with each year's passing, the greater seems to be this couple's need of him.

The milking done, Klaus comes slowly back down the lane. The sight of Larry's Granada in its blanket of snow makes him remember, for the first time that particular morning, all the afternoons of the building of the pool, with the light going, with Larry urging him on, with the mosaic slowly, inch by inch, taking shape. In his heavy snowboots, he crunches round past Larry's silent and shuttered house and stands some way from the swimming pool, looking with a perplexed smile at what remains of it – a shallow basin in the soft contours of the snow, an indentation. Gone, he thinks. Gone, as if it had never been.

Then he hears an insistent tap-tap-tap, tap-tap-tap and he throws his head back and looks up at the empty trees and the blue sky and sees, at the Maréchal's high window, Gervaise beckoning him in. He waves to her and turns towards the lane. The sun dances on his golden head. For a man his size, his tread is light.